ROGUE ELEMENTS

Hector Macdonald grew up on the coast of Kenya and now lives in London. He began writing thrillers soon after completing a zoology degree at Oxford University. When not inventing twisted plots for troubled characters, he works as a strategy and communications consultant in industries as diverse as telecoms, banking, pharmaceuticals and healthcare. He has, on occasion, provided consulting services to various agencies of the British government.

www.HectorMacdonald.com

THE MIND GAME

'An ingenious thriller' – *The Times*

'A splendidly engineered tale of deceit and illusion' – *Guardian*

THE HUMMINGBIRD SAINT

'Hard to put down' – *Time Out*

'One of the most unusual thrillers of the year'
– *Yorkshire Evening Post*

THE STORM PROPHET

'The perfect race meets the perfect storm' – *Mirror*

'His best yet … a one-sitting read' – *Sunday Express*

ROGUE ELEMENTS

HECTOR MACDONALD

Published by Advance Editions 2015
Advance Editions is an imprint of Core Q Ltd
Global House, 1 Ashley Avenue, Epsom, Surrey KT18 5AD
All correspondence: info@AdvanceEditions.com

First published as an advance ebook by Advance Editions 2014

ISBN 978-1-910408-02-5

A CIP catalogue record for this book is available from the British Library

Designed & typeset by K.DESIGN, Somerset
Printed and bound in Great Britain by Clays Ltd, St Ives plc

www.AdvanceEditions.com

for my father, who liked this one

Alasdair Macdonald

1942–2014

INTELLIGENCE GLOSSARY

ABIN	Agência Brasileira de Inteligência (Brazil)
ACTOR	Codename for SIS
AQ	Al-Qaeda
CIA	Central Intelligence Agency (USA)
CNI	Centro Nacional de Inteligencia (Spain)
CSIS	Canadian Security Intelligence Service
CX	Intelligence 'product' (SIS)
DCRI	Direction Centrale du Renseignement Intérieur (France)
DEA	Drug Enforcement Administration (USA)
DGSE	Direction Générale de la Sécurité Extérieure (France)
DHS	Department of Homeland Security (USA)
DIA	Defense Intelligence Agency (USA)
Dry cleaning	Checking for and evading surveillance
DS	Directing Staff (training officers)
EPV	Enhanced Positive Vetting
FCO	Foreign and Commonwealth Office (UK)
Five	The Security Service, also known as MI5 (UK)

Fort	Fort Monckton: SIS training centre near Portsmouth
Friend	Informal term for SIS officer
GCHQ	Government Communications Headquarters: UK signals intelligence agency
General Service	Technical and administrative SIS officers
H/NARC	Head of Counter-Narcotics (SIS)
H/SECT	Private Secretary to the Chief of SIS
H/TERR	Head of Counter-Terrorism (SIS)
H/TOS	Head of Technical and Operations Support (SIS)
HPD	Head of Personnel Department (SIS)
I/OPS	Information Operations: propaganda and psychological operations
Intelligence Branch	Fast-stream SIS officers
IDF	Israel Defense Forces
Increment	Special forces detachments supporting SIS
IONEC	Intelligence Officer's New Entry Course (SIS)
ISC	Intelligence and Security Committee: oversight body of UK parliamentarians
JIC	Joint Intelligence Committee (UK)
Kidon	Mossad unit responsible for assassination
Mabahith	Saudi Arabia's domestic security service

Magav	Israel's border police
Mossad	Israel's external intelligence agency
NCA	National Crime Agency (UK)
NIS	National Intelligence Service (South Africa)
NSA	National Security Agency (USA)
OSA	Official Secrets Act (UK)
PD	Personnel Department (SIS)
PMPD	Prime Minister Protection Detail (RCMP)
Porthos	Secure internal electronic messaging system (SIS)
RCMP	Royal Canadian Mounted Police
Shabak	Israel's domestic security service (also known as Shin Bet)
SIS	Secret Intelligence Service, also known as MI6 (UK)
SO15	Counter-Terrorism Command of London's Metropolitan Police, formerly Special Branch (SO12) and Anti-Terrorist Branch (SO13)
SOCA	Serious Organised Crime Agency, now part of the National Crime Agency (UK)
TOS	Technical and Operations Support (SIS)
UBL	Usama Bin Laden
WMD	Weapons of Mass Destruction
YZ	Highly classified

THE SPIES

Independent

Simon Arkell	(ex-SIS)
Madeleine Wraye	(ex-SIS)
Gavriel Yadin	(ex-Mossad)

Secret Intelligence Service

Jeremy Elphinstone	former Head of Requirements and Production
Linus Marshall	former Head of Counter-Intelligence Section
Jane Saddle	Private Secretary to the Chief
George Vine	Head of Middle East and Africa Controllerate
Martin de Vries	Head of Technical and Operations Support
Tony Watchman	Head of Counter-Terrorism Section
Edward Joyce	Treasury officer, seconded to Personnel

Other

Avraham Boim	former Deputy Director (Shabak)
Shel Margrave	Deputy Director, Operations (CSIS)

PROLOGUE

ENGLISHMAN'S BAY, TOBAGO – 23 May

The staff at Emerald Sea Resort had grown familiar with the routine of the tourist staying in the garden villa suite. He ran on the beach every morning before breakfast, and at night he drank well and tipped generously. In between, he disappeared with his companion in a rental car for much of the day. On their return they shed muddy boots, bird books and cameras, and spent the remaining daylight hours sunbathing. The supine companion drew admiring glances from male guests and staff alike; Emerald Sea's activities coordinator offered the couple a free kite-surfing lesson off Pigeon Point in the hope that he might get to lay a guiding hand on various parts of her anatomy. But it seemed she didn't speak much English, and the tourist brusquely declared that his girlfriend was afraid of the sea.

No wonder, then, that they spent their days trudging through damp rainforest instead of enjoying the easier pleasures of Tobago's fine beaches.

Despite his tips, the tourist was not much liked by the staff at Emerald Sea. They sensed something unfamiliar about him, a rigidity of purpose even in his sunbathing, an intensity that was out of place in a Caribbean resort. His lithe, sweat-free body should have impressed; instead, it unnerved. When discreet but searching questions were later asked by foreigners with clipped accents, a number of the staff cited his disquieting manner, although none would go so far as to say he was anything other than he purported to be. There was no memory of unusual equipment, or overheard telephone calls, or an alien language that might have suggested the Middle East.

The only recollection of substance came from a teenage waiter who had served the companion a rum punch by the pool. Attempting to clear a space for the drink on their table, he had picked up a tablet computer with a view to stacking it on top of a German-language novel. He never got that far. Instead he found his wrist rigidly, agonizingly seized. What did he remember most of the man staying in the garden villa suite? The bleak iciness of his gaze as their eyes met over that simple misunderstanding. The threat implied.

On the last day of his vacation, the tourist requested a late check-out, which was granted on payment of an unofficial consideration to the reception manager. Then, as usual, he and his companion put on hiking boots – scraped clean of yesterday's mud – and carried binoculars, mineral water, a packed lunch and two bird books out to the rental car. Neither of the resort staff loitering in the car park noticed the small black suitcase already stowed in the boot of the Ford saloon.

The night had brought heavy rain, and along the Claude Noel Highway pools of water steamed lightly under the flamboyant trees. The tourist did not observe the 50kph limit more conscientiously than any other driver, although he matched his speed to the slowest of the vehicles around him. From Scarborough he cut north across the island on Providence Road, deftly navigating the confusion of unsigned junctions in the capital's northern suburbs to reach the lush rainforest of the interior. At Les Coteaux, he stopped by the roadside stall with the colourful Rasta paintwork, as he had done every other morning of his holiday. The companion remained in the car while he greeted the radiant proprietress in figure-hugging pink and paid for the four mangoes and bunch of bananas she had set aside for him.

At the viewpoint above Castara Bay, the tourist noted the same three police cars that had kept watch over the scant Northside Road traffic for the last three days. He allowed himself a casual glance in their direction, and was rewarded with a wave from one of the officers. His daily routine had been noticed even by the police. He waved back and continued on, keeping his speed just below the limit.

Two more police cars were parked on the verge beyond Castara, their officers standing in what little shade was available and scanning eastbound vehicles with rather more vigilance than might have been expected on a regular balmy day in paradise. Nevertheless, the tourist doubted they knew why they were there. They had almost certainly been told to watch for anyone 'unusual' approaching Englishman's Bay.

There was nothing unusual about two holidaymakers in a rented Ford saloon.

Belvedere House stood in eighty-three acres of private hillside estate, midway between the fishing villages of Castara and

Parlatuvier. Once a splendid colonial mansion, it had been rebuilt after Hurricane Flora demolished its hipped roof, Victorian fretwork and carved teak columns in 1963, and then lavishly refurbished by its new American owner in 2008. From its abundant verandas and balconies, the views across the Caribbean were a match for even the most dazzling cocktail-hour conversation. Some hundred metres below its steeply sloping lawns, Englishman's Bay lay untouched by developers, a sliver of golden sand just visible through the sea almond trees and palms. The rainforest took hold in the valley behind the beach and rose uninterrupted through the Belvedere estate. From there it continued up the hillside into the Main Ridge Reserve, the backbone of Tobago.

Said to be the oldest rainforest reserve in the western hemisphere, the Main Ridge was the vantage point from which the tourist had for six days observed the layout and activity of the Belvedere grounds. The island's most popular forest hiking trails lay to the south and east, but the tourist had identified a small river that flowed north to the Caribbean coast, meeting Northside Road just past the turning to Englishman's Bay. Each day, he had pulled over by the river and made his way on foot upstream. The companion would slip into the vacated driving seat and continue on to one of the trails on the Roxborough–Parlatuvier Road. There she passed the time photographing manicou crabs and leafcutter ants, before returning to pick him up at the same spot four hours later.

The plan on this final day was only a little different.

An unmarked truck was parked a short way up the track leading to the Belvedere estate. The tourist gave no sign of having seen it, but drove on into the valley behind Englishman's Bay and parked under a large immortelle tree. A minibus blaring rapso came roaring down the hill towards them. The tourist raised a map, simplistic and colourful, half-covering his face. When the road was clear he stepped out of the saloon, collected the suitcase from the boot and disappeared into a stand of giant bamboo. The companion switched seats and drove off.

The next car didn't pass the spot for ninety seconds, and by then the tourist was deep inside the rainforest.

He lay on a broad, damp branch overhanging the perimeter fence. Epiphytes clung to the branch – fleshy orchids, bromeliads the size of garden ferns – while below delicate aerial roots trailed towards the forest floor. There was little to see: the rainforest, dense and heavy with moisture, blocked all view of Belvedere House and the small army of technicians, political aides and security officers currently in occupation. The fence itself was barely three metres high, easy to scale, but the tourist had no intention of touching it. In a previous life, he had spent months studying perimeter protection, and were he responsible for security here he would have fitted motion sensors along the length of the fence. For that matter, he would have instituted regular patrols with dogs. But in the twenty-three minutes he'd been watching, no one had appeared.

He let two more minutes tick by, then dropped the suitcase to the ground and followed it down, landing with a neat five-point roll.

In his pocket was his own map of the Belvedere estate, compiled from sketches made over the previous days, high in the hills above. He didn't need it. Every detail was already committed to memory. He knew the exact extent of the rainforest in this sector of the estate, and the distance to the open gardens around the house where elite officers from three nations patrolled. He knew the bearing to the derelict outhouse below the garages. And he knew precisely how many steps lay between the outhouse and the array of generators in the driveway.

He walked with great care, stepping only on exposed roots and fallen bamboo to avoid leaving footprints in the mud.

The outhouse had been searched by a team of three security officers two days earlier. He had watched them enter from his vantage point on the Main Ridge, and seven minutes later he had watched them leave. A strip of yellow tape across the doorless entrance read SECURITY: NO ENTRY. The building smelt of damp and rot, and the excrement of forest creatures. It had once housed a smoker, and what was left of the roof was black from years of wood fires. Rusty hooks that had long ago held curing fish and pork still hung from a rail over the stove. The tourist set his suitcase on the rubble-strewn floor and checked his watch.

10:26. Two minutes ahead of schedule.

He opened the case. Inside was a battered toolbox, a carpenter's belt and a set of very ordinary clothes. The tourist changed into the jeans, white cotton shirt and plain brown boots, and bundled his muddied hiking clothes into the case. From a concealed compartment he withdrew a photo identity card and a badge, yellow with a distinctive blue triangle in the centre. He clipped the ID to his shirt pocket and hung the badge on a lanyard around his neck.

In covert work, there is a time for stealth and a time for boldness. On leaving the outhouse, the tourist walked directly out of the trees and up the lawn to the drive. Sixteen paces and he was alongside the generators. Another eighteen took him past a throng of electrical engineers, junior producers and make-up artists. Six more placed him at the foot of the steps leading to the front door of Belvedere House.

A walk-through metal detector stood next to an X-ray scanner. The tourist placed his toolbox on the conveyor belt.

'That also,' said a security officer in dark suit and shades, pointing to his carpenter's belt. The identity card clipped to his lapel bore a small Dutch flag.

'I haven't seen you before,' said another officer, this one with a Brazilian flag on his lapel. He made a close examination of both badge and identity card.

'I haven't seen you before either,' shrugged the tourist, passing through the metal detector.

Two more security officers met him on the other side. These were Canadians, and while one opened the toolbox and inspected each item, the other patted him down. 'Isn't the set done already?'

'It's done,' nodded the tourist, buckling the carpenter's belt around his waist. 'I'm here to dismantle. Mr Davis wants everything cleared away right after transmission.'

The officer's search of the toolbox was thorough: spirit level, framing square, power drill, tenon saw, screwdrivers, tape measure – no knives, chisels or hammers. He closed it up. 'Nice handle. Ergonomic.'

The air-conditioned interior of Belvedere House was elegantly modelled in teak and polished granite, with cream walls and cool blue furnishings. Kartouche had been able to obtain the architect's plans drawn up for the recent refurbishment, and the tourist now stepped assuredly from the hall into a capacious walk-in closet where he deposited the toolbox and carpenter's belt among a clutter of fishing rods, scuba equipment, lifejackets and boat fenders. The jeans and boots had fitted the carpenter story, but they were clean and unmarked and now served just as well to suggest a hands-on technical manager.

At the end of the hall a trestle table covered in papers was surrounded by a cluster of production executives. Caught up in an argument about title sequencing, they barely noticed the tourist pass by. He took one fleeting look at the papers and as he walked on he processed what he'd seen – in particular a studio plan showing three armchairs. Each was marked with initials: TM, AvdV, MA. Picking up an abandoned clipboard, the tourist pushed through double doors into the imposing space known to him from the architect's plans as *Main Reception*.

It was alive with activity. The great French windows that gave onto a terrace overlooking the Caribbean had been blacked out with thick fabric. In front of them, the furniture had been cleared aside to make way for a temporary television studio, with a plain white backdrop and three chrome-and-black-leather armchairs. Along the back wall was a chaos of cameras, lights, screens and wires. Dozens of production assistants, electricians, sound engineers and runners generated a terrific hum of chatter and motion. Most were dressed like him in jeans or cargo pants and loose, cool shirts. Although a couple of junior assistants eyed him with vague curiosity, he was largely ignored by the rest.

From the double doors, the tourist walked a line that was perfectly parallel with the back wall. His steps, seemingly casual, were precisely uniform. When a harried camera operator charged across his path, he paused to let the man pass rather than deviate from his course. When he had taken fourteen steps, he stopped.

He was directly alongside a large camera rig. No good.

Three more steps brought him level with a thicket of LED panels on stands. Better. Behind the lights, much of the back wall was taken up by a large oil painting, a leaping blue marlin, framed in teak. Inconvenient, but not an insuperable problem. Once the lights were switched on, no one would see anything back there.

With his attention focused on the clipboard, the tourist slipped between the light stands. Leaning briefly against the back wall, he glanced behind the painting. Electric wires. He noted the height of the alarm, eighteen centimetres above his head, and of the heavy-duty hooks on which the painting was suspended, eight centimetres above that.

Then he left the room.

There was still more than half an hour till transmission. None of the principals had yet emerged from make-up.

'Welcome to a broadcast that could change the world. For many years now, a debate has been quietly raging. It speaks to social policy, to morality, to law and order, to public health. And it is deeply controversial. Today we will turn up the volume on that debate.'

The host addressed the camera in the composed, solemn tone on which he had built his reputation as one of Britain's foremost political interviewers. Behind him were the three empty chrome-and-leather armchairs.

'Three like-minded, progressive leaders will shortly propose a brave new approach to one of society's greatest challenges. Is it a viable solution? That is for you to decide. Our speakers seek to initiate a global debate and build a better public understanding of an issue that has for too long been obscured by stale political posturing. You can have your say on the Think Again website or using the hashtag displayed on your screen. Please take part. Your opinion matters. Your voice needs to be heard.

'And now it is my privilege to introduce three remarkable individuals: President Murilo Hernandez Andrade of Brazil, Prime Minister Anneke van der Velde of the Netherlands and Prime Minister Terence Mayhew of Canada. The floor is yours. The world is listening.'

It was forgivable hyperbole. The transmission was being relayed via satellite to fifty-eight different broadcasters around the globe. The schedules of CNN and France 2, of Al Jazeera, Rai Uno, BBC1 and ABC1, had been cleared to accommodate twenty-five uninterrupted minutes of live feed. Think Again's liberal-minded benefactors had hired dozens of PR agencies to build a massive multinational audience. And yet, to the many viewers across multiple time zones, there was a sense of anti-climax in the appearance of the three politicians. It was the absence of applause. There was no studio audience to provide the usual comfortable blanket of approval. These three stood alone.

* * *

The Dutch prime minister spoke first. 'Friends, politics is sometimes about choosing the lesser of two evils. None of us stood for election because we wanted to raise taxes. None of us dedicated our lives to public service in order to deny patients expensive treatments.' She paused to share a look with the men on either side of her, a moment of solidarity. 'And not one of us went into politics to put drugs more easily into the hands of our children.

'And yet when a greater evil proves itself through long years of bitter experience, it is our duty to consider the alternative, however unpalatable.

'Friends, the problem of the illegal drugs trade has become so embedded in our culture that many of us barely see it any more. We drink coffee, watch football, play with our kids, gossip with friends, all the time ignoring the rivers of adulterated, uncontrolled, potentially lethal substances flowing all around us. We close our eyes to the mass murder and anarchy inflicted on developing countries, to the billions of dollars falling like rain into the pockets of criminals. We close our eyes and tell ourselves we have the situation under control. Friends, where drugs are concerned, we lost control a long time ago.'

Drug use is illegal in Trinidad and Tobago, as it is in most countries. Consequently, the Think Again conference was among the most closely guarded secrets ever held by its leaders. One of many small nations caught at the sharp end of the War on Drugs, its Cabinet had been immediately sympathetic to the reformist charity's appeal for an anonymous space from which to broadcast to the world – even if it brought stiff disapproval from all-seeing Washington.

Another reason for the secrecy was, of course, security: far easier to protect the high-profile participants in a controversial event if no one knows where it is.

The secrecy was a heroic achievement on an island more used to relaxed gossip and a free-for-all attitude to other people's business. The retired Italian owner of the Belvedere estate had been invited to take a vacation in Europe at the government's expense, in return for making his home available for a symposium on banana pest management. The film crew and security teams had been flown in at 3 a.m., when the airport at Crown Point was closed down and no staff were on hand to observe the studio equipment, generators and satellite transmitter being offloaded. The three premiers had been conveyed to Belvedere House in a customized windowless vehicle disguised as a builder's truck. Two cars filled with plain-clothes Trinidadian Special Forces officers formed a discreet escort. The local police, along with the caterers, were told only that a reclusive Venezuelan oil man, the subject of frequent kidnap attempts, was on holiday with a few dozen close personal friends.

It should have been watertight.

'The dismal truth is this: we will never be able to suppress the illegal trade in substances that have such widespread and enduring popularity.' Prime Minister Mayhew was silver-haired and straight-backed, with a patrician profile but an earthy, guttural voice. 'In 1998, the UN General Assembly set an objective of eliminating or significantly reducing narcotics cultivation and trafficking by 2008. Opium and cannabis production doubled in that time. The US government alone spends 15 billion dollars and makes 1.7 million arrests every year in its War on Drugs. An American citizen is arrested for possession or sale of cannabis every thirty-eight seconds.

'Think about that a moment. Cannabis is a mildly psychoactive substance, in most cases less harmful than alcohol or tobacco. It is legal in four US states. Forty-two per cent of Americans have used cannabis. That's around 127 million men, women and children. Are these people criminals? Technically, most of them are. As a law-maker and a former law-enforcer, I have to ask myself: how can it make sense to criminalize so many millions of ordinary people?'

Behind the back wall of the great reception room now serving as a TV studio lay Belvedere House's master bedroom suite. It was possible that one of the less indispensable members of the crew might feel the need to lie down or relieve themselves at some point. But sandwiched between bedroom and bathroom on the architect's plans was a third, windowless room containing nothing more than a whirlpool bath and a very expensive sound system. It seemed unlikely anyone would want to use either during a live television transmission.

The tourist had reclaimed his toolbox, and now he jammed the door of the whirlpool room shut behind him with a thick rubber wedge. He paced out four steps and set a chair from the bedroom against the wall. With a pencil, he marked on the wall the position of the blue marlin painting's alarm and of the picture hooks. Stepping up on the chair, he cut a neat plug of plaster from the wall above the marks with the surprisingly sharp edge of his framing square. Then he began drilling.

The power drill was not, despite appearances, standard carpenter's issue. For one thing it was slow. The polycrystalline diamond drill bit, guided by a rail system braced against the wall that allowed for millimetre-by-millimetre control, would take over ten minutes to cut through the Victorian brick. But it was powerful. And it was very, very quiet.

Murilo Andrade strode animatedly about the set. A passionate, dark-eyed giant, he kept his arms in constant motion as he spoke. 'Let me make a public confession that will surprise no one. For many years, as a young man, I smoked marijuana. In Brazil, this is normal. Over my lifetime, I have, who knows, spent ten thousand dollars on weed. Not *one cent* of that money went to anything useful. None of it went to the government to pay for drug treatment programmes. None of it fed directly into the mainstream economy to strengthen my country.

'Instead, it went to organized crime. It bought guns. It bought the cooperation of police officers, prosecutors and judges. It bought mansions for drug lords. The world spends more or less 400 billion dollars on illegal drugs each year. As long as Prohibition remains, most of that money will go – untaxed – into the wallets of the worst scum on the planet.'

A change in colour of the material being sucked through the drill's clear plastic waste tube warned the tourist that the drill bit had reached plaster. He lowered the speed still further, raising the torque and scraping away the last millimetres. Removing the drill, he put his ear to the hole and listened. Andrade was still speaking.

With a damp cloth, he cleaned the traces of masonry dust from the wall and floor, and erased the pencil marks. Next he took the largest of the screwdrivers from his toolbox and eased off the tip to reveal a scalpel blade. The shaft was extendable, and he pulled it out to its full length of 120 centimetres. Slowly he inserted it into the drilled hole, careful not to catch the blade on the rough brick, until its razor-sharp point was resting against the back of the Blue Marlin canvas.

Squinting along the shaft of the screwdriver, he carved a small circle of canvas out of the great fish's flank.

The Dutch prime minister leaned forward in her chair. She had long ago mastered the knack of ignoring the crowds of technicians and the blinding studio lights to focus entirely on the camera. 'Is it possible to legalize drugs? No one argues that the tax revenues and cost savings would be welcome in this Age of Austerity.' A rueful smile. Anneke van der Velde was a politician who had reached the top through inclusiveness and informality. 'More importantly, many of us feel instinctively uncomfortable prohibiting adults from activities that hurt no one but themselves. But still . . . is it truly possible to make these dangerous substances legal? Because they *are* dangerous. No one is disputing that. Just as alcohol and skiing and chainsaws are dangerous. Can we responsibly allow our supermarkets to sell MDMA that might induce a psychotic episode? Or ketamine that might rot your bladder? Or heroin that might kill you?'

* * *

The handle of the toolbox was ergonomically shaped, it was true, but that was not the reason for its generous proportions. It split open at the touch of a concealed pin to reveal an even more exquisitely crafted device. The dart gun had been designed for one very particular application: firing through restricted apertures. In such situations, a normal scope is impractical; instead, a tiny camera had been set into the muzzle of the gun, wirelessly connected to the tourist's smartphone.

He inserted the barrel into the drilled hole and switched on his muted phone. The image was crisp, clear, magnified: the dart gun was presently pointed at the back of an LED panel. A slight shift and the lines of the reticle found his target's shoulder. Another minute adjustment, and they crossed just above her left breast.

Anneke van der Velde felt the tiny dart penetrate her flesh, but she did not understand what it was. She had been bitten several times by mosquitoes during her short stay in Tobago, and with her mind so entirely on the broadcast she dismissed this sharp little pain as yet another vexatious tropical bug. It did not interrupt the flow of her speech for one moment.

'Drugs *are* dangerous. But the bigger danger lies in the way addicts are forced to obtain their fix. Heroin and cocaine may be cut with brick dust, drain cleaner, even rat poison. Some supplies are too concentrated and the user overdoses. Syringes may be contaminated: the primary route of transmission for HIV in Western Europe and North America is through shared needles. The criminalization of drug use means that people who need support from health professionals risk imprisonment if they approach the authorities. So they hide underground, mugging and stealing and selling their bodies to fund their habit. Over half of all acquisitive crime in Western Europe is committed by drug addicts desperate to buy heroin or crack cocaine. The solution is a safe, regulated, taxable system of narcotics supply accompanied by well-funded health education. Allow us . . . Allow us to explain . . .' She grimaced suddenly, put her hand to her side. For a long, uncomfortable moment, she was silent.

'Perhaps, President Andrade,' she said finally, in a voice that was stripped of its usual dynamism and vigour, 'you would explain how it could work.'

The Dutch prime minister was still alive when the tourist left Belvedere House.

'Boss changed his mind,' he grimaced to the Canadian security officers on the door. Walking out into the damp Tobago heat, he surveyed the seventeen vehicles crammed into the sloping driveway. Most were local hire cars, anonymous white saloons and silver Suzuki SUVs. He chose a Nissan for its open windows. Once in the driving seat with his toolbox, it took him just sixteen seconds to start the engine.

Both security checkpoints – at the gate and on the dirt track beyond – waved him straight through. No one had any great interest in vehicles leaving the Belvedere estate.

At Emerald Sea Resort, cocktails were still being mixed. Families played contentedly in the pool. A small TV at the back of the terrace bar showed frantic debate between far-off political commentators, but the volume was too low for anyone to notice.

They checked out, with only a slight quibble over the bill, and drove the short distance to the airport. Monitors at A. N. R. Robinson International showed CNN clips of the Think Again transmission, but none of the passengers watching were aware of their proximity to the event. The tourist and his companion boarded the 19:05 British Airways flight to London Gatwick amidst a murmur of commentary about the shocking death. She seemed so young for a prime minister, they all agreed. So nice. Such a shame.

The distraught guardians of Anneke van der Velde's body were unwilling to entrust it to the Trinidad and Tobago Forensic Science Centre, and so it was not until nine hours after the tourist – or Gavriel Yadin, as he could now once more think of himself – touched down in southern England that deliberate poisoning was established as the cause of death by toxicologists in The Hague. Even then, it took a sharp-eyed pathologist over an hour to locate the tiny puncture wound where the soluble polymer dart had buried itself in the prime minister's pectoral muscle. Up to that point, no one had noticed the plaster plug that had been carefully reinserted in the wall of the whirlpool room. The damage to the Blue Marlin painting had been blamed on careless lighting engineers.

Finally, three days after Gavriel Yadin left Tobago, an officer in the Canadian Prime Minister Protection Detail recalled, during what was effectively an interrogation, the carpenter who had departed shortly before Anneke van der Velde collapsed. By then, the stolen Nissan hire car had been found on a forest track, although no one had thought to connect it to the death of the Dutch prime minister. Consequently, no DNA or fingerprint analysis was conducted before its ignition was repaired and it was valeted and hired out to a family from Scotland.

The assassin's trail, always tenuous, had become the coldest thing in the Caribbean.

PART I:

THE SPY

MILAN, ITALY – 7 June

The rendezvous was an underpass on the outskirts of the city. Madeleine Wraye knew it wasn't going to be the meeting point. If it was, she'd got the wrong man.

No CCTV units. The grimy pavement was wide enough for them to pull over without obstructing the traffic. Edward Joyce activated the hazard lights and raised the bonnet in accordance with their instructions.

'See that?' he said, pointing to a heap of abandoned crates, a vagrant's shelter, fifty metres off. He marched purposefully to the dilapidated encampment, peered inside. Wraye watched him with amusement. 'What?' he said, aggrieved, when he returned to the car.

'Nothing.'

'*He* wouldn't have checked?'

'Yes, he probably would have.'

Joyce leaned against the BMW, feigning nonchalance as he studied the water stains on the decaying concrete overhead. 'He could have chosen somewhere less grim.'

'He wants the cover. In case we have drone or satellite surveillance.'

'Jesus. The man really is paranoid.'

'He has reason to be, unfortunately.'

A car had come to a halt on the opposite carriageway. White, a Fiat. Comfortably anonymous. In it, the lone figure of a young woman. Moments later a similar model in silver pulled up behind the BMW.

'Steady,' murmured Wraye. 'Hands in the open. We don't want any misunderstandings.'

The driver of the silver Fiat stepped out. 'Good evening,' he said in accented English. 'My name is Carlo. Thank you for your punctuality.' He was short and skinny, with a thin moustache and two delicate gold chains around his neck. Addressing Wraye, the man added, 'Our friend asks that you travel a little further. Your colleague must remain here. Is this acceptable?'

'Absolutely n—' Joyce began, but Wraye interrupted him.

'It's acceptable.'

'You will leave all weapons, phones and radios behind.'

'I'm not armed,' said Wraye, handing her phone to Joyce.

'Thank you,' Carlo smiled, as if greatly relieved. 'Your driver is waiting for you.' He gestured across the busy road.

'Great,' muttered Wraye. A steel barrier separated two flows of continuous traffic. She was going to have to perform an undignified dash and an even more undignified clamber over the barrier, all for the amusement of the young woman still sitting coolly in the white Fiat.

Joyce grabbed her arm. 'Are you sure he's worth it?'

'Worth what?'

'The risk! You said yourself TALON might have turned

hostile since you knew him. You don't have any idea where that woman's taking you.'

'Yes. He's worth it.'

'There are other people who could do the job.'

'Who? *You*?' Wraye stared at him. 'You want to hunt Yadin?'

Joyce drew himself up. 'It's not such a ridiculous idea.'

She laughed hollowly. 'He'd eat you for breakfast.'

The young woman did not speak at first. She drove fast but sensibly, checking the rear-view mirror more often than was really necessary. Someone had shown her what to do, Wraye decided, but she wasn't service-trained. Their route led into the centre of Milan, via a lot of empty backstreets and seemingly random right turns. Even if Joyce had found a gap in that steel barrier and executed a swift U-turn, he would never have caught up with them. Wraye estimated it would have taken five or six surveillance vehicles to beat that simple underpass gambit without giving themselves away.

'Is he always this careful?'

'No one has traced him in nine years.' The driver wore white jeans and a citrine blouse. Her hand on the gear stick betrayed only a hint of tension. The skin was tanned but butter-soft.

'That's because everyone thinks he's dead.'

A slight shrug. 'Exactly.'

Their destination was a large and anonymous modern hotel near the Giardini Pubblici. From the underground car park, an express elevator carried them to the sixth floor. Wraye studied her escort in the elevator mirrors. A beautiful face, intently focused. High cheekbones. Perfectly straight ash-blonde hair.

The kind of woman one couldn't imagine doing the washing-up. 'Is he here?'

'I'll be taking you to him shortly.' Her accent not quite English.

The room was a standard four-star offering, with only a framed print of the Gothic cathedral to hint at their location. Laid out on the bed was a long sapphire dress of elegant but conservative cut, a pair of matching heels, a set of underwear, and a small make-up kit.

'We're going to a party?' asked Wraye, lifting an eyebrow. There was no telephone in the room, she noticed.

The woman produced a cotton sack. 'All clothes, jewellery and personal items go in here. Carlo will return them to your associate.'

Wraye considered her. 'What's your name?'

'Beth,' came the reply, after a short hesitation.

'Well, "Beth", how about telling me what the plan is?'

'I don't like to talk a whole lot.'

Australian, decided Wraye, but well hidden.

'So what are you – his girlfriend?'

'His employee,' said the woman, her voice neutral.

'Like a PA?'

'Sure. Like a PA.' A hint of humour.

'I'm not bugged. No tracking devices sewn into my collar, if that's what this is about.'

'We haven't got much time. Please get undressed, Ms Wraye.'

'How do I know this is genuine?' she demanded. 'The man I'm looking for is officially deceased.'

Beth reached into her pocket. 'He said this would help with any doubts.'

She held out a strip of animal hide, discoloured and stiff with age. Wraye stared at the thing, took it with visible reluctance.

'Do you recognize it?'

'It's from one of the devices we used to torture him.'

For the first time, the cool little assistant seemed off-balance. She took refuge in repetition, holding out the sack and saying, 'We haven't got much time.'

'Are you going to watch?'

'Yes.'

Turning irritably away, Wraye stripped off her jacket, boots and trousers. She did not like this young woman seeing her naked. The age difference was too stark. Though her mind felt sharper and quicker than ever, her body – despite frequent visits to an expensive Knightsbridge health club – was too obviously past its peak. At fifty-three, Madeleine Wraye could no longer pretend that her breasts were firm or her stomach flat. Removing her underwear and dropping it along with her rings and handbag into the cotton sack, she felt unreasonably resentful of the other woman's impassive gaze.

'Raise your arms, please.' The woman inspected her armpits, the small of her back, beneath each breast and between her legs. She ran her fingers across her scalp, felt behind her ears, looked in her mouth and between her toes.

'Satisfied?' snapped Wraye.

'I'll leave you to get dressed now.'

They returned to the underground car park, but not to the same car. Beth led the way instead to a black Mercedes and opened the rear door. 'You are Lady Celia Buxton. This is your invitation.'

The stiff white card swarmed with golden copperplate, except for the line detailing the location of the event. That had been scraped bare. 'You're presently summering in Monaco. You've known the Count since he visited London in 1996 to paint the Naval College at Greenwich. You met at Christie's, where he outbid you on a small Renoir.'

'I've never "summered" in my life,' muttered Wraye as she got in. 'Who dreamed up that absurd legend?'

'The person you are looking for is known to the Count as Jeffrey Morton. Please remember that. Jeffrey Morton, a security consultant from Portsmouth, formerly an officer in British military intelligence. That's all. We won't be speaking again.'

'Wait, I need to know where—'

But the door was already closed and, much to her annoyance, Wraye discovered that the partition between driver and passenger was shut. Both rear doors were locked and the windows could not be opened. A black film on the glass cut visibility almost to zero.

Madeleine Wraye was not someone who suffered such loss of control with good grace.

, ITALY – 7 June

The journey lasted around two hours. Devoid of her watch and phone, with only the setting sun to inform her, Wraye couldn't make a more accurate assessment of the passing time. The drive was fast and smooth, some of it flat, some hilly. At one point she caught a hint of sea air transmitted through the car's air-conditioning system. But most of the time she could see nothing through the heavily tinted windows but the skimming headlights of autostrada traffic, and the occasional sequence of fluorescent dashes as they passed through a tunnel.

It was fully dark by the time the Mercedes came to a halt. The rear window slid down, and Wraye looked up into the ebullient face of a man dressed in a frock coat, embroidered waistcoat and powdered wig. '*Buonasera, signora*,' he said. Still Italy, then. Probably.

Wraye held out the gold-scripted invitation.

The car door opened and a deep red carpet extended before her, flanked by flaming torches, rising up a marble staircase to a neoclassical portico.

Wraye gazed up at the great house. Floodlights illuminated classical statues in niches and orange trees in giant terracotta pots. Guests in evening dress crowded the ornate balconies and terraces. A string orchestra was playing Rossini. Waiters in Renaissance-patterned waistcoats and skullcaps glided amongst the guests bearing magnums of Dom Pérignon.

'My God, Simon,' breathed Wraye to herself as she stepped out of the car. 'How you've grown up.'

He was not in the hall or drawing rooms downstairs. Nor was he part of the younger crowd that had assembled in the courtyard loggia, with loosened bow ties and wandering eyes. Wraye accepted a glass of champagne from a waiter's tray and climbed the magnificent curving staircase. She recognized amongst the men on the upper floor a handful of Italian parliamentarians from the right of the political spectrum, as well as several high-profile media figures and business leaders. On each one, she could have recalled a substantial body of data, some in the public domain, some rather more intimate.

At the end of one corridor, she found herself in a library. It was less crowded than the other rooms: a small group by the piano; two couples not quite entwined on the couches. And over by the windows a man with his back to her, three young women clustered about him. He was the right height, still slim, hair a little darker than she remembered, back and shoulders solidly drawn beneath his modish silk dinner jacket. His words had his debutante audience captivated. A joke, a toss of the head, a wink to one of the girls, and Wraye caught a glimpse of his face.

It wasn't him.

She turned to go – and stopped still. Positioned exactly where he ought to be – away from the windows, close to an exit, with a clear view of all doorways – was a ghost. Dead to the world, and most especially to his former colleagues, yet unquestionably real in his charcoal suit and blue striped tie, the man was engrossed in conversation with the oldest guest at the party. He had seen her, of course, long before she identified him. He would have been informed of her arrival, would have judged her progress through the palazzo, decided on the door she would come through. And still he managed to give no sign of it. His attention seemed entirely focused on the matriarch in the Rococo armchair, and only a trained observer would have noticed that he kept Wraye always within his peripheral field of vision.

The sight of him, now, after nine lost years, brought back a moment from long ago. A Georgetown drawing room.

Watching her new, undeclared officer through a filter of congressmen, aides, lobbyists and the more respectful members of the DC press corps. Peripheral vision only, always careful to avoid any suggestion that she knew the young man with the dark blond hair and the playful blue eyes who didn't quite seem at ease in his jacket and tie. And when some well-meaning Washington wife decided to introduce the two Brits – 'He's with the *London Times*, Madeleine, one of your rising stars' – she had shaken hands with a polite smile, searched valiantly for common ground, and then moved on to more important people.

'Mr Morton.'

The head turned a fraction. Those eyes had once been full of life. Now they were unreadable. 'Lady Buxton.' His voice, spellbinding to the Washington establishment, was so instantly familiar it made her catch her breath.

He held out a hand which she took, flesh and blood, for a measured two seconds. Slight creases in the warm skin. Smile lines around the mouth – a reassuring sign. His teenager's beauty had metamorphosed into something more appropriate to his profession. There was a hardness to his jaw now, a hint of jeopardy in the magnetism that still defined his gaze.

'*Mi scusi*,' he murmured to the matriarch. Guiding Wraye with a respectful hand not quite touching her back, he led the way to an adjoining room. 'Celia, it's been a long time.'

'It really has. You should have written.'

'Well . . . here we are, anyway.'

'At a society party, no less. Wouldn't a bar at Milano Centrale have done?'

The next room turned out to be less comfortable than the library, and was empty of guests. Some kind of archive, it offered only hard wooden chairs and rolling stepladders to reach the higher shelves.

'This is safer.'

'That answers a number of questions. You view me as a threat.'

'A potential threat.'

'Then despite the elaborate precautions of your charming Australian assistant, you've arranged an escape route out of here.'

'She'll be gutted you nailed her nationality.'

'And the Count is . . . ?'

'A client.'

'I see. The security consultant. That's why you're the only guest dressed like an employee. Didn't I teach you to blend in?'

'Bow ties and cummerbunds?' he smiled. 'I haven't changed that much.'

'Shall we sit down? There's a lot to talk about.'

'Let's stand. We don't have long.'

'Because you don't trust me.'

'It's possible you've already borrowed a waiter's phone to call in our location.'

'Which is?'

The smile returned for a second.

'Just how long do we have?'

'I leave in four minutes.'

'After nine years? No!' She grabbed two wooden chairs and thrust one at him. 'Sit down! You owe me that much for the funeral you put me through. Who was it, by the way, that unlucky man in the kitchen with your wife? Four minutes, my *God*. You expect to get what you want from me in four minutes?'

He remained standing. 'What makes you think I want anything from you?'

'You agreed to see me, at what you evidently consider to be great personal risk. There must be a reason. Is it information you're after? About the bombing? Our investigation was inconclusive.'

'I wanted to be able to look into your eyes. To know if you had a part in it.'

She went cold. 'And what do you see?'

He scowled. 'Inconclusive.'

'You were like a son to me! I loved Emily. To suggest I could have harmed either one of you—'

Impatiently, he said, 'I leave in two minutes. What do you want, Madeleine?'

'Simon, *look* at me! I'm the same person you trusted with your life in Kyrgyzstan. The friend who sat with you in Almaty while you waited for news of your father's stroke. Have you forgotten the Swat Valley, stuck all night in that freezing ditch? Does that mean *nothing*?'

For an instant his face softened involuntarily, and she recognized in his eyes a flash of the man she'd known – the adventure and life and joyful curiosity. Seizing the moment, she said, 'I have a job for you.'

He laughed out loud.

'At least let me tell you what it is.'

'I have plenty of work.' That spark of connection was gone. Coldly suppressed.

'So I see,' she sneered. 'Italian counts! What else? Korean toothbrush manufacturers? You've sold out.'

'And you haven't? They say your new house has a sauna in the basement.'

'My clients are still the right people.'

'Sure about that?'

'The job is important.'

'It was always important,' he sighed. 'But I'm not Simon Arkell any more. I can't afford to be. If I step back into that world, someone might find out their bomber missed his target.' He turned away. 'It was good to see you, Madeleine.'

He was gone in a second, but she was as quick, catching him on the stairs. 'Hear me out and I'll give him to you.'

'What?'

'The bomber, Simon. The man who killed your wife.'

He didn't stop moving, didn't flinch even. 'So you *were* involved,' he said blackly.

'We don't know who ordered it. But there was a CCTV record – a private unit outside the corner shop. It caught a van leaving, with a usable frame of the driver's face. Simon, I have the bomber's name.'

He stopped on the threshold of the hallway. 'Give me the name and I'll consider the job.'

'First we discuss the job.'

There was something there, briefly, a glimmer of the old lust for living, for the unknown. The thirst for adventure that had propelled him through some of the most inimical corners of the planet without a hint of self-doubt. But there was also something ominous which made her feel uneasy, a glaze of suspicion that swept her right back to an interrogation cell in Abuja. A British subject invading sovereign Nigerian territory under a French flag. A potential diplomatic nightmare. A prospect.

The suspicion faded – or seemed to fade. It was all she could hope for at the moment. Maintain contact at all costs. 'Simon, I promise you—'

'Come with me,' he said.

ABUJA, NIGERIA – sixteen years earlier

It was a stitch-up by Tony Watchman. Or Jane Saddle. Either her or Jeremy Elphinstone. One of those scheming rivals who played the political game with a little more attention than she did. They had been quicker to recognize that after the fall of the Berlin Wall it was no longer enough to have a shining record in SovBloc intelligence. In fact, with former KGB officers being invited to parleys at Century House, it could even count against you. What mattered most was who you had batting for you in the committees. And the truth was Madeleine Wraye had never devoted sufficient attention to recruiting batsmen.

She'd wanted DC, had expected the Balkans, had been dealt – following the 'Christmas Massacre' that saw much of the Secret Intelligence Service restructured – a career-numbing joke in Abuja, the new capital of Nigeria. The last place on earth for an aspiring spymaster to build her political clout. With the intelligence community still hunting – after the shocking demise of the Cold War – for a new purpose, Wraye needed to be in Belgrade or Beijing, Beirut or Berlin. Abuja held nothing but new concrete and old corruption. Four years of filing the tittle-tattle of Nigeria's kleptocratic military-political class, never to be read by the Joint Intelligence Committee or even published in the CX Book, would break her.

The first priority, then, was to select new targets for the demotivated staff of two General Service officers and three secretaries that she inherited. Following the growth of international heroin trafficking and racketeering networks operated by the Nigerian diaspora, organized crime was an obvious choice. Madeleine Wraye was quick to see the potential for some real spy work on the networks' home ground, generating substantive, relevant CX that might actually get circulated back in London. The laborious investigation she initiated yielded scant results in the first months. One of her officers, alarmed by the new regime requiring him to associate with 'slum-dwelling criminals', resigned. But the remaining officer took up the challenge, and by the second year they had together assembled a fair picture of the organized crime syndicates operating from Nigeria. By the third year, a headline-grabbing series of drug seizures and arrests had been triggered across Britain.

During those three years, Wraye made a special effort to get close to her CIA opposite number, an old Africa hand with a great deal of influence back in Langley – perfectly placed to talent-spot 'a Brit we can do business with'. The two station chiefs cooperated to shine a light on illegal bunkering operations in the Niger Delta and secure advance notice of tanker hijackings. Indeed, by the end of her time in post, the relationship was such that she was able to request, for a particularly unusual liaison operation, the covert aerial surveillance services of a Lockheed S-3 Viking based off a US carrier in the Gulf of Guinea.

'What I don't get,' said the CIA chief over a late-night whisky and soda in the US embassy, 'is why you're involving yourself. Hell, I'm no fan of the French, but aren't they supposed to be our allies?'

It had started with a report from an asset in Djibouti, far from Wraye's West African patch. The asset was a long-time SIS agent within the French Foreign Legion's East African base. His cryptonym was SABLE, and he was believed to be a Welshman with the rank of lieutenant in the Bureau des Statistiques – the Legion's intelligence division – although his identity was known only to his Nairobi case officer and two directors in Head Office. He had marched stiffly – it was joked by those who knew of the Legion's peculiarities, at a rate of exactly eighty-eight steps per minute – into the British embassy in Paris during his first leave, to offer his services. He loved the Legion and planned to make a career of it; but he loved Wales more, and seeing as Cardiff didn't run to an intelligence outfit the British one would have to do. Whatever the truth of that particular yarn, for years SABLE kept the Service closely informed of covert French actions throughout sub-Saharan Africa.

His most recent communication had read: *Legion black incursion Nigeria pm14/am15 May. Target Chadian rebels Borno state.* A grid reference was given, nothing more. SABLE was renowned for his brevity.

Having arrived in Nigeria with no love for the place whatsoever, Madeleine Wraye had come to feel protective of her adopted turf. Large and oil-rich though she may be, Nigeria is surrounded on all sides by Francophone countries. The unwritten rules were clear: the French could stir up as much trouble as they fancied in Togo and Benin to the west, Niger to the north, and Chad and Cameroon to the east, but they stayed the hell out of (British) Nigeria.

By then, she had worked the Abuja cocktail circuit long enough to have built up strong relationships with all the key players in the military government. It was a simple matter to pick up the phone and pass on SABLE's intelligence. His grid reference pinpointed a village thirty kilometres south of Lake Chad which served as an occasional training camp and weapons store for Chadian insurgents. On the morning of 14 May, the Nigerian Army High Command quietly evacuated the village and brought in two companies of the 3rd Armoured Division to lay an ambush.

Wraye had attached one fundamental condition to her tip-off: the legionnaires should be released within a week of capture. The goal was to shame France, not condemn her mercenaries to long prison sentences. Above all, there must be no casualties.

When the call came from the US Navy Viking loitering high over the Legion field base outside Massakory, Wraye and her CIA counterpart put down their whiskies and decamped to the secure conference room to watch the infrared video feed. At 1 a.m. exactly, the engines on a plane parked beside the camp's dirt airstrip underwent a rapid change of colour and twelve glowing bodies climbed aboard. As the aircraft departed to the south-west, Wraye phoned the Army High Command. The Viking tracked the French plane through Cameroonian airspace and across the Nigerian border. Wraye made a second call when it was five nautical miles from the target village. She watched as twelve bodies tumbled from the plane, then she bid her American host goodnight, drove home and went to bed.

The following afternoon, Madeleine Wraye was invited to Army Headquarters Garrison – a rare honour for a declared spy. The ambush had been a great success, she was told. All twelve of the legionnaires had surrendered without a fight. There was just one curious detail. When it came time to handcuff the prisoners and transport them to Abuja, only eleven legionnaires remained.

After an extensive search by over 400 troops, the twelfth was recaptured just one kilometre from the Cameroonian border. He was, to everyone's surprise, English. Would Ms Wraye like to see him?

If the Army High Command had expected Madeleine Wraye to intercede on behalf of a British subject, they were to be disappointed. On the contrary, intrigued by his disappearing trick, she encouraged them to sweat him. After observing the first four hours of his interrogation, she was more than intrigued. The Englishman showed not the slightest concern at finding himself in a foul cell, strapped to a steel chair and roared at by a bearded Hausa giant. He offered up a name and rank immediately, followed almost teasingly by a date of birth and regiment number. But on the subject of the Borno raid, and on every other subject, he was silent.

'That's not his real name,' Wraye told the interrogator when he returned to the darkened observation room. On the other side of the one-way glass panel, the young man calling himself

Corporal Jonathan Reeves sat peaceably, with manacled hands in his lap and curious eyes hooded against the savagely bright lights. 'The Legion issues each recruit with a new name for the duration of their service. Make him tell you his real name.'

The Hausa giant tried hitting the legionnaire, first in the gut, then in the face. He punched him hard enough to split the skin on his jaw and tip the steel chair over. He hosed cold water into his mouth and nose. With Wraye's agreement, he beat him with a stick and then a whip made of strips of animal hide. He even tried a little electricity work. Nothing had any effect.

The presiding officer said, 'We will get results if we go harder, but is there a reason? What can he tell you that it is worth crippling him?'

Wraye nodded. 'Keep him awake forty-eight hours, no water, then I'll talk to him.'

That evening, she issued an urgent requirement for SABLE: *Require civilian name Corporal Jonathan Reeves*. She hoped the Welsh lieutenant would appreciate her brevity.

The legionnaire was kneeling in a stress position with a hood over his head. The pool of urine had largely evaporated, adding a new note to the background stench of the cell. Two guards, whose job it had been to prod the prisoner with batons whenever his spine softened, came lazily to attention as Wraye entered carrying a small pile of books.

'Go,' she said.

When the door was locked behind them, she removed the hood and gazed at the dirty stubble, swollen jaw and bloodshot eyes of the man she had decided to recruit.

'Hello, Stephen.'

His head jerked up.

'You'll have to learn to disguise your reactions. That is, if you want to go on using false identities. No good if you give yourself away like that.'

She pointed him to the steel chair and took the other, padded seat. He stood up warily, and with some difficulty. When he sat, his back remained straight, his cramped legs half-tensed.

She gestured to the pile of books. 'They tell me you've been asking for some reading material on the region.'

He picked one up with cuffed hands. 'These are wildlife guides. I asked for histories.' His voice was contorted by thirst.

'You're in Abuja. A manufactured city. It has no history.'

Wordlessly, he let the book drop.

'Why did you run, Stephen? Why did you abandon your comrades?'

'My name is Jonathan Reeves.'

'Well, now, that's what's confusing me. The name of the prefect expelled from St Michael's following the death of a classmate was Stephen Gordon. The name of the seventeen-year-old Guardsman kicked out of the Coldstream – his father's old regiment – for aberrant and unbecoming behaviour was Stephen Gordon. The name of the boy who presented himself at the recruiting office of the French Foreign Legion in Lille three weeks later was Stephen Gordon. What do you think they're saying about you, Stephen? Stephen? The men you abandoned. What happened to that glorious *fraternité* we hear so much about?'

The legionnaire didn't answer. He kept his gaze on Wraye, but gave nothing more away.

'I expect you'd like a drink.'

Nothing.

'No?' She produced a plastic bottle from her briefcase. 'It's mineral water. Safe. Cold. The Nigerians bottle it on some mountain or other. Have a drink, Stephen. After I'm gone you may not be offered another for some time.'

She held out the bottle, but he made no move to take it.

'I mean, really, what is the point? Põldoja's been chattering away for hours. So have Kraft, de Souza and the others. Why put yourself through this pain when all Abuja wants is an admission of guilt before they let you go. Christ, you were caught red-handed, bearing French arms on Nigerian territory. It's not like you're telling them anything they don't already know. They just need to hear you say it. African pride, Stephen. Stephen? Just a rough operational sketch and you're on a plane back to N'Djamena. Back to the warm, welcoming breast of La Patrie. Croissants and garlic for breakfast. Otherwise it's more thirst, more beatings, more pain.'

He was smiling. Dark, antagonistic, nonetheless a smile. 'You think this is pain?' he said. 'You should try a Legion jail sometime. You should try a Legion training camp. Our NCOs would have a lot to teach your friend with the beard.'

Wraye suppressed a flutter of excitement. He was perfect. He'd made a mistake responding – any engagement, however defiant, is a way in for a skilled interrogator – but the resilience and attitude were just what she wanted. There weren't twenty officers left in the whole of the Service who could summon up a smile under these circumstances.

'Is that right?' she said. 'Beau Geste has teeth again? Because word is the Legion's a shadow of the force it was in Algeria.' There are many ways to manipulate, and Madeleine Wraye knew and used them all. But her preferred technique was prodding. Goading her subject to reveal what he shouldn't, with little pricks to his vanity and his self-esteem.

It didn't work on the legionnaire. He gazed at her thoughtfully, then said, 'A general Nigerian history would be fine.'

'Stephen, let's cut the crap,' she said, swiftly changing tack. 'You're not in a good position here. The Nigerians can hold you as long as they like. They'll claim they let you go, deny all further knowledge of you. When you don't show up, the Legion will write you off as a deserter. Meanwhile you'll be rotting in a cell that makes this place look like Shangri-La. You want that?'

No response.

'I can help. I can get you out of here today.'

'What does that make you? Military liaison?'

'Something like that.'

'Oh,' he grimaced. 'That's what you are.'

'Maybe you do want to rot. Maybe that's why you joined the Legion. For the pain. The forced marches. The punishments. Breaking rocks all day. Confined to a hole in the ground for a week. They still do that? Maybe that's why you took the Coldstream branding game too far. You wanted the pain of that steel burning into your chest. All because you killed a schoolboy. Thomas Parke, organ scholar and shoo-in for Cambridge, beloved by his mother and three younger sisters, drowned in a storm drain because you dared him to follow you. Do I have that right, Stephen? I heard they had to use a garden rake to get his body out. Your best friend's corpse. Do you want the Nigerians to throw away the key so you can finally forgive yourself? Would twenty years here salve your conscience?'

She'd reached him. At last she'd got through. He didn't say anything for three long minutes, but she knew from the slight shifts in the muscles of his face that she'd found something real, something that cut deep.

When eventually he spoke, his desiccated voice had a new hollowness to it. 'I never dared him.'

'You called him a coward, right? Heavy rains put the sports fields out of commission. Bored pupils. An audience. Big strong Stephen Gordon shows the world what a tough guy he is by swimming forty metres through an underground pipe. Fucking stupid stunt, but you made it. Good for you. Another bloody schoolboy hero. Except now you have to go and push your best friend into copying you. Dying for you.'

'I didn't call him a coward. I didn't say anything.'

'But you didn't stop him.'

The prisoner looked down. His manacled hands hung lifeless between his legs.

'You let him try to match you, even though you knew he wasn't as strong.'

'What business is it of yours?' he growled.

'What business of mine? Are you serious?' She was shouting all of a sudden, standing over him. 'A fucked-up British loose cannon roaming around Africa with French weaponry in his hands, invading a major trading partner and strategic ally of the United Kingdom? Are you absolutely serious, Stephen? You don't see what business that is of mine? We've shot British subjects for less.'

'Then go ahead. Shoot me.'

She watched him silently for a while. Taking her seat, she whispered, 'Are you really this self-destructive? Or is it an act?'

'I'll take that water now.'

She gave no sign of hearing him. The bottle remained on the floor beside her chair. 'Stephen, why are you giving your considerable talents to France? If your original sin was in Wiltshire, why pay Paris?'

He lunged forward and grabbed the bottle with his cuffed hands, ripped off the lid with his teeth and emptied it down his throat.

'Whatever part you think you played in that boy's drowning, you're no use to me if you have a death wish.'

He blinked at her. '*Use to you?*'

'What do you hope to achieve in the Legion, other than self-annihilation? I've seen your record: a hell of an achievement in an elite unit. Top of the class in close combat and survival. Top five in marksmanship, navigation, boat handling, covert infiltration, demolition and guerrilla tactics. The Djibouti trainers love you. They even rate your singing.'

'Vehicles.'

'Excuse me?'

A dull, lifeless voice now. 'Vehicles. Your informer left that one out. Top five in off-road and urban driving.'

'And all for what?' Wraye leaned back in her chair and treated him to her most pitying stare. 'You've got your corporal's galons, but they'll never make you a sous-officier. Did you know that? It's in your file. Bold print. You're not French, and you're not considered loyal or stable enough to make up for that defect.'

'That's bullshit.'

'Face it, Stephen, they still see you as a troubled teenager. "*Grandes lacunes*" in your moral and emotional development. Got to hand it to the French for linguistic style. We'd have just called them "gaps". *Grandes lacunes.* Highly intelligent, devastatingly effective in the field, but simply not leadership material.'

'So I should be a spook instead?'

She matched his stare. 'You should.'

He laughed, the sound coming from his loosened throat richer and deeper for the water. 'If I'd wanted to sit in an ivory tower and dream up theories about the resurgent Soviet threat, I'd have knocked on your door in London.'

'Fighting neocolonial wars for France is more relevant?'

'At least it's real.'

'The Service has a new agenda. Global Tasks, we call it. Terrorism, organized crime, nuclear proliferation. That's as real as it gets.'

'The *Service*?'

'Oh, I'm sorry. I haven't introduced myself. My name is Madeleine Wraye. I'm Chief of Station for the Secret Intelligence Service in Nigeria. In two months' time I take up a new position as Deputy Chief in Washington. My career is accelerating and I intend to gather around me a small number of people loyal only to me. People who, in different ways, are . . . useful.'

'You want a soldier in Washington? I don't see it.'

'I want an outsider. Someone the FBI doesn't know about. Undeclared. Deniable. Officially we don't spy on the Americans: we're there to liaise and collaborate, not steal secrets. Unofficially, both sides collect whatever they can get. I need someone not afraid to take a few risks, get hurt, possibly face a couple of years in prison.'

'Sounds appealing.'

'And I need brains. You were on track for Oxbridge, just like Thomas Parke. Your Coldstream application was as erudite as they come. I need someone smart enough to ask the right questions, push the right buttons with people a whole lot more dangerous than your Legion NCOs. The kind of man able to disappear under the noses of 400 Nigerian soldiers.'

The prisoner said nothing, but a flicker of a smile appeared in his eyes.

'I also need social confidence. Even in here, you have it in spades. Perhaps that comes from your mother's hotel career? Those five-star palaces where you spent the school holidays hanging out with staff and guests alike. Hong Kong. Rajasthan. Mayotte – that was where you first encountered the Legion, wasn't it? Lombok. New York. Buenos Aires. Florence. How many languages is it now? With French?'

'Four.'

'Four languages,' purred Wraye with real pleasure. 'And you know how to hold a glass of wine.'

'These days I prefer Corsican beer.' The legionnaire glanced at the empty plastic bottle crumpled in his fist. 'Thank you for the water and the books, but you're wasting your time. Even if I wanted to sign up with the kind of outfit that scavenges for recruits in Nigerian prisons, a Legion contract is five years, no exceptions. I've served three.'

'So desert.'

'Obviously your informer hasn't briefed you on what that means.'

'You'll be arrested if you ever set foot in France. Your name will be mud in the regiment. So what? Jonathan Reeves will no longer exist, and if you come with me to DC it certainly won't be as Stephen Gordon. Who cares what the French think of you? They won't have the first idea who or where you are.'

'I happen to like the Legion.'

'I happen to like Chekhov. Doesn't mean I want to spend my best years watching nothing but Russian tragedy. Look, Stephen, you've proved yourself out here. You've atoned, closed the book on Thomas Parke. It's time for you to move on. For what it's worth, you'll be reasonably paid. For what it's worth, you'll be directly advancing the interests of your country. But above all, you'll be using everything you've got – not just the muscle, not just the stamina. Everything, Stephen. That's what I want from you. Everything. Do you know how good it feels to give everything you have for something that matters?'

The prisoner was silent. He let the crushed plastic bottle drop to the floor.

'What would I be called?'

'Whatever you want. So long as it fits on a credit card and has no discernible connection to your previous life.'

He considered that. Reaching for the fallen book, he examined the cover. *An Illustrated Guide to the Birds of West Africa.* The author's name was short, punchy. Had a certain ring. He showed it to her. 'How about that?'

'Fine,' she smiled. 'All right, Mr Arkell, let's get out of here.' She put the stress on the second syllable – to rhyme with *hell.*

'A meal, a bath, the Official Secrets Act and a soft bed – in that order, OK?'

The newly christened ex-legionnaire insisted on doing one thing before giving himself over, body and soul, to Madeleine Wraye. He wanted to return his Legion rifle.

'Deserting is bad enough,' he explained. 'Deserting with your weapon is a whole different level of sin.'

'It's the stupidest idea I've ever heard,' said Wraye. 'They'll lock you up the moment you show your face.'

But Simon Arkell was adamant, and so Wraye arranged for him to pick his Clarion out of the pile of confiscated arms in a small shed at the back of the Abuja cell block. She stripped him of his Legion combat fatigues, replacing them with the chinos and short-sleeved cotton shirt of an oil worker on holiday. She issued him a rented 4x4 with space under the back seat to conceal the gun, a new passport, and just enough nairas for fuel, food and border bribes. He was back three days later.

After the diplomatic dust had settled on its abortive and politically embarrassing adventure into north-east Nigeria, the French Foreign Legion recovered eleven of its twelve men but only one of their weapons. The serial number of the assault rifle found on the commandant's desk at the Massakory field base identified it as that of Caporal Jonathan Reeves, previously known as Stephen Gordon, deserter.

Its return has since become a minor legend in the Legion.

LIGURIA, ITALY – 7 June

He'd put a towel over her head for the short drive – excessive precaution, wise in this business – but she could talk without difficulty. 'Am I allowed to know what you've been doing all this time? Why you disappeared? Don't say amnesia.'

'You start. Why did you leave the Service?'

'That won't see us past the first traffic light. Politics. Always politics. Male egos conspiring for the top jobs. Same tired old story.'

'And now?'

'I bring people together. I facilitate. I work across organizational boundaries in a way that was impossible in SIS. So when, to pick a relevant example, the Canadian Security Intelligence Service needs a dangerous man identified, they come to me. And when they decide they want that man terminated in a way that won't come back on them, they ask me to find the right candidate for the job.'

'That's what this is? You want me to kill someone?'

'You've killed before. Chad and Somalia for the Legion. Pakistan for us. God knows where else since you disappeared.'

'I don't do that kind of thing any more.'

'Oh? And why is that?' When he didn't answer, she said, 'If Emily's death taught us anything, it should be that there are bad people out there – bad enough to need eliminating.'

'And there are plenty of other independents who'll do it,' he said roughly. 'I'll give you some names if you like.'

Wraye took a breath. Slow down. The towel against her face was making her clumsy. 'So you don't kill any more. What *do* you still do? Blackmail? Eavesdrop? Steal secrets? Or are those sins also off the table?'

'I do whatever my clients need done. Within reason.'

'You still fight with a stick?' She said it with a smile in her voice – half admiring, half mocking.

'Not much reason to fight these days.'

The smile disappeared. 'You've gone soft,' she said accusingly.

He didn't reply.

Simon Arkell had learned fast in Washington. On his own, below the radar, he had succeeded in penetrating parts of the US defence and political establishment from which Wraye, as a declared SIS officer, was politely but resolutely barred. Befriending Treasury lawyers on the racquetball court, flirting with congressional staffers in Adams Morgan bars, and offering hard cash to Pentagon janitors – all with a nonchalant innocence that only a young and charming English newspaperman could get away with – Arkell had harvested intelligence of the first water. Revelations about the back-room deals done by the outgoing Clinton administration. A list of wealthy donors still channelling funds to the IRA. American military spending projections. Insight into the questionable intelligence sources on which the State Department was basing its Mideast policies.

And he was not even officially employed by SIS. Wraye had chosen from the outset to keep him off the books for as long as she could, unregistered with SIS and therefore unknowable to CIA eyes within the Service. The job at *The Times* had been organized through a civilian friend who owed her a debt of gratitude for the safe recovery of a kidnapped foreign correspondent. Arkell filed many a story under the name Andrew Tiller, as he was known in Washington. One or two were even quite valuable scoops. But the best stuff he kept for Wraye. And on their return from America, when it came time to recruit Arkell formally into the Service, she was meticulous in crediting him with every scrap of intelligence collected.

'Tell me the truth, Simon,' she said now. 'Are you doing anything more with this new life of yours than escorting rich men's children to school and rescuing their iPods from the playground bully?'

'You know I can't discuss operations.'

'*Operations!* At best, you're planting bugs in the offices of the Count's business rivals. Admit it: you're pissing your life away using one fiftieth of the skill set I gave you. Wouldn't you rather draw on everything you have, Simon, to do something truly important?'

'That line isn't going to work on me a second time.'

'It's still valid. Even more so. Then, you were a soldier, tough as nails but directionless and unformed. Now . . . I couldn't even say that for you.'

'Then find someone else,' he said simply.

The cottage was isolated, surrounded by woodland, dark. The end of the track. Arkell parked facing the way they'd come. With a torch, he checked three tell-tales around the oak front door – a fleck of silver paper in the lock, a scattering of sawdust on the door mat, the end of a vine trapped against the jamb.

Her first impression, once inside: he didn't live here; it was a loan from the Count, temporary digs for the hired help. Kicking off his black oxfords, Arkell padded across worn stone tiles to the fridge. 'Chianti or Verdicchio?'

'Some choice,' she said. 'Can't get your Corsican ditchwater here?'

He took the Verdicchio and two plain tumblers into the next room – empty but for a desk and a couple of armchairs. The fireplace had been used recently, despite the season. Pieces of half-burnt kindling outlined the ashy hearth. 'I remember you loathed it.'

Splashing wine into both glasses, he passed one to her and downed the other without appearing to taste it. No cheers, no clinking of glasses. He'd never been this cold before. His upbeat attitude, his boundless energy, had once been a source of great comfort and inspiration to Wraye. Her duties in Washington had included liaison with Defense Intelligence Agency weapons-proliferation experts, and at times her growing comprehension of the rogue nuclear threat had come close to sinking her. Simon Arkell's youthful optimism had helped her overcome the gnawing despair and step up to the tremendous responsibilities she had worked so hard to acquire.

She remembered his wedding as a moment of rare humanity in her fraught world. The speech: most of it directed straight to Emily; all of it from the heart. The first dance, with the two of them entwined like honeysuckle. Enough emotion in the air to carry Wraye back to her own short-lived marriage. Enough to wet her cheeks for the first time in years. She was one of just three SIS colleagues to be invited, and the only one he thanked in his speech, however obliquely. And Emily, who by then knew who she was and what she did, came over to her and hugged her with real warmth while whispering fervently, 'Keep him alive for me, will you? Please?'

That was two weeks before Wraye was made Director of Counter-Proliferation. It was an appointment that took her – and Arkell with her – all through the East European and Central Asian states that had previously, as constituent parts of the Soviet Union, been her enemy. Counter-Proliferation was one of the few spheres of SIS activity in which pure intelligence-gathering needed, on occasion, to be supplemented by covert action. In that, Simon Arkell excelled.

He refilled his glass, stripped off his tie and sat in the chair by the desk. 'Let's get this over with.'

Setting her wine untouched on the floor, Wraye took the other chair. She glanced at the desk: a laptop and a pile of hardback books on the history of Liguria. Somewhere deep in the night, an owl uttered a low cry. 'His name is Gavriel Yadin,' she began. 'He is a former Mossad officer, a member of the Kidon unit – an assassin. He is the man who killed Anneke van der Velde at the Think Again conference.'

This time, Arkell merely sipped his drink. 'It was a heart attack. We've all seen the clip.'

'It was hydrogen cyanide, delivered via a soluble dart.'

He hesitated. 'Not a single news report—'

'Who's going to admit a prime minister was murdered in front of three security services and a global television audience?'

'You said this was for the Canadians.'

'They reckon their man may be next.'

'As part of Think Again?'

'The theory – and it is only a theory – is that someone has hired Yadin to take out the three pro-legalization premiers, *pour encourager les autres*.'

'Then why not kill them all at once?'

'Perhaps to give the others a chance to recant? Or perhaps it's just more terrifying one by one.'

'There could be a thousand other reasons why van der Velde was targeted. Her clampdown on organized crime. Her immigration stance. The Dutch military cuts . . .'

'Nevertheless, the Canadians are nervous. They want the killer found and neutralized. You know what CSIS are like – friendly folk who identify themselves to the public and collect most of their intelligence within their own borders. They aren't set up to do this themselves.'

'How did you identify Yadin?'

'There was DNA from a set of abandoned hiking clothes, but the profile wasn't known to any police database. And Yadin managed to avoid showing his face to a single one of the CCTV units at the Tobago venue. But by chance a technician running a test on a reserve studio camera caught him on video for 1.8 seconds. CSIS couldn't make a match. Nor could the CIA or NSA or any European service. This guy is a ghost as far as the intelligence community is concerned. So they came to me. In the end, one of my contacts in the South African Secret Service nailed it from an old NIS–Mossad partnership archive.'

'Can I see the video?'

'It was on a memory stick your assistant confiscated in Milan. She's very beautiful, by the way. Are you . . . ?'

Arkell replenished his glass. 'Carlo will bring it here tomorrow.'

'The same data package is on my secure server. If you have broadband in this fleapit, I'll show you now.'

'It can wait.'

Wraye gazed at him, trying to gauge whether he recognized the trap he had just sidestepped. Computers were never his strong point, but in nine years that could have changed. Certainly, his simple online presence was well conceived: the social network profile carried no photo or contact details – just a mailbox through which bidders for his services could register their interest, if they were well enough connected to acquire his username.

For a long time, Wraye had remained entirely unaware of his survival. Then, a whisper of a rumour: a particularly effective freelance spy operating in the corporate market, who happened to have a background in the French military and British Intelligence. She was astounded, then hopeful, then tormented. But she did not look for him. If Simon Arkell really was alive, she reasoned, he had chosen to remain dead to his former SIS colleagues. She would respect that choice.

Until CSIS came calling. For the Yadin commission, there was simply no one else in the same league. It was a German industrialist, an old contact from her Counter-Proliferation days, who steered her to Arkell's webpage. *Remember Abuja?* was all she wrote. It was enough to elicit a response from beyond the grave.

'You've tried Mossad.'

'*Address unknown*,' she smiled. 'Yadin was kicked out twelve years ago. The charges were serious: rogue behaviour, ungovernable attitude, even a suggestion – unproven – that he took money from Hamas in exchange for advance notice of assassination targets. The Mossad claim they've lost track of him. It's unlikely, but there's no way they'll give up one of their own to a foreign service, even a blacklisted liability like Yadin. I stamped my foot with the DG, who still owes me from our A. Q. Khan collaboration, and he allowed me a glimpse of Yadin's personnel file. He also let slip that Yadin has been working for the same master ever since he left Israeli government service. That's as much help as we're going to get from them.'

'What's his story?'

Wraye nodded towards the laptop. 'May I? All my notes are on the server.'

Arkell didn't take the bait. 'Give me the headlines.'

'His mother was a PT instructor for the army, a sabra with a sharp tongue and undying loyalty to the state. Father quite the opposite: a mild-mannered university lecturer from Berne with a passion for model trains. The psychs speculated that little Gavriel reacted against what he perceived to be a gender imbalance between his parents. He became single-minded, occasionally vicious. There was an unfortunate incident involving his younger brother and a razor blade. You'll have to read the notes . . .'

'Go on.'

'Not that he's a sociopath. The Mossad steer clear of the mad and the bad. If he made it through selection, we can assume he's reasonably well balanced. But remember what we're dealing with here. There are fewer than fifty Kidon combatants in service at any one time, and their training is superb. Sophisticated killing techniques, weaponry, tradecraft, the psychology of fear. They want their enemies to feel vulnerable wherever they are, and utter ruthlessness is a crucial weapon in that psychological war.

'I saw an example of their work in Abuja. Israel used to buy most of its oil from Nigeria, for obvious reasons. A couple of Hezbollah strategists got it into their heads to bribe the relevant ministers into cutting off the supply. We had the Petroleum Corporation wired, and we picked up a lot of chatter about these two Lebanese gentlemen. I passed on the gist to Shabtai Shavit. Within twelve hours a Kidon team had flown in. They didn't just kill the Hezbollah men; they took them down to the Delta and fed them, alive, to crocodiles. I was given a copy of the video tape as a . . . courtesy. Hezbollah got the other copy as a warning.'

'From the van der Velde killing, I'd say Yadin's more subtle than that.'

'It's not a question of subtlety. Yadin understands the importance of the message behind a kill. His file lists a dozen hits in Arab capitals that were blatant, broad-daylight shootings, guttings and sliced throats, where the objective was to discourage Syria, Jordan, Iraq and the Gulf states from offering Palestinian terrorists safe haven. The mess and mayhem was the point. On the other hand, Yadin also assassinated two Swiss bankers, one French weapons scientist, one British solicitor and two American lobbyists, all allegedly working on behalf of Israel's enemies. Three were declared to be natural deaths, one a road accident and one a suicide.'

'He's versatile. Comfortable with gore, but also adept at hiding his tracks.'

'His methods are tailored to the ultimate objective, and that gives us our first clue about the Think Again murder. A straightforward shooting would have made Anneke van der Velde a martyr to the drug-legalization cause. A premature natural death, on the other hand, makes her look unhealthy in body and, perhaps, in mind. If you were religiously inclined you might even conclude that God had taken a view on her politics.'

'So whoever's contracted Yadin wants to derail Think Again,' nodded Arkell. 'A cartel looking to keep prices high? A trafficking syndicate? A conservative or religious group, even?'

'All strong possibilities, but let's not forget the countless government and commercial entities that owe their existence to Prohibition, particularly in the US. The DEA has ten thousand employees dependent for their livelihoods on drug laws that also keep an army of prosecutors, judges, attorneys and specialist law-enforcement units employed. There's an entire industry constructing and servicing all those prisons that won't be needed if drug offences disappear. A lot of interested parties must be getting very anxious right now about the way the world is going. Portugal decriminalized all drugs and cut abuse by fifty per cent, an outcome that has impressed a lot of people in Washington. Four American states have legalized marijuana, with more likely to follow. Beneficiaries of Prohibition can see the world's biggest narcotics consumer teetering at the top of a very slippery slope indeed.'

'Perhaps Andrade and Mayhew will take the hint and shut up.'

'On the contrary, they're scheduled to make a joint address to the European Parliament in eight days. Provisional title: "Why Europe Must Lead the Way in Drug Law Reform".'

Arkell looked up sharply. 'It'll be cancelled, it has to be. Their protection units won't allow it.'

Wraye sighed. 'Much to the frustration of my Canadian clients and their Brazilian counterparts, both men are determined to go to Strasbourg. "In memory of Anneke van der Velde".'

'Eight days . . . *Eight days?* Are you serious? How am I supposed to find a professional assassin in eight days?'

'You found Petrov when everyone said he was dead. You tracked down Deuterium Dmytro in the most godforsaken corner of Jizzakh province. Four of the most dangerous proliferators you bagged with no help from the Increment.'

'They were civilians. Scientists. They made basic errors. Yadin isn't going to leave the same traces. The only way to catch him in eight days is to put out an international alert.'

'We do that, Yadin will see it instantly. At the moment he doesn't realize we know who he is. That's your one big advantage.'

'I'm not taking the job.'

'The contract is half a million dollars. Unlimited expenses.'

'Doesn't matter. It's not feasible. Tell your clients to keep Mayhew in Canada.'

'Gavriel Yadin can just as easily—'

'No more about Yadin.' Arkell held up a warning hand. 'The bomber, Madeleine, the man who killed Emily. Who is he?'

Wraye spread her hands apologetically. 'I can't tell you.'

'You promised me his name.'

'Yes, but—'

'No buts. I've fulfilled my side of the bargain. I heard you out,' he thundered. 'Tell me his name!'

She flinched minutely at his anger. 'I can no longer discuss him.'

'Why the hell not?'

'Because you've just forbidden it.'

Arkell stared at her. Slowly, disbelievingly, he sank back into his chair.

'Now you understand why it has to be you.'

'Bullshit,' he growled.

'You never saw the Special Branch report on the bombing at 43 Dault Street. "All the hallmarks of an Al-Qaeda attack". Right explosive chemical traces, right fragments. And of course you'd just rushed back from Yemen without authorization. The obvious conclusion was quickly drawn. Except that some of us never felt entirely comfortable with it, for the simple reason that Al-Qaeda doesn't blow up private homes in the UK. So what should we conclude? That you were targeted by a highly skilled assassin who tailored his method to produce a specific but misleading impression.'

'Bullshit.'

'It's the same man in both clips, Simon: the Dault Street corner shop CCTV and the Think Again conference footage. They're on my server if you don't believe me.'

He didn't hesitate for a second. Seizing the laptop from the desk, he tapped in a password and thrust it at her.

'You have wireless here?'

'Show me!'

'All right,' she murmured, taking the machine.

* * *

The tracking programme that was initiated in a remote data centre when Wraye logged into her server was not especially complex, but it co-opted a far more sophisticated battery of code originally written by software engineers at the USA's National Security Agency. This code swiftly chewed through a chain of anonymizing proxies to establish the Italian internet service provider from which the URL request had come, and then even more swiftly traced the relevant landline on the Ligurian coast. No record of the trace was left on the ISP's own systems. The only evidence was an automated email arriving in the inbox of Edward Joyce.

Simon Arkell had turned the colour of death. 'Yes,' he muttered.

Wraye frowned as, for perhaps the thousandth time, she watched Yadin take those few critical steps in front of a Tobago camera. 'You haven't seen the Dault Street clip yet.'

'I don't need to. That's him.' His voice was empty, robotic. 'I saw him.'

Now it was Wraye's turn for surprise. 'You saw Yadin? When?'

Arkell closed his eyes. 'Outside my house. That's why I'm alive.'

'You recognized him? You *knew* him?'

'I'd never seen him before.'

'Then why . . . ?'

Arkell held up a hand, brow creased in memory. 'We were about to have dinner in the kitchen – Emily, Saeed and I. But the Service rang again, George Vine this time, and Emily was sick of pretending I wasn't there. So I went upstairs to take the call. I told George I was coming in first thing in the morning.

Full report, everything explained. I was still hoping I'd be able to reach you before then.'

'Reach *me*?'

'You were in Kyrgyzstan. I had to know your answer before I took Saeed to Head Office.'

'My answer? To what?'

'The Porthos message I sent from Yemen. About Ellington. About the GRIEVANCE warning.'

'*GRIEVANCE?* This was two years later, Simon. What *warning*? I never got any message about GRIEVANCE from you.'

Arkell was silent for a while, trying to read her. 'I *sent* you . . .' He stopped himself, as if suddenly wearied beyond measure. 'I went up to our bedroom,' he resumed quietly. 'Emily's jeans were on the floor. I remember that. While George was delicately meandering around the subject, all I could think was how strange it was to have Emily's jeans lying crumpled in front of me after three months in Yemen. Then something made me look out the window. George was going on in that gentle, disappointed way of his about chain of command and respect for the rules, and I noticed an NTL van parked across the street. And there was a man in the driving seat, like he was on a job.'

'So? He was on a job, so what?'

'At 8 p.m.? In a street with no cable?' Arkell closed his eyes. 'There was an extra aerial. And the bodywork wasn't quite right. Looked like Five. I guessed they'd found out about Saeed, and it seemed best just to have a quiet word with them. I didn't want to scare them off by marching out the front door, so I went through the garden and looped round the block. Left George pontificating on the line. There was no one around except the guy in the van. He was watching our house so intently he didn't see me approach. And with the engine running, he didn't hear me. Another three seconds, I'd have been knocking on his window. But that was when it . . .'

Gently, Wraye helped him: 'When it went off.'

'When it went off,' he echoed monotonically. His hands had become fists, crushed against his thighs. The rigid muscles in his neck were shivering.

'Go on,' she said.

'He never saw me. The moment it detonated I hit the ground, like it was Chad or Pakistan. I didn't understand it was my house. My wife. Not right away. A second, maybe. Two seconds. Before I realized. By then the van was driving off, the bomber right there, hurtling past me, never seeing that he'd missed his target.' Arkell's voice cracked. 'That pavement. I was lying on that pavement, watching the flames, the smoke, everything gone, knowing Emily was dead and . . .' He swallowed to loosen his constricted throat. 'And knowing you must have ordered it.'

He looked up at last, and she saw that from nowhere he had produced a thin rope and that it was looped around both his fists, a noose ready for her neck. 'Did you?' he asked. 'Was it you?'

Madeleine Wraye kept her unwavering gaze on him while she reached for the tumbler and took her first sip of wine. 'Simon, who was Saeed?'

AL MAHWIT GOVERNORATE, YEMEN – nine years earlier

The emergency posting followed directly from the endless catastrophe that was Iraq. With those elusive weapons of mass destruction to find, an insurgency to crush and, later, terrifying sectarian violence to contain, it was inevitable that Baghdad would fill with CIA and SIS spooks. They had to come from somewhere. So it was that Arabic-speaking staff were pulled from stations all over the region. And in their place, officers with no experience of Middle Eastern politics, culture or language were drafted in to mind their assets and keep alive the hunt for Usama bin Laden.

Simon Arkell was in the Transdniestrian region of Moldova, on the trail of a Latvian arms dealer with pretensions to nuclear grandeur, when he was recalled to London and reassigned to Sana'a. His cover was British Council. As Martin Bayley, he brushed up on his classics, attended the drab little British Club with rare enthusiasm, and diligently sought out members of the Yemeni artistic community for tiny cups of sweet, strong coffee and earnest chats about the decline of Western morals. The Yemeni culture took some getting used to – niqab-shrouded women and AK-47-toting men who chewed qat all afternoon, their cheeks bulging like hamsters with the macerated drug. But Arkell was quick to acclimatize, and soon he was quietly making contact with his predecessor's assets: a cleric in Hadramawt, a shipping agent in Aden, two civil servants in Sana'a and a Hamdan tribal elder in Al Mahwit governorate named Ali Al-Gadhi. It was this last who introduced him to Saeed Bin Abdullah Al-Khaneen.

Al-Gadhi lived in a small mountain-top town, four hours' drive from Sana'a. His towering square house, a crumbling relic of grander times, was intricately decorated with geometric white patterns and built precipitously on the edge of a cliff. Wild fig trees clung with trunk-thick roots to the sheer black rock face below, and eagles drifted in the currents above the flat roof. For miles around there was nothing but abandoned terraces cut, during a more productive agricultural age, into the parched mountainsides.

Arkell and his translator were welcomed at the courtyard gate by Al-Gadhi's three wives. They ushered him out of his desert boots, up ancient stone steps and into the majlis. Nine men sat on mats against the walls, their legs covered in blankets against the mountain cold, their cheeks bulging with qat. Above each man was a rifle, suspended from a heavy iron hook – AK-47s, old Lee-Enfields, one Chinese Type 56. Two of the men shifted a fraction, and Arkell was invited to sit beside the host.

For some time, very little was said. The translator coaxed Arkell through the usual greetings. Tea and qat were offered and accepted. A gift of an English leather wallet was presented in return. Arkell knew enough of Yemeni culture by now to understand that many hours might pass before they reached the real substance. The polythene bag of qat leaves was passed to him repeatedly, and soon a mildly euphoric mood came over him. Draped in a blanket the colour of mulberries he smiled endlessly at the hardened mountain men, but he kept his contributions – both translated and in halting Arabic – to a minimum.

Then, suddenly, it was time. The men around them rose as one, took down their rifles and filed out of the room.

Al-Gadhi muttered something to Arkell's translator, who, without reference to his employer, also left. Perhaps it should have worried Arkell, at that point, to see a stranger walk through the door. But the qat had done its work and his only substantive feeling was one of vague curiosity.

The newcomer offered thanks to Allah and took up position on the mat opposite Arkell. His suit trousers bore a trace of mountain dust, but otherwise looked as new as his crisp ivory shirt and silver butterfly cufflinks. A barber had very recently drawn razor-sharp lines on the man's nape and sideburns. The only thing out of place was the savagely crushed nose. It had healed some time ago, but the new tissue had done nothing to disguise the damage.

'This . . .' muttered Al-Gadhi, speaking English for the first and only time, 'is Saeed.' Abruptly, he rose and walked out.

Arkell took one look at the desperation in the man's eyes and spat the wad of qat into his tea cup. 'Hello,' he said, offering his hand.

If the man saw it, he didn't respond to the gesture. Instead he began talking, fast. 'Are you who they say you are? Do you have credentials? I will feel more comfortable after you show me your credentials. Ali says you are CIA?'

Arkell wasn't surprised. It was not unusual for assets to confuse SIS with the better-known agency, and sometimes little distinction was drawn between American and British officers. Also quite possible that his predecessor had passed himself off as CIA when recruiting Al-Gadhi. And so Arkell nodded, thinking nothing of it, curious to understand what this highly strung city creature was doing in the mountains of Yemen.

'Thanks be to God. I was afraid you are British MI6. Your face seems British. Do you have credentials, please?'

After two years in Washington, Arkell could summon up a solid Ivy League accent with no difficulty. 'What's wrong with the Brits?'

'They betrayed me,' said the man gravely. 'They did this to me,' he added, touching his wrecked nose.

Arkell was intrigued. An Iraqi, perhaps? Had he crossed paths with the wrong British army patrol in Basra? 'Doesn't sound like them,' he shrugged. 'Polite bunch, what I've seen.'

'Because of them, I was arrested in Riyadh.' His eyes were a flickering chestnut. 'I gave critical information to the British embassy. The same day, the Mabahith came for me. Less than twelve hours after I warned Mr Colville. You think this was coincidence? Locked in a cell underground for twenty-one months. No trial. Just beatings. I should have gone to the American embassy. It was a foolish mistake. I thought I knew the British. I studied at London Queen Mary. I read Jane Austen and Charles Dickens. It was a matter of familiarity, you see?'

'You said you gave this Colville some kind of warning?'

'Which he ignored,' said Saeed hotly.

'What makes you say that?'

'Because two weeks later hundreds of innocent people were murdered in Chicago, and no one did anything to stop it!'

Arkell felt suddenly weary. He had driven four hours to meet an asset who had nothing for him but the ravings of yet another GRIEVANCE fabricator. New as he was to the Middle East, Arkell had already had plenty of would-be sources offer to sell him the inside story on the sarin attack on O'Hare's Terminal 3. With the qat euphoria wearing off, he could barely be bothered to keep up the American accent.

'So you knew about the plot before it happened, huh? What does that make you?'

'I was secretary to Sheikh Salih Abdallah Ibrahim. He liked my handwriting. I have a fine penmanship for English, and my Arabic script has won prizes.' He glanced down at his right hand, and Arkell noticed it was shaking. 'It's not so good now.'

'Who is Sheikh whatsisname?'

'You don't know?' Saeed was astonished. 'Doesn't the CIA have extensive—?'

'Over in Intelligence, sure. I'm just a humble Operations grunt.'

'The Sheikh is a very powerful man in Saudi Arabia. In fact worldwide. He has business interests on all continents. He is a supporter of many Salafi fundamentalists.'

'That's nothing unusual in Saudi.'

'An extremely generous supporter. You could say he bankrolled the airport attack.'

'Is that right?' said Arkell. 'And you just happened to stumble across the plans on his breakfast table . . .'

Saeed recognized the tone. Visibly hurt, he persevered: 'I was working late. I remained usually in the Sheikh's offices, but this time I went to the kitchens for a glass of milk. You understand?'

'I'm just about keeping up.'

'I heard them! Talking in the majlis, agreeing the—'

'Who? Who was talking?'

'I don't know. Three, perhaps four men. I couldn't go in. But I heard such things!' His eyes rose to the heavens as he recounted a cascade of telling details: the ingenious pressurized canisters, disguised as Coke bottles; the decision to target the landside area of the terminal so the devices wouldn't have to pass through scanners; the IT systems attack which caused long queues to build up at check-in, and the staged disruption at security that resulted in a similar logjam there; the rigorous training of the poisoners, preparing them to perform their suicidal role calmly and discreetly, invisible in the restless crowds of their victims.

GRIEVANCE in the raw, when it was still just a horrific idea. 'They didn't say a date, but it was enough, yes? To catch the terrorists and save all those people. It should have been *enough*.'

When it became clear that the man had finished speaking, Arkell said, 'What exactly is it I can do for you, Mr Saeed?'

'You don't think this is important information?'

'To be honest, it's a little late.'

'About Mr Colville of the British embassy! Don't you understand the significance?'

Arkell sighed. 'Why don't you tell me the significance?'

'I gave the British MI6 full warning of the sarin attack on your country and they did not stop it!'

'If I hear you right, you spun a diplomat a wild story without evidence. Frankly, I'm not surprised the poor guy did nothing. He was probably in charge of passports or tea parties or whatever.'

'Then why was I arrested?' hissed Saeed. 'That same day, seized off the street by the Mabahith. I did not say Mr Colville did nothing. He did exactly what a spy would do if he is in league with the jihadists. Do you not understand what I am telling you? Your allies, the British, let the attack happen. Perhaps they even arranged it!'

'OK, I think that's plenty,' said Arkell, rising to his feet. 'Thank you for your information, Mr Saeed. I'll be sure to pass it on to the relevant department.'

'You don't believe me,' said the other man dully.

'Not my job to believe. I'm just a humble field grunt. Up to Intelligence to assess your testimony.'

Saeed gripped his arm, a last desperate appeal. 'I need help. My family spent everything to have me released. I was expelled from Saudi Arabia. I came to our relatives . . .' He cast an arm around Al-Gadhi's majlis. 'It is well known Ali has American friends. But I cannot stay here. The jihadis have long arms. So do the British. I have to go to America.'

With gentle but effective force, using only forefinger and thumb, Arkell broke the man's grip. 'That's not gonna happen, Saeed.'

'Please! Consult your superiors. Tell them what I have said. I will be here three more days.'

'Sure, Saeed. I'll tell them what you said.' He opened the door. Al-Gadhi was waiting to escort him out.

'Mr Bayley!' cried Saeed.

Arkell glanced back, impatient to be gone.

'I lost everything.' He looked pitifully alone in the centre of the majlis, his crushed nose distorting his whole face. 'I tried to help your country, and I lost everything.'

* * *

Something about that final moment bugged Arkell as he sat on his terrace in Sana'a's historic Old City the following morning, eating fresh date rolls washed down with thick, bitter coffee. It was the sheer guilelessness of the man. The helpless honesty of a lost soul pinning everything on one last bet. For a fabricator, he was disturbingly convincing.

And yet not for one moment did Arkell believe him.

He was willing to accept, at a stretch, that Saeed might have overheard something and gone to the embassy to report it. That was as far as Arkell's credulity would go. The overworked junior diplomat who heard Saeed out – whether or not he was a Friend – would likely have paid little attention to yet another vague, alarmist terror alert. As for the claim that SIS had orchestrated Saeed's detention, Arkell smiled at the idea. If only the Service really did have that kind of influence with the Saudis. No, Saeed had got careless in some way: maybe he'd filched the Sheikh's cash; maybe he'd leered too long at his daughter. It was nothing new for the trusted lieutenant of a powerful man to find himself peremptorily flung into the gutter. Nor was it a surprise that after twenty-one months' incarceration, Saeed had managed to concoct a story blaming the Service for all his woes.

He certainly wasn't the only conspiracy theorist with SIS in his sights.

By 11 a.m. Arkell had found an excuse to drop in to the embassy and place a call on the encrypted line to London. The desk officer with responsibility for the Arabian peninsula was a caustic old soldier who did not respond well to idle chatter, and Arkell had invented an operational query of sufficient substance to justify the call. He had a possible asset in Hudaydah, he said, an Iranian engineer who claimed first-hand knowledge of a biological weapons programme. But the man was asking for resettlement in Britain and fifty thousand a year.

'Twenty,' came the terse response. 'And only if he delivers a concrete WMD lead.'

'Twenty it is,' agreed Arkell. 'By the way, do we have anyone in Riyadh using the name "Colville"?'

'Not any more.'

'Meaning?'

'That was Rupert Ellington's cover.'

Next, he called Personnel Department. 'File check, please,' he said, trying to keep the agitation out of his voice. 'Rupert Ellington.'

A pause. 'That file is closed.'

'I just need the date of death.'

When the answer came, after a long bureaucratic silence, it seemed to him that the whole world stopped breathing.

He drove directly from the embassy to Al Mahwit governorate, not pausing to get a new travel permit from the police. At the road blocks, he flashed the previous day's *tasriih* and referenced the British Ambassador until they let him through. On the way, he made one more call, this time to a mobile in Damascus. 'Dermott, it's Martin Bayley in Yemen,' he said in a chipper voice. 'How's the aubergine salad?'

The man in Damascus had only been called Dermott for nine weeks. Prior to that, he was Rollo, a shipping consultant in Singapore. Prior to that he was any number of people, among them Charlie Pearman, his real name. 'Aubergine salad' had become a running joke during a rushed Arabic language course the two re-tasked officers had shared in London.

'Martin,' he responded smoothly. 'How nice to hear from you. Actually the Syrians do it superbly. Lemon juice and paprika, really makes it zing.' Just the kind of thing a business analyst in Damascus would say, should anyone be listening.

'Wonderful! We must catch up properly sometime. I was thinking about you because I came across an old English teddy bear in the Sana'a market the other day. Checked yellow trousers and scarf, red jumper. Most unlikely, and it reminded me you had a favourite bear not far from here until a couple of years ago?'

There was silence from Damascus. When he spoke again, Pearman was newly brusque. 'That's right,' he muttered.

Arkell was relieved. He had been confident the Rupert Bear reference would be lost on any Yemeni or Syrian listeners; he wasn't at all sure his Accelerated Arabic classmate would get it. 'I was trying to remember where that bear ended his days. Was it under our flag?'

'It was last seen in bed, close to our flag.' *Rupert Ellington died in his sleep in the diplomatic quarter of Riyadh.*

'So nothing . . . odd?' Arkell tried to phrase the question gently. Ellington had been Charlie Pearman's closest friend in the Service, and he had taken his death very badly.

'No. Completely unexpected, but natural.'

There was a measure of anger in Pearman's voice. Arkell thanked him quickly and brought the call to a close.

So Rupert Ellington hadn't been gunned down in a Saudi street by Islamic militants desperate to seal the leak created by Saeed. No, it was much, much worse than that.

LIGURIA, ITALY – 8 June

'Let me get this straight,' interrupted Wraye. 'Without consulting your superiors, breaking all protocol, you decide to scoop up this Saeed character and rush him back to London. Why?'

'Isn't that obvious? If his story was true, we were looking at a major conspiracy involving someone in the Service. Saeed was the star witness. The Chief and Jeremy needed to hear what he had to say. *You* needed to hear it. I wasn't going to let anyone else near him until we knew exactly what had happened to Ellington.'

'How did you get him out of Yemen?'

'Via Aden. I put him on a freighter to Mombasa.'

'With what funds?'

'Two thousand dollars from the Exceptional Circumstances Fund.'

'So immediately half a dozen people on the ECF committee know something is up,' said Wraye. 'Mombasa?'

'I flew ahead and met him off the ship. We decided he could pass for a Greek. There was a charter flight to Rome, direct from Mombasa. I travelled via Nairobi. Hired a car and picked him up.'

'Passport?'

'Central Facilities supplied it while he was on the ship.'

'So they knew all about Saeed?'

'They didn't have his identity or nationality. Just a request for a Greek passport in a false name.'

'You must have sent a photograph.'

'Deliberately obscure. I got a man in Aden to touch up the ears and jawline. No recognition system could have identified Saeed from it.'

'They had his travelling name. Which means they could have obtained CCTV images at Rome immigration. Did you bring him into the UK on that passport?'

'We came through the Tunnel. They barely glanced at our passports.'

'But they had your registration. You used a Service identity to hire the car, I presume?'

'There was no link to Saeed.'

'Every petrol station CCTV system between Rome and London could have captured his face beside that number plate.' She shook her head. 'Any tourists fiddling with cameras on your Eurotunnel shuttle?'

Arkell reddened. 'The Service doesn't have the resources to run that kind of operation without a very good reason.'

Wraye stood up angrily. 'You've just told me this man was incarcerated on the same day a perfectly healthy SIS officer dropped dead, barely hours after he was passed a warning about one of the greatest terrorist atrocities of our age. Show me a "very good reason" if that isn't it.'

He didn't reply.

'So you assumed I was the one who sent Yadin to kill you, because I was the only person you knowingly informed. Yet in three minutes you've suggested any number of other SIS personnel whose paranoia you might have pricked if they had something to hide about GRIEVANCE.'

She stared pointedly at the rope still hanging from his left hand. He tossed it aside. 'You agree it was someone in the Service, then?' he said roughly.

'And here's another thing: I never received your Porthos message. So you have to ask yourself, *who did*?'

'Porthos was totally secure.'

'Except from the directors with snooping rights.'

'*What*?'

'"Who watches the watchers?" Answer: the most senior watchers. What did you expect? The Porthos messaging system was a rich seam of intelligence on the thinking and intentions of our officers. It was inevitable that we were going to mine it.'

'Who? Which directors had access?'

'We'll come to that. I want to be very clear about the possible implications first. Let's choose a cryptonym . . .' She cast her eyes around the room, the desk, the fireplace. 'ASH. Maybe it's a man, maybe it's a woman. Maybe it's more than one person. We'll hypothesize an entity within the Service named ASH who somehow became aware of your interaction with Saeed. Assuming both Saeed's story and your story are true, what can we deduce about ASH?'

'You mean besides the fact that he ordered Ellington killed, Saeed arrested, and my house blown up?'

'He, she or they,' she corrected.

'We can deduce that ASH knew about GRIEVANCE in advance and didn't want the attack disrupted.'

'Or didn't know, but when informed by Ellington had reason to want it to go ahead,' cautioned Wraye.

'Or was one of the plotters himself,' said Arkell grimly.

Wraye did not bother to correct the gender assumption a second time. 'And if we accept what the Mossad tell us with respect to Mr Gavriel Yadin's exclusive loyalty to a single master since he left their employ, what else can we deduce which unutterably complicates our current investigation?'

Arkell stared back into her stony eyes. 'That a senior SIS officer has ordered the assassination of three world leaders.'

The room had grown claustrophobic. They moved to the kitchen, where there was better light and more air. Wraye picked up a pad of paper and a Pentel rollerball.

'Let's be methodical. Who knew you were asking questions about Ellington?' Tearing off a single sheet of paper, she set it on a glass chopping board that would capture no trace of her handwriting. In large block capitals, she wrote ASH at the top of the page.

'Charlie Pearman, I suppose,' began Arkell reluctantly. 'Two or three people on the Arabian Peninsula desk.'

'Along with anyone else from the controllerate who happened to be in Head Office that day. Then you go off-piste . . . George Vine gets to hear you're missing. He initiates an investigation that uncovers your interest in Ellington . . . Who would have handled that?'

'One of the field coordinators. Or George might have done it himself.'

She wrote down three names, pausing almost superstitiously before adding that of the Service's most senior regional director. 'You said George telephoned you just before the bombing? Kept you on the line?'

Arkell nodded, a new rage building.

'Then there's Personnel Department,' said Wraye quickly. 'That could bring another six officers into the frame. Who else?'

'Central Facilities. The passport for Saeed.' He gave the names of the two forgers he'd spoken to, along with their managers.

'And of course the good people of Technical and Operations Support who were probably called on to locate you,' she said, writing down a cascade of names. 'All right, that leaves your Porthos message. What did you write?'

Arkell had no difficulty, after nine years, recalling the message word for word. '"Saudi citizen Saeed Bin Abdullah Al-Khaneen claims gave full warning of GRIEVANCE attack to ACTOR officer Rupert Ellington day of his death Riyadh. Have Al-Khaneen in my care. Request urgent advice in light of possible ACTOR complicity in GRIEVANCE."'

Wraye looked up, an expression of mild fascination on her face. 'That was a remarkably naïve message to send.'

'My wife died.' His jaw was clenched. 'I don't need to be told I made a mistake.'

'I'm sorry.'

He nodded. 'So who had special access to Porthos? Who could have intercepted the message?'

'It started as a Counter-Intelligence function. The idea was that Linus Marshall should have sight of all Porthos traffic – looking for unusual behaviour that might signal treacherous designs. But there were objections from some of the other directors – they worried it would give Linus too much power. It became quite political. So then access was extended to the Chief and a number of the directors. Perhaps nine other people might have been able to read your message.'

She completed the list and counted the names. 'Twenty-eight possible candidates. And that's without considering all the colleagues who might have heard some casual mention of your activities in the time Saeed was on that ship. Evaluating them all without proper access to Service records is going to be a nightmare.'

'No.' Arkell rocked forward. 'No, it's simpler than that. Don't you see it? You never got my Porthos message, which means ASH deleted it. He has to be one of the nine directors with snooping rights. Forget Charlie Pearman and the forgers and field coordinators. None of that matters.'

Wraye nodded slowly. 'You're right. Well . . . you would be right, except for one problem . . .'

'What?'

'We had snooping rights, Simon. Not deleting rights.'

'Someone must have done,' retorted Arkell. 'Porthos messages didn't get lost. It never happened.'

'You're sure you addressed it to me?'

'Oh, please . . .'

Wraye tapped the pen against her teeth. 'There is one possibility. We couldn't *delete* other people's messages, but in the first few months there was a small glitch in the Porthos surveillance functionality. Some of us discovered – by chance – that we could *edit* messages.'

'You are kidding.'

'No one worried about it all that much. It didn't occur to us that anyone would exploit the glitch. The whole point of snooping rights is to keep an eye on things without leaving a trace. Interfere with the object under observation and you give yourself away – first rule of surveillance. TOS rectified the glitch eventually, but the idea that anyone would have actually meddled with a Porthos message . . .'

'You received *something* from me, didn't you?'

Suddenly, it hit her. 'Your last words. That's what they were to me. Damn it, I read them out at your funeral!'

'Tell me.' It was little more than a growl.

Closing her eyes, she took herself back to that sad little church, the casket with the ashes of a few misidentified body parts. His sister, his parents. God, his *parents*. Did they know he was still alive? And Wraye, calling herself Angela Redfern, a procurement director at the Department for International Development, scraping together what lines she could to convey her officer's great service to his country without giving away the slightest hint of what he had actually done.

'"Having a lovely time in Sana'a. Weather's perfect. Wish you were here."'

There was a long silence.

'That's not even funny!' shouted Arkell.

'Believe me, I spent weeks trying to understand the hidden message in your words. I was convinced there was something there that could explain what had happened to you. I called up the Yemeni meteorological records. I tried every code key we'd ever shared. Nothing. They were just words.'

'Words I never wrote.'

'Which proves the case against ASH. A deleted message might possibly have been a technical error. An altered message, on the other hand . . .'

'ASH is one of those nine directors.'

'Yes.'

'Their names, Madeleine. Linus Marshall, the Chief, who else?'

'It couldn't have been Linus. Even in Kyrgyzstan, I checked Porthos daily. ASH got to your message before I did, meaning ASH had access to a Porthos terminal on the day you sent it. Linus Marshall was hiking in the Drakensberg that week. He's off the list.'

'Their names.'

'And I think we can clear the Chief straight away. Since his retirement, he's been a generous supporter of Think Again. He makes speeches in favour of drug reform in the Lords. If ASH is behind the van der Velde murder, it isn't him.'

'Their names!'

She looked suddenly drained. 'You know their names, Simon. You know exactly who we're talking about.'

Some of the fight went out of Arkell. It was as if both of them were overwhelmed by the simple act of contemplating treachery at such an exalted level.

'Jeremy Elphinstone,' he said quietly. 'Requirements and Production, the heart of everything: he would have been first in line after the Chief.'

'Yes.'

'The regions? Did the controllers have access?'

'Selective access to messages sent by their own people. George Vine, in this case.'

'I'll bet Jane Saddle wheedled her way in there somehow.'

'Of course. There wouldn't be much point in the Chief having a personal secretary if he didn't trust her with everything he saw.'

'What about the section heads? Same rule as the controllers?'

'Not quite. For us, it wasn't a question of who sent the message but what words it contained. For Counter-Proliferation, I could see messages that referenced "Yongbyon", "centrifuge enrichment" and so on. For Counter-Terrorism, Tony Watchman could access any message mentioning "Zawahiri", "USS Cole", "9/11", "O'Hare" . . .'

'"GRIEVANCE",' added Arkell glumly.

'Undoubtedly,' agreed Wraye.

'That leaves the three TOS directors. Did they have access?'

'They did. The Chief reasoned that if we didn't give the architects of Porthos full access to Porthos, they would take it anyway behind our backs. But remember, Susan didn't join the Service until after GRIEVANCE . . .'

'And Alec was on sabbatical at MIT when I went to Yemen.'

'So that just leaves . . .'

A slight shudder, but it might have been the chill of midnight. 'Martin de Vries.'

'Exactly.'

Simon Arkell hesitated before concluding: 'Five possible names then, or . . .'

She glanced up. 'Yes?'

'Never mind.' Taking a lighter from his pocket, he set fire to Wraye's list and dropped the burning paper in a colander.

She let it go. 'Five suspects: Elphinstone, Watchman, de Vries, Saddle and Vine.'

'Shouldn't be hard to narrow down,' he said, rising.

She caught his arm. 'Simon, I appreciate Emily's death is driving you to act. God knows I'd feel the same for that sweet girl. But you're in no position to investigate ASH. I still have some access and plenty of contacts. Let me do this.'

'And put ASH in some cosy prison cell? Out for good behaviour in three years?' He shook his head.

'That won't happen,' she assured him. 'A public trial would be an impossibility for the Service, especially with the GRIEVANCE connection. In fact I'll make you a deal: hunt Yadin and ASH is all yours. That's in addition to the half-million-dollar fee. Should ASH happen to meet with an accident shortly after I've proven his or her guilt to the satisfaction of the Joint Intelligence Committee, well . . . no one in Whitehall will be overly troubled.'

Simon Arkell drained the last of his wine. 'You can forget the fee,' he said.

'So you'll do it? You'll terminate Yadin?'

He turned his violent gaze on her, and in his eyes Wraye saw the memory of a savagely obliterated love.

'Of course I'm going to bloody kill him.'

By the time the wine was finished the clock on the electric cooker read 01:49. Collecting a pillow and a blanket, Arkell escorted Wraye past the tight little staircase, through a back door and out into the moonless night. 'What's this?' she said suspiciously, as he opened the weather-beaten oak door of a windowless annexe.

'There's a mattress at the back. It's comfortable enough.'

'Jesus, Simon! I thought we just made a deal. You still don't trust me?'

With a firm arm, he steered her into the annexe. 'Until I have proof you never got that Porthos message,' he said, tossing her the blanket and pillow, 'yours is the sixth name on the list.'

Wraye did not sleep well. She strongly suspected the annexe had been used, for much of its rustic history, to keep livestock, but beyond testing the door to confirm it was bolted on the outside, she didn't try to get out. The lumpy mattress was murder on her back. Her head swarming with memories, she dozed fitfully, half-recalling, half-dreaming.

Reconstructing.

'Is this, in reality, a discussion about our officers' security?' Martin de Vries speaking. That dust-dry voice, not a speck of concession to human feeling. 'Or is it a pre-emptive assault on Five in the matter of how this outrage is to be spun for the newspapers?' The only emotion was machine-like anger. Outrage, a word all the more potent for the Afrikaner's heavy emphasis on the first syllable.

'Five want to know, as well they might, why this happened and whether it is about to happen again.' The Chief, magisterial but always softly spoken. '*I* want to know. Can anyone tell me? George? Tony? Some data would be very nice just now. Is it UBL? Are all our officers at risk in their own beds? Or should we open our skirts and let Five establish for us what we seem unable to determine ourselves?'

She had had to fight her way, almost literally, into the room. Straight off the plane from Bishkek, worn out by a sleepless transit in Istanbul, she was in no mood for Jane Saddle's pettifogging ways. Clutching a sheaf of documents tight to her chest, as if afraid Wraye might catch a glimpse of their contents, the ageless personal secretary to the Chief was at her meticulous worst.

'It's not a question of rank, Madeleine, but of relevance. No one is challenging your place at the top table. This is not a meeting of the top table. It's a side table, with a specialist menu, to which certain members of the top table have something to contribute. Counter-Proliferation does not fall into that category. This was not a WMD event.'

'I hired him,' growled Wraye, physically forcing her way past H/SECT. 'I trained him. I put him in harm's way.'

'You shouldn't blame yourself, Madeleine . . .' It was a standard technique of Saddle's to lurch, when she felt in danger of losing a point, into false sympathy. She liked to play the motherly figure. It worked better with the men.

'Rest assured, the last person I blame is myself.' Gaining access at last to the conference room, she had laid eyes immediately on George Vine, on Jeremy Elphinstone, on Tony Watchman. 'I'm here, Jane, to find out who I should blame.'

Elphinstone and Watchman both saw her arrive but pretended otherwise. Vine, naturally, was quick to play the part the others had spurned, hurrying across to her and taking both her hands in his plump fingers. 'Madeleine. My heart is broken for you. Truly. If I could only convince you that I share your pain. You saw his talent before any of us. You built the bond long before I had the honour of knowing him. But I can honestly say, notwithstanding the limited time we worked together, he was like a son to me.'

'Thank you, George.'

It was almost true. George Vine had taken the trouble to brief Arkell personally for the Yemen posting, inviting him to his opulent home in Isfahan and commenting afterwards to Wraye,

'He is rather gorgeous, isn't he? A dash of Lawrence about the man. I do wonder, though, if he ever plans to mellow, to settle down. He's like an oversized Peter Pan, don't you think?'

An apt comparison, Wraye had felt at the time: boyishly high-spirited, yet lethal. Simon Arkell would leap at the chance to try something new, learn another skill, explore the unknown. But those mental lacunae identified by the Foreign Legion were still there. However much he developed as an intelligence officer, his moral and emotional instincts remained fixed at the level of a gifted seventeen-year-old. Not that he was immature – just stuck, somehow, in a youthful frame of mind. It was as if a protective curtain had come down over part of his brain when his best friend drowned, preserving for ever a remnant of his teenage psyche: an impatience with planning and reflection; a tendency to leap to judgement; a bravery that bordered on recklessness; a blindness around women.

Now, like Peter Pan, he would never grow up.

'I feel desperate,' Vine was saying. 'You entrusted him to me and I've let you down.'

'I didn't entrust him to anyone. I don't remember being consulted in the matter of his reallocation.' Her gaze returned to Elphinstone, who had his broad, Service-bearing back to her. She didn't begrudge his high-handed approach to resourcing; manpower was always stretched in SIS, and someone had to make the difficult decisions. She just wished Elphinstone would make better decisions. 'Nuclear simply isn't the priority at the moment,' he had told her over the secure line from London, while Arkell packed next door and echoed the elementary Arabic phrases coming from his minidisc player. Not the priority! Wait till a device is detonated in Piccadilly, Jeremy my dear, and then tell me nuclear's not the priority.

But in a way he had been proven right, hadn't he? It wasn't an atomic bomb, after all, but your basic terrorist's plastic explosive that had ripped up a stretch of Dault Street. And Tony Watchman's star had crept another few inches higher with this further validation of his section's relevance.

A question of relevance, Madeleine. Relevance.

Was she in danger of becoming irrelevant?

'Five will need to answer some questions of their own,' Watchman was saying in that blasé tone which, evidently, he saw no need to curb for the sake of a dead officer. 'How did the explosives enter the country? Who planted them? Was there any warning chatter they failed to pass on to us? We should push hard for answers. It's our man down, after all.'

'Hear, hear,' murmured Elphinstone, making a note on a yellow schedule sheet. His mind was elsewhere, realized Wraye. The support he was giving Watchman was automatic, unthinking, and that worried her. Those two together, if they really were together in the sense she now feared, could be formidable. It was a bad time for Linus Marshall to be away.

'Then no one can tell me anything useful?' mourned the Chief. 'I must go to the Foreign Secretary empty-handed and advise him to look to the Home Office for information? We don't even know what Arkell was doing back here, George?'

'*Mea culpa*, sir.' Vine did actually wring his hands, a piece of theatre they had all expected and all saw through. 'I should know and I don't. I have no doubt there was an excellent reason. He was an unimpeachable officer. One of the best. And I did talk to him, I did. But the reason why was not forthcoming, not on that occasion, though I was confident he would explain all as soon as he was able. His wife died as well, of course. We should – we *must* – spare a thought for her.'

Somehow, Madeleine Wraye managed three hours' sleep despite the discomfort of the mattress and the distraction of rodent activity somewhere nearby. When she awoke, narrow strips of sunlight marked the floor. From outside came a muted pounding.

She could only guess at the time. Where the hell was Joyce? Stiff and cold, she put her eye to the gap between door and jamb and caught a glimpse of Arkell hurtling past. A moment later it happened again.

Exercising. The bastard was exercising.

She tried a different crack, and watched her former officer work effortlessly through one hundred straight burpees. In the sunlight he looked as young and vital as the day she had recruited him. A little bulkier around the chest, but his shoulders and legs had lost none of the definition drilled into them by the Legion's NCOs. She remembered him doing one-arm press-ups in the Swat Valley, his feet hooked over the bull bar of their Land Cruiser; some images never fade. With no pause to rest after the burpees, he swung a rucksack on his back – filled with rocks from the look of it – and disappeared.

No, he certainly hadn't gone soft.

When, later, he unlocked the door, sweating and dusty but wearing a clean grey T-shirt, he looked irritatingly refreshed on so little sleep. 'Good morning,' he offered, in cheerful defiance of her glare. Outside stood a weather-roughened pine table on which were laid the rudiments of breakfast. A pot of coffee. A melon, a pile of toast and an unlabelled pot of some dark berry conserve.

'Living well on your corporate wages,' observed Wraye. But she could not maintain the sarcasm, because beyond the unimpressive table was the most wonderful view. They were standing, she realized now, on a high cliff top. Spread out below them, the Mediterranean. A couple of yachts, a liner in the distance. Sea birds flocking and whirling overhead.

She glanced back at the house. Only a few metres separated it from the cliff. 'Didn't I teach you always to keep an escape route open? How would you get clear if someone came down that track?'

'BASE jump,' said Arkell. 'I have a rig inside and a dinghy moored below. The best escape routes are the ones no one can follow you down. Melon?'

The toast was made from stale bread, and the jam was too sweet. But the melon was fresh and flavoursome, and the coffee was superb. It took the edge off Wraye's irritation.

'I'm curious about one thing,' she said. 'The Dault Street investigators didn't find very much of . . . Saeed, I suppose, to put in your coffin. But there was enough to do a DNA check. It matched your profile. How did you manage that?'

'Bribery,' he shrugged between mouthfuls of toast. 'I followed one of the forensic investigators home, gave her five thousand pounds and a few millilitres of my blood. Would have added the usual threat to nearest and dearest, but she was actually quite sympathetic: she could see that if someone with access to plastic explosive was trying to kill me I would be better off dead.'

'And then you disappeared off the face of the earth. How?'

'Why don't we concentrate on Yadin?'

As he said the name, she noted the tightening of the muscles in his face. But it wasn't the paralysing fury of the night before. He had moved past that. This was anticipation. A trace of excitement. Inwardly, she cheered: a decade on, the fire-starting spirit that made him so good at this work was still there.

'I can only suggest one lead,' she said. 'Mossad won't talk to you, but I have a contact at the Shabak who owes me a few favours. Avraham Boim – as tough a nut as Israel has got. Old-school, file on everyone, endlessly suspicious. He won't like you any more than he likes anyone else. On the other hand there's no love lost between Mossad and Shabak officers. Usual story: the Shabak does all the hard work, protecting the Knesset, hunting down suicide bombers, while Mossad agents strut about the world getting all the glory. He'll have something on Yadin . . . How are you for passports?'

'Fine, thank you.'

'What nationalities?'

He smiled without responding.

'Simon, we have eight days. Not trusting me isn't an option.' When he didn't react, she asked, 'You can travel to Israel today?'

'Sure.'

'Equipment? Weapons?'

'I'm just going to talk to the guy.'

'I mean for later.'

'I have a few suppliers.'

'This is ridiculous. I could get you official documentation from twelve countries, special forces weaponry, NSA surveillance kit, whatever you want.'

'I'll contact you if I need something. Let's leave it at that.'

She leaned back in the creaking chair to hide her annoyance. She also wanted to cover the very faint sound of an engine she thought she might have heard. 'I suppose it'd be foolish to ask if you need cash?'

Arkell stood up. 'I'll keep a note of expenses,' he offered, walking to the house.

'Where are you going?' she called, anxious that he too might have heard the engine.

'Shower,' he replied over his shoulder. 'I have a plane to catch.'

Wraye was at the front of the house four seconds after the water began flowing upstairs. He'd removed the laptop, phone and car keys, she noticed.

She peered into the trees beyond the parked car. No movement. Nothing. She raised one arm and waved.

There, hidden in the shadows of an oak, the flicker of a moving arm.

This time, Wraye made an even clearer signal: with both arms, she beckoned the unseen watchers in.

The shower had stopped. Wraye hurried back to the living room. Only one cupboard large enough to hold a parachute rig. She eased it open, tense against the imagined creak of old hinges. Nothing inside but Ligurian tourist brochures, long untouched. Where, then? Near the back door, an old armchair with a newish spread draped over it to hide the stains. And to hide the space beneath?

Wraye dropped to her knees and pulled back the printed cotton. Under the chair was a nylon pack: harness straps, bulging contents. And loosely fastened to the top, a small bundle of silky material. The pilot chute.

Quickly unfastening it, she tied the pilot chute around a heavy iron lampstand as Arkell's footsteps sounded on the stairs. By the time he came into view, she was leaning against the opposite wall with an old magazine in her hands.

He was dressed in jeans and a clean white shirt, and carrying a backpack. On his feet were a pair of the old desert combat boots she remembered trying to wean him off in DC. Those desert boots were a longstanding favourite. He'd worn similar models all over central Asia and the Balkans, even into luxury hotels and embassy receptions. A good-luck charm to him, they'd seemed to carry the sands of Djibouti and Chad into the chilliest reaches of the former Soviet Union.

'Come on,' he said, 'I'll drop you off in town. Your people can arrange transport from there.'

Wraye caught the flicker of a shadow behind him. 'I think they can do rather better than that,' she said quietly.

Simon Arkell's response was immediate and electric. He spun round, saw the figure of a man appear in silhouette where the front door should have been, saw the outline of an assault rifle in his hands and hurled his backpack directly at the intruder's face. A second man appeared as the first staggered backwards, and Arkell launched himself into the air.

His left boot smacked the man's rifle aside while his right hand grabbed an oil lamp hanging on the wall and smashed it against his head. Glass fragments exploded around them, but the man stayed on his feet and swung the rifle like a club. Arkell blocked it, seized the butt and thrust it in the same instant hard up against the man's jaw.

He crumpled to the ground.

Arkell turned to the first man, who was reaching for his fallen weapon. One punch to the throat floored him. There were more outside. He slammed and bolted the front door. Hauling the parachute rig from its hiding place, he burst out into the back garden. To left and right more men appeared, all armed, coming round both sides of the house. Arkell tugged the harness over his shoulders and swiftly buckled the straps as he ran to the cliff edge. Then, reaching back to free the pilot chute, he realized what was wrong.

He looked round and saw the trail of cord and parachute silk reaching all the way into the house. The canopy was already half-deployed.

Shrugging off the useless rig, he stared furiously at Wraye. One of the men thrust an HK45 in his face and yelled, 'On the ground! Now!'

Arkell considered him: the nervous energy, the lust for action. His weapon was too close. Arkell could have taken it off him with a quick swipe. But the other men had gathered round, nondescript ex-soldiers' clothes, assault rifles sensibly deployed. Silently, Arkell laid himself flat across the grass.

Wraye took the semi-automatic from her lieutenant's rigid hand. 'As you can see, I didn't entirely trust you either.' She crouched beside Arkell and put the muzzle to his forehead. Her voice dropped to a whisper that only he could hear. 'If I wanted you dead, this is how easy it would be.'

He stared up the line of her arm, unblinking.

'I never received that Porthos message. Do you understand? I did not blow up your house or kill your wife, nor did I commission anyone to do it for me. If we're to work together again, I need you to be clear about that.'

His eyes never left hers.

'And we're going to have to find a way to rebuild the trust we once had.'

Slowly, he nodded.

'How many names on that list?'

'Five.'

'All right, then.' She stood up. 'Report when you've spoken to Boim.'

PART II:

THE HUNT

LONDON, ENGLAND – 8 June

'It will almost certainly be designated Retracted,' Wraye had said on the flight back from Milan. 'You do know how to pull up Retracted terror alerts, don't you?'

Not for the first time, Edward Joyce felt aggrieved at how little credit he was given by those whose good opinion he craved. He had been one of the highest-rated students in his IONEC, earning praise from the DS for his diligence, attention to detail and analytical skills. That was why Wraye had picked him, after all. Her little talk about gathering together a group of capable and loyal people had touched his vanity, and he had been right to feel proud – he was the only recruit she had requested for the East European Controllerate that year. In return he'd given her everything, committed himself body and soul to the Madeleine Wraye flag.

He had enjoyed three heady years of rapid career development in her slipstream before looking up from his Balkan political corruption reports one day to discover she was gone. There had been no suggestion that Joyce was implicated in her proscribed activities. But the new controller did not want Wraye's acolytes, and nor did any other controllerate or section head. He was offered a couple of invisible station postings that he strongly suspected to be General Service roles, unthinkable for a fast-stream Intelligence Branch officer. By refusing them, he lost whatever remaining credit he might have had with Jane Saddle, HPD and the other clandestine apparatchiks who held the threads of his fate in their bloodless hands.

The transfer to Treasury had struck him as a surreal joke. He was an expert in Russian military force readiness, in the politics of eleven nations, in Moscow's intelligence-gathering operations across Europe. He had been taught to resist interrogation, to lie, to cultivate agents, even to kill. And all they wanted him to do was shuffle money?

His first impulse was to resign, to throw in his lot with Wraye and her newly formed consultancy. She did indeed offer him an unofficial salary, on condition that he stuck with the Service. 'But *Treasury*!' he lamented. It did not matter whether he was chief microdot-counter or official registrar of carbon credits, she said. The important thing was that he was inside the citadel. So long as he kept his nose clean and his EPV certificate current he would be useful to her.

Useful, for example, because he had access to SIS's Terror Alert Database.

Only one alert had been logged from Riyadh on the date in question. It had been retracted within thirty-eight minutes. Joyce printed out the details, made himself a decaffeinated coffee, and started to read.

He was still trembling two hours later when he reached Wraye, discreetly ensconced in a booth at the back of a gay bar in the Vauxhall railway arches.

'I found Ellington's alert.'

'Was it Retracted?'

'Yes. Madeleine . . .'

'Who by?'

'Sorry?'

She was even more impatient with him than usual. 'Who does the database say retracted Ellington's alert?'

'Er . . . Ellington.'

'Fuck.' She sighed. 'All right. That would have been too easy. What were the times of registration and retraction?'

'Respectively, 07:23 and 08:01 Zulu.' He wondered where he'd been at that moment – in bed asleep, probably, worn out by another long night of playing catch-up in quantum computation, nanomaterials or statistical thermodynamics. He knew exactly where he'd been two weeks later, when the horrific pictures started coming in from Chicago. 'Madeleine, I really—'

'How specific is it? Have you brought a copy?'

Holding out the folded sheet of paper, Joyce's fragile composure gave way. 'Christ, Madeleine, it's GRIEVANCE! Everything we should have known.' He felt close to vomiting. 'Who was Ellington? Why didn't the Service act on this? Jesus, Madeleine, what *is* this?'

Busy scanning the printout, she didn't answer at first. The bar owner brought Joyce a mineral water. A softly spoken transsexual, for years she had been tipping off Wraye to any Service business discussed within her hearing.

'Are you settled now?' Wraye asked coolly.

'Yes.'

'Analysis is meant to be your strong suit, Edward. Analyse this alert in the appropriate context. GRIEVANCE hasn't happened yet. These names mean nothing to you at this point. International airports turn up in every fifth terror alert. Chemical weapons have been repeatedly discussed by terror groups but almost never successfully deployed at scale. You're reading a bunch of alerts over breakfast. Perhaps, if you're unusually dedicated, you might decide to come back and have another look when you get into work. But by then the alert has been retracted. It's disappeared from view. You forget about it.'

'Until GRIEVANCE happens!' he cried.

'True, you might remember that one alert among the thousands of wild claims and fantastical stories that come in every week from around the world. But would you hold up your hand and say, "I saw a warning and I did nothing"? Do you think, given the mood at the time, that would have helped your career?'

Joyce reddened. 'Ellington's reason for retracting the alert was "Source admitted hoax".'

'You're assuming it was Ellington who retracted it.'

'Do you mean someone falsified the terror alert record?'

'Within SIS?' She smiled grimly. 'It is hard to imagine such underhand antics, isn't it?'

'But they would have been . . .' He stopped. He was suddenly and very obviously terrified. 'Those five names you gave me. Those five directors. Are you suggesting one of them deliberately retracted a genuine alert?'

'Let's avoid speculation for the moment. I need data. All the data you can acquire on those five individuals. I want to know where they were and what they were doing on two particular days. The first you know – in fact we now have a very specific window of interest on that day, between 07:23 and 08:01 GMT. Call that Alpha Day. Bravo Day comes two years later.' She wrote down the date for him. 'Most importantly, I need to know which of the five was in a position to access Porthos on Bravo Day. Search central registry for travel arrangements, Whitehall meetings, dinner invitations. Anything at all. If they signed something, I want to see the ink. If they requisitioned a can opener, get me the paperwork.'

'They're going to wonder why I'm digging.'

'They're not going to know.'

'But if what you're implying about GRIEVANCE—'

'I'm not implying anything.'

'Madeleine, I'm not stupid. I can join the dots.'

'Then you'll understand how dangerous this is, and how careful you need to be. Stay below the radar, Edward. Do what you've been trained to do: dig, and dig deep, but don't leave a trace.'

TEL AVIV, ISRAEL – 9 June

Avraham Boim lived in a simple white bungalow on the southern edge of Tel Aviv. Two blocks away, the orange groves began. A hint of Mediterranean salt carried across the coastal plain. The security provisions were discreet but robust: anti-climb mesh fencing, cameras, infrared motion sensors and a clear line of fire from every tinted window.

It was 4.45 a.m. local time when Arkell parked his rented Hyundai at the end of the clean-swept street. He was unsurprised to see a light come on half an hour before sunrise: Boim was a former paratrooper, old enough to have served in the Yom Kippur war, and veterans tend to get up early. He was more surprised to see the shrunken intelligence officer hobble out into his yard with the first glow of the new day, dressed in dungarees and carrying two sacks. A minute later, the suburban calm was broken by the low growl of a cement mixer.

Arkell approached the reinforced steel gate and rang the bell. The man in the yard looked up, eyes creased with suspicion. A lifetime on the frontline of Israeli domestic security had left him wary of any stranger.

'Good morning, Mr Boim. My name is Samuel Chester. I'm sorry to disturb you at home. I've come with a request for help from Madeleine Wraye.'

'If she sent you, we can be sure your first statement was a lie,' muttered Boim, crossing to the gate. 'But I give you credit for choosing a good Jewish name. What does that sly bitch want this time?'

'A former Mossad agent. Gavriel Yadin. We need to get in touch with him. Madeleine thought you might be able to point us in his direction.'

'Because the Mossad won't,' nodded Boim. 'So why would I?' He glanced back towards the growling drum mixer. 'My concrete needs my attention. Take your time constructing your answer.'

As he shuffled away, the gate slid open on noiseless rails. Arkell followed him across the yard.

A pile of sand and another of crushed stone stood either side of the mixer. With an encrusted spade, Boim shovelled equal quantities into the machine.

'I could begin by appealing to your long friendship with Madeleine . . .' started Arkell cautiously.

'Hah!' Boim never took his eyes off the rotating paste in the mixer. 'Twice. Not once, *twice* that woman has interfered directly in a Shabak investigation on Israeli soil. The first time, the suspect disappeared. The second time, an extremely helpful source lost his memory completely. Why do you think she isn't here herself? She knows we'd arrest her the moment she stepped off the plane.'

'So perhaps I might instead look for areas of common interest,' suggested Arkell. 'Understand better how we might help you.'

'I need no help. I'm retired. Doesn't she know that? All I need in life is right here.'

Retired, thought Arkell gloomily. So much for quick access to the Shabak file on Yadin. 'Actually, I was thinking I could help you with your mosaic.'

Boim looked round curiously. Arkell nodded towards the pile of coloured glass pieces, and beyond it the pattern emerging on the ground as night receded.

'You want priceless intelligence in return for manual labour? You have some chutzpah, I will say this for you.'

'Do we have a deal?'

'What do you know of mosaics?'

'I know how to lay concrete.'

'She sends me a builder?'

'A soldier. I was once tasked to build the floor of a barracks.'

'This does not sound like the British army,' observed Boim.

Arkell didn't reply.

'A mercenary, then?' The old spy smiled to himself. 'The *Légion étrangère*, perhaps? And Wraye's man. Yes . . . now I know who you are.' He turned back to the cement mixer, tipping it so that fresh concrete sloshed into a dented wheelbarrow. 'They said you were dead.'

Arkell was appalled at how swiftly this stranger had deduced his identity. Maintaining a neutral expression, he picked up a shovel and walked over to the patch of ground marked out by timber shuttering. Boim dumped fresh concrete into the formwork, and Arkell used the shovel to spread it out. Another load, and the formwork was full. Once the concrete was approximately level, Arkell cast around for, and quickly found, the screed rail, a length of timber dusty with old cement. The two men each took an end, and in silence worked it up and down the concrete, flattening the surface. To finish, Arkell used a bull float to smooth off the surface.

Boim watched his technique with grudging approval. 'Good,' he admitted. 'But I could have paid an Arab boy eight shekels to do the same. Now get out of the way. Legionnaires know nothing of art.'

Selecting a handful of ruby red glass pieces, he knelt by the wet concrete and embedded the first fragment. Each piece of glass was meticulously inspected before it was committed to the artwork. A curling tongue of fire began to unfurl.

'Have you heard of this Yadin?'

'Of course,' shrugged Boim. 'I know everyone.'

'Is he in Israel?'

'That I can't tell you.'

'What do you know of him?'

The Israeli considered the piece of glass in his fingers. 'Have you heard talk of Leviathan?'

'I tried to read it once.'

Boim shook his head. 'Bring me more red,' he commanded.

Arkell picked out the glass pieces and said, 'He's killed someone. Someone important. We need to talk to him urgently.'

'I understand what it means when someone like you wants to talk urgently to someone like him. If it was anyone but Yadin, I would be anxious for them.'

'Meaning he's good?'

'Meaning, my friend, you would do better to go into the building trade.'

'Let me tell you what I have,' tried Arkell, recalling the dossier he had read and re-read on the night flight from Schiphol. 'We know he served as a highly successful Kidon combatant for twelve years, eliminating forty-one targets in thirteen countries. He's able to pass for an Arab, and has operated covertly in Beirut, Baghdad, Cairo and Damascus. He's proficient with blades, poisons, sniping, explosives, garrotting and a wide range of unarmed techniques.'

'So you know nothing,' observed Boim dryly. 'This could apply to sixty men.'

'Then help me understand this one.'

'Help a foreign spy kill an Israeli citizen?' Boim bent low over the concrete.

'Surely you have no reason to protect him. At best he's a rogue agent; at worst, he's a traitor to Israel.'

'If that is the conclusion of those in authority, it is for Israel to act, not you.'

'My job is to stop him assassinating someone else.'

'Futility. This is what Kidon combatants do. I do not attempt to stop my grandson staring at the girls.'

The first direct rays hit the mosaic then, lighting up every piece of glass in a swirl of glittering colour. Arkell decided to trust Boim with the facts. 'Yadin murdered Anneke van der Velde. It wasn't a heart attack. We expect him to target Murilo Andrade and Terence Mayhew in Strasbourg one week from now.'

Boim raised an eyebrow. 'The drug peddlers? Then perhaps Yadin is doing the world a favour. Bring me some black glass.'

'Killing premiers is the best way to maintain the status quo? Is that how the Shabak excuse the Rabin assassination?'

A low growl met this impertinence. People were appearing on the street now. Early commuters, children. A police car gave a double tap on the horn as it passed. Absently, Boim raised a hand in salute. 'Israel has close to half a million drug users,' he said coldly. 'Each one of them is a drag on a country that needs every drop of strength to survive. Forgive me if I do not wish to make it easier for our future sentinels to throw themselves into the sewer.'

Arkell set a pile of black glass pieces beside him. 'But then how much police time – *Shabak time* – is consumed in the War on Drugs? How much better would you be able to protect Israeli streets from suicide bombers if you weren't distracted by illicit heroin shipments?'

Boim considered him. He seemed almost amused. In a milder voice, he said, 'Get me the emerald pieces, my friend.'

* * *

They sat in the shade of an old parasol, gazing at the extended mosaic gleaming in the hot sun. A tray of iced coffee and dates stood on the table between them. Boim was sweating in his dungarees. His hands, thick with short hairs whitened by cement dust, rested on his knees.

'Yadin is a man like any other,' he began, 'but you will not be able to stop him. I say this now to comfort myself that my contribution will make no difference. I will never accept the legalization of drugs. Never. This is scripture for me. You understand? I help you only because killing politicians cannot be the answer.'

'What do you know of his methods?'

'I have seen two of his victims. It was my unpleasant duty to clean up after him in Beit Hanina. They were jihad recruiters, the devils who call on any family that has not yet given up a child to the struggle. Yadin cut open their abdomens, tied their intestines together like Satan's umbilical cord, and wrapped them in suicide vests so that none of their friends dared help them while they were slowly dying. A powerful message, yes?' He snorted. 'We had no choice but to destroy them together with their devices in a controlled explosion.'

'Is there any technique he favours?'

'I'm afraid he's extremely versatile.'

'How good is his counter-surveillance?'

'Will you be able to sneak up on him, you mean? With the right wind and God's blessing, perhaps. Kidon combatants usually move too fast to need worry who's following them . . .' But he did not sound convinced.

'Places he frequents? Bars, health clubs, temples?'

'He reads, I hear, but there is little sentiment in the man. He knows better than to develop a habitual pattern. He is not the kind to become attached to bricks and mortar.'

'What about his parents?'

'Estranged. His father could not accept his choice of profession.'

'Any weaknesses?'

'There is so much hope in each of your questions, and I must keep disappointing you. Yadin is not an alcoholic, a paedophile, a religious extremist. He is well balanced, heterosexual. It is said he is rough with women, but it is also said they come back for more.'

Recalling the report from Tobago, Arkell asked, 'And is there any particular woman?'

'Ah,' smiled Boim. 'Yes, I believe there may be.'

'In Israel?'

'In Germany. Hamburg, if I have it right. Of course, he may have tired of her by now.'

'Her name?'

'I don't recall. It's a long time since I saw the file.'

'But you could access it?'

He shook his head. 'I'm retired.'

Although he had anticipated this particular brick wall, Arkell couldn't help a stab of disappointment.

'Of course,' went on Boim, 'any wise officer plans for his retirement. He assembles his dossiers. He caches a couple of extra passports. And, if he is able, he builds loyalties amongst the next generation.'

Arkell glanced up sharply. 'Who?' he said.

LONDON, ENGLAND – 9 June

For Madeleine Wraye, the skies were darkening. Memories of gnawing distrust, previously swept under the Vauxhall Cross carpet in the name of corporate unity, now surfacing once more. Tony Watchman, flatly denying the surveillance operation he'd run against her asset in Warsaw. Jane Saddle, whispering poison in the Chief's ear about the declining productivity of the Counter-Proliferation section.

Dig deeper. Dig further back.

Freetown.

Jeremy Elphinstone wanting back-up in his little civil war intervention. 'Not your patch, of course, no right to drag you away from the comforts of Abuja, but if you could possibly spare a couple of days . . .'

They were supposed to be meeting the president; to what end, Elphinstone would not specify. Courteous as always, he was being maddeningly holy with his secrets. Wraye knew a little of Valentine Strasser, the Krio soldier who had led a protest march on State House at the age of twenty-five and found himself running Sierra Leone. Nigeria was supporting with troops and aircraft his campaign against the Revolutionary United Front, and Wraye had collected copious intelligence on Abuja's intentions. That was why Elphinstone wanted her there: she could be presented as the shadowy leverage Britain exercised over Sierra Leone's military backer. He was much more vague on what he was hoping to achieve.

'There are interests,' he had muttered. 'We need to reassert our influence.'

By then she knew Jeremy Elphinstone and his chess master's mind well enough to anticipate that there would be more to it than that.

They were kept waiting for long hours, in a ramshackle hotel with no electricity, in the back of an overheated army truck, in an abandoned mosque, in a primary school with bullet holes in the wall, in at least three different bars the president was said to like. Their minders were sullen privates from the Northern Province who handled their Kalashnikovs like playthings. Refreshments were irregularly offered, the choice limited to warm Cokes or a dusty enamel cup of water from an unknown source.

Elphinstone, effortlessly cool in spotless linen jacket, appeared immune to flies, sweat and dirt. He passed the time writing his diary, but beneath the surface he grew increasingly tense. He seemed to take the endless delays as a personal snub, made worse for having to be endured in front of Wraye. His deep-rooted civility was sorely tested, his conversation grew curt and dismissive, until she said in exasperation, 'Jeremy, I'm missing important meetings in Lagos. If you want me to stay, I need to know exactly why we're here.'

He had concocted a sort of answer then, concerning UN votes and the Royal Navy's unfettered access to Freetown's port, but she knew he was lying. When eventually Strasser appeared, complete with beret, aviator sunglasses and combat jacket, she was shut out of the meeting after just six minutes. She received a perfunctory apology from Elphinstone at the airport before flying back to Lagos in a state of infuriated bewilderment.

Only when the mercenaries of Executive Outcomes arrived in Freetown did Wraye begin to understand just what kind of game Jeremy Elphinstone might have been playing – with her unwitting collusion. 'We aren't a superpower any more,' he had said some time afterwards. 'But we are still good at making connections. You know that as well as I do, Madeleine. This business was never just about collection.'

On the top floor of Wraye's new house in Markham Square was a single open-plan room, a sloping-walled sanctuary in the converted roof space, with a row of secure filing cabinets along one side. Her most sensitive documents were not stored here; a three-hour journey and a great deal of anti-surveillance dry cleaning in the lanes of Herefordshire were necessary any time she wanted to access those. These filing cabinets contained moderately confidential material that ought to stay out of the hands of burglars – or intelligence officers posing as burglars – but there was nothing in them that might incriminate her or lead to a conviction under the Official Secrets Act. Madeleine Wraye was ever mindful of the possibility of a visit from SO15, the Metropolitan Police's Counter-Terrorism Command, with a search warrant helpfully arranged by one of her former colleagues.

Sitting on a cushion on the floor, her aching back against the wall, Wraye contemplated the prickly question of ASH's sponsor. It was not SIS policy to assassinate friendly premiers, therefore ASH must be serving some other entity determined to maintain the Prohibition status quo. Had the same sponsor also instructed ASH to suppress the GRIEVANCE warning? Was ASH the agent of a single master, following orders for almost a decade? Or might ASH be a rogue spymaster, for sale to the highest bidder, using the Service's resources – and Yadin – to fulfil commissions from a range of clients?

To answer that question, she needed Linus Marshall. The great spycatcher. The man who should, by rights, be conducting this investigation. But Linus was as good as dead these days – to the Service and to Wraye. She closed her eyes, wearied by regret for a lost partnership.

She would start with Linus, she decided. He could only say no, after all.

EAST JERUSALEM, THE WEST BANK – 9 June

The temporary Shabak interrogation centre had been established in an abandoned block of apartments near Shu'fat, an Arab suburb of Jerusalem. The building lay hard against an anonymous highway interchange in the Israeli-controlled sector of the West Bank, a short distance from the Shu'fat Refugee Camp and the infamous separation wall. The current function of the building was not advertised, but two plain-clothes officers with silver mirror aviator Ray-Bans and unconcealed hip holsters stood guard at the entrance. No pedestrians strayed anywhere near the place.

Arkell parked the Hyundai directly outside the interrogation centre. He left it unlocked. No one was going to touch a vehicle under the gaze of the Shabak.

'Rafi Hayot,' he requested of the men at the front door.

One of them lifted a radio and muttered a single rapid-fire sentence in Hebrew. Four tense and silent minutes later, the door opened and another man looked out. Older than the two guards, he was a hardened forty-something, with a receding hairline trimmed to within millimetres of his scalp. His short-sleeved shirt was damp with sweat.

'You are Chester?' he demanded in English.

Arkell nodded. 'Thank you for seeing me.'

'Thank Boim,' he said brusquely. 'Come.'

The Shabak officer led Arkell into an unlit hall that reeked of mould. 'The elevator's broken,' he muttered. 'Maybe it never worked. Arab building. What can you expect?' Leading the way to the stairs, he added as an afterthought, 'Air con's broken too.'

Shouted orders came from above, a mixture of Arabic and Hebrew. Arkell raised his eyes and saw seven more floors above. Squares of deadening halogen light picked out patches of the stairwell. A film of dust coated every surface.

'How about your computer system?'

'This is not broken. You want to know about Gavriel Yadin? The Shabak database is very modern. You will know everything we know in five seconds.'

At the third floor, Hayot used a passcode to open a newly fitted security door. From habit, Arkell memorized the six digits. A long grey corridor stretched out ahead, with twelve doorways to left and right. The original apartment doors had been removed, and as they passed the first Arkell caught a glimpse of a large metal cage. Three men stood inside, their hands shackled to the bars. All were naked.

Across the corridor, another room held a single prisoner strapped face down to a table. Two Shabak officers stood over him with plastic sticks in their hands. A third was seated at the same table, his notebook and audio recorder vying for space with the prisoner's bound thigh. The seated officer spoke in a low voice. When no reply came his colleagues hit the prisoner three times across the back with their sticks. Each blow produced a scream.

Barely bothering to look, Hayot said, 'That one climbed over the wall with a suicide vest. They're asking him who it was for. You understand we must discover the intended martyr's identity.'

'And those?' asked Arkell, sickened by the sight of two teenage boys tied to small chairs, both of them naked, with hessian sacks over their heads. The chairs were constructed at a seventy-degree angle, putting the boys' joints and limbs under intolerable stress.

'A supermarket was burnt down. Those were identified by an informer. If they did it, we will know soon.'

Arkell resolved not to look into any more of the improvised cells. This was not his war.

Focus on Mayhew and Andrade. Focus on Emily.

Despite the cries and groans, he would have made it to the end of the corridor without deviation had one voice not cut through the rest: loud, terrified, and speaking English.

'Please listen, God, I'm just a student, I'm just a tourist!'

Arkell paused by the last apartment-cell and stared at the shivering figure inside. From his accent, he was American. He looked not quite old enough to order a beer at home. Thick black curly hair, fleshy nose. A light, incomplete stubble took the shine off his pink cheeks. The once-white T-shirt featured Homer Simpson and a couple of spots of blood. Arkell couldn't tell whether he was wearing anything else: from the waist down he was immersed in a tank of water.

One of his two interrogators picked up a bucket and tipped a couple of kilograms of ice into the tank.

'I'm American. Jewish! I'm on your side!' His voice quavered with the cold and fear.

Arkell asked, 'Is he a suicide bomber or an arsonist?'

Hayot glanced back impatiently. 'That one is unlucky. A thief who picked the wrong mark.'

He led Arkell into the end apartment, recently repainted a stern white and furnished with military-issue desks and chairs. Computer terminals, box folders, Post-it notes and coffee cups covered the desks, with a scattering of handcuffs and batons to remind visitors not to get too comfortable. Hayot kicked a chair out for Arkell and took another in front of a terminal.

'What kind of thief?' The water had been freezing cold, too, in the storm drain at St Michael's. Tom Parke's last sensation on earth had been the miserable chill of icy water.

'Gavriel Yadin . . .' muttered Hayot, entering a long sequence of letters and numbers to gain access to the Shabak database. 'The American kid? This kind,' he replied, gesturing to the computer. 'Very clever with a keyboard.'

'You're torturing a hacker?' Arkell couldn't hide his disgust.

'A cold bath.' Hayot's eyes fixed momentarily on him. 'You call this torture? Your country dominated the world. How was that done, I wonder?'

Arkell said nothing. The frantic pleas of the American boy could be heard even through the apartment door. Accent aside, he even sounded a little like Tom.

Hayot sighed. 'OK. I'm not proud of this. The man whose bank account he emptied is well connected. A rich Russian Jew. An "oligarch", you say? He has demanded retribution as the price of his continuing investment in Israeli industry.'

He stabbed another couple of keys, and Yadin's younger face appeared on the screen. 'There. Everything the General Security Service knows about ex-Mossad officer Gavriel Yadin. Avraham Boim says you are to take what you want. So take.' He stood up.

Arkell scratched his chair forward across the tired linoleum. The screen was filled with Hebrew square script. 'Would you mind translating?'

'I have work to do.'

'I only need the relationship details. There should be mention of a girlfriend in Germany?'

With a show of irritation, Hayot bent over the terminal. He scrolled through the lines of text. 'We have his mother's address . . .'

'Just the girlfriend, thank you.'

'Germany?' The sweat line on his back had extended another centimetre. 'Here . . . Hamburg. Klara Richter. Steindamm 53. Flat 86. You need a pen and paper?'

'No. Thank you. Anything else about her?'

Hayot gazed at the screen for a moment. A minute shift in the shape of his mouth suggested a smile, but he said, 'That's all there is.'

On the way out, Arkell couldn't help looking in at the American boy again. He was still standing in the ice bath, but now one of the interrogators was gripping his shoulders from behind. As Arkell watched, the interrogator seemed to lapse into a frenzy, violently shaking his suspect back and forth so that his head rolled uncontrollably about. A long stuttering cry came from the boy's lips.

'What the hell?' muttered Arkell.

Hayot glanced into the apartment-cell. 'A good technique to make people talk.'

'But you don't need him to talk.'

Hayot shrugged. 'A good technique to make people regret stealing from oligarchs.'

'You know it can cause blood clots in the brain?'

'Those cases are rare,' said Hayot, continuing on.

Arkell saw again the frightened look on Tom Parke's face as he lowered himself through the manhole and into the swirling, filthy water below. The look that had haunted him throughout the Legion years . . . still haunted him. He gave himself the length of the corridor to think very fast through the consequences of action. In just five seconds he ran two scenarios, estimating his chances in each. Then he made his decision.

He let Hayot get as far as the cell with the built-in cage. 'You've been very helpful,' he said. 'So I'm sorry about this. It's not personal.'

Hayot turned, frowning. 'What—'

Arkell hit him full in the face, and again in the stomach to rob him of the air to shout. His third punch landed less than a second after the first, and propelled the Shabak officer into the cage cell. His fourth knocked the man unconscious.

With a finger to his lips to silence the astonished prisoners, Arkell quickly removed the Jericho 941 from Hayot's belt. He cuffed the Shabak officer's right hand to the cage, and tossed his radio across the apartment. With the semi-automatic pistol concealed inside his shirt, he started back along the corridor.

The pain was subsiding. Danny Levin didn't know whether that was a bad sign. His legs were numb, his feet dead lumps of rock. His balls, gone. And now the pain was going too. Was he ever going to feel again? Would he walk again?

Another bucket of ice. Like the water could get any colder.

I'm just a tourist!

Numb.

Places like this, people like these, he'd seen them in movies.

Black sites.

Please . . .

He could feel the frostbite take hold. His toes, dead already. Have to cut them off. His dick too. How would he piss?

I'm just a kid!

He was slow to notice the new arrival. Senses dulled by the cold. The two interrogators had stopped still, were staring open-mouthed.

What?

The guy with the gun was definitely not from around here. Blondish hair. Grey-blue eyes. A casual, confident smile. Voice straight out of some old war movie: 'Very quiet now. Nice and still. Step back against the wall. Hands high as they'll go.'

British?

The man stood with feet at ninety degrees and well apart, his right arm fully extended and his left hand cupped under the butt of a gun. Looked kinda awesome.

He used his left hand to haul Danny out of the tank. Didn't seem to find it much of an effort. Certainly didn't spoil his aim.

'I'm just a student. A t-tourist.' Danny realized he was sobbing, still struggling to focus after that last bout of shaking.

'That's fine,' muttered the man, gripping him round the waist. He seemed to know already that Danny had no control of his legs. 'It's time you gentlemen tested the water. Come here, please.'

Both interrogators approached the ice tank like they were headed for the slaughterhouse.

'I'd like you to show me how tough Shabak officers are. You're going to put your heads underwater and stay down for 120 seconds. Come up early and I shoot you dead, so count nice and slow. Understand?'

They nodded anxiously. The stranger beckoned them forward. 'Big breath . . . Go.'

Then he dropped the gun, threw Danny over his shoulder, and ran.

Silently. Really, he made no noise.

Incredible.

Danny started to wonder, started to hope, but still – this was insane. You didn't get to run out of a Shin Bet prison!

Sure enough, halfway down the corridor an officer stepped out of an apartment-cell, cigarette pack in his hand.

The British guy just ran him down.

The collision was effective but noisy. The officer swore loudly, hit the concrete floor with a solid smack. They lurched on to a security door with a keypad. The man seemed to know the code. A green light winked. Two more officers emerged further down the corridor. One yelled and drew his gun. Danny, upside down, clenched his eyes shut.

Then they were through the door and charging down the stairs, one flight, another, shouts above, chaos.

One floor from the ground, the stranger slipped from stairwell to corridor, heading for the front of the building. This floor was deserted, the apartment doors all smashed in. Some still hung from their hinges, others lay in pieces. In the end apartment, Danny was set on his feet, and together they looked down from a broken window at a car parked by the kerb.

Right under the window was a guard.

He was facing the entrance of the building, gun drawn, hyperalert. As they watched he called out to someone inside the building.

'What's your name?' whispered the British guy.

'Danny,' croaked the boy, amazed to find he could speak at all.

'How good are you at jumping off diving boards, Danny?' He helped him balance on unsteady legs. Danny was wearing jeans, soaked through, but no shoes. Noticing this, the English guy kicked a piece of broken glass away from his foot.

'All right, I guess.'

'See that man down there? Reckon you could land on him? He'll break your fall.'

Alarmed, Danny said, 'He's got a gun.'

'I'll take care of that. But we've got to jump together. And we've got to go right now.'

Danny stared fearfully down at the guard. 'OK,' he muttered, although it was definitely very far from OK.

'Good lad,' muttered the mad British guy, lifting him up on to the window ledge. He climbed up beside him, and as they heard the stairwell door thud open, he whispered, 'Go!'

Danny dropped straight down, smacking into the guard's back. Did not expect it to hurt that much. Cracked his jaw against something, maybe broke a tooth? But it worked! The guard just crumpled beneath him. The Brit, landing neatly beside them, chopped down hard on the guard's wrist. Gun gone.

'Get in the car.'

Danny staggered to the Hyundai, belatedly realizing he could feel his feet again. A commotion in the foyer of the building, two officers racing out of the stairwell. Another at the apartment window above. The British guy threw himself into the driving seat. Danny was having a hard time with the seat belt.

A shout from above. Running feet close by.

The stranger had the car moving almost on the first cough of the engine. He coaxed the gas – a split second of care before powering away.

The first round missed the car completely. The second entered through the roof and lodged in Danny's seat.

'Oh shit oh shit oh shit!' The third round shattered the rear window. 'We're gonna die!'

But there were no more shots. The man had taken the stick shift so swiftly through the gears that they were already round the block and careering onto a busy street.

'We've got maybe a minute before we need to ditch this car,' he said, one hand bringing up the satnav on his phone. 'What do you know about the West Bank?'

Danny gazed at him in bewilderment. 'I'm Jewish, OK? Don't ask me for a balanced political assessment.'

'I was thinking more of geography,' smiled the man. 'Crowded markets, hidden backstreets, places the Shabak won't find us . . .' He took his eyes off the road to check the little screen, then swung into a parking lot, drove straight across it and bumped over a ditch and a kerb to reach the street beyond.

'Oh . . . I have no idea. This is kind of my first visit.'

'Me too. We'll just have to explore,' said the man. It was freakily like he was enjoying himself.

LONDON, ENGLAND – 9 June

They had never met outside Zone 1 before. Churton Street in Pimlico had been their drinking refuge when they were a team, when they shared everything and had nothing to hide from each other. Wraye knew any attempt to resurrect that level of trust now would fail. She also knew Linus Marshall wouldn't be seen dead with her so close to Vauxhall Cross. Brixton was a convenient compromise: just two stops on the Victoria line for him, and minimal danger of bumping into a civil servant, a politician or – Heaven forbid – another spy.

He was not much changed in appearance. The career frustrations of the last few years did not show on that mirror-smooth face. His eyes, always too amenable for a spycatcher, were just as alert. She was aware of some of the sadder aspects of his current life: no more hiking trips in exotic places; a lot more pills; an adulterous wife who was growing increasingly indiscreet. But he seemed to bring a sense of serenity with him into this empty basement bar. Perhaps, since their last, violent words, he had found a kind of peace.

'Linus. This is kind of you.'

'Madeleine.'

'Single or double?' Scotch had always been his drink, by preference Balvenie DoubleWood. 'They only have Glenfiddich, I'm afraid.'

'Water is fine.'

'Aren't we allowed one drink, for old times' sake?'

'The old times didn't do me much good.'

His hair was thinning, and the skin of his throat had slackened. It had been his vigour that once defined him, an unstoppable intellectual force, a whirlwind blowing in from across the river and shaking up the more settled elements in the Service. It was strange to see scalp showing through that still-dark hair.

'What can we drink to, then?' she said, handing him his Evian and raising her own white burgundy. 'European integration? Fishing quotas? The cricket?'

'Look, Madeleine,' he said, setting the water down untouched. 'I know you want to cultivate a network. I realize you need to drum up business. I'll support you where I can. But let's not pretend it's the way it used to be.'

'You still blame me, then?'

'No. No. Not really. If I'm honest, I'm still angry, but not at you any more. Not even Elphinstone and Watchman.' He paused. 'I think, if I'm honest, what makes me angry is that I've been out of that job three years and it just doesn't seem to matter – not to the Service, not to anyone.' He shook his head. 'It seemed so important at the time.'

'It was important.'

'It was a game, and the only decent opponent had left the table.'

She hesitated. 'I thought you might go back to Five.'

'Would have looked like I was running away, don't you think? Perhaps even an admission of guilt.'

'There was never any suggestion you were involved.'

'No? The close friend of the man responsible for guarding the Service's secrets manages to smuggle a stack of those secrets past the security measures he's just instituted. How exactly do you imagine the Chief interpreted that?'

'With respect to the Chief, any of our field officers ought to be able to sneak a memory stick out of Head Office. If not, we aren't training them right.'

'Our terminals don't have USB ports for memory sticks.'

She smiled. 'Well, that was the clever bit.'

'I'm glad you find this funny,' he snapped. 'It will help the long days in Audit pass more quickly.'

'I'm sorry,' she said quietly. 'I know how much you loved Counter-Intelligence. You paid a high price for my mistake.'

'We both did.' He reached for the water and took a sip, a gesture she chose to interpret positively.

'You could always join me if Audit gets too dull.'

'Don't take this the wrong way, Madeleine . . . I wish you well, and will do what I can for you. But our friendship – our partnership – was built on trust.'

'You don't honestly think I was passing names to the Russians?'

'I don't know what you were doing. What I do know is that I could never work with you again.'

'I'm sorry to hear that.' She was sincere, and it showed enough for him to soften slightly.

'My skills wouldn't have much of a market, in any case.'

'Oh, I don't know. Wait for the next big scandal at CIA and they'll be begging for an independent to go in and purge them.'

'Those scandals don't happen any more. It's all petty corruption and cyber now. Counter-Intelligence has become a hygiene function. I'm not much worse off in Audit.'

'There's always the potential for a rogue element, though, isn't there? I'm sure over the years you've had the occasional doubt about one or two of our brethren. Who does your gut say could be playing for a different team?'

'I'm not going there.'

'Elphinstone? Always used to be the public schoolboys, didn't it? Or George Vine, perhaps? He went native long ago. Or is it the quiet one we least suspect? God help us, *Jane Saddle*?'

She was laughing, hamming it up. But Marshall didn't take the bait. He was staring at her, smooth brow creased, alert eyes unblinking. 'This is what you're after,' he said. 'It's why you called me.'

Pretending not to hear, she kept going: 'Watchman? He's done suspiciously well, don't you think? Or de Vries, perhaps, with electronic access to all our secrets. What's the new Chief like? Could *he* be a traitor?'

Linus Marshall sat back and said, 'Do you realize how extraordinarily inappropriate this is? Please tell me you aren't simply fishing for dirt on the people who fired you.'

She stopped laughing then. 'Whatever you choose to think of me, Linus, surely you know me better than that.'

He considered her carefully. 'If you're working for a rival service . . .'

'I'm not.'

'But you're after something you can use against an SIS director.'

'I just want to know if there *is* anything.'

'Because . . . ?'

'I have reason to think you may have a bad apple.'

'Not me. Not my bag any more.'

'That doesn't mean you're not concerned.'

'It means exactly that. I worry about the money and leave the human beings to Alec.'

'Linus, I'm not asking for gossip. I want your gut instinct. If there is a traitor in SIS – at the very top – who is it?'

'I won't do it, Madeleine.' He stood up to leave. 'I won't blacken a director's name for your satisfaction.'

'So it's all dandy?' she shouted after him. 'Nothing to fear in Babylon-on-Thames? The great ziggurat is pure to its lead-lined heart?'

He stopped in the doorway, blinding sunshine from the street above giving him an aura that briefly restored the old sense of vitality. 'Will you lower your voice?' he hissed.

She walked swiftly to him. 'Linus, a steer. That's all I'm asking for. Do you smell anything out of place?'

He turned into the light. 'It used to be so simple, didn't it? Burgess, Philby, Blake: the crafty old Soviets planting doubles everywhere you looked. If only the Chinese *were* stepping up and recruiting in their place. But that's not where the contest is any more. You want to waste a few months chasing new spectres under the bed? Have a look at the awkward places the Service knows well. Iraq. Egypt. Serbia. Pakistan. Afghanistan. Then ask yourself which multinationals are doing unexpectedly well in those places. Maybe I'm imagining it – it's not my concern anyway now – but once upon a time I would have been curious to see if there was any connection.'

'Who's in the frame, Linus?'

He shook his head. 'Do I believe you passed names to the Russians? No. I never believed that. But you hurt the Service just as badly when you let Elphinstone and Watchman take over the roost. It should have been us, Madeleine. The Chief as good as said so. He was counting on us, his dream team. You broke a great deal more than the law when you copied those files.'

'I know,' she said, clasping his arm. For a second she sensed their old warmth, their shared feeling, their lost bond. 'Trust me, Linus. I'm trying to make amends.'

SHU'FAT REFUGEE CAMP, THE WEST BANK – 9 June

They abandoned the car among a dozen others and, under the guidance of Arkell's smartphone map, walked swiftly towards the refugee camp. Danny had taken only nine steps when he buckled with a cry of pain. Arkell removed his desert boots and handed them to the boy.

'Thanks,' muttered Danny, rubbing the sole of his foot.

The first thing they saw was the security wall. A meandering line of eight-metre slabs of grey concrete, it looped between two Jewish suburbs to encapsulate the camp, a teardrop stretching towards old Jerusalem. One road led through a break in the wall. It was blocked by an imposing new six-lane checkpoint.

A line of vehicles queued on the Palestinian side, waiting for the extensive security search that stood between them and Israel's shopping malls, buses and nightclubs. There was no barrier for cars entering the camp, and a fenced pedestrian corridor led to an unmanned one-way full-height turnstile. In theory, there was nothing stopping them simply walking out of Israeli-controlled territory.

Arkell stared at the empty pedestrian corridor. If they took it, they would be hemmed into a narrow fenced space in plain view of the Magav, Israel's border police. Cameras and barbed wire overhead. What if the call from the Shabak came then? Trapped. Every instinct told Arkell to avoid it, but there wasn't any other option.

'They won't have had time to circulate your picture,' said Arkell, pulling a blue shirt from his backpack. 'But there'll be an alert out. Our basic descriptions. Lose that shirt and put this on. Can you manage a French accent?'

'I could do Italian?' said Danny, stripping off his wet Homer Simpson T-shirt.

'Perfect. You're Giuseppe Rossi from Milan, a devout Catholic medical student, come to see Bethlehem and the Church of the Holy Sepulchre, but you're also considering volunteering in a refugee clinic. If they give you trouble, let it slip that your father is a minister in the Italian government who sits on the European

External Action Service's Middle East subcommittee. Can you manage that?'

'Hold it. You're not coming?'

'They'll be looking for two Westerners together. We have to go separately. Head straight down that sidewalk and through the gate. Don't stare at the police. Act like you do this every day. They probably won't even cross the road. If they do challenge you, they'll ask for ID. Apologize politely and say you left it in your hotel. You're staying at the Grand Court.'

'Jesus,' whispered Danny, eyeing the narrow corridor between the fences. 'I don't know that I can do this.'

'Act relaxed and you'll be fine.'

'I'm serious.' He turned back to Arkell, jaw trembling. 'They'll arrest me and throw me back in that ice bath. I can't do this. I can't.'

Arkell looked around in frustration. There were no cars driving into the camp. Perhaps he could hotwire one, hide the boy in the boot, play the aid worker. A story that would stand up to about three seconds of questioning.

Then a small white bus decorated with diagonal green stripes appeared on the road leading to the camp.

'Let's go,' he said, grabbing Danny's arm. The bus bore a route number and a destination in Arabic. Arkell stepped into the road to flag it down.

The driver was sweaty and irritable, but he took Arkell's shekels and handed him two tickets and a couple of coins in change. The bus was half-empty, its passengers all Arab and mostly female. Arkell pointed Danny towards a seat two rows from the front; he positioned himself near the back.

Within seconds they were at the checkpoint.

It was clear from the sudden braking that the driver had not expected to be stopped. This was a route he followed many times a day, each time driving straight into the camp without pause. The security checks were for the return journey. It was always so.

Except this time a magavnik had flagged him down.

Reluctantly, the driver swung open the door. Three magavnikim climbed in. None of them could have been older than twenty. One looked so young the assault rifle in his delicate hands seemed an alien, monstrous thing. The leader approached Danny, after the first two passengers had meekly displayed their identity cards. He spoke to him in Hebrew.

'I'm sorry, I don't understand,' said Danny, with only a slight tremor accompanying his passable Italian accent. 'Do you speak English?'

'You're American?' demanded the magavnik.

'Italian.'

'Your passport.'

'Excuse me. I left it at the Grand Court.'

From his seat at the back, Arkell watched with the air of a curious onlooker.

'You must show me identification.'

'Sir, I'm sorry, I left it in my hotel room. My name is Giuseppe Rossi. I'm here to help the refugees.'

'Stand up.'

'I can call the Grand Court. My father—'

'Stand up!'

'Corporal, perhaps I can help.' Arkell was suddenly there, standing close enough to ensure they didn't see his socked feet, not so close that these edgy policemen would feel threatened.

'Who are you?'

He already had a passport in his hand. Belgian, chosen from a set of five concealed in the padding of his backpack. 'My name is Michel Jamoulle. I am the personal security detail assigned to Signore Rossi by Minister Rossi.' In most covert situations, Arkell had learned to disguise his military background with a slouch or a laziness of speech. Now, he laid it out clearly enough for any private to spot. His back was straight, his bearing relaxed but alert, his gaze unwavering and the passport in his hand presented at a crisp right angle to his arm. To these teenage conscripts the message presented by the older man was clear: officer class.

The Israeli's gaze flickered between the proffered passport and the face. Arkell's expression was neutral: free of aggression, but there was no suggestion of friendliness either. Just a hint of warning. Above all, his eyes declared, he was master of the situation, whatever the current distribution of weaponry.

'Why are you sitting apart?' demanded the magavnik.

'Signore Rossi prefers to see the Holy Land without security always on his shoulder. Regrettably his father's senior position in government makes protection necessary, but he has requested I remain at a distance.'

'He needs identification.'

'Of course, Corporal. He will not make this mistake again. For today, I give you my assurance I will remain with him at all times in the camp and then escort him straight back to his hotel.' He had learned from Wraye that it was better not to ask permission in these situations.

The corporal, confused by Arkell's absolute confidence, waved him aside and snatched at the next identity card. A minute later, the policemen were gone and the bus was proceeding forward into Jerusalem's Palestinian heart.

It was far removed from the popular conception of a refugee camp. Shu'fat looked like any other suburb in the developing world. Most of the land was occupied by squat concrete buildings, some of them several storeys high. Steel reinforcing bars protruded from buildings left unfinished for lack of funds or energy. The streets were filled with the same confusion of electricity cables, piles of rubbish and tattered advertising hoardings found in any number of chaotic cities. Or perhaps the problem was worse here. Freed from daily interference by Israeli security forces, the twenty thousand residents of Shu'fat were also denied the basic sanitation, health and education services the rest of Jerusalem enjoyed. The potholes were understandable, but the uncollected filth was shocking, given its proximity to some of Israel's smartest districts.

They went first to a shoe shop, where Arkell bought Danny a pair of fake branded trainers. At the neighbouring store, they picked out stonewashed blue jeans from a limited selection to replace his still-wet cargo pants. Then Arkell sat him down in a garish red plastic chair outside a café still decorated with a faded representation of Yasser Arafat and ordered strong black coffee and a plate of baklava.

'Well,' he said.

'Uh-huh,' answered Danny.

'You've made things rather complicated.'

'Sorry.'

A boy had taken their order, but it was an older man who brought the coffees and baklava. He insisted on shaking hands with both of them and refused any suggestion of payment. He reminded Arkell of George Vine.

'You are my guests,' he beamed. 'Welcome to Shu'fat.'

'Very kind,' said Arkell, easing his wallet back into his pocket. He knew better than to insist. 'Tell me, are there any areas we should avoid? We don't want to cause trouble . . .'

The man's sunny disposition clouded only for a moment. He pointed down the street opposite. 'It is better not to go to the left side. There is nothing interesting to see there.'

When they were alone again, Arkell asked, 'What exactly did you do?'

'Hacked into the portfolio account of Dmitri Laskov at the Evron Investment Company and drained the cash balance.'

'How much?'

'Four million, two hundred and seventy-eight thousand, three hundred and eighty-nine dollars and seven cents.'

'Get to keep any of it?'

'Nope. Like, the first thing those Shin Bet fascists did was beat my account details out of me.'

'This Laskov . . . ?'

'Total shithole. Poisoned half the workers in his mines with mercury. And it's not like he would even notice losing four mil.'

'Clearly he did.'

'Yeah, well, he's the first who has.'

Arkell looked at him in surprise. 'You've done this before?'

'Only to shitholes.' Some of the swagger went out of him.

'I guess I only took small amounts before, though,' he admitted.

'Why did you come to Israel? Couldn't you hack the account from the US?'

'Evron have some pretty sophisticated firewalls. A couple of open ports only accessible via the same ISP – so I had to be local. You want me to get specific?'

'That's all right.'

Danny sipped his coffee distractedly. 'Man, it's cool you came to rescue me, but . . . I mean, like, who are you? Hundred bucks says you're not really called Michel Jamoulle.'

'I didn't come to rescue you.'

'Oh . . .'

'I happened to be passing.'

'Passing a Shin Bet interrogation cell? Oh, I get it,' he said with a curled lip. 'You're one of those spooks who get foreign agencies to do your torture for you, right?'

'Sorry, no. I was just there to get some contact details.'

'And you decided to bust up the joint?'

Arkell sighed. 'Not my smartest move.'

They sat in silence for a while. Across the litter-strewn street, two young girls with matching pink backpacks played with toy pistols. Beyond them, a mother in white headscarf and embroidered thobe shepherded three even younger children through a pile of rubble, stooping to help one pull a bright yellow plastic tractor clear of a chunk of steel-studded concrete.

'All the same,' said Danny at last. 'Thanks. I was freaking out back there.'

'You want to call your parents? Let them know you're OK?'

The American boy snorted derisively. Then, sounding less

brave than he might have wished, 'Am I OK? Like, how do we get out of here?'

'We'll think of something,' promised Arkell.

LONDON, ENGLAND – 9 June

'Anthony Watchman served in the Royal Marines before joining SIS, and his first experience of leadership was taking command of a troop after a gruelling fifteen-month training course.' The speaker was a young woman, fresh from Edinburgh University's History department. Very much a civilian, she seemed highly impressed by the idea of the Marines and even more impressed by the idea of Tony Watchman. The tufted blond hair and knowing smile of the longstanding Head of Counter-Terrorism were projected on the wall behind her. 'Mr Watchman was first posted to Ankara, where he took over a complex surveillance operation when the station chief was hospitalized with food poisoning . . .'

It had been a stroke of genius, no need for modesty. Watching his young charges make their presentations, Edward Joyce quietly congratulated himself. It was the perfect solution. Even Madeleine would have to admit it.

'It must have been very hard for Ms Saddle to leave the field after her achievements in Vienna. Leaders have to face up to difficult decisions, and she decided that her children needed their mother to be home every night. So she learned new skills, demonstrating continuous improvement, and applied her analytical talents to Treasury and Vetting, before taking on the critical role of personal secretary to the Chief.'

The challenge had been the record. The personal files on each SIS officer are jealously guarded by Personnel Department; not even the Chief can see his own file. But a smart researcher can reconstruct much of a colleague's service history from less restricted sources, including operational files, station logs and gossip. As an Intelligence Branch officer, Joyce was perfectly entitled to access a wide range of files pertaining to a particular superior. But as a humble Treasury officer, on secondment to Personnel as IONEC directing staff, he had no legitimate reason to do so. And since many of the files had been digitized, it was now impossible to so much as glance at them without that glance being entered automatically into the record.

Curiosity about one senior director might be explained away, but investigating five top-ranking individuals would bring an unpleasant degree of upstairs attention. The files were all accessible; Joyce just couldn't be seen to be interested in them. And he certainly couldn't go around asking suspicious questions.

'Since then, Mr Vine has been commended by three different US presidents on the extent of his Arab network and the quality of the CX it generates. CIA say without him AMB would have lost three times as many contractors in Iraq . . .'

So to the stroke of genius. Among the many skills Joyce was supposed to teach the Service's new intake was 'leadership'. Conveying such a nebulous concept was a challenge at the best of times, especially for someone – and Joyce was honest about this much at least – not overly endowed with leadership attributes himself. The solution was elegantly simple: combine the challenges. The eight IONEC students would research 'what makes a great leader', each with a case study to guide them.

And what better case studies than their very own Elphinstone, Watchman, Vine, de Vries and Saddle? Five officers of the highest repute, with three dummies thrown in to make up the numbers.

Simple, clean *and* efficient. He didn't even need to do the legwork.

'I'll be straight with you, I didn't much like the look of this Elphinstone bloke at first.' An Essex lad, ex-City, ex-offender, this student had given Joyce some trouble over the weeks since induction, asking the difficult questions, taking the piss. 'Posh bugger. But give him credit. The man really turned this ship around. Requirements and Production is the heart of everything, right? You need a real leader there. Someone who's proved himself. His greatest hits: Somalia, Geneva, Pakistan and Sierra Leone. The only reason Somalia's a harmless basket case and not a fully functioning AQ client state is Jeremy Elphinstone.'

Armed with a list of textbook leadership traits, the IONEC students had been dispatched that morning to gather their intelligence and present a report at end of day – with all source data appended. Young, unaware of the politics that would come to dog their careers, they could ask the unguarded questions, digging where older staff might fear to venture. They could ransack central registry and scour the central computer index. They could pester and charm and tease out information, exactly as intelligence officers were supposed to do, all the time protected by a legend made watertight by their unthinking belief in it.

Ironically, it actually was quite a useful training exercise.

'People say Martin de Vries can play chess blindfolded. He was obsessed with the Soviet Union, even more than everyone else back then.' This said by a sparky type with extraordinary hair and a natty taste in thin ties who viewed anything that had happened in SIS prior to the Vauxhall Cross relocation as akin to founding mythology. 'He personally bugged sixteen SovBloc embassies before he was twenty-eight, and rearranged the wiring of over two hundred telephone exchanges across Europe and the Middle East. As director of Technical and Operations Support, he created the Porthos messaging system—'

'That is not accurate.'

The voice, dry and dusty, came from the doorway.

'Ladies and gentlemen, this is a real honour,' said Joyce quickly. 'Mr Martin de Vries in the flesh.'

'Porthos was the work of over one hundred people, both h-here and in GCHQ and partner c-commercial organizations. It was a *team* effort.' Martin de Vries focused intently on Joyce. 'Would this individual be David Tucker?'

The student straightened unconsciously. 'That's me, sir.'

The searing glare transferred itself to him. 'And why, please, Mr Tucker, were you r-rootling around in my CoDeka file this morning? Furthermore, why did you then choose to investigate my 1988 visit to Moscow and interrogate multiple members of my staff as to my emotional t-temperament?'

Joyce intervened hurriedly as the unfortunate Tucker wilted beneath the director's gaze. 'A training exercise. Nothing sinister. We've just heard a fascinating account of your service career from David, along with similar accounts of seven other directors.'

'And were all these "accounts" of a c-c-comparable quality to the nonsense I just listened to?'

Joyce flushed, temporarily lost for words.

'Mr Joyce, what is the purpose of this exercise, to which you appear to have devoted a substantial proportion of this intake's valuable training schedule?'

'Leadership,' he coughed. He longed to be back in Italy, holding a gun, commanding a team of Wraye's mercenaries, crushing the cocky TALON. That had felt so good. 'Understanding what makes a good leader.'

'A word, Mr Joyce.'

Crimson now, Joyce followed de Vries out into the corridor. He closed the door on the rapt students.

'Far be it from me to question why cubs who've yet to r-recruit their first agent need to know how to lead,' began de Vries. 'But may I respectfully request that you prioritize instruction in the capabilities we might actually require? If it's not too much trouble, you might consider teaching them how to build a legend, how to protect themselves against electronic surveillance, even how to read a map. Unless you think I'm being old-fashioned?'

'Of course,' muttered Joyce.

'And for goodness' sake make sure the little buggers who have been into the files are fully cognizant of their data security obligations.'

'First thing we teach them,' Joyce promised.

De Vries tilted his head and gave him his dustiest stare. 'I am relieved.'

Joyce paused on the threshold of the training room to recover after de Vries's departure. The man was inhuman, he decided. Half machine, half . . . malevolence. Distracted and on edge, he nearly missed the tail end of the conversation inside. David Tucker had deliberately excluded the gossip from his presentation on de Vries, aware it was ethically troublesome, too new into the Service to have become inured to such concerns. But after Joyce's dressing down, the students had been unable to resist a colourful debate on H/TOS's character. It was only a matter of time before Tucker revealed his reserved card: 'We shouldn't judge him. His sister was murdered in Zimbabwe. Gang-raped and then beaten to death during the farm invasions. That's going to make anyone bitter.'

Tucker swallowed the last sentence as he became aware of Joyce's return. For his part, Edward Joyce pretended he hadn't heard.

Madeleine Wraye knew all about bitterness. She had first felt its deathly grip on her humanity in the hours following GRIEVANCE, as it became clear that one of her closest friends from her Washington days had been killed. Paul Connor, a Naval Intelligence officer with a rare expertise in atomic weapon delivery systems, had been scheduled to fly home from a Chicago conference that day. He'd left behind a young family whom Wraye still had not found the strength to visit.

She had got control of the bitterness, had shaken it off and gone on to pursue the proliferators all the more diligently. But now the bitterness was back, doubly intense, as she contemplated the former colleagues who might have been responsible for Paul's death. She tried to imagine each ASH suspect putting a gun to his head. Elphinstone and Watchman, yes, they would pull the trigger in a heartbeat, and go on to dinner afterwards without the slightest qualm. De Vries was more of a stretch, but she dressed him in Rhodesian khaki and gave him a scout's rifle and then she could see it. Jane Saddle? The idea seemed outlandish, but not impossible. Only Vine defied her thought experiment. Could a man as lovable and generous as George Vine kill?

A memory. Faded but intact. Egypt.

'I can see you don't like boats,' Vine had said as he helped her board the felucca. 'The thing is, hotel rooms are just too easily bugged. Vasily feels safer on the water.'

'Where is he?' Trying to cover her nervousness, Wraye was brusque and direct. It didn't help that she had contracted diarrhoea within a few hours of arriving in Cairo.

'No idea. We'll potter downstream for a while; somewhere along the way, he'll wave to us from the bank. Rather bothersome protocol, I know, but one must do everything one can to protect one's agent, mustn't one?'

She understood this was not an idle observation. Pushing aside concerns about toilet access and the dreadful first impression she was likely to make in her debilitated state, she said, 'I'll look after him, George.'

Vine patted her hand in gratitude. 'I know you'll do your utmost.'

He hadn't always been Vine. Madeleine Wraye had established as much during a seemingly casual drinks party at her political theory tutor's Summertown flat, an event which in retrospect might just possibly have been engineered around her.

'Do you know? I am so pleased. I was afraid it would only be dons.' He was slimmer then, the heavy Arabian tan and pinstripe suit giving him the look of a successful barrister just back from the slopes. 'There weren't any girls in my day. It still feels the most delicious treat.'

'There weren't any Vines, either,' she had said coolly over her glass of warmish Blue Nun. At twenty, pert and precocious, she prided herself on being no one's dupe. She had read him well enough at the college's fund-raising garden party to recognize that girls were the least of his interests.

'Goodness,' Vine blinked. 'You've been investigating me. So you conclude that I'm a fraud?'

'Not necessarily. You might be a genuine alumnus with a desire for anonymity.'

'And why might that be?'

'Perhaps you have something to hide. Perhaps your proposition is not entirely proper.' She was going through a phase of being pleased with herself for clever wordplay.

'Proposition?'

'Isn't that why you're here?' A little too pert perhaps, in those days, to compensate for her insecurities. 'I can't believe it's for the wine or the reheated Marxism.'

He smiled delightedly. 'All right, Miss Wraye, I *will* make you a proposition. The firm I work for is embarrassingly short on women, and I did so enjoy our conversation on the sundial lawn. This is your final year? I would like to invite you to apply for a job – on condition that you manage to unearth my real name.'

'What kind of job?'

'Work that out too and I'll recommend you for the fast stream.'

He had been the Honourable George Aubrey Villiers-Neville. The title had been discarded and the name savagely abbreviated the day he left Oxford. Wraye, who had come up from a provincial grammar school – what she liked to think of as the Mrs T route – found herself both awed and irritated by this privileged sloughing off of an unwanted aristocratic skin. Occasionally Vine dusted down the old identity and flaunted his baronial legacy in certain quarters of the Middle East. 'They do like these little English embellishments in Riyadh and Abu Dhabi,' he admitted. 'What they do not like, I am sorry to say – at least not to entrust with their secrets – are women. No, much as it grieves me to admit it, you'd be far better off in SovBloc.'

As a consequence of that sage career advice, Madeleine Wraye saw little of George Vine over the years, until she joined him at the Chief's top table. The agent handover on the Nile was a rare crossing of their divergent paths, and it had made an impression. He briefed her while they sailed. The asset was a Soviet embassy signals clerk, identified as a potential turncoat by a contact in the Egyptian Mabahith. Vine had approached him in the souk with an innocent question about cumin, and then cultivated him over eight long months. 'I find it best,' he observed, 'just to talk to them until they tell you a secret. So much easier if you don't have to ask for anything.' Now Vasily was being rotated back to the USSR and out of Vine's sphere. 'You'll have to judge for yourself if he's worth keeping on the books. The truth is we've already had the best of him. I've drained him dry; now it's a question of what he can do for you in post – and it is quite a lowly post. But you never know: all kinds of communications pass through these people's hands. He may just be able to tip you off when the tanks start rolling westward.'

'Why's he doing it? Money?'

Vine used his Panama hat to fan away a fly. He was sweating lightly, having given her the only shaded seat. 'If that's what he wanted, we'd have lost him to the Americans. No, he's frustrated, fed up with seeing lesser men promoted ahead of him, angry that no one's fully recognized his talents. It's worth reminding him of that occasionally, very gently provoking that sense of grievance.'

'Lovely.'

'Madeleine, my dear, traitors aren't nice, normal, well-adjusted people, by and large. We have to work with what we get.'

'What role should I play today?'

'Be his friend, simply that. He hasn't been able to talk openly to anyone but me for almost two years. Be sympathetic, indulge his resentments and anxieties. He won't trust you at first, but he'll desperately want to. Simply to have someone else in his life he can talk to. He may fall in love with you at some point, of course . . .'

'Is that why you picked me?'

'He certainly likes pretty faces, and there aren't many of those in the Service. I've found it helpful to procure the odd mistress for him. Up to you whether you want to make similar arrangements in Minsk. It might take the pressure off you. It will also help you lead him very gradually to a point where he really feels he has no choice but to keep on working for you.'

Wraye glanced uneasily at the boatman. Vine had assured her he spoke no English. 'You mean blackmail?'

'Certainly not. But the fellow is married, and the more secrets he betrays to you and illicit pleasures he accepts from you, the harder it will be . . . let's just say, the easier it will be to keep doing as you ask.'

George Vine was, by common agreement, the most gentlemanly of intelligence officers. And yet if Wraye could pinpoint a moment when the scales had finally fallen from her youthful eyes, when she had truly understood how deep she would need to bury her arms in shit to serve her country, it was that day in George's sun-bleached and leaking felucca.

Maybe, after all, he could find it in him to pull a trigger.

SHU'FAT REFUGEE CAMP, THE WEST BANK – 9 June

They had strayed, Danny noticed with alarm, into the exact area the café owner had warned them against. The Englishman seemed relaxed, arms loose by his sides as if out for a stroll, although his eyes never stopped scanning the people around them. Most were kids, inventing games amongst the rubble and scrap metal, or silent women laden with babies and torn grocery bags. But every now and then a street corner would be held by two or three young men. They wore faded blue jeans, fake Timberlands or old army boots, and most had a red-and-white keffiyeh looped casually around their necks. Some chatted in low voices over a cigarette; others were silent, watching these outsiders with suspicion. Handguns protruded from several belts.

For some reason, Danny was alarmed to note, his rescuer always seemed to turn into the streets manned by these unnerving sentinels.

Eventually they were blocked. Turning a corner, they found themselves facing four men with handguns openly displayed. Danny instinctively turned back, only to see three more approaching from behind. Surrounded by Palestinian weaponry, he had never felt more Jewish.

That was when the Englishman started speaking Arabic. Danny watched him lay his right hand against his chest, as the indecipherable words tumbled out. Then he pointed at Danny and spoke a single, forceful sentence in which the only decipherable word was 'Shabak'.

They were led into a well-guarded apartment block and made to sit next to a window that looked out on the security wall. Open sewers ran downhill towards it; if nothing else, the people of Shu'fat could demonstrate their contempt for the wall by sluicing it with effluent. Beyond lay the green and orderly – if illegal – Jewish settlement of Pisgat Ze'ev. Kids on bicycles, cleaners and gardeners at work in villas boasting satellite dishes and double garages. It struck Danny as surreal to be surrounded by automatic rifles so close to a scene of such suburban calm.

The man giving the order was no less alarming than his foot soldiers. He leaned in close to Danny and said, 'Israeli.'

'No,' stammered Danny. 'American.'

'Jew?'

The man was around fifty years old, a greying beard covering much of his face, with teeth that were stained but perfectly straight. His nut brown eyes were heavily creased. He wore a collarless tunic of rough grey cloth, and his black-and-white keffiyeh was tightly wrapped around his head so that a fringe of tassels hung over his left eyebrow.

'Yes, he's Jewish,' the Englishman answered quickly for him.

The Palestinian scowled. 'This man says the Shabak tortured you. Why do they torture a Jew?'

Helplessly, Danny said, 'I guess they were pissed at me.'

A disconcerting scrape of metal from one of the young sentinels broke the silence that followed. Not understanding English, he'd chosen that moment to check the breech of his automatic. Irritably, the older man ordered him from the room. He turned back to Danny with a grin. 'You pissed on the Shabak?'

Danny nodded towards his rescuer. 'Not as much as he did.'

The grin widened. 'You pissed on the Shabak.'

'Uh . . . yeah.'

'And you need my help.'

Danny glanced unsurely at the Englishman, who said, 'We need to cross the border. You have ways to bring in . . . supplies from Jordan. Vehicles with modifications, perhaps. With your permission, we could be the return cargo.'

The Palestinian considered them both, all signs of mirth gone. 'You have money?' he demanded. 'Two thousand dollars? This is the transit tax you must pay the Authority.' He waved airily towards the window. 'For our schools and clinics.'

'Seems reasonable,' said the Englishman, opening his backpack and extracting a bulky envelope. 'We need to leave immediately.'

One of the foot soldiers led them to an alley behind the apartment block where a gleaming white 4WD Toyota stood waiting. On the doors were the scraped remnants of a UN agency's markings. Danny waited until the engine had started.

'You realize what they're gonna use that money for?' he demanded in a furious whisper.

His rescuer looked at him curiously.

'Shit, you just funded terrorism!'

A little perplexed, the Englishman said, 'I suppose that's possible.'

'*Possible?* What else is he going to do with it?'

'My guess is a new TV and a gold necklace for his girlfriend.'

The Toyota moved at pace through the streets of the camp. Pedestrians stepped smartly out of its way and two cars pulled over to let it pass. Within a few minutes they were clear of the concrete warren and moving into open land, with only a few older buildings scattered across the parched landscape.

'And what if he spends your two grand on a stack of suicide vests headed for Tel Aviv buses?'

'I've seen too many real tragedies to worry about hypotheticals.'

The vehicle picked up speed as they left the village of Anata and turned onto the main highway through Wadi Qelt. Other than an IDF base to the right, there was nothing around them but the grey-brown hills of the Judaean Desert.

'Maybe you should check out a demolished nightclub sometime. See what a pile of Semtex can do.'

'That won't be necessary,' said the Englishman. Danny heard the warning in his tone and fell silent.

The journey to Jericho was swift and uneventful. The ancient town, a collection of squat grey and dirty white buildings that blended into the background desert hills, seemed tired and faded. An abundance of greenery fed by the Ein es-Sultan saved it from disappearing completely into the surrounding sands. Twenty thousand people lived in Jericho, many of them refugees, but there was little sign of life.

The transfer from Toyota to smuggler's truck took place in a dusty yard protected from view on all sides by a high brick wall. The Tata vehicle was dirty, rusty and entirely unremarkable. It looked to have been used to transport all manner of legitimate cargoes, from livestock to building materials. Its owner was a cheerful Jordanian who assured them in broken English that he and his truck were well known at the King Hussein Bridge and there would be not one small problem.

Then he sprang a hidden catch on the underside of the chassis, invited them both to urinate against the brick wall, and helped them into the chest-crushingly small compartment concealed above the fuel tank.

The short drive to the border was worse than uncomfortable. Their shoulders and hips were quickly bruised by the jolting of bad suspension on potholed roads. Danny muttered something, an attempt at a joke, but the other man silenced him immediately.

At the Israeli border post, the truck queued for an eternity before receiving a cursory examination from the Magav. They were not interested in an empty vehicle returning to Jordan. The driver pulled up a couple of kilometres into the Hashemite Kingdom and released them from their steel priest hole. 'You see?' he beamed. 'No problem. Never problem.'

At the Englishman's request, he drove them straight to the US embassy in the western suburbs of Amman. As they climbed out of the Jordan River valley towards the affluent outskirts of the hilltop capital, Danny asked, 'What happens now?'

'Now you go home.'

'What if I don't want to go home?'

'You have no passport, no money, no clothes. You're still in shock. You're going home.'

'And you?'

'I've got a job to do.'

'What kind of job?'

He didn't answer.

Danny shifted in his seat, trying to find a more comfortable position between the driver and his rescuer. The gear stick was pressed against his leg and a metal spring protruding from the bench seat was digging into his buttock. 'I could help you,' he ventured.

'I don't need help.'

'You don't know what I can do.'

'I know you're very clever and not all that smart. Which is why you're headed back to college. Tell the embassy you were robbed while visiting Petra. Ask for a temporary passport and a phone call to your parents. They can sort out a ticket home for you. For Christ's sake, don't mention the Shabak or your activities in Israel to any diplomats. You'll only embarrass them.'

Two blocks from the squat, sand-coloured fortress designated United States territory, the Englishman asked the driver to pull over, well clear of the CCTV and armed police units that surround every American embassy in the Middle East. He gave him a $300 tip and they parted with much invocation of God's blessing upon them.

'Aren't you coming?' asked Danny, gazing down the wide, clean boulevard. The outline of a police truck mounted with a machine gun was visible in the distance, guarding one corner of the antennae-strewn building.

'Your story is you were travelling alone.'

'How about a drink first?'

'Sorry. No time.' The Englishman hailed a taxi.

'So, like, can we keep in touch? What's your name, anyway?'

The guy just smiled. 'Do me a favour. Choose your marks more carefully in future.'

Danny felt genuinely hurt. 'You won't even tell me your name?'

The Englishman climbed into the yellow saloon. '*Matar*,' he murmured to the driver. As the taxi pulled away, he looked up and said, 'Stay out of trouble, Danny.'

PORTSMOUTH, ENGLAND – 10 June

'His *sister*?' queried Madeleine Wraye. 'Martin de Vries doesn't have a sister.'

'Not any more.'

'I wasn't aware he ever did. We looked into all that when we made him a director.'

'She was actually his half-sister,' said Joyce. 'Different surname.'

'Beaten to death? You're sure about that?'

'There's a photograph on a Zim Opposition website,' he said, reaching for his smartphone.

'I don't want to see it. Christ, poor Martin. He did press us to intervene in Zimbabwe. He was convinced we could stop

Mugabe in his tracks with a few I/OPS or Increment actions. Of course we stonewalled him. We had no idea his sister was on one of those farms.'

'It's a hell of a motive.'

'It's a *possible* motive,' she corrected. 'Keep an open mind. There are four other names on that list.'

Edward Joyce gazed through his binoculars at the wharfs and streets below. 'Jane Saddle is in the clear. Three days' leave, covering Bravo Day. Her daughter's school organized a camping trip to the Brecon Beacons. She was one of the volunteer parents.'

'You checked she actually went?'

'The school posts photographs from every excursion online. She's in half the pictures from that year. Bright yellow raincoat, posing with the kids on a dozen windy hilltops. No way she could have accessed Porthos.'

Wraye nodded, satisfied. Her fingers were skimming across the screen of a tablet. 'These are good,' she acknowledged. She had issued Joyce with two tiny pieces of equipment in that Vauxhall Arches bar: a miniature digital camera with which to photograph logbooks, requisition forms, memos, travel receipts and journals in SIS's central registry, and a highly unusual flash drive for all the data collated by the IONEC students on the ASH suspects. To smuggle the devices in and out of Head Office, she had shod him in black lace-ups with generous heels, inside each of which was a copper-lined compartment. Proper old-school kit.

The flash drive had no USB interface, but rather a delicate moulded body designed to fit between an Ethernet 8P8C connector and its port on a desktop terminal. To copy the students' files, Joyce had stayed late in the office, lingering over a set of accounts from Buenos Aires. He had encouraged a pencil to roll behind his terminal, had reached to retrieve it, and had swiftly inserted the device between connector and port. No alarms had gone off. It was as easy as Wraye had promised.

Wraye looked up from the data haul on the tablet and gazed out over Southsea. 'How are they doing?'

'Pretty well.' He handed her the binoculars. 'Allwood is impressive. Green shirt with blue daypack.'

Wraye found the IONEC student and followed him as he sauntered, with casual purpose, through the tourist crowds scattered around the shops and restaurants of Gunwharf Quays. 'Who's the target?'

'TD7. Blue jacket, thirty metres ahead.'

From Deck 1 of Portsmouth's Spinnaker Tower they had a god's eye view of the surveillance operation. Three other students had adopted a workable formation around the senior training officer known as TD7, modified to allow for the canal that ran through the middle of their route. One student walked forty metres ahead of the target, guided by radio instructions from Allwood. Another, the back-up, followed behind, out of sight should TD7 turn. The fourth was across the canal.

'Your front-runner is ballooning a little, and the boy in the red shirt is staring more or less continuously – he'll show out the moment the target looks round.' She handed back the binoculars. 'What was he thinking, wearing red?'

Joyce said nothing. TD7 had paused at a shop display. Allwood handled it just right, continuing naturally past while his back-up took over the eyeball position. The student in front had stopped to take a photograph of the Spinnaker Tower, a manoeuvre that allowed her an oblique view of the target. 'Look again,' he said, giving Wraye the binoculars once more.

Red Shirt had disappeared. Wraye finally spotted him on a bridge across the canal, now sporting a white T-shirt and blue baseball cap. As the target abruptly started off in a new direction, the four watchers slipped effortlessly into a revised formation around him.

'Not bad,' she offered. 'What do you have on the others?'

'Nothing on Elphinstone. The man left no footprint that I could find on Bravo Day. Vine was in Damascus station, presumably with access to Porthos. Watchman and de Vries were both in Head Office. A bunch of meetings logged, as well as a conference call with Langley for Watchman at 15:30.'

'All right. Is Elphinstone in London at the moment? I'll start with him. Nothing more suspicious than a blank slate.'

'Start with de Vries,' said Joyce forcefully. 'If you're looking for a traitor, he—'

Wraye interrupted him with a raised hand: a group of noisy schoolchildren were being herded past them by a frazzled teacher. Two were leaping up and down on the transparent section of the floor, seemingly intent on cracking the toughened glass and plunging to their deaths.

When they had ebbed away, Wraye said quietly, 'Because his sister was murdered? That's your analysis?'

'He wrote letters to Blair, to the whole Cabinet, arguing for intervention in Zimbabwe. There are copies on file, the scrupulous bastard. He goes on about "the team" but he despises most of us. I've been reviewing the decisions he's made since the farm invasions: he's stopped valuable projects, withheld new kit on the flimsiest of grounds, denied logistical support to important missions. This is a man who hates the Service for doing nothing to stop Mugabe – hates it so much he's willing to sabotage our vital interests. Maybe retract a genuine terror alert.'

'Unfounded speculation.'

'Maybe even kill an SIS officer.'

Wraye looked cautiously around. There was no one within hearing distance. 'Where did you get that idea?'

'I know Ellington died in Riyadh on Alpha Day.'

'In his sleep. Nothing suspicious about a ruptured aneurysm.'

'Read the TOS travel log. A courier was dispatched to our embassy in Saudi two hours after the retraction of the threat alert. Ellington died that night. Now guess who sent that courier.'

Wraye packed the tablet away. 'All right. I'll start with Martin.'

LONDON, ENGLAND – 10 June

The IONEC student tasked to research Martin de Vries had picked up some useful tittle-tattle from off-duty TOS officers. De Vries had missed his own birthday drinks at Head Office to make an unscheduled journey to Istanbul, reason unknown. He had requisitioned some valuable surveillance kit shortly before the Think Again conference, later declared lost. He had disciplined one of his secretaries for the trivial offence of searching for a pencil in his desk drawer. He had recently developed the habit of going out on to the terrace overlooking the Thames to make calls from a private mobile.

None of which, Wraye reflected, probably amounted to anything. There had always been unwarranted question marks hovering like tsetse flies around Martin de Vries. His initial SIS application, made just six months after his emigration from the newly christened Zimbabwe, had been rejected on grounds of questionable motivation. Some worried, after his time as a scout in the Rhodesian Bush War, that he might be a racist fanatic. Others took the opposite line: that he might hold a grudge against Britain over the sanctions regime, the Beira Patrol and the Lancaster House Agreement. Still others took against his Afrikaner roots and refugee odour, even though he held British citizenship.

He remained persistent and was tossed the odd freelance bone – hired to courier equipment behind the Iron Curtain or to install radios in awkward places. When he proved capable, they gave him more taxing assignments – dead drops, radio repairs in the field, recovery of lost assets. Further successes brought him to the attention of senior officers with sufficient clout to overcome the quibbles of Personnel Department, and the stateless misanthrope was brought in-house. Once given full access to the Service's resources, de Vries had quickly shown a remarkable aptitude for design and engineering. Nevertheless, for years his loyalty continued to be questioned.

Wraye remembered how struck she had been on first meeting him by his extraordinary memory for objects, places and people. He was able to keep track of SIS equipment and weaponry right across Eastern Europe and the Soviet Union. If she was planning to meet an agent in a particular town in Romania, or Poland, or Yugoslavia, de Vries could tell her, without reference to the records, exactly where the nearest radio and survival pack were cached. And he would do it without pride or any obvious desire to be helpful; his style was always that of the academic contemplating an intellectual problem.

She found him at his favourite Battersea pub, seated at a table with four other men. Who were they? A secret informant network? His brothers visiting from South Africa and Australia? Fellow exiles reminiscing about a lost land?

'My goodness, what a surprise!' she said, avoiding using his name.

Martin de Vries did not bother to conceal his displeasure. He could do it – she had seen him dissemble masterfully when dealing with NSA liaison officers and certain government ministers – but he did not relish it as Vine and Elphinstone did. He marched her away from the table. 'W-what do you w-want?' he hissed.

'Have you been on a diet, Martin? You look thin.' She remembered him as a slender man, but now his eye sockets had taken on a cadaverous look and his cheekbones had grown painfully prominent. She wondered if he might have cancer.

'You can't just c-come up to me here,' he protested.

'Why not? You don't imagine I'm going to be indiscreet, do you?' She judged it finely – not so loud as to be audible to the drinkers, but loud enough to disconcert.

'What do you want?' he repeated.

'Why wouldn't you respond to my meeting request, Martin? So we could do this the civilized way?'

'You're out.'

'And that makes me untouchable?'

'You broke the law.'

'I copied some files for my own personal reference.'

'A flippant tone d-doesn't make it any less illegal.'

'Christ, Martin, everyone does it.'

'*I* do not do it! My *team* does not do it.' He looked genuinely furious. Was he dissembling now, she wondered. Was he, with his apparently black-and-white ethics, the best dissembler of them all? 'The information on that flash drive could have blown a hundred agents. It could have made us vulnerable to our enemies in every arena. It was grossly irresponsible! You're no better than Snowden – worse, considering your rank. That is why I will have nothing more to do with you.'

The blood had drained from his cheeks, leaving sunken white skin marked with a few brown spots, sun damage from his African youth. He looked entirely alien to her, a different species. She was starting to understand the nickname popularized by those who had failed to live up to his standards: Martin the Freeze. Yes, there was ice in the man.

'All right, Martin, I'll swallow your sanctimony. But you're going to have to swallow my presence for a few more minutes. The more readily you answer my questions, the sooner you can get back to your pint.'

He didn't respond. It was a kind of acquiescence. She led the way out of the bar, away from curious ears.

'A few years ago, you took a six-month secondment with SOCA. Why?'

'They needed specialist support. Why not?'

'What areas of investigation were you primarily involved in?'

'Counter-Narcotics.'

'That's what I thought. Must have seemed trivial stuff after the work you'd been doing on Pakistan.'

'On the contrary. It had an immediate relevance and effectiveness that was appealing.'

'Stopping a couple of shipments of coke, so advertising execs in Soho have to fork out a few quid more?' Her laughter was gently mocking, not unkind.

'I see you take as careless a view of our controlled substances legislation as of Section 8 of the Official Secrets Act.'

'Quite right,' she smiled. 'The law's the law.'

'I happen to think,' he said, rising to her bait, 'that heroin and cocaine are the most pernicious influences in our society today. I am very proud of the contribution I made to stemming their flow.'

'Whatever must you have to say about Think Again?'

'Dangerous lunatics,' he snapped.

'Best dead?'

He stared at her. 'Are we finished?'

'We haven't started, Martin. That was just warm-up chit-chat.'

'For God's sake, get on with it.'

'I want to take you back to a particular directors' meeting.' She gave the date. 'Primarily we discussed WMD, but there was another agenda item that might place it for that prodigious memory of yours: an argument about replacing a broken table football machine in the junior officers' rec room.'

'Yes.'

'At that meeting, you made a surprisingly impassioned statement about disciplining officers who operate unilaterally without regard to correct protocol in the field. It was quite random. We were all left wondering who you were talking about. Do you remember?'

'I do.'

'Was it one of my officers?'

'It was A-A-Arkell.'

'You had been provoked by his leaving Yemen without consulting London?'

'C-correct.'

'Are you all right, Martin? You've started stammering again. Is something disturbing you?'

'*You* are disturbing me,' he said, with a great effort. 'As you well know. What is your point?'

She folded her arms. 'The thing is, Martin, when I later made my inquiries into Arkell's death, you denied earlier knowledge of his off-piste activities, claiming you only heard about his unauthorized itinerary after he was killed.' Fixing his wavering eyes with her own rock-solid gaze, she said, 'Now why would a man of your integrity lie about a little matter like that?'

His expression had turned sullen. 'I don't recall.'

'You remember the table football, but not why you covered up your personal investigation into Simon Arkell's journey back to the UK?'

'Perhaps it felt in-d-decent,' he spat, 'to question the behaviour of a man who had just been killed in the service of his country.'

'That's all you have? Good taste? That's your explanation?'

'Like I say. I don't remember.'

'All right. Then I'd like to take you further back. Riyadh, two weeks before GRIEVANCE. You requested an expedited Saudi visa and access to the diplomatic quarter for a declared courier with a package for the Ambassador. The courier was travelling under the name of Sidney Dawson. In the TOS log, the *Purpose* column is blank—'

'How did you get access to the log?' he demanded.

'Don't worry, I haven't kept a copy. Why didn't you state the purpose?'

'I can't tell you.'

'Because it was sensitive?'

'Extremely.'

'What was Sidney Dawson's real identity?'

'I don't know.'

'Martin, you dispatched him!'

'I did *not*. The courier was not one of our people. My only involvement was the Saudi clearance and the last-minute plane ticket.'

'Then who sent the courier?'

'You are no longer entitled to such information.'

'Oh save it, Martin, or do you want me to go in there and repeat the question in front of your friends?'

He regarded her with deep loathing. 'It was an exceptional arrangement for Counter-Terrorism,' he said at last. 'The courier was sent by Anthony Watchman.'

HAMBURG, GERMANY – 11 June

Klara Richter lived on the eleventh floor of a 1970s apartment block, a short walk from the old city centre. Arkell stood across the road from it with his fixer, Carlo, watching the entrance.

He was dressed quite differently now. Gone were the desert boots and jeans. In their place he wore a crumpled black suit and black shoes, together with a priest's black clergy shirt and clerical collar from an ecclesiastical supplies store. Within the intelligence community there is an unwritten rule that officers should avoid posing as NGO staff or members of the clergy, to prevent real priests and aid-workers coming under suspicion of espionage. Arkell no longer considered himself a member of the intelligence community, and besides, Hamburg was hardly Equatorial Guinea.

'There's no other exit? No garage?'

Carlo shook his head. 'She went out for bread at 7.20. Back eight minutes later. Definitely still in the building.'

'You have any contacts with the local police?'

'Sure. They've got nothing on her. Pays her taxes. Model citizen.' He held out a small bag. 'I've tested them – all working fine.'

Arkell took the bag and transferred the small devices it contained to his pockets. Over the course of nine years as a lone operator, he had grown proficient at finding his own sources of equipment for the various private assignments he had undertaken. It was never as straightforward as ordering kit from the Directorate of Special Support, but then there were no bureaucratic hurdles to jump, nor reprimands for damage or loss. And often the options available on the open market – Carlo had obtained these devices from a former Stasi officer in Berlin – were better than equivalent items expensively developed in-house.

'Thanks. How are you for cash?'

'Plenty left in your account.'

Arkell nodded. 'Stand down for now, but stay in town. We may need surveillance on Miss Richter.'

At the entrance to the apartment block, Arkell studied the rank of buzzers. Sensing a woman behind him, he put his finger to one at random. The woman hesitated until she saw the clerical collar, whereupon she unlocked the glass door and held it open for him.

'*Danke*,' he smiled, insisting she go first.

He followed her to the elevators, let her choose a button first, then pressed 9. When she got out at the fourth floor, he waited for the doors to close before selecting 11.

He knew his story inside out. Still, he rehearsed one more time. His fingers checked the bugs in his pockets as his face settled into a look of hapless concern. The effusive apologies at wasting her time. *Entschuldigung, Fräulein, I'm in a bit of a mess. I'm borrowing a friend's apartment and I've gone and let the washing machine flood . . .*

The words were still running through his mind as the elevator doors opened on the eleventh floor. He stepped out into a long corridor of light-grey paintwork and dark-grey carpeting. As he did so, a man took his place in the elevator. Arkell turned, faintly surprised by the sudden proximity of another human being, but the man was facing away from him and the elevator doors closed a second later.

Entschuldigung, Fräulein, I'm in a bit of a mess . . .

Number 86. He knocked, and was surprised again, this time by the speed with which the door opened.

'I didn't mean it, my darling, I promise I . . .' Accented English. The woman broke off when she saw Arkell. '*Wer sind Sie?*'

Arkell stared at her: the smudged mascara, the rumpled hair, the silk dressing gown hurriedly drawn closed, the red welts on her neck that it didn't quite hide.

'I'm so sorry . . .' he muttered, turning abruptly. *You're a priest: walk, don't run.*

The man in the elevator. Dark, cropped hair. Very fit, a strong neck. The image was back in Arkell's mind, fresher and clearer than before. Black leather jacket, small brown messenger bag. Free hand lightly curled. And as he stepped past? A momentary impression of a face, the same side-view captured by a studio camera in Tobago.

He ploughed through the swing door to the stairs and ran down four steps at a time, cursing himself for not considering this possibility. Yadin, *here*! He had no weapon. The shoes were hopeless: a loose fit, and slippery leather soles. The clerical collar constricted his throat. Four storeys down. Five. How fast did the elevator move? Seven storeys. Eight. His foot slid out of control on the worn concrete, and he had to catch himself on the railing. More than anything, he needed the unfailing grip of his desert combat boots.

Bursting out of the stairwell, he sprinted to the elevators. Open and empty. Into the street, but no sign of Yadin. The Kidon combatant had left a car parked outside. Or he'd hailed a taxi. Or he'd set off at a fast march to one of the nearby U-Bahn stations. Whichever way, he was gone. Arkell ran the 800 metres to the main railway station. He scanned the passengers milling around the concourse, boarding the S-Bahn train to the airport.

No Yadin.

Reluctantly, Arkell had to admit he had just let slip a golden opportunity.

When Simon Arkell presented himself for the second time at Klara Richter's door, she was fully dressed in jeans and branded T-shirt, with fresh make-up around hazel eyes. Her long sun-kissed hair, still damp from the shower, was partly covered by a loose-knit beret. A silk scarf, yellow stripes on grey, hid the marks on her neck. Her tanned feet were bare.

'Hello, yes, sorry, me again,' he smiled sheepishly. 'Apologies for interrupting earlier. Wrong flat. Sixty-eight, I was after. You're eighty-six. Stupid mistake, but then we put the verb at the end in German, don't we, so why not numbers too? You do speak English, don't you, Fräulein? I think you spoke English when I . . .' He broke off, summoning a quick blush, a trick Wraye had taught him in DC.

Her questioning gaze was direct but very slightly off-centre, so that one eye seemed brighter than the other. 'Is there something you need? Can I help you?' she said. Perfect English. The accent was almost undetectable now. Perhaps it only emerged at moments of stress. Also lacking was any suggestion of warmth or welcome. The clerical garb had won Arkell a few moments' formal politeness, but he needed a way in fast. The washing-machine story was unusable now.

'Really, I was wondering if I could help *you*,' he said, the smile starting to sag. 'I couldn't help noticing earlier . . .' An embarrassed gesture towards her neck. 'And the truth is I see a lot of high spirits on the base, the lads always ending up with scrapes and bruises, but when they're laughing about it you know they'll be all right. On the other hand, you seemed . . .' Pausing, as if to choose the right word: '. . . *Distressed*.'

'I'm fine,' said Klara Richter with quiet dignity. Her long brown fingers tightened on the door, a second from closing it. One silver thumb ring; an adventurous mulberry nail varnish lapping against chewed cuticles. 'Thank you.'

Arkell's hand joined hers on the door, firmly insisting. *Don't use a foot*, he'd told himself. A chaplain wouldn't use a foot. 'The thing is, Ms . . . ?'

No response other than a deepening frown at his obstructive hand.

'The thing is, as a servant of God I have a duty, really, let's call it an obligation, not to walk by on the other side. You know the parable of the Good Samaritan?'

A reluctant nod from her. Dialogue.

'First thing they teach you in theology school: it's the people who don't want to talk about it who most need our help. So even if it seems like an invasion of privacy, we really have no choice. My name's Anthony, by the way. Strictly speaking, it's the Reverend Anthony Pearson, Chaplain to the Forces, third class, but everyone just calls me Padre. And it's honestly just a three-minute chat, an emotional check-up, if you like.'

'Look, Mr Pearson . . .' she began wearily.

'Or I could ask a German priest to visit if you'd prefer?' he said brightly, as if he'd only just thought of it. 'I know a couple of excellent fellows here in Hamburg, both visit us regularly at Bergen-Hohne. I can rely on them to see you're all right, and in German, too . . .'

It wasn't exactly a threat. Wraye used to call that kind of

well-meaning promise of future hassle *an incentive to cooperate in the present.* It found its mark with the assassin's girlfriend. Exasperated, she shook her head and let him in.

The living room was spacious and airy, with a floor of laminated ash and high windows framed by floral print curtains. None of which was as interesting to Arkell as the location of her mobile phone, on a side table near a small cane armchair. Klara gestured him towards a couch, but he pointed to the armchair, saying, 'That looks like it might be kinder to my back. If you don't mind?'

She nodded and he took the chair. 'We don't carry weapons, of course, but they still like to put us through the same assault courses as the regular troops. My lumbar vertebrae have never recovered from falling off something they call the "confidence pole". Nor has my confidence, if I'm honest,' he laughed awkwardly. The laugh turned into a cough, dry and rasping.

'Do you want water?' A half-hearted offer, but he seized on it.

'Tea would be lovely if you have it, actually. Black, green, peppermint . . . Anything hot. Helps my throat. We were out all night on exercise last week and I still haven't thrown off this cold. Not that it's infectious.'

With a resigned nod, she drifted through a side door into the kitchen.

Arkell had her mobile phone in his hand within a second. The NN-3U from Berlin was already switched on and ready to use. He plugged its universal connector into the data port, and the device began two tasks simultaneously. While it copied every saved number, every text and all records of received, dialled and missed calls, it also uploaded a small program to the phone.

Henceforth every text sent and received on it would be copied to the NN-3U and every call relayed.

It was done in thirteen seconds, long before any kettle could boil.

By the time she returned with a cup of black tea, no milk, Arkell had also planted two microphone transmitters the size of aspirins. One bug went under the cane chair, the other in amongst the wiring behind her stereo. He was rubbing his back when she entered, stopping the moment he saw her and standing to take the tea with an abundance of gratitude.

He gestured at the photographs on the wall. 'These are very good. Yours?'

'Yes.'

Each was framed in black lacquered wood. Arkell recognized Hausa, Tuareg, Aborigine and Quechua faces. The others, he guessed, were Mongolian and Papuan. In each photograph, the subjects were posed naturally but alertly, reaching beyond the lens with their eyes. It was uncanny, that reaching expression, replicated on four continents. What direction had she given them to achieve it?

'Are you a professional?'

'Photographer?' She snorted. 'I wish I could be. I am training as a physiotherapist.'

He steered clear of the Hausa faces – too close to his own story. 'I've been to Peru. Beautiful, beautiful land. Is that where you took these ones?'

'Ecuador.'

'Ah. The Galapagos!'

'No.'

His face fell. Another trick Wraye had taught him. *Make them feel bad for not sharing your enthusiasm.* 'I'm sorry, you must think me the most awful busybody.'

She looked down, as if wishing to hide her thoughts behind the lopsided beret. 'My boyfriend is a little bit . . . physical, that's all,' she said, one hand brushing tangled golden strands of hair from her cheek. 'It's nothing serious. Just his way.'

'His way to hurt you?'

'It doesn't hurt.'

'Before I joined the army, my parish was in south London. A number of young women told me they didn't mind their boyfriends hitting them. Then one of the women killed herself.'

She laughed abruptly. 'I'm not going to kill myself!' Her hand flew to her mouth in dismay. 'I'm sorry. I'm not laughing at her death.'

'That's all right.' He sipped the tea. It was strong and bitter, and reminded him of patrols in Chad. 'I just want to make sure you know what you're doing.'

'We love each other. The rest is not important.' That direct gaze, off-centre again, with the same dominant eye commanding all attention. The full mouth remained slightly open, as if anxiously awaiting his reaction, two white incisors the only teeth visible between her lightly glossed lips. She had an irregular dusting of freckles, he noticed, on her nose, to go with the Caribbean tan.

'Does he get angry with you?'

'Never with me . . . With life, perhaps. Gavriel said something once – we should "have contempt for life", to make death easier. He said, "We are buried in our coffins already." I don't think he believes it. His parents died when he was a boy . . . It's hard for him, sometimes.'

Yadin had given her his real name. Perhaps it was serious, then. 'How did you meet? He's not German?'

'In London, four years ago. I was studying for a masters.'

Arkell pictured a studious girl bent over her books in some Bloomsbury café, catching the eye of the assassin on his way to a covert meet with ASH. 'Not in physio?'

'I wanted to work at the British Museum, so I took the UCL MA in Artefact Studies. A childish dream, but at least my English is better.'

'Fragments of the past,' he smiled.

'Why do you say that?' she asked curiously.

'I . . .' He realized he'd slipped briefly out of character. Looking into Klara Richter's sincere, searching face, he couldn't help being himself a moment longer. 'I've spent a lot of time trying to piece together random bits of history from those fragments,' he admitted. 'Just as an amateur,' he added hurriedly.

'What period?'

'It's about the place, not the period,' he found himself saying. Why this sudden openness? 'Wherever I am, I like to find out the local history, as far back as possible. It helps you understand the place. And the people.'

'It does.' She was smiling too now. 'What about Hamburg?'

'Like I say, I'm just an amateur.'

'You know how it began?'

He hesitated. It wasn't an act this time. 'Charlemagne? His castle, Hammaburg, defending the confluence of the Alster and the Elbe.'

'Bravo!' She clapped delightedly, and for half a second her approval made Arkell forget why he was here, what he was meant to be, most importantly who had been making love to this spirited woman just an hour earlier. That off-centre gaze had shifted minutely, and in that brief moment there was a perfect balance between her two rounded eyes, symmetry so flawless and unexpected that the effect was blinding. 'And Hohne?'

'Excuse me?' He was quite lost.

'You're stationed at Bergen-Hohne, no? What have you discovered about Hohne's history?'

Arkell managed to keep smiling. 'Fräulein, you know so much about me, and I don't even know your name.'

'I'm sorry. Klara. Klara Richter. I'm rude.'

'Not at all. I barged in here, asking personal questions. You've been very tolerant. But, Fräulein Richter, may I test your tolerance a little further? I would very much like to meet Gavriel. To reassure myself that you are in good hands.' He blushed, deliberately again, at the unfortunate metaphor. 'Might that be possible?'

The enthusiasm dampened and then died in her eyes. 'No,' she said quickly. 'No, Gavriel would not want that.'

'Could I speak to him on the telephone? A couple of words of kindly guidance from a chaplain – even a Jewish lad couldn't object to that.' He tried to make it a joke, although he knew he was losing her.

'He won't talk to you.' She had retreated into suspicion and worry, her arms crossed, brow drawn beneath the beret.

'Of course,' he said soothingly. It had been too much to hope for. 'I understand.'

'I'm sorry, I have to go out now. I am late for work.'

'I've taken up too much of your time.' He put the cup down. 'Thank you for reassuring me . . . a little, at least.'

'I'm fine, really,' she said again, a touch of aggravation creeping into her voice.

'May I possibly use your bathroom?'

Frowning, she pointed down the corridor.

Where the living room had been immaculate, the bathroom was a mess. A long tiled ledge either side of the basin was scattered with cosmetics, hairbrushes, toilet rolls and clogged razors. Two wet towels clung to each other on the floor by the bath. What was the story here? Who was this woman who kept part of her life so neat and let the rest chaotically unravel?

Klara was waiting for him in the corridor. There was no opportunity to do more than glance into the bedroom: a rumpled bed, black high-heeled boots and a short grey dress abandoned on the floor. No chance to plant the third bug he had ready in his hand.

'Take care of yourself, won't you?' he asked of her.

He wondered, after the door had closed, whether that had been the Padre's plea or his own.

There was no *Gavriel* in Klara's list of contacts. Arkell forwarded all eighty-three numbers from her phone to Wraye. In a utilities cupboard outside the apartment he installed the booster transmitter that would relay the signals from his bugs via a local wireless network to Wraye's multilingual listeners. As he was leaving the building the NN-3U beeped twice, an outgoing call to a saved number: *Dejan*.

'It's Klara,' she began in English. 'Can you pass Gavriel a message?'

'Go ahead.' The man's voice was a domineering growl.

'Someone came here. English. A priest. Gavriel said to call if anyone asks about him. His name was Anthony Pearson, chaplain with the British army at Bergen-Hohne.'

'Description?'

'Strong. Alert. One metre eighty-five. Blue eyes. Hair dark blond.' A small pause. 'Good-looking for a priest.'

'Contact me again if he comes back.' Just enough words to betray a Slavic accent before the line went dead.

Arkell called Wraye. 'Dejan is the priority. She doesn't have a direct line to Yadin.'

'We have thirty-eight results back . . . We have Dejan. The number is registered to an Ingrid Bernhardt of Dresden.'

'I need the current location of that phone.'

'Give me fifteen minutes.'

Arkell looked through the rest of Klara's saved numbers. Most were German mobiles or local landlines. No Israeli numbers. He walked across the street to the hostel where he'd stored his backpack. The tattooed girl at reception smiled respectfully at his clerical garb, then more lewdly when he re-emerged from the bathroom in jeans and desert boots.

Wraye called as he was walking to the station. 'Dortmund. Ingrid Bernhardt's phone is in Dortmund. Dejan is sitting in the regional headquarters of World Hunger.'

GLOUCESTERSHIRE, ENGLAND – 11 June

It was not the first time Wraye had visited the country estate of Jeremy Elphinstone, although it was a new experience to be invited. Elphinstone had made a habit, in contravention of SIS rules, of hosting high-value assets from time to time amongst the drystone walls and broadleaf glades of his Gloucestershire pile. When a particularly obliging foreign general, minister or intelligence officer visited London, if a ruse could be devised to dupe their babysitters, Elphinstone would have them smuggled down the M4 and would order the silver polished and the cellar ransacked in their honour. A hostile intelligence service could have learned a great deal by mounting a permanent watch on his estate. Wraye, having cultivated a number of informers in the Service's car pool, had the advantage of knowing when a covert visit was being arranged. If her schedule permitted, she would drive to the convenient wooded hill overlooking Elphinstone's gardens, and through binoculars determine which assets were currently held in highest esteem by Requirements and Production.

It mattered because R&P made the weather in the Service. The Chief called the shots, but Elphinstone set them up for him. Ever since Abuja, Wraye had made a point of knowing what was going on in R&P. Her remarkable – even uncanny – knowledge of SIS's most secretive activities, drawn from a wide and creative range of sources, had impressed both the Foreign Secretary and the Joint Intelligence Committee. Whenever she was able to refer to operations that other SIS directors seemed convinced were known only to them, she rose another notch in the estimation of Whitehall customers. Ministers and mandarins began to seek her advice on all aspects of intelligence; began – most dangerously of all – to talk of her as a possible Chief, a development that could only set her on a collision course with Watchman and Elphinstone.

It would have been inconceivable, in that era, to receive an invitation from Jeremy Elphinstone, Prince of the Service and heir expectant to the Chief's green ink. Yet now that she was cast out, beyond the pale, he was prepared, eager even, to receive her. 'You couldn't have called at a better time, actually. At least if I've understood correctly what it is you do these days.'

She half expected a liveried footman to open the heavy oak door, but instead it was a mop-headed, mascara-coated teenager – most likely a boy, she judged – who answered the clanging bell.

'Hello,' she offered. 'Angela Redfern from the Foreign Office. I'm here to see your father.'

With a mumbled acknowledgement, the boy turned and led the way across a hall hung with ornate mirrors and oil paintings in gilded frames. In the drawing room beyond, sprawled across a Queen Anne chaise longue, a second boy looked up from a PlayStation. 'Dad,' muttered the first, managing to load the syllable with infinite scorn. The second boy snorted and returned to his virtual world.

'In there,' conceded her guide, pointing to a panelled door at the far end of a wide corridor. He slouched away, uninterested in her thanks.

Jeremy Elphinstone had been writing in his diary. A leather-bound book with thick cream pages lay cracked open beside a wingback chair. A fountain pen lay across the confident black copperplate. Next to the diary, a half-empty tumbler of whisky. It was revealing to Wraye that he should prefer to remain in his study even when not working.

He said, with a flicker of irritation, 'Did Antonia let you in? I'm sorry, I didn't hear the bell.' Beethoven, swiftly turned down, had been playing when she knocked.

'It was one of the boys.'

'Right.' The irritation intensified. 'Didn't bother to introduce himself, then?'

She tilted her head.

'Used to. They were both delightfully polite. Now they barely speak to me. Of course it's my fault. I spent the first fifteen years of their lives buried in work, only to look up and find my wife had turned them against me.'

'I'm sorry to hear that.'

'You're lucky you never had children, Madeleine.' He gestured to a row of crystal decanters. 'Drink?'

'I'm driving.'

'I don't remember alcohol having much impact on your cognitive faculties at the Fort.'

'That was a long time ago.'

He poured a glass of mineral water and gestured her to the wingback chair, while he took the less comfortable oak chair by the window. He had always been gallant in that way, even at the height of their little Cold War. Stretching out his legs, elegantly crossing them so that one leather-slippered foot bobbed a little, he said, 'I gather you've already seen Martin. And presumably Linus. Were they able to offer anything?'

'Excuse me?'

'Work-wise.'

She had the shape of his thinking now, and decided to go with it. 'Sadly not.'

'But you're looking for something? You're available?'

'Broadly speaking.'

He gazed at her almost fondly. 'I must say, I'm surprised you'd try me. But pleased. We tied ourselves up in such ridiculous knots, didn't we? And the unpleasantness was never necessary. It wasn't personal – you know that, don't you?'

'It was politics.'

'That none of us got right.'

'Clearly. How is the new Chief? Must be strange, having an outsider at the top.'

He ignored that. 'I'll admit I had no idea Jane Saddle had so much bite. You know it was her that lit the blue touch paper with the ISC? You didn't like her much, I remember, nor she you. But she was outraged at what happened to you, saw it as an attack on the sisterhood, I dare say. And so Tony had his knuckles rapped . . .'

'And you were demoted.'

'Hardly that.' He uncrossed his legs and crossed them again, in clear discomfort. 'It's good to be closer to the action. And West Europe is still a vital controllerate. The CX we were able to offer the banks on sovereign debt positions in the southern Eurozone bought us a lot of credit in Whitehall.'

She only smiled. 'I thought you might resign when they gave R&P to Rachel.'

He was about to object, to continue the pretence, when

suddenly he seemed just too tired to bother. 'I couldn't afford to. The pension implications . . . Well, you know all about that.'

'Indeed,' she said coldly.

'I admire you, Madeleine. What you've built for yourself since you left. I'm not sure I would have had the entrepreneurial oomph to do it. And, frankly, my stock was too low just then to feel confident of a decent directorship in the City. I needed to stay, if only to leave on better terms at a later date.'

Glancing out of the sash windows at the croquet lawn, the wisteria-smothered pergola and the extensive box topiary, Wraye said, 'I never realized you were in it for the money.'

He gave a mirthless laugh. 'This place? All Antonia's. She controls the capital, which is a polite way of saying she cut me off a long time ago. Nevertheless, I'm expected to pay the school fees and the bills – on a government salary. It's beyond a joke.'

Wraye offered her best sympathetic face, while her mind raced. The possibility that money might be a motive for Jeremy Elphinstone had never occurred to her. Power yes, ideology possibly, but straight cash? Had the public-school spymaster simply been bought?

'So you'd like me to find some dirt on your wife,' she smiled.

'There is none,' he said blackly. 'Other than her complete contempt for the institution of marriage. No, I need you to help me with something particularly sensitive. Something I can't be seen to do myself, and can't ask anyone in the Service or Five to do. I want you to investigate Tony.'

Of all the many things Elphinstone might have said, this was surely the most unlikely. 'Are you serious?' Wraye spluttered.

'Things have changed.'

'Since Tony got to keep his job when you didn't?'

He bristled. 'Tony and I still have a good working relationship. That is not the issue. We may not be quite as chummy as we once were, but I would have no doubts at all concerning his continuing fine stewardship of the Counter-Terrorism section if it were not for a particularly alarming development.'

'Go on.'

'You understand that this is YZ information, that I would lose no sleep at all having you locked up under the OSA were you to disclose it?'

'Jeremy, please. I am still in the business of keeping secrets.'

He fixed her with a cautious gaze. 'Do you know Javier Diaz?'

'At CNI? Vaguely. He looks after South America, doesn't he?'

'Amongst other things. I've seen quite a lot of him since taking over Western Europe. He's turned into a bit of a drug warrior, feels personally insulted that Spain has become the gateway for so much of Europe's trade. How much do you know about cocaine smuggling?'

'Brief me.'

'The Caribbean was the main route for years, both to the US and, via drug mules and banana boats, to Europe. When maritime and aerial patrols made that difficult, US-destined narco-traffic shifted to the overland route through Central America while European consignments were stashed on cargo vessels. Neither is spectacularly convenient for the drug lords, given the gang warfare in Mexico and the suspicion European customs officers place on vessels originating from South American ports. So some of them had the bright idea of transferring their operations to West Africa. One in particular has made quite a success of it.

'His name is Rodrigo Salis, formerly of the Cali cartel, bit of an unknown until recently, if we're honest. A few years back he set up a warehouse operation in Guinea-Bissau, and since then he's been shipping product in and out at a heroic rate. The local military and politicians enjoy a few crumbs from the big man's table, and Salis has really made himself at home: hacienda in the bush, big SUVs, expensive women, the lot. Meanwhile his cargo can hitch a ride on any number of vessels heading up the west coast of Africa. Fishing boats meet them offshore at night, fat bribes for the crew, and no one's the wiser about that nice clean South African freighter carrying grapefruits or manganese to Rotterdam. Other consignments are driven north through the Sahara and either hauled aboard European ships en route to Baltimore and Hampton Roads, or ferried directly across to Spain.

'That's what drew Javier's attention, and he's mounted an impressive surveillance operation in Bissau. Now who do you imagine he claims has shown up in that unlikely city, shoes shined and bottle of Scotch in hand? Who, of our acquaintance, has been spotted by CNI shaking hands with the noble drug lord and generally carrying on like a long-lost amigo?'

Wraye could barely speak for her astonishment. Had the answer simply dropped into her lap? 'Tony Watchman went to Guinea-Bissau to meet a drug baron?'

'So Javier claims.'

'He has pictures. Video.'

'*No, señor*. Classic ops support cock-up. Javier was watching the live feed from their cameras, swears he identified Tony, but the sequence was never recorded.'

'So there's no proof.'

'That's why you're here.'

'Tony hasn't taken a sabbatical in Counter-Narcotics, has he?'

'He hasn't stepped outside C-T in sixteen years. Terrorism is Tony as surely as the Middle East is George.'

She paused to absorb the extraordinary charge. 'Is there any legitimate reason,' she began carefully, 'why Counter-Terrorism might have an interest in Salis? A source of funding, perhaps? Afghan heroin supports Islamic terrorism; cocaine presumably keeps FARC in AK-47s. Perhaps Colombian drug money is starting to impact our own security interests?'

'I've looked into it, and so has Javier. When he realized he was spying on an SIS director, he got very nervous. Tried admirably hard to find a reasonable explanation. Tried, but failed. Salis has no known connection with any terrorist group. His bank accounts show no transfers to anyone on our watch list. That's why Javier came to me.'

'Have you spoken to Tony?'

'I can't afford to do that. Maybe you can – once you've found proof of the link. It goes without saying that you can never mention this conversation to him.'

'I haven't said I'll do it.'

'There's not much cash around these days, but I can probably find you forty thousand from the Salamander fund.'

She smiled to herself. 'Can I ask you something first?'

'Go on.'

'Indulge me, Jeremy. I'm trying to reconstruct a particular

day, nine years ago. Hard to find data, now that I'm on the outside. You're the only person I know who's had the discipline to keep a diary all this time.' She gestured to the leather-bound book. 'Still managing to write every day?'

'Without fail.' He moved to the bookshelves. 'What date?'

She gave it to him, and he reached without hesitation for a caramel-coloured journal on the top shelf. Flicking it open, he leafed through the pages. 'Sorry. Nothing of any interest.'

Brazenly she said, 'May I see?'

With a slight frown, he handed the diary to her. Checking the date at the top of the page, she quickly skimmed the copperplate. 'Newcastle?'

'Recruitment. We were trying, if you remember, to draw in a more diverse range of applicants. Personnel Department had identified three interesting candidates in Bradford and four more in Newcastle. I went up to look them over.'

'You'd stayed in Leeds the night before?' she said, glancing at the preceding entry.

'Evidently so.'

'We don't have any secure offices in those parts, do we? Nothing with a Porthos terminal?'

'God, no.' He closed the diary and replaced it on the shelf. 'Why do you ask?'

'Thank you, Jeremy,' she said, rising. 'You've been very helpful.'

He stood up hurriedly. 'So you'll take the Watchman commission?'

She paused on the threshold. The sound of a morose teenager plucking aimlessly at untuned guitar strings could be heard. 'Why not.'

DORTMUND, GERMANY – 11 June

The office and warehouse complex plastered with the insignia of Europe's third-largest famine relief charity was closed by the time Arkell arrived. Except at moments of crisis, the managers and administrators of World Hunger kept remarkably fixed working hours. Local taxi drivers joked that they could set their watches by the flood of staff exiting the building at exactly 5 p.m. The reception was locked, and not even a night security guard appeared when Arkell pressed the bell.

He circled the building and found a loading bay at the rear. Four different warehouses abutted the oil-stained access road. All of them were locked and silent. The evening sunlight glinted off a heavy silver padlock on the World Hunger loading bay gate. To one side a flight of five concrete steps led up to a small door. Beneath it, a strip of white light.

Arkell tried the door and found it unlocked.

A hangar-like space, crowded on all sides with sorted mountains of clothes, shoes, books, household goods and sports equipment. Most of the items were used, but there were also appliances and kitchen utensils in the manufacturers' packaging, and dresses on hangers with the labels still attached. Crammed street donation bins stood ready to be emptied between the piles, together with hundreds of bulging plastic bags in branded orange. Along one wall stood industrial washing machines, tumble driers and dry-cleaning units. And at the far end of the space, beside a small forklift truck, were stacked hundreds of cardboard boxes, each with a neat printed label and the World Hunger logo.

During the day, Arkell estimated, a sorting, cleaning and packaging operation of this magnitude might easily employ thirty people. At night, it seemed, eight young and ill-dressed Slavs were sufficient.

They were distributed around the warehouse, six of them picking through the donated goods piles, the other two pressing suits and dresses alongside the humming dry-cleaning and washing machines. None of them looked up from their work and none of them spoke. Noiselessly, Arkell approached the nearest, a thin youth who had just pulled a box-sealed digital radio from a heap of electrical goods. His haul, laid out on the concrete beside him, was substantial: four pristine LCD televisions of varying dimensions, two car GPS units still in their boxes, a selection of MP3 and Blu-ray players, radios and even an unused air ionizer.

'Good evening,' murmured Arkell from just behind his left shoulder.

The youth swung round anxiously.

'I'm looking for Dejan.'

The electronics picker pointed wordlessly past the mountain of clothes to a small office formed of grey panel walls and lodged unceremoniously against the concrete wall of the warehouse.

A dozen strides brought Arkell to the open doorway. He gazed in at the shaved skull and bull neck of the man sitting at a vinyl-topped office desk, with his broad back to the door and his meaty fingers punching numbers at surprising speed into a calculator. His other hand scribbled the results into a notebook with a stub of pencil.

Although Arkell had not moved, he suddenly dropped the pencil and swivelled round, rising from his chair as he did so. '*Was haben Sie hier zu suchen? Das Lagerhaus ist geschlossen!*'

The initial impression was of fury, with a tinge of guilty fear. There was nothing hospitable in those eyes. A discovered scam made him a cornered rat – antagonistic and dangerous.

It was no time for boyish charm. Had Arkell anticipated the illicit operation he had stumbled upon in the World Hunger warehouse, he might have chosen a different moment to approach Dejan. But time was short, and this man had a secret to hide. Perhaps this was the right time, after all.

'I'm here about Yadin,' said Arkell pleasantly.

Dejan, on the verge of another exclamation, fell silent. He watched Arkell closely, considering, then said, 'You're the British priest.'

'If you like.'

'Parson.'

Arkell smiled. 'Pearson,' he corrected. 'It's as good a name as any.'

Dejan tilted his head, stretching the heavy neck. 'Did Klara tell you about me?'

'No.'

'Then you're hacking her phone. A spy.'

'I need to speak to Yadin.'

The other man glanced over his shoulder into the warehouse. Three pickers looked hastily down.

'Let's go somewhere we can talk,' said Dejan.

He led Arkell across the warehouse, past the mountains of donated goods and the toiling pickers. Suddenly he was expansive, convivial. 'You had me worried,' he said breezily, one oversized hand lightly resting on Arkell's shoulder. 'I thought you were some new *verdammt* manager working late and ruining my little pension scheme.' His other hand waved vaguely towards the piles.

'You keep the good stuff for yourself.'

Dejan paused by the clothes mountain and showed him an evening gown picked out by a woman in oversized jeans and collapsing sneakers. 'You see this? Armani. Perfect condition. Worn once, maybe. Some rich bitch who can't be seen in the same outfit, easing her conscience by giving away her cast-offs. We put this in a World Hunger store, the price tag is sixty euro maximum. What's the point?' He returned the dress to the pile of spoils. 'I press it, label it, send it to the right people, I can get a hundred and fifty euros for this. They sell it for three hundred, the customer gets a bargain on a dress worth two thousand. Everyone's happy: rich bitch, customer, seller, my unemployable Bosniacs, me. There's too much stuff donated for our shops to handle anyway.'

'Whatever you say. I'm only here for Yadin.'

'Gavriel, yes,' mused Dejan, ushering Arkell through steel double doors into a linoleum-floored corridor anaemically lit by fluorescent tubes. 'But, you see, he's a secretive fucker. Doesn't like people knowing too much about him.'

'You know about him.'

'Me?' Smiling self-deprecatingly, he said, 'A little, perhaps. Gavriel comes to me when he needs things. We go back a long way. He trusts me to keep an eye on his girl.'

There was a purpose in Dejan's stride which belied the easy

tone of his conversation. Arkell glanced briefly at his hands, checked they were still empty.

'Where is he now?'

'That's always hard to say.' Still the casual tone. 'What do you want with Gavriel, Mr Parson? He has a few enemies. I have to be careful. In here.'

He opened a steel door into a windowless storeroom and switched on the lights to reveal stacks of boxes on open-frame shelving. The top boxes were spilling leaflets: World Hunger, in a dozen languages. There was no other exit.

Arkell hesitated on the threshold.

'It's a personal matter.'

'Please, enter.' Dejan's great hand pressed again on his shoulder. Arkell was acutely aware of the solid bulk of the man. 'Here we can talk as long as we want without one of these *verdammt* Bosniacs interrupting us.'

The man's leather jacket was too thick and too loose to tell what was underneath it. Arkell glanced around the storeroom. A section of shelving was yet to be assembled, and a cluster of steel rods, shelves and wooden posts of various sizes were stacked in one corner. It was all he needed.

Arkell walked into the room and was not surprised when the other man locked the door behind them. 'This personal matter,' said Dejan flatly. 'Why don't we talk it over, you and me?' His right hand reached inside his jacket.

'I'd rather not.' Arkell continued forward to within a metre of the shelving posts before turning.

Dejan was holding a switchblade. 'Talk, Mr Parson.'

He'd anticipated a knife – carrying a firearm in Germany

was just too risky. And a man of Dejan's strength would not expect to need a gun. All the same, Arkell was relieved. You never could be certain.

'Put that away. I'm not here to hurt you, and I'm not going to report your Armani scam. Tell me where to find Yadin and you won't hear from me again.'

Dejan laughed, fingering the blade of the knife. 'Do you have any idea who Gavriel Yadin is? Even if you walk in here offering one hundred thousand euros . . . But you don't do this. You come here and demand priceless information for free.' He raised the knife, using it like a conductor's baton to emphasize each word. 'Who are you? And why are you looking for Yadin?'

Taking a step back, judging the distance, Arkell said, 'One last time: put it away. I don't want to have to hurt you.'

The warning incensed the larger man. 'Hurt me?' he snarled. Launching himself forward, he repeated the words with even more scorn. 'Hurt *me*?'

The momentum of his weight carried the knife unstoppably forward as Arkell swung around, seized the longest of the wooden posts in both hands and flipped it with a twitch of his wrists so that it smashed with shocking force into Dejan's right thumb.

They both heard the thumb break a second before the blade clattered on the concrete floor.

The post felt good. A comfortable weight, about a metre sixty long. A round pole would have been easier to slide through his fingers, but the hardwood was strong and dependable. Arkell rolled the post in his hands, getting used to the shape of it.

No sound came from Dejan. His astonished face reddened;

he stared at his shattered thumb, then at the knife by Arkell's feet. He raised his prize-winning left fist and charged.

Sprawled on the floor, Dejan tried to comprehend what had just happened to him. The Englishman stood back, letting him recover. That wooden post had whirled so fast. Dejan had felt the savage impact first in his ribs, then across his left forearm, then on the side of his head. The knife was nowhere to be seen. Rising to his feet, Dejan shook his head to clear it, and glowered at the improvised weapon the Englishman held so casually. His hands were positioned about fifty centimetres apart, loosely tensed. Dejan now knew how quickly they could spin that post around, the force they could exert through it.

But he had fought all his life with his fists, and he refused to accept that a smaller man could hold him off with a mere stick. It was just a question of getting hold of it, wrenching it from his hands, and then finishing the bastard off.

Dejan feinted left, the old move that always fooled cocky kids in the ring. No one ever expected a man of his size to swing back so fast. The post lashed out where he would have been, and Dejan's left hand snatched at it.

He couldn't understand how he missed it.

His fingers closed on air and he felt a staggering pain in his shoulder. Somehow the post, too, had swung back, only to drive point-first into his collarbone, which snapped like a baby's finger. The post continued on, over his useless shoulder, and skidded sideways, picking up new momentum to smack the back of his head.

This time, Dejan briefly passed out.

He came round to find the post resting on his throat.

'Yadin,' said the man. 'Where is he?'

'Fuck you.' The pain in his thumb and shoulder made Dejan wince as he spat the words.

'Try again,' said the man, using one foot to nudge his broken collarbone. Dejan screamed.

'I don't know! France. Somewhere in France.'

'Where in France?'

'I don't know.' He screamed again as the foot pressed harder. 'Really, I don't know! He doesn't tell me!'

'That's a shame,' said the man, stepping back and cracking the post across Dejan's nose.

This time Dejan roared like an enraged bull, spattering blood over his chin. Before he could move, the post was back on his throat.

'I don't like doing this,' said the other sincerely. 'I really don't. But I have to keep hurting you until you give me Yadin.'

By now the roar had subsided into a choked whimper. Blood was trickling down the back of Dejan's mouth. He said nothing.

Grimacing, the Englishman stamped down on the broken collarbone.

The blood in Dejan's throat gave his new scream a sickening rattle. 'I don't know where he is, I swear! He's going to Cyprus tomorrow, that's all I know.'

'Where in Cyprus?'

'Lemona,' he gasped. 'There's a chemist . . . Kolatch. He needs to see Kolatch.'

'Why?'

'I don't know! Gavriel told me to set up the meet. Make sure

Kolatch is home tomorrow. Said he had to collect something. He didn't say what.'

'How do you contact Yadin?' the man asked finally, reaching inside Dejan's leather jacket and pulling out his phone.

'The number is saved as *Gerhard*. I leave a message. Always a message. He never answers.'

Arkell left Dejan bound to the shelving and locked the storeroom door. What he had just done sickened him. It brought to mind Wraye's old pep talks about the operational necessity of extreme methods – about the requirement for those tasked to preserve what was good to get their hands dirty. They had never helped. He walked out through the warehouse with a tight smile to each of the uneasy pickers. When he reached the access road he called Wraye.

'I'm sending you photos of Dejan and his German ID,' he said once he'd relayed the Cyprus lead. 'I'll courier his phone to Markham Square. *Gerhard* is Yadin: probably an anonymous postbox service, but check it out anyway.' He read out the number. 'You might want to have someone keep Dejan out of contact until this is over – if you know anyone near Dortmund?'

'I have associates in the area,' confirmed Wraye. 'There's an overnight charter flight for Paphos departing Frankfurt at 23:30. Gets in at 05:35. Can you make it?'

'Sure,' said Arkell, vaguely irritated. He didn't need administrative support from Wraye, and he was still uncomfortable with her knowing his exact movements.

'I'll arrange for a weapon to be sent up from Akrotiri.'

'No need,' replied Arkell, too brusquely. 'I make my own arrangements.'

A pause from Wraye. 'All right. If you're sure.'

'Just take care of Dejan. I don't want him warning Yadin.'

LONDON, ENGLAND – 11 June

From Gloucestershire, Madeleine Wraye had sent a carefully worded message to Joyce's anonymous webmail account: *Bravo Day personnel recruitment activity. Landmark, 11 p.m.*

'I think the registry keepers are getting suspicious,' said Joyce when he sat opposite her in the Mirror Bar at London's Landmark Hotel. But he looked very pleased with himself.

'Show me.'

'Not even a drink or a hello first?'

Wraye scanned the photographed recruitment records and quickly determined that Elphinstone's diary had been telling the truth. His notes on the seven Newcastle and Bradford candidates, in that familiar copperplate, were dated and countersigned by PD/3. Even his expenses for the trip were neatly set out.

Jeremy Elphinstone was off the list.

'Good,' remarked Wraye, somewhat to her own surprise. She looked up at the reflections around them. The Mirror Bar was one of her favourite meeting spots, ideal for detecting watchers. 'Yes, Edward, we must get you a drink. I have a somewhat more challenging job for you.'

She waited for the barman to mix him an Old Fashioned, and then set out her requirement. He put down the squat glass untouched. 'I can't do that,' he gasped.

'It's important you don't open the file. Any fingerprints and DNA traces in it must be preserved.'

'Madeleine, I can't just walk into central registry and steal a file!'

'Why not?'

'Well, Christ, look what happened to you.'

Her jaw hardened. 'So don't get caught.'

He had no answer. 'And if I did manage it . . . how would I get it out of the building? You know the guards check our bags.'

'Post it to yourself.'

'*Post* a YZ file? Are you crazy? Don't you remember how the post room works? It's only got more paranoid since you left.'

'Send it to yourself at the Fort. That's still considered internal mail, isn't it?'

'Yes . . .'

'Package it up, nice and boring, and pop it in the Fort's postbag. When it arrives, just drive it out in one of the training cars.'

He considered her with awe. 'That is a genuinely genius idea.' His face darkened. 'I'm not saying I can get the file, though.'

She leaned across the table. 'Edward, listen to me. Whatever you may think, I have full confidence in you.' Patting his arm, she reiterated the words: '*Full* confidence.'

Could it be Tony Watchman? Wraye lingered in the Mirror Bar after Joyce had left, pondering the idea. She had got on well with him on the IONEC, when they found themselves learning their very first tradecraft together and shivering with nervous delight at talk of Moscow Rules and Lubyanka interrogation techniques.

He was sparky, different, tough. A little like Arkell in that way. And he had been completely devoid of sexism at a time when female Intelligence Branch officers were still a disturbing novelty to many in the Service. He had known she was as good as any man, and had not been afraid to say so. But the rivalry had been quick to develop, first humorously, later with real venom as career-determining choices were made and political games enacted.

Abuja!

He had performed spectacularly while she had been stuck in West Africa. Plenty of colleagues had been happy to keep her informed of Tony Watchman's achievements in the Arabian peninsula, and relay the praise heaped on him by George Vine for networks cultivated and plots averted. Perhaps out of jealousy, she had been unwilling to view him as the future leader others envisaged. And later, when she saw herself as bearing some of the burden of responsibility for the continuing health of the Service, she had gone to Elphinstone and warned against giving Counter-Terrorism to Watchman. That, in retrospect, had been her biggest mistake. Not that she could have known how close the two men, with their diametrically opposed backgrounds, had grown in her absence. She had genuinely believed that Tony running Counter-Terrorism would be bad for business.

Why? It was hard to remember now. Some of the things he'd said in passing over the years, perhaps:

> *People are afraid of terrorism. I'm not. We need some kind of enemy, or we might as well retrain as ballet dancers and insurance salesmen. I'd rather have a bunch of Fenians and ragheads as my enemy than the USSR.*

The Service needs to develop a much more clearly articulated house view on terrorism. We've got to make it our own. Otherwise Five will call the shots and we'll be reduced to chasing the upstream elements of whatever foreign conspiracies they deem worthy of their investigation.

Terrorists are just regular people with a grievance.

Terrorism is a tactic, not a character trait. It's the most effective means of warfare for anyone significantly weaker than their opponent, states included. Let's not forget we've used terrorist techniques often enough ourselves.

And then, when he had been appointed H/TERR in spite of her efforts, and he had called her out onto the terrace overlooking the Thames to celebrate with champagne their simultaneous elevation to the top table, he'd joked, 'So much of Counter-Proliferation is about keeping WMDs out of the hands of terrorists, isn't it? Perhaps that means you should report to me . . .' She'd managed half a glass before finding an excuse to leave him – and Elphinstone, who'd joined them – to finish the bottle.

A man was eyeing Wraye in one of the mirrors. It was a kind of nervous invitation. She considered his thinning hair, his good suit, his brown eyes and strong, capable fingers. Younger than her, but only a little. Spanish, perhaps, in town on business. A good expense account and a reasonable degree of authority in his working life. Probably still married.

She picked up her wine and walked over to his table.

LEMONA, CYPRUS – 12 June

It was a small, forgotten village; thirty-eight residents by the last count, three of them English. Two early risers knew of Kolatch, and they provided directions to his house, set on a hillside between an olive grove and an untended apricot orchard three kilometres outside Lemona. But neither knew anything about him. He never appeared at the taverna in the neighbouring village, did not buy his bread from the bakery or his wine from the Tsangarides Winery. He had a car – a white car – but no wife, girlfriend or maid. The last time any builder, plumber or electrician had been near the place was eight years ago.

They estimated he was between forty and seventy years old.

By 8.30 a.m., Arkell was established on the same hillside, two hundred metres above Kolatch's house. In Paphos, he had found a hardware store whose proprietor lived in the apartment above and was prepared – after much grumbling – to open up early. He had bought canvas, a shovel, a clasp knife and a roll of agricultural bird netting. The Olympus 12x50 binoculars, dark glasses, soft khaki hat and sunblock came from Frankfurt airport. He had made one further stop on the way out of town, at a convenience store, collecting twelve litres of mineral water and a bag of assorted cereal bars, dried fruit, electrolyte sachets and salami. The hire car he had left on the other side of the hill, a safe distance from his observation post but close enough for a swift departure if necessary.

He had selected a position on the jutting edge of a terraced vineyard. It commanded excellent views down the deserted hillside to the chemist's house. The only approach to the vineyard was a winding path that showed no recent tracks. Small-bore irrigation pipes took automated care of the day-to-day needs of the vines; there was no sign of regular human attention.

Crouched low, Arkell dug a shallow trench in the soft dusty earth between two rows of vines. He lined the trench with the canvas and positioned bottles of water along each side. The food and binoculars went at the end of the trench. Stretched out on the canvas, Arkell layered the bird netting over himself as makeshift camouflage. Satisfied that no part of his body protruded above the ground – that a casual observer would catch not so much as a glimpse of him unless they happened to walk along this particular row of vines – he turned his attention to the house.

The windows were broad and clean, allowing him a perfect view into Kolatch's sizeable kitchen, his bedroom and his well-stocked library. There was no sign of any laboratory, chemical apparatus, or indeed any chemist. Arkell scanned each room carefully through the binoculars, noting every object on view, however trivial. He called Wraye.

'His car's there. No Kolatch or Yadin yet. What about the airlines?'

'Last-minute bookings to Larnaca and Paphos from all over Europe. None in the name of Yadin, of course, and we don't even know if his reservation was last-minute. So it's up to you to pick him up.'

'"Pick him up"?'

'You know what I mean. Have you got a weapon?'

'Of course,' said Arkell.

'Good, because we found something strange in Dortmund. Our friend Dejan wasn't in great condition when my guys reached him.'

'I had to hurt him a bit. He was—'

'Nevertheless, I would guess you didn't put the Sig .45 round in his brain.'

Behind his dark glasses, Arkell's eyes blinked. He stared out across the dry Cypriot landscape. 'The Bosnian pickers?'

'All gone. The place was empty, unlocked, lights on – little piles of high-value goods abandoned. Oh, and someone had very cleverly wiped the CCTV.'

'You think it was Yadin?'

'Or someone watching Yadin's back. Be careful, Simon. He may have been alerted.'

LONDON, ENGLAND – 12 June

For a few hours, Edward Joyce had been buoyed by Wraye's words. Long enough to devise a plan. He had considered simply ordering up the Salis file, but then he would be personally liable for it. 'Losing' a YZ file was a sackable offence, and he was on thin enough ice already. The only answer was to smuggle it out of central registry, and after Wraye's rare flattery he was ready to believe he could do it. But as Joyce worked through the night, compiling fictional Social Security records and Special Branch reports, scribbling imaginary letters, printing out reams of loosely related news articles and hurriedly fabricated CX reports, his confidence began to sag. By the time he had showered and shaved in the gym on the ground floor, the lunacy of his proposed action was blindingly clear to him.

The paper records of the Secret Intelligence Service are

monumental, dating back to before World War One. Much of the material has now been digitized, but there is art in intelligence analysis and many officers still prefer to look for truth in original documents. One never knows what insight might be gleaned from the texture, scent or condition of a document, what stories a slight stain on the back of a letter might tell. Some of the older archives are stored in a variety of undisclosed locations around London and the Home Counties; everything else is housed in the purpose-built central registry at Vauxhall Cross.

Weighed down by a document box full of his night's work, Joyce arrived in the registry to find the most notoriously ferocious keeper presiding. Jeanette Fortune had already eyed him with great suspicion as he searched operational logs and expenses records for Wraye, surreptitiously photographing documents in various CCTV blind spots behind the stacks. Now that he was embarked on an even more foolhardy venture he was sorely tempted to retreat with all speed and nevermore venture into her lair. But he remembered what he was supposed to be – what he *wanted* to be more than anything else – and he forced a smile to his lips and said, 'Jeanette, good morning! Lovely to see you again.'

'Mr Joyce, do you realize that yesterday you left a WE/ZUR file open on a reading desk?' She had not looked up; her hand continued to make notes in a ledger. 'You do understand this is a *secret* service?'

'Won't happen again,' he promised. 'I wonder if I might beg your assistance on a training exercise for IONEC.' He hefted the document box. He had already made sure the guard by the elevator had clocked him bringing it into central registry.

The keeper looked at the stack of papers in the document box with undisguised disgust. 'And this is?'

'Eight imaginary villains. My finest creations. We've got a Saudi prince funding Islamic State, a Chinese visiting professor spying for the Ministry of State Security, an Iranian ballistics expert, a—'

'I'm sorry, Mr Joyce, what are these fabrications doing in central registry?'

'With your permission I'd like to plant them for my eight students to locate.' *Eight*. It was important to keep repeating the number.

'Impossible. We'd have to assign them all registry numbers, catalogue them on the system—'

'Actually, I've already assigned them numbers,' he said with what he hoped was a helpful grin. 'I've made sure they aren't already in use. And there's no need to put them on the system. Each of the eight students will find a reference to their villain's file number hidden away in a set of documents they'll be given.'

Fortune considered this outlandish proposition with an expression of great weariness. But she could find no solid objection to make. 'I'll need a list so we can ensure all the files are removed. We can't have works of fiction floating around indefinitely.'

'Of course,' promised Joyce. 'I'll purge them myself straight after the exercise. Might it be possible,' he ploughed straight on, heart beating wildly now, 'to borrow some empty registry files? Used and battered, ideally, to keep it authentic.'

'I don't know that we have any old ones,' Fortune muttered bleakly, but her assistant, who had been silent throughout, looked up and said, 'There's a load I was about to throw out. From the re-org of the Syrian security services records.'

He led Joyce to a side table on which a pile of empty pink and powder-blue files had been neatly stacked. Each still bore a white label on its spine, with a registry number written in black ink. 'You can stick a new label over the old one,' said the assistant, handing him a roll of adhesive labels. 'Do write clearly, though,' he said, with a warning nod towards Fortune.

Joyce worked fast, increasingly frightened that another officer – God help him, even Martin de Vries – might appear and demand to know what he was up to. The fabricated dossiers were already assembled, and it was the work of moments to slip them inside eight powder-blue files. But when it came to writing out the labels, he found himself jinxed by the assistant's parting words. He kept making a hash of it, writing too big, too small, smudging the ink, having to discard label after label. Finally he had the files ready, and he approached the keepers' desk with a casual, 'I'll just slot them into place and be out of your hair . . .'

It had been too much to hope for. 'Leave them on the desk. We'll do it.'

Joyce realized his hands were numb. He had to get this right. 'Mind if I come with you? Get a feel for where they sit in case anyone needs a steer? Otherwise the students will only bother you again.'

Fortune sighed monumentally, glanced at her watch – could any player imbue that action with more meaning? – and stepped out from behind the desk. 'Give me the first one,' she commanded.

Following meekly in her wake, fictional dossiers clutched in his arms, Edward Joyce felt the pressure of the stacks building around him. The secrets of a nation – of an empire – were piled high on all sides. He had arranged the files in accordance with the registry's layout, and Fortune, recognizing this thoughtfulness, thawed slightly. After the third registry number had proved to belong in the neighbouring stack to the second, she demanded the fourth in a slightly milder tone. Nevertheless, to Joyce her manner seemed increasingly terrifying, for they were now approaching SQ/ alley, as he thought of it, home of SQ/83774, also known as the Salis file.

He handed her the fifth file, in his nervousness – and for the first time – reading out its number: 'SQ/83281.' His voice sounded absurd. Squeaky. Surely she must know! He compounded his appearance of guilt by involuntarily choosing that same moment to glance up at the ceiling-mounted cameras.

'That one's an African despot with a stranglehold on strategically important mineral resources,' he gabbled helplessly.

If he was caught, what then? A secret court and a lifetime in Wakefield? What would it be like to be imprisoned for espionage? Murderers and rapists could be frighteningly patriotic, he'd heard. Would they consider his crime as unspeakable as paedophilia?

'Then you've given it an entirely inappropriate number,' snapped Fortune. 'SQ is organized crime.' For a moment he contemplated with horror the possibility that she might actually insist on renumbering the file, taking them away from SQ/ alley. Could her librarian's sense of propriety be so offended by the idea of even a fictional villain berthing in the wrong category that she would be willing to waste her time correcting his carelessness? But with another, different species of sigh she started down SQ/ alley and found her way swiftly to the right shelf.

Seconds, now, he had just seconds to locate the Salis file, and do it nonchalantly for the camera behind them. Fortune had a finger on her shelf, had the spot, was parting the files, making space for the cuckoo. SQ/83712, SQ/83736, SQ/83781 . . . The African despot was sliding into place, uneasily, between two criminals of the organized persuasion. SQ/83774. There! But it was too late. Her hand still on the African despot, Fortune was turning back to him. 'Next?' she demanded, giving the file a last, expert tap to ram it home.

Mutely, he offered her the sixth file.

She glanced at the number, rolled her eyes, and said, 'I suppose this one is a long-dead KGB officer? You do know all TZ files are pink?' Without waiting for a reply, she brushed past him and marched towards the next bank of stacks. Last chance. His back was to the camera. Fortune, too, was blocking the CCTV line of sight. Slipping finger and thumb around the base of the powder-blue file he tugged it sharply off the shelf and palmed it under the remaining two dummy dossiers. In the same movement, he turned and followed Fortune.

Had they seen it? Were the guards in their control centre three storeys above even watching? Joyce imagined Martin de Vries standing beside them, insisting on constant surveillance. *Follow him everywhere. I want to know what he does in the toilet, even.* The guard by the elevators was in radio contact with the control centre; was he even now rising from his seat under de Vries's instructions and marching towards SQ/ alley? The Salis file felt clammy in Joyce's hands, soaked with guilty sweat, ridiculously heavy. His footsteps were insanely loud. Why didn't Fortune turn and stare? She was sliding the TZ file into place, tutting at the powder-blue anomaly in a sea of pink. Accepting the seventh file from him. Another sarcastic comment, lost on him, and then on to a new stack. Cuckoo in place. Christ, this was a lunatic idea! Fortune reaching for the eighth file, please God can she count, the hesitation as he gave it to her, the frown, the bureaucrat's stare, and then –

'You said *eight* files.' An accusatory tone, but to Edward Joyce it was like the Hallelujah Chorus. Oh, wonder!

He looked down at the innocent powder-blue file in his trembling hands. Were they really trembling? He couldn't tell; his vision was blurred. 'That's right. Have we done eight?' Too innocent! He sounded like a kindergarten child reaching for the biscuit tin.

'Yes, Mr Joyce, this is the eighth.' Referring to the file in her hands but staring still at the file in his. Could she tell? Was she so master of her universe that she could recognize this very file? Could she *smell* Rodrigo Salis?

No possible excuse could explain why he was holding SQ/83774. His hand over the spine number, he had to trust in powder-blue anonymity. Had to believe in his own plan, though his heart was battering in triple-fast time against his lungs. 'How odd . . .' The next part was so rehearsed in his mind that it happened almost as if he were nothing more than an observer. The sheet of paper extracted from his jacket pocket and smoothed flat over the red-hot powder-blue. 'Let's see . . .' The finger counting moronically down the typed list of fictional names and file numbers. 'Bloody hell, you're absolutely right!

I made up nine. How stupid of me! Could have left the office two hours earlier.' Tucking the Salis file swiftly under his arm, spine down, he concluded, 'Well, there's only eight students. I'll hang on to this one for next year.'

There it was: his part played. Now it was for the audience to decide whether to clap or jeer. He smiled a foolish smile and waited for the Fortune verdict.

He nearly missed it through the blur of his distressed vision. The slightest rolling of eyes and then she was off to the final stack. The last of the eight fictional files planted – Christ, he mustn't forget to have the students come and collect them – and the job was done. Or nearly.

He pulled out a Pentel rollerball and crossed the last name and number off his typed list before handing the sheet over. 'The imposters, for your records,' he said.

'If you could try to ensure,' said Fortune, in her best martyr's voice, 'that your students come here only when we're not busy . . .'

Glancing around the empty, silent space, Joyce nodded sympathetically. He tossed the Salis file casually into the document box. 'Thanks so much, Jeanette. You're an angel.'

At the lifts, the guard, an ex-Grenadiers sergeant with a permanently red nose, jolted himself out of a long reverie and staggered to his feet. 'A shufti in the box, if I may, sir.'

Heroically casual, Joyce glanced back at the keeper, a quizzical look on his face that would have made even Madeleine Wraye proud. She called out, 'It's all right, Charlie. He brought that material in with him.' Though the word *material* was loaded with distaste, Joyce could have hugged her.

'Very good, sir.'

The padded envelope was already addressed and waiting in the bottom drawer of his work station. He stopped there only to collect it, unwilling to take out the Salis file where others might see. On the route to the post room he knew of three CCTV blind spots. The first was deserted, and he paused just a few seconds to slip the file into the envelope. Even inside the bubble padding it felt stickily hot. With a sense of profound relief, he dumped it two minutes later into the Fort Monckton post bag and went to get a drink on the terrace. It was only when he reached the bar and found it shut that he realized it was not yet 9.45 a.m.

LEMONA, CYPRUS – 12 June

The chemist appeared at 11 a.m. exactly. He walked into the kitchen, switched on the coffee percolator and set a laptop on the counter. While the coffee brewed, he browsed the web. Arkell's binoculars were good enough to make out the movement of his fingers on the track pad, but not the words on the screen.

Kolatch was around sixty years old, portly, slow-moving but fast-fingered. His hair was thinning white, his glasses thick-framed in black plastic. He wore a grubby white long-sleeved shirt and, despite the heat, a grey woollen cardigan. He poured his coffee without looking up from the screen, drank it with no sense of pleasure or awareness. When the cup was empty, he snapped the computer shut, scooped it under one arm and disappeared again to another part of the house.

To his laboratory?

What did Kolatch actually do all day?

A partial answer came shortly after noon. By then, the burning Cypriot sun had soaked Arkell's shirt and jeans in sweat, and he had drunk two litres of water and swallowed an electrolyte sachet to compensate. The bird netting afforded some protection from the midday glare, and he had been careful to cover every inch of exposed skin in sunblock. When the phone vibrated silently against his thigh he found that it, too, was damp with sweat.

'Another ex-Mossad rogue element,' said Wraye. 'Arni Kolatch, research chemist from Tel Aviv. Forced out in the late nineties when the legacy of his poisons became too embarrassing.'

'So he's supplying Yadin with the compounds to kill the Think Again premiers.'

'He was arrested seven years ago for supplying banned nerve agents to private defence contractors, including a couple that used them fairly indiscriminately in North Africa. Fled the country and disappeared. Mossad claim they have no idea where he is.'

'Just like Yadin.'

'Just like you, until a few days ago. That's the trouble with old spooks. They do know how to make themselves invisible.'

Arkell ate two cereal bars to keep himself alert. He'd slept on the plane, but not enough to withstand completely the soporific effects of the dry heat and the relentless hypnotic clicking of cicadas. Kolatch's lunch lasted from 1.30 until 2 p.m. exactly. He ate two boiled eggs, a flatbread and a salad of chopped cucumber and tomato. Again, the focus on the laptop screen outweighed any visible interest in the food.

With the kitchen once again empty, Arkell lowered the binoculars and wiped the sweat from his face. He felt something on his back, a weighty, sliding sensation. Remaining still, he waited for the snake to pass across him. About a metre and a half long, he estimated. When it was clear, he raised his head a fraction above the trench and watched the blue-black whip snake slip away through the vines. He had checked three things on his smartphone in the boarding lounge at Frankfurt airport: Cypriot summer temperatures, rural population distributions and venomous fauna. Only the blunt-nosed viper was a concern. As for the local population, he was bearing witness to the truth of what he had read: there was almost nobody left in this area.

By 3 p.m. Arkell had seen only four people, aside from Kolatch. All four passed along a narrow and overgrown path some distance away. The dusty track that led from the nearest paved road to Kolatch's house remained undisturbed. Even the road was barely used: just a small, speeding hatchback and a few ageing farm vehicles had passed this way.

He had drunk five litres of water and urinated twice, crouched between the vines, by the time the heat started to fade. He took off the damp hat and stretched beneath the bird netting to loosen his cramped limbs. Remaining in position overnight would be no problem, except insomuch as it would suggest Yadin wasn't coming. Dejan's tip, he felt instinctively, was sound: Kolatch's Mossad career and the poisoning of Anneke van der Velde both pointed to a connection. But if Yadin knew he was being followed, he would have changed his plans, sourced his murder weapons elsewhere. Disappeared.

And then how the hell was Arkell supposed to find him?

A cool breeze drifted up the valley, making the vine leaves around him flutter. Arkell brought the binoculars to his eyes once more, but they only confirmed what he already knew: Kolatch was not in the kitchen, bedroom or library.

A solitary grandmother appeared, picking her steps with difficulty along the path. Arkell waited until she was out of sight before raising his head and checking, as he had done periodically throughout the sweltering day, that no one was on the hillside above or to the side of the terraced vineyard.

The place really was deserted. No wonder the fugitive chemist liked it here.

Arkell's mind had begun to wander badly when at last a car appeared and turned off towards the house. He called Wraye, binoculars tracking the car. The sun was behind him; no danger of light reflecting off the lenses. 'He's here. Suggests he landed Paphos one hour ago or Larnaca two hours ago.'

She responded within fifteen seconds. 'Three possible flights. We'll check the last-minute names.'

'No visible car-hire branding. Stand by for registration.'

The track put the vehicle side-on to his position, but the final fifty metres to the house brought it round and Arkell was able to read the number plate. Wraye repeated it back to him, and he hung up.

'Let's get a proper look at you,' he murmured as Gavriel Yadin stepped out of the car.

He carried the same brown messenger bag. The leather jacket was gone; Yadin was dressed in a pale green shirt and light cargo pants. Through the binoculars he looked taut, impatient.

Wraparound sunglasses obscured his eyes. Thinner than Arkell remembered from Hamburg, he looked almost frail on the wide, empty hillside.

Kolatch opened the door and the two men hugged. The chemist kissed Yadin on his left cheek and ushered him inside. They reappeared in the kitchen, where Kolatch seated his guest at the table. He produced a plate of pastries and a beer, which he set before the Kidon combatant. Then he withdrew.

Alone in the kitchen, Yadin rose immediately and moved to the window, staring out with shaded eyes at the deserted hillside. Arkell remained absolutely still, confident he was too remote to be seen, but aware that even a slight movement might be detected. Yadin's gaze passed over his position and moved on to a nearby clump of stunted trees. He focused on the trees for nearly a minute before emptying his beer down the sink, washing away the traces and returning to the table.

Glancing at the clump of trees, half a kilometre from his vineyard, Arkell wondered what Yadin had seen there.

When Kolatch returned, he was carrying two small boxes. He handed them to Yadin, who offered a white envelope in return.

The transaction complete, the two men left the kitchen.

Arkell waited until Yadin was in his car with the door closed before flinging off the bird netting and running, crouched amongst the vines, to the track. He left everything behind; there was no time to eliminate his traces and therefore no point taking with him the bulky canvas, water bottles or shovel. Even the €250 binoculars were abandoned. Only the clasp knife in his pocket remained from his morning purchases.

Unburdened, the evening sunlight in his face, Arkell sprinted over the crest of the hill and down an old goat track to his hire car. He had the local roads memorized; he knew the route Yadin must take to return to the coastal motorway that led to both Paphos and Larnaca airports.

He drove fast on the narrow, winding lanes until he caught a glimpse of the other car. Then he slowed to a comfortable cruise, out of sight most of the time, adding a little speed after each junction to ensure his quarry remained within range.

Wraye called. 'The car was rented to José Cumes at Larnaca International at 17:12. Same name on the manifest for an Air Malta flight that landed 16:50. Passenger's origin was Orly. Booked to fly out of Larnaca, Aegean Airlines, 08:20 tomorrow. Where is he now?'

'Just leaving Kolatch. I'm on him. Any hotel bookings?'

'Not in that name. Simon, don't leave it too long.'

His jaw was tense. Breathe. A simple stabbing, that was the plan. A death that could be written off by the local police as a tourist mugging gone wrong. He'd done it before. In the anonymity of an African night. In the souk in Tangier. On a night train in Russia. He'd done it before, but it was never easy. And it had been a long time.

The road dropped through the brown, treeless hills to the west coast. Arkell slowed as it straightened out. The setting sun was in his eyes, but he had no difficulty seeing Yadin's white car take the turning onto the South Cyprus coastal motorway.

The man who killed your wife.

It was never easy, but there was no doubt whatsoever in his mind.

* * *

Washington? She made a face.

That's where I live.

Of course it is. I could tell from your accent.

Around her, he was always laughing. The looks she gave him, they made the world a sunnier place.

You could come and visit.

And why would I bother? Plenty of men in London, you know.

None like me.

None like you. She rolled over and kissed his chest. On the branding scar. She never asked about it – then or later. *And if I came, what sights would you show me?*

None. We'd never leave my apartment.

Goodness. He writes for The Times *and he has his own apartment. My mother will be assembling my dowry as we speak.*

If I'm honest, it's the paper's apartment.

Does it have a good shower?

The best.

A double bed with clean sheets?

Most of the time.

He caressed the lobe of her ear and wondered what on earth he could do to keep hold of her.

She closed her eyes and laid her cheek against his scar. *Perhaps a little holiday abroad isn't completely out of the question.*

PORTSMOUTH, ENGLAND – 12 June

Two men in suits were waiting for him on Level 3 of the multistorey car park by the Cascades Shopping Centre. They said very little, other than to identify themselves using one of Wraye's security phrases. Both wore latex gloves. Both assumed expressions of violent disapproval when Joyce proffered the Salis file with his bare hands.

Guiltily he said, 'I haven't opened it.'

One of them had a plastic case ready. The file was quickly sealed inside. 'Take his data,' the man muttered to his colleague.

An electronic device with a glass panel materialized from nowhere. 'Press your thumb and fingers here,' said the other man in a low voice.

'Wait, I . . .'

'We need to be able to eliminate your contamination from the analysis,' said the first man, as if to a child.

His colleague was preparing a swab. 'Open your mouth.'

Edward Joyce had arrived bearing his prize and expecting adulation. Instead he was being treated like disease-ridden livestock. Suddenly he realized he had no idea even of the significance of the Salis file. What the hell did Wraye want with a Colombian drug baron anyway? Not knowing the answer was as humiliating as the mouth-swabbing and fingerprinting.

Once they had his DNA and prints, the two men drove off without another word, leaving Joyce to wonder at the network Madeleine Wraye had assembled since her exit from the Service. Who were these people? Along with a team of mercenaries in Italy and an intimidating forensics unit in England, what other freelance assets could Wraye call upon when needed? Were they even freelance? Or were they moonlighting government employees like him?

It was a sobering moment for Joyce, who had grown used to

thinking of himself as Wraye's right-hand man. Nevertheless, he was unique, wasn't he? He was her one asset within the Service, the only man able to smuggle a YZ file out of the SIS fortress. For a few indulgent minutes, Joyce felt triumphant, his fragile self-esteem restored. Not even Wraye's nameless golden boy could do that.

LIMASSOL, CYPRUS – 12 June

Gavriel Yadin was not headed for Larnaca. Not yet. The A6 had cut through bare rock and crossed desiccated canyons, and now, as the light faded, Yadin turned off towards the southern port city of Limassol.

Whether he was stopping for dinner or spending the night, Arkell decided, it would happen here.

Yadin drove first to a shopping mall in a suburb of square concrete houses topped with identical water tanks. He made a call from a phone booth. It was too brightly lit, too public. Arkell stayed in his car, using the time to check the knife. He tested the locking mechanism, closed his fingers around the handle and pictured the act.

The man who killed your wife.

Next stop was a tourist restaurant on the edge of the old town. Yadin took his time parking, idled over the menu. The restaurant was open-fronted; Arkell kept an easy watch from a café across the street. While Yadin dined on king prawns and kleftiko, Arkell ordered short black coffees to fight off the effects of too little sleep.

He needed them. Yadin was killing time, dawdling over his meal, waiting for something. The restaurant, full at first, gradually emptied. One waiter disappeared. The other, with few calls on his attention, started flirting with a girl outside.

Arkell watched the last two groups pay their bills and leave. A small dispute over the price of the wine. Nothing to interrupt the flirting for long.

Yadin was still seated, his back to the now-empty restaurant, picking at a plate of kourabiedes. The waiter had given up on him: the girl outside was far more interesting. Arkell could sense the moment coming. He set a handful of euros on the table by his empty coffee cup, ready for a fast departure. Giggles from the girl rang through the deserted street. Arkell bent down and rested his hand briefly on the sun-warmed ground.

The waiter cast one last glance towards his customer, and stepped into the street and the open arms of the girl. Arkell moved.

He crossed the street, drawing the knife from his pocket and easing the blade open as he reached the threshold of the restaurant. A quick scan confirmed there were no cameras, no other eyes to see what he was about to do. He walked calmly through the empty restaurant, right hand caressing his thigh with the blade, Greek muzak masking the slight pad of his desert boots on the tiled floor.

Again, that side view of Yadin. Just as in Hamburg. Just as in Dault Street. Only this time the shoulders were slumped, the eyes wearily gazing at his half-eaten dessert, a picture of a man lost in gloomy reflection.

Two more steps, blade to the back of the neck, just below the base of the skull. No sound. Out again in two seconds.

Gavriel Yadin. The man who killed your wife.

Staring at a plate of sugared almond cakes.

The image was sudden and completely unexpected: Emily, dunking a cookie in her coffee while he made scrambled eggs and complained she was ruining her appetite. The cookies were from Wraye, sent anonymously every couple of weeks with coded instructions under the lining paper of the box. Normally he chucked them in the trash, but Emily couldn't resist the white chocolate ones. *I'm warning you, my love – try and control what I eat and we won't get on.* That flirtatious twitch of her mouth as she faked a frown. A single crumb caught on her lower lip.

He hadn't seen her this clearly, this disturbingly real, for years.

Standing two metres from a Mossad assassin.

Frozen by the past.

Abruptly, he turned and left the restaurant, didn't look round, kept walking, didn't stop until he was two streets away.

I'm warning you, my love –

Christ.

What the hell?

A simple enough assignment. Find a man and kill him.

Go back. Now. Get it done.

The restaurant was empty. A fifty-euro note beside the unfinished kourabiedes. The waiter still engrossed outside. Arkell walked fast to his car, resisting the urge to run, saw Yadin's headlights come on down the street, heard the engine fire. His pulse slowed. He'd been lucky. He hadn't lost him yet.

Now Yadin drove with purpose, directly to the port. He parked on a broad avenue leading to the passenger terminal and slipped down a side street. The messenger bag in his hand, the leather jacket on for the first time. Cold? Or a sign of wariness?

Arkell followed, silently padding fifty metres behind him. Watched him push open the grimy door of a dockers' bar. A casual glance through the smeared window gave Arkell the measure of the place: small, suspicious, intimate. Not a door you could open without drawing attention to yourself. Arkell walked on.

He gave it thirty seconds, then sauntered back past the window. Again, just a fleeting glance, the lost tourist looking for somewhere to get a nightcap. Yadin was at a table with another man, short with a broken nose and coal-black eyes. Kolatch's two boxes lay between them. One beer, almost empty. Nothing for Yadin. Arkell continued to the end of the street and looked back in time to see a figure emerge from the bar. Too dark to see a face, but the slim silhouette was right.

The man set off in the opposite direction, then turned down an alleyway. Passing the bar for the third time, Arkell confirmed Yadin was no longer inside. The man with the broken nose was standing, both boxes cradled against his ribs as he finished off his beer.

Arkell reached the alley as Yadin turned the corner. He covered the distance swiftly, and found himself in a street of closed-up chandleries. His quarry was on the threshold of another alley, pushing deeper into the dark and silent maritime quarter. He knows, Arkell reluctantly acknowledged. He knows he's being followed. It was the only explanation for this odd route through a deserted area of town. Yadin was drawing him away from the boxes, possibly into a trap.

He had no choice but to follow.

As if to confirm his fears, Yadin headed for the darkest, narrowest alley leading off the street. Arkell had to admire his tradecraft: not once did the Kidon combatant glance back, or try to use shop windows or car mirrors to see behind him. There was absolutely no suggestion of suspicion.

If it weren't for the strange route, Arkell might have relaxed.

He tightened his grip on the knife and entered the alley.

It was long and straight, with no exit for seventy metres.

Yadin wasn't there.

Instantly, Arkell dropped to the ground, rolling sideways, not knowing where the threat was but acting instinctively to escape the trap. As he dropped, a gunshot sounded. Then a second, coming from a darkened doorway. By then Arkell was back in the street, crouching as he ran for cover behind a parked car.

Somewhere nearby, a dog began to howl.

He waited. Both men had forfeited the advantage of surprise. Now it was a question of tactics. The Israeli would be wondering what he was up against. One man? A surveillance team? Armed?

The knife was useless now. Without a gun, Arkell's only sensible move was retreat. But that meant losing Yadin. He cursed himself for not accepting Wraye's offer of a weapon, supplied unofficially from the British sovereign base at Akrotiri, just a few kilometres from where he now crouched. He cursed himself for not killing Yadin when he had the chance. Now that shots had been fired, now the battle was on, nothing would distract him from driving the blade home.

But that opportunity was long gone.

Suddenly, Yadin was standing in the entrance of the alleyway, brazen in the weak light of the one functioning street lamp. He hovered there, tensed to react, gazing up and down the street. As his eyes turned towards the car, Arkell ducked down. Not quickly enough. Two more shots, two metallic screeches in the metal above his head. The car bonnet was no protection now. Arkell ran, crouched over, along the line of parked cars, then sprinted across the road. Scared shouts from an apartment above.

Yadin fired three more shots, two of them close enough for Arkell to hear the searing whistle of their flight before he reached the refuge of a side street. He kept running, the assassin's boots pounding behind. Sirens, some way off. Down the side street, dodge into an alley – a dead end. But a garage low enough to climb. He was up the wall, fingers scraped on rusty metal guttering, before Yadin reached the alley. Not pausing to look back. The assassin had a target now, wouldn't stop until he'd eliminated it. Arkell sprinted across the roof and sprang over a narrow yard to balance precariously on the wall beyond, before tumbling into the street below.

It led to the avenue where their cars were parked, but Yadin was already close behind. No time to find the car, unlock it, start the engine and drive away. There'd be a bullet through the windscreen before he'd turned the key.

Instead he kept on running, across the avenue, through a car park, through a cluster of warehouses, always with the sound of those pursuing feet behind him. The man was as fit as he was, sprinting the whole route without slowing. There were no more shots. The scattering of people on the avenue, or the approaching sirens perhaps, restrained Yadin. Or maybe he only had one clip.

Arkell knew better than to trust in that hope.

A wire fence blocked his way. He went up it like a cat on a tree trunk. Twenty paces on, he looked back to see Yadin roll neatly over the top.

A dusty track through a yard stacked with imported timber led to a stretch of marsh. Beyond was the cargo terminal wall, and in front of it the road leading to RAF Akrotiri. Arkell hesitated before the mass of reeds. To either side of him were locked warehouses and mountains of timber. Behind, the ominous scuff of running feet.

He plunged into the reeds, his boots sinking into layers of foul soft mud.

Quickly he worked his way deep into the thickest stand of reeds. The darkness was nearly complete, only a slight glow from the port penetrating the foliage. He crouched low, knees in the muddy water, and as Yadin came running through the timber yard, he made himself completely still.

He could see only glimpses of Yadin's outline at the edge of the marsh. The Israeli was scanning the timber stacks, looking for hiding places, finding none. He approached the reeds, gazed at the mud – at Arkell's deep footprints. Looking to the road beyond, he saw it was empty.

He stood still, staring at the reeds for an age.

Arkell eased the clasp knife out of his pocket. He opened the blade and steadied his feet, ready to spring if Yadin came close. In the dark thicket of reeds, he might have a chance.

But Yadin understood that. He stepped back from the marsh and slipped the gun inside his jacket. 'HaMossad?' he called, his voice ringing loud through the reeds. 'CIA?'

He waited, though he must have known there'd be no reply.

'You were seen,' he shouted scornfully. 'Above the chemist's house. On the road, white Toyota saloon.' He gazed from side to side, as if seeking an audience. 'No weapon? No back-up? Tell them to send a professional next time.'

He spat on the ground and turned away.

Emily, what am I doing?

What are you doing to me?

He had long wondered if the SIS officer who had ordered his wife's death alongside his own had ever met her. She'd attended one staff social to which spouses were apprehensively invited. Not at Head Office, of course; they'd borrowed rooms at the In & Out. What must it have been like, to be plunged into a throng of spooks for the first time? He had felt so proud of her, holding her own among people who valued others by the secrets they possessed, secrets entirely unknown to her. She got the balance just right, asking thoughtful questions that showed an interest without veering into political or confidential territory. And though she preferred not to dance with his colleagues, she drew their attention in her quiet, thoughtful way just as surely as she had drawn his in Covent Garden.

'The main drawback for wives,' George Vine had said, his Iranian tan glowing amongst the pallid faces of his colleagues, 'is the status problem. Fine in the early years, but after a while it gets embarrassing when the husband never makes ambassador, never collects a gong for that long Whitehall service, never does anything noteworthy they can talk about.'

'What about husbands?' she'd asked.

'Excuse me?'

'How do spies' husbands cope?'

'Goodness, there you have me. I've been unthinkingly sexist, haven't I?' He glanced at Jane Saddle, at Madeleine Wraye. Lowering his voice, he said, 'The evidence suggests not well, I'm afraid. But please don't let that put you off joining us should the academic life pale.'

Could George Vine have possibly given the green light to Yadin when he knew Emily was in the house? When he had just heard her voice on the phone?

Jeremy Elphinstone she had met only briefly on arrival, hospitable and welcoming as host of the event, but quick to shift his attention to the next guests. Jane Saddle had been too busy trying to limit the bar bill to take any notice of a junior officer's wife. Surprisingly, Emily had got on best with Martin de Vries. He was nothing if not sincere, and that was a quality Emily prized, especially in a room full of professional liars. Attempting to break the ice with the awkward Afrikaner, she had said lightly, 'It's brave of you to let us outsiders see your faces. I suppose any one of us could be an enemy agent compiling a list of Britain's top spies.'

'You could be,' he had agreed gravely. 'That is the risk we have chosen to take, the price we must pay for a measure of family harmony.'

'Would you prefer not to let spouses in?'

'Look, it was agreed by the directors and I respect that team decision, whatever my own views on the security risks.'

Because he took it seriously, she took it seriously, and he seemed to appreciate that. Before long they were talking about her PhD thesis on networked behaviour, and Arkell was amazed to see how animated de Vries could become over a topic of no direct relevance to his own work.

'But it is relevant,' he'd insisted. 'Our technology is driven by your pure science, just as surely as your science is advanced by breakthroughs in technology. The phenomena you observe in networks today, we will assuredly be exploiting in our software tomorrow.'

'What a nice man,' Emily had observed later, to Arkell's surprise.

Had he been the one? Had he ordered Dr Emily Arkell blown up, torn into a thousand bloody fragments of bone and pulp and sinew?

It was late and Tony Watchman was drunk by the time they encountered him, red-faced and sweaty from the dance floor. 'She's a pretty one,' he said, ambling towards them with a champagne bottle gripped like a weapon in one fist. He smiled luminously to dispel Emily's frown. 'Want some? Amazing what you can find locked away in Naval and Military cupboards. I'm Tony. And you must be the reason Simon's always late to work.'

'Actually, I hardly ever see him. He's abroad all the time.'

'Oh well.' A wolfish grin. 'Time on your hands.'

As if sensing trouble, Madeleine Wraye appeared at that moment. 'Tony, you look dreadful.'

'And you look wonderful as ever, Maddie. It's good to see you let your hair down, literally if not figuratively. You've always had beautiful hair. Like this one,' he said, deftly curling two fingers under a lock of Emily's hair.

'Take it seriously,' Wraye told Arkell later. 'I was watching the whole thing. There was a definite look behind your back.'

He had laughed. 'Tony was wasted. He was giving looks to every woman in the room.'

'I don't mean Tony.' She let it sink in. 'He's an attractive man, Simon, an intelligent man. A powerful man. Whatever his condition, your wife saw something she liked in him.'

Emily. What are you doing to me? Nine years in the ground, and still . . .

And still.

Did Tony kill you?

LEMONA, CYPRUS – 13 June

This time Arkell drove straight to Kolatch's front door.

He had waited a long time in the marsh, feeling the muddy water seep into his boots and the cramp set into his tensed legs. He knew it was likely Yadin was long gone. But he also knew the Kidon combatant might be lying in wait in the timber yard, or on the road that lay between the marsh and the port. That's what he would have done, after all.

Shortly after 1 a.m. he had checked into an anonymous three-star hotel, where he could clean up and catch a few hours' much-needed sleep before heading to Larnaca airport for a 6 a.m. stake-out of the Aegean Airlines check-in. Yadin never showed up. With a little charm, he was able to elicit from the airline staff confirmation that passenger José Cumes had missed the flight.

Gavriel Yadin, it seemed, had made other arrangements to leave the island.

He'd pulled Madeleine Wraye out of bed to confess the outcome. 'Let me get this straight,' she said blearily. 'You had Yadin and you let him walk away?'

'I'll get him,' Arkell promised.

'You said he gave the poisons to a sailor?'

'I said he gave two boxes to a man in a bar near the port.'

'Don't get smart with me,' she snapped. 'You've lost the right.'

'I'll find out what I can from Kolatch,' he offered.

'Maybe you should go back to babysitting corporate executives,' she said, hanging up on him.

The return drive to the west side of the island had done nothing to improve Arkell's mood.

'Yes?' said Arni Kolatch, opening the door just enough to expose one eye.

Arkell slammed it open, pushed past him. 'We need to talk.'

He went first to the laptop in the kitchen, inserted a flash drive and copied the mail files, internet history and document folders. Over Kolatch's mounting protests, he picked up the mobile phone on the side table and copied all numbers and messages to the NN-3U. Finally, he sat the chemist down at his own kitchen table, picked up a steak knife and said, 'I've got a headache, so let's not piss about.' He pressed the man's limp arm to the table and held the steak knife over his wrist. 'You know what your own people are capable of. I'm no different.'

'I doubt that,' said Kolatch softly.

'Do you doubt my willingness to hurt you?'

The older man shook his head. 'I heard what you did to Dejan.'

Arkell stared at him, revealing nothing.

'You have a nice life here,' he said. 'I'd rather not wreck it. Please, make it easy for both of us.'

'I intend to.'

Surprised, Arkell said, 'You'll tell me about Yadin?'

'Whatever you want to know.'

He was instinctively suspicious. But, on the other hand, this man knew how to survive. Maybe cooperation was his secret weapon. 'I need to know what was in the two boxes you gave him. And I need to know when and how he'll use them.'

'Ah,' smiled Kolatch. 'So it *was* you. He said he saw someone in the trees.'

Frowning, Arkell turned to the window. He could see, high up the hill, the edge of the vineyard, and level with it that clump of stunted trees. 'I wasn't in the—'

The window exploded.

Glass fragments burst around him. A sharp sting as three shards cut into his left arm and chest. Automatically he dropped to the floor, out of sight, trying to sense whether there was anything more, a leaden impact, a bullet in one of his vital organs.

But when he looked back, it was clear where the round had come to rest. The chemist's face was a bleeding crater. His legs were sprawled over the chair, his shoulders on the floor in an expanding pool of blood.

Yadin?

Arkell didn't believe it. He'd seen the two men embrace. And with a sniper's rifle in Yadin's hands, Kolatch would not have been the target.

Then who?

As blood oozed from the chemist's head, Arkell pulled the

slivers of glass from his own body and worked through the possibilities. Did Yadin have a support team? Had the Cypriot National Guard somehow got involved? Or had Wraye sent someone else, a moonlighting soldier from Dhekelia perhaps, to clean up Arkell's mistakes?

None of those made sense.

After twenty minutes he decided to move. Whoever it was, he told himself, if they'd wanted him dead they'd have shot him first. He stood up and looked out of the shattered window. There was the clump of trees, but . . .

His eyes narrowed as he worked out the angles.

A shooter in the trees could not have seen – let alone killed – someone seated at the table. On the other hand . . .

He left the house at a fast run, and kept running all the way up the hill to the vineyard. Breathing hard, he came to a stop beside his trench.

There was the canvas, the shovel, the binoculars and the water, all just as he'd left them. Only one thing was different.

In the centre of the trench, provocatively balanced on its rear end, was the spent casing of a single .338 Lapua Magnum cartridge. A round much loved by US snipers in Iraq and Afghanistan. Arkell picked it up. A trace of heat remained in the rimless brass.

There were footprints, but they told him nothing. Two men, ordinary hiking boots. One of them had lain in his trench, making good use of his canvas, to eliminate his last lead.

And now? The footprints led to the same track Arkell had used the day before. He climbed the crest to confirm it: they were long gone.

Whoever they were.

LONDON, ENGLAND – 13 June

'Not the worst of the drug barons,' H/NARC had summed up in his distinctive prose style, 'but at the top of the second tier, with pretensions to the first. Rodrigo Salis may have more direct impact on UK interests than some of his mightier peers due to his relocation to Guinea-Bissau, bringing his operation closer to British business concerns in Africa as well as trade routes into the UK.'

The SIS file was bulky but insubstantial. Much of the supposed CX was really little more than open source reports or the stale crumbs charitably dispensed by other security services. Translated articles from Colombian newspapers rubbed shoulders with redacted DEA documents and colourful accounts from *Telegraph* and *Guardian* journalists on flying visits to Bissau. HMRC and Metropolitan Police arrest records detailed drug mules working for Salis's organization who had swallowed as many as thirty balls of pure cocaine encased in layers of cling film and wax. A CIA report, also heavily redacted, on the drug wars in Mexico, gave a flavour of his marginal involvement in the battle for control of Juárez. Salis was said to have personally murdered both his uncle and his brother-in-law in the struggle for control of the family cocaine business. Non-family rivals were regularly eliminated, often in a pointedly bloody and shocking way.

As for his activities in Bissau, much less was known. The news articles claimed local people had been threatened, and a couple had disappeared, but they also conceded that plenty of Guinea-Bissauans were doing rather well out of Salis. Hard currency was trickling down all over the place, and no one was too concerned as to its provenance.

Some vital statistics were recorded: Salis was believed to be fifty-three years old, one metre seventy-four tall, with brown eyes, five children and an aversion to poultry. Wanted for murder in three countries, and for trafficking offences in fifty-six. His relationship with his moustache was unsettled: it appeared in three photographs; the other two showed him clean-shaven.

All potentially useful information, but none of it as compelling as the forensics report that accompanied the Salis file. Every single page, that was the conclusion. Every newspaper cutting, redacted report, arrest record, extradition request and NARC assessment bore traces of Anthony Watchman's DNA and fingerprints.

It was impeccable proof, the strongest possible circumstantial evidence that Javier Diaz had correctly identified Watchman in Bissau. And even if there was a good reason for the Head of Counter-Terrorism to be taking such an interest in a Colombian drug baron, one peculiar detail made Watchman look guilty as hell. At the front of the file was a tag listing all the officers who had requisitioned SQ/83774. Neither Watchman nor any of his direct reports was named on that tag.

FRANKFURT, GERMANY – 13 June

Arkell called Wraye the moment he landed at Frankfurt airport. 'You should know I'm still doing this. And I'm angry now.'

'Well, good.'

'I'm sending you a package of data from Kolatch's computer. Nothing on Yadin but there's plenty of other interesting material you can sell to your clients. Consider it a gift of atonement.'

'That's appreciated.'

'You should also know Kolatch was killed. Not by me.' He hesitated. 'Is there anything from the girlfriend?'

'Nothing. No one has visited the apartment – the bugs are working fine, but it's just footsteps and the occasional scraping chair. She's tried to call Dejan four times. A few other trivial calls to local businesses and friends. The GPS puts her in a physiotherapy clinic on Burchardstrasse most of the day. She's a dead end.'

'How about ships leaving Limassol?'

'Too many to search without very good reason. Sailing time to Italy is two to three days, so there'd be plenty of time to get Kolatch's poisons to Strasbourg for the parliamentary address on the sixteenth. How was he killed?'

'Sniper. Right in front of me. There's another team out there.'

'I'll ask around. Be careful, Simon.'

'I will. And Madeleine – for Strasbourg – I'll accept your offer of a weapon.'

Arkell cleared Immigration and headed for the arrivals hall. There he found himself staring into the grinning face of a young Jewish American called Danny.

'*How* . . . ?' It was so ridiculous, so utterly unlikely, that Arkell's mind instantly worked it out. But still he had to pose the question. 'In a moment, I'm going to ask you what the hell you think you're doing,' he threatened. 'But first . . . How did you find me?'

Danny looked ridiculously pleased with himself. 'You're Richard Warwick. I got ya! English names leaving Amman, purchasing a ticket on the day of travel. Yours was the only one that day. I mean, it's pretty unusual, right? Like, who goes to Amman airport and thinks, "Hey, maybe I'll fly someplace today"?'

'And you found this information . . . ?'

'It's not so hard hacking into Amadeus.'

'Yes, it is,' muttered Arkell, recalling a lecture given by Martin de Vries on the subject.

'Then I just waited for your next flight. OK, so not the next one: Cyprus is kind of far, but I figured I'd meet you when you came back to Europe. I mean, I guess Cyprus *is* officially Europe, but like, *real* Europe. Man, you really love booking last-minute, huh? I had to haul ass to get here.'

Horrified as he was that a kid had been able to track him, after nine years of staying off the grid, he had to admit a grudging admiration. He made a mental note to ditch the Warwick passport along with his Michel Jamoulle identity. 'Why were you so determined to find me?'

'Like I said.' The boy's smile had faded. He looked suddenly nervous. 'You saved my life.'

'They weren't going to kill you, Danny.'

'Still. I owe you. I want to help.'

'I don't need your help.'

'So, like, tracking someone who doesn't want to be found – that's not a skill you could use?'

Arkell was silent. It was just possible this kid could do stuff even Wraye's people couldn't. Hacking the Amadeus flight booking network. Emptying an oligarch's bank account. These were not small achievements.

'How old are you?'

'Twenty-five.'

'Don't lie to me.'

'I am! It's a Jewish thing. We look younger than we are.'

'Uh-huh. How old are you?'

Danny met his intense stare. 'Twenty,' he confessed.

'You're in college.'

'Awh, I wasn't learning anything. I was teaching the professors, mostly.'

'Modest.'

Danny shrugged. 'I won't get in the way.' He tapped the laptop under his arm. 'Just set me up with wireless and tell me what you want to know.'

The lives of a prime minister and a president were on the line. And, after all, what was Arkell doing at twenty? How many men had he killed for France by then?

'As it happens, there is someone I'm looking for.'

'All right!' nodded Danny excitedly. 'What's the name?'

'Good question,' Arkell muttered, leading the way to the car rental desks. 'You'd better start with José Cumes.'

In the soul of the man who had on occasion travelled under the name of José Cumes, contradictory instincts were at war. There was the instinct for survival, bred deep into his bones by a long line of survivors, then reinforced by the acculturation of the Golani Brigade and a string of Mossad instructors. But there was also the instinct for honest self-reflection, passed on to him by an academic father who had always insisted that, above all else, he spurn the temptations of self-delusion and recognize and respect the truth of himself, whatever it happened to be.

The truth, as Gavriel Yadin had for a while now accepted, was troubling.

It wasn't that he killed people for a living. No sudden outburst of scruples challenged his long-held view that killing was a natural part of animal life. He was very good at it; people found his talents useful: that was enough. But where did it lead? What happened next?

He'd watched a movie recently, aged assassins – good-humoured Americans, wrinkly and warm-hearted – called out of retirement to do one last job. Absurd. One of them could barely walk for his decrepit hip. One was plugged into a dialysis machine. The third was half-blind and needed help from a little boy locating his target. Even then his hands were shaking too much to hold the rifle steady. It was meant to be hilarious, but it wasn't. It was humiliating.

Impossible.

How does an assassin age?

Not like that, certainly. So what, then? Stop? Retire at fifty? Transform like magic into some different creature? Other members of the Kidon had become trainers, civil servants, security guards, politicians . . . It was too depressing.

Kartouche had once sent him to kill a Chinese businessman. He didn't know why. He rarely knew why. The Chinese was a big man in plastics manufacturing; he owned several factories in Guangdong making toys and casings for electronic equipment. Yadin intercepted him as he was leaving his golf club in a

Daimler. It was an expansive, exclusive place, with a long drive through newly planted woodland. Easy to step in front of the car and, when it slowed, shoot the driver in the head. The target had said, in trembling English, before he too was killed, 'But I haven't finished building my company.'

That struck Yadin. *I haven't finished.* When he found himself staring into death's chasm, would he feel similarly unready? Was there anything not finished in his life? And if not – he suspected there was not – did that mean his life lacked purpose? It was not without effect: he had brought the lives of many significant people to a premature end, changed the course of certain strands of history. But that was different from purpose. Effect alone was not meaningful.

If he had nothing particular to achieve before he died, then . . .

Always recognize and respect the truth of yourself.

. . . then why continue to exist?

Yadin was not afraid of such questions, any more than he was afraid of the guns and knives and lethal injections that might, for him, at any point render them irrelevant. That did not mean it was an easy question.

At the beginning it had been about controlling, then mastering his fear, his revulsion, his lust for the kill. Those emotions had long since been cauterized. Then it was about technical mastery. Every skill that interested him had been perfected. So what next? Quantity? Was there any point to achieving a certain number of kills, like an athlete determined to win a set quotient of gold medals or an investment banker obsessed with pushing his bonus above a particular benchmark? If so, what was the number? It could only be an artificial construct, however he selected it. A meaningless figure with no basis in natural order or logic.

Some other elusive goal, then?

The truth of yourself. The truth was this: Yadin's lust for life was gone. He used to enjoy classical music, particularly Mendelssohn. Now, it irritated him. Making love to Klara . . . he was finding it necessary these days to work harder to achieve orgasm – and did he really enjoy it, anyway? Did he actually *want* it still? Or was it just necessary to prove to himself that he was still human?

There was no pleasure any more.

He was still capable of feeling. He felt annoyance, frustration, embarrassment even – but rarely anything positive.

The truth . . . The truth was this: he was feeling old.

New wrinkles had appeared below his eyes and the skin of his throat seemed a little slack. He wasn't vain, but it was a sign. A lesion on his thigh wouldn't heal. Previously, he barely noticed wounds before they were gone. His breath, he was convinced, had turned fetid, necrotic. He'd tried mouthwash, mints, garlic, but the sensation lingered and he now refused to kiss Klara. He was overcompensating physically, ridiculous in a man still at peak strength. He was pumping iron until his muscles trembled, sparring with a trainer at an intensity quite inappropriate to the requirements of his work. Yet even as he pushed himself, he struggled to explain to his own satisfaction *why* he was pushing himself.

He had become a perfectly tuned machine with no appetite to function.

There had always been philosophy in his parents' household. His father had lectured in a range of humanities, had had a fondness for the writings of Hume and Locke. But an essay by the sixteenth-century mayor of Bordeaux, Michel de Montaigne, was the hook that caught the young Yadin's attention. Entitled 'To Philosophize is to Learn how to Die', it made a deep impression on a boy just about to face national service and the possibility of a Hamas bullet.

So frequent and so ordinary was how Montaigne, whose youthful brother had been killed by a tennis ball, described death. And yet, he had written, *death can surprise us in so many ways.*

Most of his father's philosophers Yadin had been content to leave behind when his skills in unarmed combat and marksmanship drew the attentions of a Mossad talent spotter. But Montaigne had stayed with him, and as the questions on the continuing purpose of his life multiplied, he had sought out a book of his essays and read them all.

The writing was astonishing – insightful, humorous, bewilderingly eclectic, laced with classical wisdom. It inspired him to visit Montaigne's tower in Dordogne, his only adult excursion as a genuine tourist. A futile exercise. He had stood in the library at the top of the tower and felt nothing. He had studied the Latin and Greek maxims inscribed on the beams overhead, he had gazed out of the windows, he had sat where Montaigne would have sat, looking at bare walls that would once have been lined with precious volumes. None of it seemed pertinent to his own condition.

He had flown back to Germany and read the essays again in Klara's bed, and felt that perhaps, even though he remained perplexed by his own existence, he was beginning to understand.

LONDON, ENGLAND – 13 June

The Secret Intelligence Service maintains a modest rented office in Mayfair, two streets back from Green Park, where meetings with less trusted partners or potential assets can be held in an anonymous corporate setting. The limited company whose name appears on a small perspex badge beside the entrance is listed at Companies House, but its very ordinary revenues and costs are manufactured by Technical and Operations Support staff at Vauxhall Cross. It does not advertise.

Madeleine Wraye had used the office herself on many occasions: to flatter internationally mobile businessmen into playing unpaid snoop; to barter information with uncannily informed hedge fund managers; to go through the motions of negotiating, in the guise of an export sales director or a well-funded buyer, with some of the nastier commercial entities on the planet. It was unsettling, as well as mildly humiliating, to be sitting on the other side of the desk.

As if sensing her discomfort, Anthony Watchman lounged back in the Herman Miller chair and gave her his most charming smile. He'd always been good at the charm, when he could be bothered. It was a tap he could spin open when he wanted something. A hard-edged charm, to be sure – rough-diamond stuff – but effective nonetheless. However much you recognized that the diamond could cut you, it was difficult not to be seduced by it. It was the very hardness of the man that made his dazzle so appealing. It felt like a favour bestowed: instead of ripping you from limb to limb, he had chosen to stroke you behind the ears. For now.

'Madeleine Wraye,' he marvelled, the welcoming smile not quite making it to his eyes. 'Madeleine Wraye.' Flicking a lever on the chair, he leaned back a little further. 'How the bloody hell are you? And what the hell are you doing with yourself these days?'

'You don't know?' she smiled back. The visitors' chairs were padded but rigid – deliberately less comfortable. Well aware of the psychological disadvantage that could accrue, she had spun hers around on arrival and now sat with her arms folded over the chair back.

'I'm sure someone keeps track,' he said. A perfect put-down, she had to admit. 'Seriously, Madeleine, it's good to see you. You look well.'

'So do you, Tony.' It was true: he must be fifty, more or less exactly, but you wouldn't know it. The sandy hair – with touches of white around the ears only – was still thick, layered and styled to look artlessly ruffled. He had been a habitual marathon runner, she remembered, hitting a faster time each year until an Achilles tendon ruptured, and even then he managed annual half-marathons across Salisbury Plain. And he had kept in shape. If there was fat on that frame, his tailoring did not reveal it.

'The independent life working out OK? Enough business? I'm sure we could find a few bits and pieces for you if it's helpful?'

She did not rise to the bait. 'No complaints so far.'

'Shit, it's good to see you,' he reiterated, and the sincerity in his rounded eyes and gently shaking head might almost have been believable. 'Really, Maddie, I miss having you around. We all do.'

'That's nice to hear.' Her sincerity would have seemed to an outsider just as authentic. His pet name for her still rankled, but she had been disguising her irritation for so long she wasn't sure he even remembered it was a goad. 'Although apparently you don't miss me enough to offer tea at Head Office.'

He spread his open palms, the honest, regretful friend. 'That would be a tough sell to the boys on the door. A woman of your abilities that close to our servers? They wouldn't like it.'

So he was going to play rough. His allusion was not subtle. Worse, she reflected, it was more than a little triumphant. And that was just not on. For Tony Watchman had been the agent of her fall from grace. Others were involved, of course – but it had been his hand on the dagger.

The charge, in the grand scheme of things, had been a minor one, but in the Service it was treated as the gravest of crimes. Copying secret files for personal use. And she was guilty, it was true, although she was by no means alone. Officers routinely cached files of particular importance to their own circumstances. No treacherous intention; it was simply too easy, despite the safeguards, to do it. Impossible to search every officer exiting Head Office – especially those trained in confounding such security measures – so in the end the system had to fall back on the Official Secrets Act and positive vetting. SIS simply had to trust its staff not to do anything too stupid with its data.

But if someone were to be caught red-handed, well, then there could be no mercy.

Wraye had only done it for insurance, that was the irony. She knew the menfolk were feeling threatened, wanted her out. Well, just in case they found a way – and for the likes of Elphinstone and Watchman there always was a way – she needed to prepare herself for life on the outside. If she wanted to stay in the intelligence game, it was simple: she needed intelligence.

The take was enormous. Over a period of seven weeks, Wraye copied everything the Service held on a plethora of governments, armies, weapon systems, central banks, proprietary technologies and corporations. She left not a trace of her activity. But Watchman knew she was doing it. And she knew he knew.

She even knew the day he was going to order the raid on her little house in Tryon Street.

On that day, a pleasant June morning with only a chance of rain later, she had postponed a meeting with the East European Controllerate team and strolled across the sixth floor to his office. Elphinstone was there, of course. Together, they were raptly watching one of Watchman's three desktop screens. When she knocked, Watchman hit a button, changing the display.

'Got a moment, Tony?'

Elphinstone excused himself with a murmur about a call to Langley.

Watchman said, 'I'm busy.' He was not always charming. It had taken a few years for Wraye to interpret correctly the coded laments of secretaries and junior case officers who reported to him. The rough edges of this self-polished man lay only a little way below the surface. He had been described in more than one confidential assessment as a bully.

'I brought popcorn,' she said brightly. 'I thought we could watch it together.'

He understood in an instant. 'You've moved it,' he accused.

'I don't know what you're talking about.'

'Where have you hidden it? I hope you realize any number of hostile agencies may have you under observation – may already have taken possession of the data.'

'Don't be self-righteous, Anthony. We both know you've done far worse. May I?' She leaned across him to reopen the live feed from Oscar Lima unit. 'I'd like to check they don't break anything.'

Together they watched the search team rifle through her possessions. The process was methodical and meticulous. Every item examined was replaced exactly as found.

Wraye was enjoying herself considerably, despite the violation of her home, until Watchman sighed and shifted gear. He gave her that charming smile, and she knew immediately that she was in trouble.

'It's a pity you moved the cache,' he said, as if making a purely objective observation. 'It would have been less painful this way.'

'What does that mean?'

'You don't think this is the only dirt we have on you?'

'Is that a technical term in C-T, Tony?'

'This may surprise you, but I genuinely like you, Madeleine.'

'Seeing as you're trying to destroy my career and put me in prison, Tony, yes, it does surprise me.'

'Prison? No one wants that. It won't come to that. Not unless . . .' He paused, as if to think it through for the first time. 'Well, not unless we have to move to Plan B.'

'Plan B,' she smiled thinly.

'Madeleine, we have video of your pay-off in Lviv.'

She remained entirely reactionless. That in itself, of course, was reaction enough to betray her. Not that Watchman needed it.

'It's very good quality. We have you counting the cash and then shaking Gregor Uhlig's hand. Irrefutable.'

For the first time in years, she felt an urge to cry. 'There was context!' she said furiously. 'That was Service business, and I can prove it.' But she already knew she couldn't.

'The Chief was very clear: no deals. Uhlig is to be captured and delivered gift-wrapped to Moscow, nothing more and nothing less. Instead, you're on film accepting a bribe from the very same arms dealer your colleagues in Counter-Terrorism are busting a gut to close down! Is that the evidence you want me to put before the tribunal?'

Twenty-six years of service. She was so close to the top. The first female chief of SIS. So nearly her name in the history books.

'Let us use the data indiscretion and you can walk away untouched. I guarantee it. Directorship in the City, spotless record in the wider intelligence community if that's where you want to go. Not a murmur about Uhlig.'

'Just so long as I get out of the boys' way.'

'It's not personal, Madeleine.'

'Oh, it is a little bit personal,' she snapped.

Calmly, he waited, knowing he'd won.

She gestured to the screen. 'Which rooms have they done so far?'

'Office, both bedrooms and the bathroom.'

Her voice sounded very distant. 'Tell them I'm popping home for five minutes. Tell them to clear out now and resume when I leave.' She stood up. 'I'll put it behind the fridge.'

* * *

Watchman was stroking his tie. It was an unconscious action, at least as unconscious as any made by such an experienced intelligence officer. The tie was a deep and lustrous purple silk weave. Conservative but confident. It occurred to Wraye that his suit was rather finer than anything she'd seen him wear previously. More corporate, like the tie. In that chair, behind that desk, she decided, Tony Watchman was doing his best to look the model Chief Executive. He hadn't quite pulled it off. There was still just the slightest imprint of a chip on his elegant shoulder. Still the insecurity of a man who hadn't been to university, who didn't quite belong. Yes, he'd won, by any measure he'd won – but he'd never entirely believed it.

'So, aside from the sadly impossible prospect of tea at Head Office, what can I do for you, Maddie?'

'I have a few questions on behalf of a client. A friendly, I promise. Would you mind?'

'It would be my pleasure.' The expansive CEO, ever generous with his time.

'It goes back a while. Rupert Ellington. Remember him?'

'Remind me.' Not a flicker.

'Our man in Riyadh, around eleven years ago.'

'Died on the job.'

'That's the one.'

'Poor sod. Brain aneurysm, wasn't it?'

'Turns out it wasn't.'

'Oh. Guess I don't remember him all that well, then.'

'That same day, an emergency courier was sent to Riyadh with a package of papers for the Ambassador. Your courier. Any idea what was in those papers that made them so urgent?'

He paused. 'This was before GRIEVANCE?'

'Just before.'

'Then I'm afraid I've no idea. All kinds of issues seemed important before GRIEVANCE.'

His face was entirely composed, not a thing to be read there.

'Why didn't you use a Service courier?'

'I'm sorry?'

'Martin said you asked him to clear the visit with the Saudis and organize a flight. He offered you a Service courier but you turned him down in favour a guy from outside. Name of Sidney Dawson.'

Watchman considered the desk between them. 'I remember now.'

'What?'

'What the papers were.'

'What were they?'

'I can't tell you.'

She had expected that, at least. 'And the courier?'

'The papers were time-critical. I had to get a man on a particular scheduled flight. It was a matter of rushing someone to the airport. Martin's courier wouldn't have made it. My guy was ready to go. He was a private security operative I used a number of times back then. I trusted him.'

'Any chance he might have dropped by Ellington's house? Maybe popped something in his bedtime cocoa?'

Watchman breathed forcefully. 'That's dangerous ground, Madeleine.'

'Yes or no, Tony?'

'What do you think?'

'I think possibly yes.'

'Think differently, and quick, or this meeting's over. There's a nasty whiff of accusation developing.'

'All right,' she conceded. 'But let's stay on dangerous ground. Two years later my officer, Simon Arkell, was killed.'

'I thought he was George's officer by then.'

'It was an act of terrorism on British soil. Your section handled the liaison with Five and SO13. What was the final conclusion?'

'Insufficient data but probably AQ, threatened by something Arkell had unearthed in Yemen.' Watchman looked very slightly smug. Was it his confident recall of an old case? Or something else?

'You never worked out what he might have found?'

'No means to do so. His house was obliterated, along with his laptop and phone. He'd gone AWOL for a few days, requested a passport for some Greek. That's all we had.'

'Did you identify the Greek?'

'No.'

'How about the bomber? We had CCTV.'

'No match.'

'None? Nothing since?'

'No.'

She laid the Tobago shot of Yadin in front of him. 'Know who that is?'

For the first time, something shifted in Watchman. The cockiness gave way momentarily to unease. 'I can't discuss this man.'

'Why's that?'

'He's part of an ongoing investigation by another service.'

'Then how about this one?' She put down a second picture. She'd decided to go with one of the moustache-sporting variants.

'No idea.' Not a flicker of recognition. He was very good, reflected Wraye, given that his fingerprints were plastered over this very photograph.

'Now, Anthony, I happen to know that's not true.'

'Are you calling me a liar?' he smiled.

'I imagine you'll take it as a compliment.'

'Your evidence?' Was there a hint of a break in his confidence?

'You weren't all that discreet in Bissau.'

'I see.'

'Want to tell me why you went to visit Salis?'

'No.'

'Business? Social? Shopping for personal use? Why so coy, Tony?'

'He's part of an ongoing investigation by another service.'

'Damn right he is. DEA, NCA, a dozen other counter-narcotics units. I'm sure they'd all like to know what a British Intelligence director is doing hobnobbing with a drug baron.'

'This is not something I can discuss with anyone beyond the sixth floor.'

She sat back, temporarily winded. 'The Chief knows?'

'He does.'

'So you'd have no objection if I raise it with him?'

'Knock yourself out.' He was smiling again, at ease and confident.

Wraye shook her head. 'What kind of pig shit are you swimming in these days, Tony? Rodrigo Salis, my God.'

That smug look didn't waver a jot.

She was out of ammunition. He had stonewalled perfectly,

giving away almost nothing. She stood up. 'How do you feel about your country, Tony?' It was an old joke from their earliest days together: the question Oxbridge tutors were supposed to ask of their brightest students over a cup of tea before steering them towards SIS.

'I love it dearly,' said Watchman. 'And I'm fighting to preserve it in the most effective way I can.'

It was a moment of odd sincerity that left her feeling more unsettled than anything else he'd said.

HAMBURG, GERMANY – 14 June

This time he did not dress up.

A receptionist wearing hoop earrings guarded the front entrance of the clinic. Beyond her, a pale green passageway led to four consulting rooms. Arkell approached with a large envelope and a clipboard.

'Klara Richter?'

The receptionist held out her hand for the envelope. Drawing back, Arkell mimed a signature on his clipboard. He was pointed to a seat but chose to stay standing. When Klara appeared, she stared at him in confusion and then in silent accusation.

'Step outside?' he suggested.

On the street, Klara said, 'You're not a priest.'

He waited for a pizza delivery boy to saunter past. 'I expect you've probably guessed by now that I work for British Intelligence.' When she didn't speak, he added, 'And you'll have understood this is about Gavriel.'

'What do you want?' Anxiety scratched every word.

'Ms Richter, do you know what your boyfriend does for a living?'

'He's a businessman.'

'He's not a businessman.'

She frowned. 'He sells engineering equipment for Rovman Industries.'

'Look, Klara,' he said quietly, 'there's no easy way to tell you. Gavriel Yadin is a former Israeli intelligence officer, trained to kill. An assassin.'

She stared at him in disgust. Off-centre. One incensed eye out-glaring the other. 'Is this meant to be a joke?'

'Three weeks ago he poisoned the prime minister of the Netherlands. Two days from now he will attempt to kill the president of Brazil or the prime minister of Canada – or possibly both. I have to stop him, and I need your help to do it.'

She laughed hollowly. 'Excuse me, I have to go back to work. Please don't come here again.'

'I'm going to show you something. It's not pleasant. This is what Gavriel does.'

Before she could move he had ripped open the envelope and pulled out a large black-and-white photograph. She twisted violently away. 'You're insane!'

'Klara!' He gripped her arm. 'Gavriel did this because he was ordered to by the Israeli government. Now, he's working for someone much more dangerous.'

'Why do you have this picture?' she cried, struggling to get free. 'Are you sick?'

'I know this is hard for you to—'

'It's bullshit!'

He waited for her breathing to settle, then let go of her. 'Why don't you call him and ask?' he suggested softly.

She looked towards the clinic but didn't move.

'You don't have his phone number, do you? Why do you think that is?'

Angrily, she said, 'Yes, he's married, I know that. I'm not naïve. He told me in the beginning. I'm not doing anything to break up his family.'

'Is that why you agreed to travel on a false passport? Why you both used false names when you went on vacation?'

She blinked at that, but quickly recovered. 'His wife's father works for the Israeli Police. Gavriel didn't want to . . . leave a trail.'

'Klara, he's not married.'

'He told me early on,' she said dogmatically. 'That's why I can't call him. In case *she* picks up.'

'So instead you leave messages with a violent criminal named Dejan.'

She looked at him in amazement. 'Dejan is Rovman's German sales agent.'

Arkell pulled out his smartphone, found the Rovman website, and searched for the German contact details. He showed her the screen. 'Do you want to check that?'

She stood very still, not responding.

'Or you could call them and ask about Gavriel.'

Still no answer. He pocketed the phone.

'Klara, we know you were in Tobago with Gavriel three weeks ago. A lovely vacation, lots of sun, lots of bird watching. How much of the time were you together?'

'All the time.' A chill, scared note had crept into her voice.

'That's not true, is it? At least on the last day – and I'd guess several others – you split up for a few hours, didn't you? On the north side of the island? Somewhere around Englishman's Bay?'

'How do you know these things?' she whispered. Her bunched shoulders were trembling. 'Were you spying on us?'

'What was his reason? Did he want to hike faster than you? Did he say you scared off the birds?'

'He . . . he's been suffering . . .' She stared at her ankle boots. 'How do you say? Mid-life? He's been depressed. He wanted time with himself . . . to think.'

'In the hills above Englishman's Bay?'

She nodded.

'Were you aware that the Think Again event during which Prime Minister van der Velde died was taking place above Englishman's Bay on the last day of your vacation?'

She closed her eyes and did not open them for over a minute. Simon Arkell felt acutely the pain of her comprehension.

'Then this is all a terrible coincidence,' she said, her last, hopeless bid. 'Like those poor people locked up in Guantanamo. We were in the wrong place at the wrong time, and now you are going to lock up Gavriel too.'

'You don't really believe that.'

'He's not a murderer!' She was choking on the words. 'He's not a murderer! He's not!'

Her resistance collapsed then. She sat down heavily on the pavement and buried her head in her hands.

Crouching beside her, hating the role he was required to play, Arkell said, 'It's a really simple choice, you see. We can have you arrested now on a charge of conspiracy to murder Anneke van der Velde, as well as a range of other charges of obstructing justice and so on. That will mean at least three years in prison. You will find it very difficult to get any kind of healthcare work with a criminal record. Or you can help us prevent another murder, and in return we'll make sure you stay out of court.'

RIYADH, SAUDI ARABIA – 14 June

The General Directorate for Investigations, or Mabahith, is one of the world's busier domestic intelligence services. The Kingdom of Saudi Arabia has had no shortage of internal threats to keep it occupied, from belligerent citizens returning home after the 2001 fall of the Taliban to the sparks from the Arab Spring that threatened to set light to the Wahhabi tinderbox. The jihadist targets – refineries, foreign compounds, government offices, royal palaces, Mecca itself – are plentiful and precious enough to keep the officers of the Mabahith very twitchy indeed.

Madeleine Wraye met Ahmed al-Hadlaq a few hundred metres from the Mabahith's `Ulaisha Prison. She had found it necessary to enter the prison on two occasions during her long career with SIS, and was glad not to have to do so again now. Many of the detainees had never faced trial; a few had been tortured. The two Iranian officials al-Hadlaq caught comparing uranium enrichment notes with a particularly ambitious Saudi branch of Al-Qaeda were in a pitiful state by the time Wraye was invited to interrogate them. It was not a pleasant environment.

'My apologies,' said al-Hadlaq, gesturing around the mean coffee bar in which they were seated. His diamond cufflinks glittered in a smooth arc. 'You understand, as it's not official . . .'

'I'm very comfortable here,' smiled Wraye. 'And I'm grateful you could interrupt your schedule for me.'

Al-Hadlaq waved away any suggestion of inconvenience. 'Whatever I can do.' His rich, silky tones were hypnotic. Wraye had witnessed the command they had over sleep-deprived and disorientated prisoners. She had immense respect for the man's professional capabilities.

The Mabahith officer made a coded gesture to a waiter. He pulled a laptop from a steel briefcase and flipped it open. 'The man you asked about: Sidney Dawson. Our records confirm he entered the country through King Khalid international airport. He arrived on a British Airways flight direct from London Heathrow. As a declared MI6 courier, he was met by officers from my service at Immigration and provided with a courtesy escort throughout his stay in the Kingdom.'

'He was under Mabahith observation the entire time?'

'Just like MI5 we prefer to know what foreign intelligence assets – even friendly assets – are doing within our borders.'

Two coffees arrived, small and very dark. Wraye listed cardamom among her least favourite spices, and loathed sugar in coffee, but she sipped hers with the appreciation she knew was expected.

'Are there any notes from the escorting officers?'

'Of course.' One-handed, he typed a series of commands on the Arabic keyboard. 'Routine procedurals. Subject arrived. Subject welcomed. Drive to Safarat. No traffic. Security forces checkpoint: credentials accepted. Drive to Residence of United Kingdom Ambassador. Subject entered Residence 22:47. Subject left Residence 22:53. Drive to Radisson Blu. Subject checks in 23:21. Subject goes to room. Subject receives room service 23:44. Subject receives breakfast room service 06:29. Subject exits room 07:05. Drive to King Khalid. Subject checks in to British Airways flight 07:42. Subject passes through Immigration 07:48. End report.'

'Is there a picture?'

Al-Hadlaq tapped two keys and turned the laptop towards her. A standard passport photograph next to a CCTV image. It was not Yadin. 'You know him?'

'Yes,' Wraye admitted. Yes, she had met the man. Short and overweight, owlish glasses on a fleshy face, ill-fitting clothes. One of the deniable scavengers Tony Watchman used from time to time to smuggle firearms across unchallenging borders and perform the occasional clumsy burglary. Low grade but harmless. Certainly not the type to slip out of a hotel room under Mabahith guard, talk his way back into a secure diplomatic quarter and make a murder look like a natural death.

Damn it. She had wanted it to be Tony.

'Do you have access to the passenger arrivals records for that day?'

'All passengers?'

'Adult male Caucasian.'

Al-Hadlaq typed swiftly. 'No name?'

'I'll know him when I see him.'

'Saudis too?'

'It's possible he was travelling as one. But start with the foreigners.'

The passport photographs began scrolling across the screen. Face after face after face. They flickered for an instant and were gone again: both intelligence officers were well practised in this art.

More coffees were brought, and still the faces kept coming. Arab, Western, Indian. Wraye hardly blinked. 'Stop,' she murmured. 'Back two.'

The name was Dieter Rheinhardt. Chemical engineer. It was almost funny.

Poor Rupert Ellington hadn't stood a chance.

'I know this face,' muttered Al-Hadlaq. 'We've had a Request for Identification from the Canadians.'

'Yes.'

'That's why you're here?'

'Yes.'

'We found a match.'

'Oh?' Wraye sat back. CSIS had told her no service had been able to offer anything on the Yadin image.

'He was in Bahrain recently. We thought he was one of yours – an MI6 asset, I mean. There has been bad blood recently with Canada over carbon pricing, so we chose to favour our British friends and say nothing.'

'Abu Ali,' said Wraye slowly, 'what made you think this man was one of ours?'

Ahmed Al-Hadlaq returned to his keyboard, a touch of embarrassment showing for once on those smooth cheeks. 'Please remember, Bahrain is going through difficult times. We have to be rigorous in our surveillance on behalf of our ally.

Mr Vine is a highly valued friend of Saudi Arabia but, as I have said, we prefer to know what our friends are doing.'

The photograph filled the screen. George Vine had a glass of mint tea raised to his mouth, his lips caught in an unfortunate pucker on their approach to the rim. By contrast, his companion in the Bahraini hotel lounge was perfectly composed. It seemed he had resisted Vine's inveterate hospitality, for there was nothing on the table before him. Instead of a glass, he held a tablet computer. And where Vine was dressed in slacks and open-neck shirt, this man wore a dark grey suit and crimson tie. On this occasion, it seemed, Gavriel Yadin was all business.

There was still time before her flight home, and Madeleine Wraye wanted to satisfy herself on one particular point. The detour would be noted in the Mabahith records, but it was important to be sure. Rather than head straight for the checkpoint off King Khalid Road, she had the driver take her due west from `Ulaisha into Wadi Hanifa, the valley that runs through the western suburbs of Riyadh.

On the way, she called Joyce. 'I need you to get me a meeting with George Vine as soon as possible. I'd call him myself but I don't want him working out where I am.'

'Where are you?'

'Can you meet me at Heathrow tomorrow morning? Bring everything you have on Vine.'

They followed the wadi road north-west, past orange groves and palm plantations, past warehouses and a dam, until Wraye's smartphone GPS told her they were skirting the back of the diplomatic quarter.

'Please don't be alarmed. I just want to take a quick look,' she told the driver as she stepped out of the car. He was presumably an officer of the Mabahith, but he raised no objection.

Her shoes were flat, which was good; they were expensive Italian patent leather, which was not. They were ruined by the scramble up the side of the wadi. Nevertheless there was nothing especially challenging about the ascent. A wall ran along the edge of the quarter, but it was not the sort of barrier to trouble a man like Yadin. At night, even with the occasional patrol, he could have been up this slope and over the wall in less than a minute.

That was all she needed to know.

WESTERN GERMANY – 14 June

Klara Richter didn't seem surprised to find a young American in the back of the hire car. She did not respond to Danny's cheery greeting. Arkell stopped off on Steindamm just long enough for her to collect a bag of clothes and jam a black felt fedora low over her eyes. The drive south to Strasbourg took more than six hours, and other than Danny's occasional attempts to connect, the journey passed in silence.

At a service station outside Hanover, Arkell bought coffee and belegtes Brot, which she accepted with a muttered thank you. Passing Frankfurt airport, he realized she was crying. He kept his eyes on the road, pretended not to notice.

As they crossed the Rhine into France, he thought about the Legion and the jail cell that still awaited him. Nothing happened: no gendarmes, no flashing lights, no cries of betrayal.

On impulse, he said suddenly, 'Look, I know how it feels.' She did not seem to have heard.

It was almost dark when they drove into Strasbourg. Arkell lodged Danny and his laptop in a corporate hotel with plentiful Wi-Fi, three streets from the pension he'd reserved for himself off Grand Rue. 'José Cumes,' he reminded him at the reception.

'Whatever,' said Danny wearily. 'Man, that was *the* most depressing road trip in history. Seriously, dude, you need to lighten up with that Fräulein.'

At the pension he gave Klara the bed and slept on the floor, blocking the door. His first night on French soil in over seventeen years was plagued by dreams of mutilated corpses – Yadin's victims, who had somehow become his own.

HEATHROW, ENGLAND – 15 June

Arriving at Heathrow was one of the few occasions when Madeleine Wraye really missed being a member of the establishment. For years, she had been discreetly met at the gate by a member of the UK Immigration Service and escorted through some of the less well-known reaches of the airport to a small road tunnel where a Service car would be waiting. Nowadays the car was a rather better model, but there was no escaping the Immigration queues. Just occasionally, squeezed between a brawling family and a school soccer team back from a European tour, she would spot one of the Immigration officers who had previously whisked her past all of this misery. If they recognized her they would nod sympathetically and raise a quizzical eyebrow as if to say, 'What happened to you, then?'

On this occasion, as it turned out, the car would not be needed. A text message from Joyce had brought the good news that George Vine had invited her to dinner. The bad news was she would have to turn right round and fly back to the Middle East. The only available slot in Vine's calendar was tonight. There was just time for a shower at the Sofitel and a debrief with Joyce before she would need to return to Terminal 5 for the Beirut flight.

Joyce's message was not the only one awaiting her on landing. Several urgent voicemails had stacked up from Shel Margrave, Operations Director of the Canadian Security Intelligence Service. The last had been left just twenty minutes earlier – the middle of the night for him. She dialled his office number.

'Your phone was switched off,' he began accusingly.

'I've just stepped off a flight.' Wraye counted the number of people ahead of her and estimated a twelve-minute wait. 'I'm in a public place. Will you still be at your desk in quarter of an hour?'

'We have a lead on Yadin. You need to get your guy to West Africa.'

'Seriously? That doesn't fit with our intelligence. Are you sure of your lead?'

'One hundred per cent. Comes from the Spanish. CNI was on our distribution list for Yadin's picture. They just came back demanding to know who he is. Seems he showed up in Bissau, of all places, and executed a Colombian drug lord they had under surveillance.'

Dazed, Wraye turned her back on the nearest passengers

and covered her mouth as she whispered, 'Are you saying he assassinated Rodrigo Salis?'

A surprised pause. 'Jesus, you're *good*. How do you know about Salis? Never mind. Can your guy get out there?'

'No point. The target will be long gone. We have to focus on Strasbourg now.'

Margrave hesitated. 'I don't like to think of him in the same city as Mayhew.'

'I understand.'

'You're on this one hundred per cent, right? No other little projects distracting you? Making you take long flights?'

'One hundred per cent, Shel.' An immigration officer was pointing her to a free e-passport gate.

'Your guy had better be good.'

'Oh, he is,' she promised.

'You need to get the Salis file back to central registry fast,' Wraye told Joyce. 'He was killed yesterday. They'll be wanting to update the notes.'

'And how do I do that?'

'You'll think of something. What do you have for me on George?'

Madeleine Wraye was pacing the room in an effort to get her blood flowing ahead of the next flight. She'd ordered room service before deciding she wasn't hungry. Joyce, primly seated at the desk, was working his way through her breakfast tray.

'Endless small stuff. He's implicated right across the Middle East, potentially in the pocket of just about every Arab ruler and business leader you can imagine. It's all in the file.'

'Old news. Why would he have met Yadin?'

'I haven't found anything yet.'

'All right. What else?'

'You asked me to look into corporations that might have benefited from SIS product in our key geographies . . .'

'Any connections to George?'

'All the usual official ones . . . BP, British Airways, Barclays, RBS and so on. Beyond that, there are around a dozen corporations that have been unusually successful in our hotspots. I've searched for links to the remaining names on your list. Watchman may be tangentially involved with a couple of mining companies, but the standout partnerships are George Vine with AMB and Martin de Vries with Plessis-Fischer.'

Wraye hid her surprise. 'You have evidence?'

'Nothing that would stand up in court.'

'Edward, you're making serious allegations. If an SIS director was found to be passing YZ intelligence to a foreign business of such military significance as either one of those he wouldn't just be fired – he'd be immured in the Tower. De Vries and Vine know that very well. So tell me please, Edward, how you've managed to uncover something that two very experienced officers would make damn sure no one could find out?'

Joyce turned to face her: indignant, nervous, triumphant. 'I did the Alpha Course.'

'*What?*'

He reddened. 'It was a temporary thing. After you left the Service and I got transferred, I was a bit depressed . . .'

'Edward, tell me you aren't relying on divine inspiration.'

'On my course was this guy from Oregon. Christopher. He

was working for an investment bank, hated it, had served in the DIA, wanted to go back. So I got to know him, you know, just in case. Well, anyway, he did go back. And we're still in touch.'

Wraye gazed at him in disbelief. 'Edward Joyce has cultivated an agent in the Defense Intelligence Agency?'

He laughed awkwardly. 'Oh, I wouldn't claim that exactly. We're just friends. He probably thinks he has an agent in SIS.'

Her stare turned brutal. 'You *told* him?'

'I . . .' Too late, Joyce realized what he had confessed. 'It was a very difficult time for both of us. I haven't passed any secrets, I swear.'

She let him sweat a moment. 'And he's never asked for any?'

'He asked about George Vine.'

Wraye sat down. 'I see.'

'It was maybe a year ago. I didn't give him anything. But when Vine turned up on your list, I called him and asked what it was about. He wouldn't say. Then one of the IONEC students mentioned AMB owing a lot to George in Iraq, so I went back to Christopher and tried flying that kite. Turns out DIA have an agent in AMB's accounts department.'

'Edward,' she whispered, 'what have you got?'

He opened his case and extracted a large grey file. 'Everything I could find on AMB. Most of it is open source.' He laid a single sheet of paper on top. 'That's from Christopher.'

It was a list of dates and figures – large figures, with dollar signs preceding them. Wraye swallowed up the message they conveyed in one glance. 'Don't ever reveal who you work for, Edward. And stay away from Alpha. I can't imagine what you were thinking.' She slipped the AMB file into her cabin case. 'What about de Vries?'

'I don't have anything documented.'

'Plessis-Fischer,' she prompted.

He breathed in. 'OK, so their Europe and Middle East sales division is run out of London. Headed by Johannes van Rensburg. He's on the board; there's a good chance he'll be CEO within a few years. But while he's in London, guess how he's spending his Sunday evenings?'

She knew the answer because she knew where Martin de Vries went on Sundays and she could see from Joyce's face it must be the same. 'Zimbabwe Freedom.'

'That's right. He drives all the way from Hampstead to Southfields to sit in a municipal hall with Martin de Vries.' Joyce was alive with the witch-hunter's fervour now. '*Even though he's not from Zimbabwe!*'

Wraye was unimpressed. 'Plenty of South Africans feel strongly about the situation in Zimbabwe.'

'You don't think it's suspicious that an SIS director and the next chief of a major arms manufacturer just happen to belong to the same small action group?'

'Not necessarily.'

'Madeleine, this is the one! So what if George is taking bribes from a military contractor? He takes bribes from everyone. But Martin de Vries? Whiter than white, yet he's meeting covertly with the representative of a company whose share price rose eighteen per cent after GRIEVANCE.'

A company that supplies all kinds of lethal hardware to the world's counter-narcotics agencies, Wraye silently added.

'How do you know they're meeting? It's not good enough to place them in the same building along with a hundred other people. You need more.'

Joyce swallowed. 'I have more.'

'Go on . . .' She frowned at his hesitation. 'Let's hear it.'

'They have dinner,' he said, the words running together in his hurry to get them out. 'Afterwards.'

'Alone or with other Zim Freedom people?'

'Alone.'

'More than once?'

'Regularly.' No hesitation now.

'Where?'

He looked down, then said, 'A South African restaurant in Wimbledon. Potjiekos.'

'What's your source?'

'A waitress. I asked around a bunch of restaurants near the venue. Showed pictures of both men. The Potjiekos waitress confirmed they often have dinner there. Even knew their favourite dishes. And she said a really interesting thing. She said a couple of times she tried to hand them their coats but both times she got them the wrong way round. Which she never normally did.' Joyce's eyes were shining. 'What do you think, Madeleine? Intel in one coat, cash in the other? They're similar height and build. Choose the same style of coat, and you've got the perfect exchange medium.'

'Not in summer.'

It was clear Joyce hadn't thought of that. He looked strangely embarrassed, then defiant. 'They could use newspapers in summer.'

Wraye flicked the conjecture away. 'It's Sunday today. You want to prove your case? Head over to Wimbledon tonight and video them together.'

He didn't quite meet her eye. 'Sure,' he muttered.

'I have to get to my flight. Something else I need you to do for me while I'm out of contact, Edward. I've commissioned some associates to trawl through bookings at hotels and rental accommodation in Strasbourg. It's possible Yadin may fly in, do the deed and fly out without his head touching a pillow, but my suspicion is he's already there. If my associates identify a likely booking, they will call you. I need you to pass on the details to TALON.' She handed him a slip of paper. 'TALON's pension in Strasbourg. Leave a message for "Mr Locke". Do it as soon as you hear from my associates. We're very short of time now.'

He took the paper, irritated. 'Of course.'

'Another associate is arranging a weapon for TALON. That person will also call you. Pass on the arrangements in the same way.'

'Anything else?'

She frowned at the tone. 'No, Edward. That's all.'

Martin de Vries had never thanked her. That still rankled. For eight full minutes in the Chief's office he had listened to her unreserved defence of his performance and character, and he had never thanked her.

No one else had stood before the Chief and argued that, if in no other walk of modern life, in the security services technical brilliance must occasionally trump people skills. The man wasn't running agents; his direct reports didn't need to be mollycoddled! Perhaps he was immoderate in his criticism, but weren't all geniuses? As for the suggestion that his Rhodesian roots might compromise his loyalty, who did they think he was working for? Mugabe?

He wasn't a director then. HPD had taken against him, as had Jeremy Elphinstone and Jane Saddle. He was hanging by a thread after a whispering campaign instigated by two disgruntled TOS technicians. Her intervention, Elphinstone had later admitted, was the only thing that kept a good man in post. She had risked her own political capital to save his career, and he had never thanked her.

When, years later, the itch of his ingratitude still niggling, she had referred half-jokingly to the matter, the newly appointed Director of Technical and Operations Support had looked puzzled.

'But you only told the truth,' he observed.

'There's truth and there's truth, Martin.'

'I'm not following. Are you saying you have doubts about my loyalty?'

'No, of course not!'

'You think I am inappropriately harsh with my people?'

'You're harsh. Sometimes very harsh.'

'Inappropriately harsh?'

She hesitated. The lightness with which she had unwisely tried to broach the subject was long gone. 'I couldn't say that.'

'Then what is this other truth you're talking about?'

'That's not what I meant . . . Look, did you see anyone else lining up to defend you?'

'You were in a position to give an informed opinion. Most were not.'

'God, Martin,' she exclaimed, exasperated. 'All I'm saying is it would have been nice if you'd acknowledged the effort I made on your behalf.'

'I don't see what else you could have said,' he shrugged. 'But, all right. Thank you.'

'Oh, for Christ's sake,' she'd scowled, wondering not for the first time how Martin de Vries managed to make her feel so very stupid.

STRASBOURG, FRANCE – 15 June

Klara Richter couldn't make him out, the English spy. It was bizarre, considering the circumstances: he seemed genuinely interested in the fabric of the city. They were supposed to be looking for Gavriel, yet his pivoting gaze sought out architectural curiosities as much as faces. A mansard roof. A sliver of a house squeezed between two more obviously historic half-timbered buildings. The iron bars on three round windows. A rusting hook jutting from the upper floor of a tavern.

Then, ludicrously, he had stopped altogether and was crouching in the middle of the street.

'Lose something?' she asked.

'Found something.' His left hand was spread across one of the flat cobblestones. His eyes were closed. Klara sensed a strange euphoria in him. She wished she had a camera to capture that expression.

'A stone? Wow.' There was still bitterness in her voice, although she had woken that morning with a resolve to be more civil to the broad-shouldered man stretched out on the pension carpet.

So far it had been small talk only, but the mood was lighter between them.

He gazed up at her, as if wondering how much to reveal. 'History,' he said at last.

Klara burst out laughing. She stopped herself quickly, but he seemed unbothered by her reaction. 'It's good to see you cheerful.'

'I'm not cheerful. I'm laughing at you.'

'That was a cheerful laugh. I don't care if it's at me.'

She tilted her black felt fedora back a fraction. 'Are you for real?'

But he was impatient, now, to tell her. 'In 1518, a woman called Frau Troffea started dancing here, right here.'

'So?'

'She didn't stop for six days.'

'So?'

'As she danced, others joined in. Thirty-four by the end of the week. Four *hundred* by the end of the month. It started right here.'

Caught between disbelief and irritation, Klara lapsed into German: '*Und?*'

'You have to feel it,' he said, reaching for her hand.

Klara backed away.

'It was hot,' he went on quietly. 'Midsummer. The dancing was frenetic. Exhausting. But the dancers couldn't seem to stop themselves. One had a heart attack. Another collapsed from dehydration. There were strokes, more heart attacks. People started dying. It was called the Dancing Plague. By the end of it, more than forty dancers were dead. That's . . . history.'

Tentatively, Klara spread her hand beside his.

'I don't feel anything.'

He took gentle hold of her fingers. They were rigid, and he waited for them to soften in his. 'Like this,' he murmured, curling them around a single cobblestone. 'Feel it?'

'No.' But the answer was more obstinacy than truth.

'There's a legend about St Vitus – a bad-tempered Sicilian martyr. It was said that anyone who angered him would be condemned to dance uncontrollably. He was a big deal around these parts back then.'

Klara straightened up, dusted off her hands. 'What is the point of the ground-stroking?'

'I don't know.' He seemed suddenly embarrassed. 'It helps me get a feel for a place. If I know the history . . . if I feel the history come alive in me . . . it gives me a kind of strength.'

Klara reached into her bag and found her sunglasses. 'These streets they repave all the time,' she muttered, walking on alone.

SURREY, ENGLAND – 15 June

The tree house should have been straightforward: a self-assembly pack from a reputable high-street chain; just a Wendy house on stilts, with a little plastic slide that clipped on the front. Edward Joyce had been methodical, unpacking all the pieces and setting them out in regimented lines on the terrace. The jumbled assortment of screws, bolts, wooden plugs and plastic washers had been painstakingly counted out into separate jars and placed out of reach of his younger daughter. Maya was usefully engaged in branding each plank of wood with a pink crayon smiley face, while Jasmine issued imperious directions. Sophie, with long experience of his DIY tribulations, was playing her part, bringing him beers as rewards for each completed stage, and marvelling at 'the amount of work they expect you to do'. Even the sun was shining.

But it was starting to go wrong. The bolts weren't protruding from the stilts at the correct angles. The braces weren't fitting properly. He didn't need a spirit level to recognize that the platform on which the Wendy house would rest was sloping. With Sophie watching from the kitchen, and the kids plaguing him with 'Is it nearly ready?' questions, he couldn't face dismantling the whole thing and starting again.

So he kept going. The girls weigh nothing, he told himself. If it can support me, my children will be perfectly safe. His mind drifted as he wondered how he could disguise the platform's crookedness from his wife and neighbours, and he found himself screwing the wrong sections of wood together for the Wendy house frame. As he pulled them apart in irritation, one essential baton split.

'Fuck!'

Maya looked up, pink crayon resting against a stilt. 'What, Daddy?'

Where was he going to get a replacement baton on a Sunday? 'Nothing, sweetie,' he smiled, slipping off the platform and crouching beside her to examine the half-finished face.

'She's doing it wrong,' declared Jasmine with the absolute authority of a five-year-old. 'She keeps putting the nose above the eyes.'

'Well, now, you're right about that,' murmured Joyce, putting an arm around his older daughter. 'Very well spotted. But I think Maya is drawing the gholfin people who live under the bridge. They all have noses over their eyes. Isn't that right, Maya?'

Joyce liked inventing for his children. If he were to draw up a list of his acknowledged skills in the domestic arena – to offset his inadequacies with screwdriver and spanner – making up stories would have been one of them. So far he'd only twice considered creating such a list.

'I *love* goofing people,' decided Maya, adding two arms to the chin of her pink crayon face.

It was a sweet moment, but the mood didn't last. Climbing back onto the sloping platform, Joyce knocked over his beer. Eight minutes later, he realized he'd lost three crucial screws. Fourteen minutes after that, a splinter inserted itself deep under his thumbnail as another baton snapped. His phone rang while he was hunting in the grass for a green plastic washer.

'What?' he yelled.

His exasperation faded as he listened. With Maya's pink crayon he scribbled an address on the back of the instructions booklet. He looked across the lawn at his wife, frumpy and sweating on her knees in the herb garden. He looked at the girls, locked in a tearful tussle over a stuffed toy, while a dozen other toys lay abandoned around them. He looked at the wreckage of ill-fitting joints, beer-soaked tools and splintered batons. And although he knew what he was supposed to do with this information – what Wraye had expressly told him to do with this information – he made a spontaneous decision to do otherwise.

Climbing off the sinking ship of his daughters' joint birthday present, he walked over to the herb garden and said, 'Darling, would you mind putting the tools away for me? It's work. I have to pop over to France rather urgently.'

STRASBOURG, FRANCE – 15 June

They ate lunch in a winstub with red-and-white-checked tablecloths and dark panelled walls. Copper cauldrons hung from the rafters. An antique spinning wheel and sepia prints of the cathedral reinforced the theme. Klara ordered choucroute garnie, but spoke to the waiter in note-perfect French. Arkell chose steak tartare. The thought of a genuinely French meal after all these years, even one prepared in this Teutonic corner of the country, made his tongue prickle with anticipation.

His Legion French sounded like coarse sandpaper after hers.

She glanced up at the accent but said nothing. The black felt fedora, now accessorized with a delicate silver chain around its crown, was tilted over her left eye, emphasizing that off-centre gaze. He was still having difficulty reading her. Could this hurt creature continue to love a professional murderer? Arkell didn't believe so, but Wraye had often warned him against making assumptions about women. 'You don't know us, Simon,' she'd say. 'You know tactics and mountains and ballistics, not women. You don't know what we're capable of.' She said it even after he was married.

Without thinking, he reached across the table. 'I know this must be difficult,' he said.

Klara jerked her hand away as if he'd stung her.

'Sorry . . .' He leaned awkwardly back. 'I just . . . I realize what I told you must have been a horrible shock.'

'About the Dancing Plague?' she said coolly. Her eyes were on one of the copper cauldrons, her fingers tightly gripped around her water glass.

He glanced around, out of habit noting the faces of the other diners. Two couples, one engrossed, one silently bored. A big family, preoccupied by their children. A pair of old men tucking in to an entrée of fois gras. A solitary businessman jabbing at a tablet as he ate. 'If you want to talk about it . . . About Gavriel . . .'

'Here?' she shot back. 'In front of these people?'

'No, of course not.' He felt, abruptly, that he'd lost his way with her.

'I ask myself,' she muttered eventually, 'if he's an assassin – what are you?'

She wanted time alone in the cathedral after lunch, and Arkell took the opportunity to call in on Danny. The young hacker had made himself at home in his boxlike hotel room, with towelling robes and room-service trays scattered either side of the unmade bed. The TV had been reconfigured to play music videos from YouTube, while an unrelated assortment of French rap was streaming on his laptop.

'Nothing much out there,' he said as Arkell muted the TV. 'I mean, like, plenty of José Cumeses floating around South America, but you want the one who flew into Cyprus and rented a car from Hertz on Thursday, right?' A brief, smug grin.

'Right.'

'Yeah, OK, so that one definitely isn't a real person. I can give you his date of birth, but there isn't a whole lot of point seeing as it's only been associated with the name since April. Señor Cumes of Uruguay has travelled twice in his short life: to Canada and Brazil. I've put all the dates and hotel bookings on Dropbox for you. Nothing else to offer, unless you've got another name.'

'Can you turn that down?'

'Sure.' Danny flipped the screen on his laptop, silencing the French rap.

'Do what you did with me: look for last-minute flight bookings from any Cyprus airport, leaving on Friday. Male, travelling alone. Cross-reference with flights into Strasbourg.'

'You got it. Are you being nicer to your pretty German?'

'I'll see you later, Danny.'

'European women like a bit of charm.'

He paused on the threshold. 'What do you know about European women?'

'So you do like her,' he grinned.

Arkell turned on his heel. 'At least let the maid make up your room.'

Concerned by the changing nature of US military interventionism in the twenty-first century, Madeleine Wraye had for a while taken a general interest in the Kentucky engineering and logistics group formerly known as American Metals and Bauxite. While stationed in Washington, she had heard occasional approving mentions of its three most prominent directors – David Atticus of South Carolina, Stephen Lambert of Kentucky and Hans-Rudolf Müller of Basel – although she never met them. Originally a mining business, AMB had quickly discovered it was more successful at digging stuff up than finding it in the first place. Consequently, the focus of the business shifted in the late twentieth century from exploration to the provision of engineering and logistics solutions to others. AMB grew to become a diversified services business, offering governments, mining firms and oil companies everything from construction, drilling, blasting and transport to process consultancy and security.

It is a fact of industrial life that many of the world's most valuable mining concessions are located in isolated and dangerous places. As a result AMB had developed, more or less unintentionally, a core competency in managing secure and efficient operations in challenging places. For decades, they had employed armed security guards; this branch of the AMB operation, once barely acknowledged, had gradually been professionalized with the help of veterans of several elite forces. Coupled with their ability to throw up prefabricated buildings and lay down instant infrastructure in hours rather than weeks, the disciplined but politically expendable security division had made AMB an obvious choice for US military contract work in Afghanistan and Iraq.

So lucrative, in the new world of privatized warfare, were those Pentagon contracts that AMB was soon deriving more than 65 per cent of its profits from conflict. In itself, that made the revelation that an SIS director with a great deal of influence in the Middle East was in the pay of AMB acutely disturbing. Joyce's compilation of reports, data and news articles, however, added to Wraye's concern. Following the USA's lead, a dozen countries had contracted AMB to take the load off their military machines – quietly and efficiently performing all the dull but essential transport, catering, construction and facilities management work that so many armed forces screw up. Most impressively of all, AMB had managed to ride out the Arab Spring, ending up with more clients than ever in the region. If that was in part the work of George Vine, he was worth every cent they paid him.

Had AMB profited from increased US belligerence after GRIEVANCE? Unquestionably. Might AMB have facilitated – even instigated – a terrorist attack to create a suitably destabilized international environment in which to develop this bounteous revenue stream? It was conceivable. Billions of dollars in new business made anything conceivable.

In the afternoon they took the tram to the European Quarter. Neither of them had any more expectation of finding Yadin there than in the town centre. But the English spy seemed to think it was important to keep looking and Klara, who had never been to Strasbourg before, was curious to see this French heart of EU power.

They were allowed into the elliptical courtyard of the Parliament's seemingly unfinished tower, but no further. Armed officers of the Police nationale were in evidence, reinforcing the Parliament's own extensive security measures ahead of the premiers' address. The riverside promenade around the great glass building was closed.

Architecturally, the Parliament left her cold. The white-and-black grid that paved the courtyard appealed more than the soaring pink piers and reflective glass. 'Maybe you should see what the stones have to tell you,' she suggested.

He took the mockery in good spirit. 'Imagine the things that have happened on this spot,' he said. 'Roman soldiers watching for the Germanic hordes; Suebi waiting until the Rhine froze and then pouring across it in their thousands. Attila slaughtering everyone, burning the town to the ground. Charles the Bald and Louis the German joining forces here against the Holy Roman Emperor. Citizens forced to go to war with their own bishop. The world's first newspaper, published here. Goethe at university, here. The Prussian army bombarding the city; mass evacuation in World War Two. Just imagine all the assignations, the celebrations, the terrors, the murders, the desperate schemes, the pacts, the heartbreaks, the moments of revelation that must have taken place on this one riverbank, long before the EU came along.'

Impossible not to be a little touched by his passion for those fragments of the past. 'Do you find it difficult to relate to normal people?' she asked.

He looked genuinely hurt, and before she knew what she was doing she had undermined her own taunt by smiling.

'You're cruel,' he told her, smiling back.

She liked that smile. She liked a lot of things about him.

Crossing the canal, they followed the tramlines to the European Court of Human Rights, where pitiful howls against corruption or injustice were scrawled on placards lashed to the railings. Across the street a small camp of petitioners had formed, tents hung with further declarations of persecution and abuse that made Klara seethe at the appalling hand life had dealt these people. In silence, they passed them by, taking refuge in the Parc de l'Orangerie, where a cheerier Sunday crowd of families, lovers and pensioners was strolling and picnicking amongst the fountains and colourful flower beds.

'What did you mean, you know how it feels?' she asked.

'What?'

'In the car, you said, "I know how it feels". You know how *what* feels?'

He was visibly uncomfortable. 'I suppose I meant losing someone you love.'

'I haven't lost someone,' she said sharply. 'I haven't lost anyone.'

He didn't answer.

'Gavriël is not who you say he is. I'm only here with you to prove that.'

'OK.'

'Who did you lose?'

He flinched at her tone. 'My wife.'

She hadn't expected that. He didn't seem the type. Too much of a loner.

'She left you, that's clear,' she said, deliberately brutal.

'She died.'

It was a beautiful summer's afternoon in a historic city beside one of the world's great rivers and, although the bitterness crumbled inside her, she couldn't find an adequate way to apologize.

The apartment was on the sixth floor of a drab, off-white tower block near the university. Most of the block's residents appeared to be students, and Joyce did not have to wait long for someone to hold open the communal door for him. Once inside, he quickly recognized that this was not an environment in which he could easily loiter. The corridors were plain and uncluttered. There were no cupboards to hide in, no open seating areas where he might act the older boyfriend waiting for his lover to return from a seminar. He would either have to approach the target directly or stand like a lemon by the elevators until some resident reported him to the police.

Edward Joyce faced the apartment door, fingers gripped around the moulded butt of the Sig Sauer in his pocket. The gun was a comfort for what it represented. Wraye had ordained that this particular weapon should be used to kill Gavriel Yadin. The fact that someone else's finger was meant to pull the trigger could surely be overlooked. Joyce had already impersonated TALON with ease – the nervous little Czech outside the station had handed over the Sig Sauer, ammunition and suppressor without question on hearing the requisite code phrase. He had played Wraye's golden boy once; he could do it again.

Joyce stared at the panelled door, thick with uneven white paint. He wondered how TALON would handle it. Probably just burst in and blast the place to hell.

He flexed his fingers.

No, he couldn't do it. Not with a Mossad killer on the other side of the door.

Joyce stepped back from the apartment. Along the corridor, the elevator opened. Flicking the safety lever on the Sig Sauer, he shifted his feet into a shooting position. But it was a girl who emerged from the elevator. She walked towards him with a slight frown. He smiled at her, gave a vague nod towards Yadin's door to explain himself. His thumb eased the safety lever back up.

She didn't smile back. Visibly on edge, she unlocked an apartment door. Two away from Yadin. It was an opportunity, Joyce sensed immediately, a chance to get out of this impossible position. He waited until she had the door open before striding forward and snapping his left hand over her mouth. They were inside the apartment with the door shut in less than two seconds.

'Anyone else here?' he whispered, pressing the Sig to her ear. She was rigid under his grip. Mute. The only noise was the muffled trickle of her urine on the linoleum floor. '*Est-ce qu'il y a quelqu'un ici?*' he tried again, hoping his shock at his own impulsiveness was coming across as an icy determination.

She shook her head.

'Stay completely silent,' he continued in classroom French. 'I won't hurt you.'

Releasing her, he saw the red mark around her mouth where he'd gripped her, and for a confused moment he thought of Sophie, and then of Maya and Jasmine waiting for their tree house. Grimacing, he used the Sig Sauer to wave her forward into the living space.

'*Il faut . . .*' He was struggling with the French. 'You speak English?'

She nodded blankly.

'I have to stay here a few hours,' he said, relieved in his confusion to be able to express himself properly. 'It's nothing to do with you. I just need the flat, understand?'

She wasn't going to speak at all, he sensed.

'Where's the bathroom?'

The question evoked a new look of terror. She was pretty,

except for a mole on her chin; tall, with very fine eyebrows and a trace of childhood still in her cheeks. Joyce realized that his stolen mission, supposed to be exhilarating, noble even, had turned sordid.

'So you can clean up,' he said impatiently. 'Where is it?'

She led the way. He kept the door open and the gun raised as she used a towel to dry her bare legs. The lower part of her skirt was soaked, as was one ballet pump. He wanted her to change, but worried she might freak out if he suggested taking any clothes off. There was a towel rail, serving as drying rack, firmly fixed to the wall. He touched the metal to check it was cold, then bound her wrists to it with a pair of tights.

'I'll get you a chair,' he offered, but when he came back with one of the two aluminium stools from the kitchen she wouldn't sit on it. 'Suit yourself,' he muttered. He filled a mug with water and made her drink. Then he stuffed a sock from the rail in her mouth, checked she was breathing through her nose, and closed the door on her.

BEIRUT, LEBANON – 15 June

Never a great Middle East enthusiast, Madeleine Wraye found it hard to think of Beirut as a place one could go for dinner. But she had always known that when it came time to confront George Vine it would have to happen on his turf. Aside from reluctant visits to London for funerals and directors' meetings, he had barely set foot outside the countries of the Eastern Mediterranean and the Persian Gulf in decades.

An old quip around Head Office: 'George is coming . . . Lock up the gold and summon the hookahs!' A joke with various shades of humour to it, although all were intended respectfully. Whatever his predilections and his weaknesses, the sheer weight of experience the veteran camel driver had accumulated during thirty-eight years in the field, and the remarkable network he had assembled, could not be matched in the Service. The CIA were assumed to have more agents in the region; few intelligence professionals believed they had better.

'Madeleine, how lovely.' He kissed her on both cheeks before pulling out her chair and seating her with immaculate care. He was dressed in a black shirt, open at the neck and hanging loose over soft white linen trousers. The clothes were Western but the effect was Arabian. She detected a hint of frankincense, a scent he had wisely never worn on his rare visits to London. Here, she supposed, he felt free to be his true self. 'How utterly lovely, after all this time.'

He was shaking his head, as if in wonder, as he fussed about her, making sure she was comfortable, offering a cushion against the hard teak of her chair, summoning the drinks waiter with an effortless gesture that spoke of many long evenings in this gilded place. 'Champagne? Pastis? Everything's on me tonight. You've been so kind to come all this way.'

She thought about resisting, demanding they split the bill if only to enjoy his insistence. He was a famously generous man. He sincerely loved treating people to whatever they would accept. How he paid for it all . . . well, now.

'Thank you, George. I'm just grateful it wasn't Isfahan. Spending the evening under a sheet isn't my idea of a good time.'

'We'll break you in slowly,' twinkled Vine. 'Lebanon today, Iran tomorrow. The important thing is to understand the poetry of the hijab. It isn't actually a restriction, you see. In fact it sets women free.'

Two tall-stemmed flutes of champagne were set before them. Vine had not touched anything but water before she arrived. Old-fashioned manners. Dumb, but hard to resist.

'Let's agree to disagree about Islamic dress codes, shall we?'

He beamed at her. 'You're absolutely right. Of course you are. Now tell me everything you've been doing.'

'Oh, life is very dull these days without you around, George.'

Reaching across the table to take her hand, he said effusively, 'I love you for saying that. Thank you. We know each other so well, don't we, Madeleine, and you know I know there's a splash of sardonicism in your words. But I also know there's warmth there, I do. Genuine warmth, and I thank you for it.'

He squeezed her hand a few seconds longer than most people would tolerate, but with George Vine it was somehow acceptable. He was everyone's favourite father figure, kind-hearted and well intentioned, and his quirks were there to be excused and enjoyed.

Meze arrived with the second glass of champagne. Vine insisted on talking her through each dish, as if you couldn't order all of them in the Edgware Road, without needing to come within a thousand miles of a Hezbollah citadel or a Palestinian refugee camp. 'Fatoush. The bread is intentionally stale. That lemony taste is in fact sumac. Persians add it to rice and Turks put it on lahmacun, but here they prefer it on salads. Did you know that Islamic doctors were using sumac as an effective medicine while Europe was still sunk in the Dark Ages? Extraordinarily advanced. Now this is kibbeh nayyeh. Don't worry, I know the kitchen. They're very responsible with raw meat . . .'

She let him meander on a few minutes longer, and then interjected: 'George, do you know why I'm here?'

'You mean it's not a social visit? I'm going to ask them to bring us a Cabernet from the Bekaa, if that suits? We can get jolly good Bordeaux here if you'd rather, but really it's a tiny bit insulting to an excellent domestic industry.'

'It's about time, don't you think, that we had a little chat about the circumstances of my exit from the Service.'

Vine looked pained. 'I know. I do know. I'd hoped, I suppose, that we could simply glide over it, but really I'm grateful to you for making me confront the past. It wasn't good. I have to be honest about that. We didn't give you the support you needed – that you deserved after decades of public service. It was wrong of us. You had a right to expect better from your colleagues and – I hope I can still say this – from your friends.'

'*Support*, George? Really?'

'I should have been there for you.'

'You're actually going to sit there and pretend you had nothing to do with it?'

'Dearest Madeleine, there are so many more pleasant things we could be talking about. Please . . . let me apologize profusely for all my past failings and then we can turn to the future. *Your* future. I want to hear everything you're up to.'

'Sorry, George, I want to stay in the past a little longer. And the person I really want to talk about is Dmitri Rostov.'

With a long, drawn-out sigh, George Vine said sadly, 'Must we spoil this lovely evening?'

'Then you do remember what you asked of me? The favour you flew all the way to Warsaw to request?'

'It's in the past, Madeleine.'

'A critical asset, you said. Held the key to Russian financial and logistical support of the Assad regime. The Service had lent him two hundred thousand dollars, you said, in case he needed to make a speedy departure from Syria. Now, extraordinarily, he was ready to return the money, only you couldn't be seen with him. Who could you trust to take charge of all that cash on your behalf? Who could always be relied upon in a sensitive East European operation?'

He spread his hands in boundless apology. 'Tell me what I can do to make amends.'

'There was no such person, was there, George? You might think I should have recognized Gregor Uhlig from Counter-Terrorism's most wanted list. Strangely, though – and I did manage to look back through my Porthos messages before my access was terminated – Uhlig's profile was missing from all the C-T bulletins sent to me. So what can I conclude? An unholy alliance between Tony Watchman, Gregor Uhlig and George Vine to implicate me in a fictional pay-off that I would be unable to disprove. Is that really what you've sunk to?'

There was silence for a long time. When at last he spoke, it was with a deep and troubled regret. 'I do so hate that we had to do that to you.'

'Had to!'

'You'd made it very clear that in the event you should find yourself in the Chief's seat, the services of a decrepit old fellow like me would no longer be required.'

'Age had nothing to do with it. The plethora of little deals you have across the region generating regular payments into your Singaporean bank accounts were, if you remember, of more immediate concern to me.'

'And you were quite right, quite right,' he said vigorously. 'I'm not proud of myself. And I dare say if Tony hadn't felt he might rather like the top job himself, and hadn't come to me with a ready-made plan, I probably would have laboured on in my little sandy burrow for as long as I could, and then cheered heartily from the stocks as you purged the Augean stables. I wish I had, I really do. I feel wretched.'

'As wretched as you felt when Rupert Ellington died?'

'I don't follow.'

Was there something there? It was hard to tell in the dappled light from the candelabra. And the alcohol had probably dulled both her perceptions and his reactions.

'You do remember Ellington?'

Loud giggles from a bling-laden group of kohl-eyed women at the next table. An unhelpful distraction.

'I certainly do. A good man. A very good man. We were much the poorer for his loss. Look, I hope you've left some room. We've got a whole leg of lamb coming, slow-roasted with cinnamon, pine nuts and apricots.'

'I think I've lost my appetite.'

'Some wine, then.' Vine lifted the bottle, but her glass was still half full.

'Of those many deals across the region, there's one in particular I want to ask you about.'

'Madeleine, anything I can help you with, just say the word, but do please tread softly. You never know who's listening in this place.'

'I bet you do, George. I bet you've got this place and a hundred others wired up just the way you want it.'

'If only I had your talents in that area,' he answered wistfully. 'I'm a dinosaur who knows a few useful people, that's all.'

'People like AMB.'

'Now that really is a name we should avoid mentioning again. After Iraq and Syria, they aren't at all popular with certain gentlemen in this town.'

'You're on good terms with them, though. Sixty thousand dollars last year and the year before. Two hundred and ninety thousand this year. Why the sharp increase? How have you suddenly become more valuable to the good folks in Louisville?'

Vine gave up trying to distract her with the wine bottle. 'Goodness, how can you know that?' He sat back dolefully. 'Now I'm embarrassed.'

'*Now* you're embarrassed?'

'What can I say? It's a win–win intelligence-sharing arrangement with absolutely no downside for Her Majesty's Government. I have always been careful not to indebt myself to any party to a degree that would give them leverage over me, and to every transaction I always apply the simple test: does this hurt Britain or mankind? In this case, as in every other I have acted upon, I can assure you there is no harm.'

'George.' She leaned forward. 'What have you done for AMB this year that's worth so much more?'

He made a vague gesture. 'They have interests . . .'

'Interests that would make it worth turning a blind eye to a terror attack?'

He was staring at her in bafflement. 'You've lost me.'

'How long have you been taking money from AMB? Does it go back, say, more than ten years?'

'Do you mind if I let that one go unanswered? You seem to have quite enough upsetting facts at your fingertips without my adding to the pile.'

'You need to tell me why AMB paid you over a quarter of a million dollars this year.'

'Well, you see, I'm not sure I agree with you about that. It may not be completely legitimate in your eyes, and I do understand that, but nevertheless it is a private arrangement and I would be breaking my word to the aforesaid organization if I were to disclose the details.'

'How about I disclose the details to the Chief?'

His brow wrinkled extravagantly. 'I wish you wouldn't. And you know, I trust you not to. I don't think it would make any difference, but it would put the Chief in a difficult position and I wouldn't wish to do that to him.'

'That's it?' she marvelled. 'You're not even going to try and defend these payments?'

He smiled sadly. 'You know what I am, Madeleine. It hurts me to think how you must judge me, but I am too old to change my spots now. It seems to me I still perform some useful function for the old country, even if I can barely recognize it these days. When my failings start to outweigh my contribution, then I shall go gently into whatever dark night is my just deserts. Heavens, what an appalling metaphorical mess that sentence was.'

'Shall I tell you who killed Rupert Ellington?'

His fatalistic smile evaporated. A reaction, certainly, but what kind of reaction?

'I confirmed it yesterday. Your friend, Gavriel Yadin. He also killed Simon Arkell. Remember him?'

'Yadin? I don't know the name.'

The photograph was on the table before he'd finished the sentence. Vine studied it resignedly.

'Not awfully flattering of me. Bahrain. The Mabahith took it, I presume?'

'AMB pay you over a quarter of a million dollars four days before you meet with a man who's murdered two SIS officers. George, what's going on?'

He looked away from the photograph. 'You've clearly made up your mind that there's some connection between this man and my friends in Louisville. Is there any point my saying that I believe him to be a private wealth manager by the name of Carlos Pérez? The information he was able to provide on a certain Qatari gentleman proved both accurate and rather useful. However, if you tell me that Rupert Ellington was murdered and that this gentleman is a killer—'

'A former Kidon assassin, to be precise.'

'Well, then . . .' He seemed genuinely at a loss. 'Well . . . I must say . . . ah, there's the lamb.'

'How did you come to meet him, this "Pérez"?'

'Do please have some before it gets cold.'

'Did he approach you? Did an agent introduce him?'

'Look at the way it just falls off the bone. Marvellous!'

'George, you need to answer my questions.'

'Well, yes, but . . . as it happens I'm not sure that will do me much good.' He used his napkin to remove a spot of grease from his shirt cuff. 'I'm beginning to think I've been played for a fool, although the motive eludes me. You've presented me with such startling facts – none of which I'm in a position to dispute just now – that I fear saying anything further on the subject will only add to my foolishness. Forgive me, Madeleine, I really must insist we talk of pleasanter things.'

Even George Vine was capable of steel, and Wraye saw it now in his face. He would not be answering any more questions. There was a 23:45 Alitalia flight to Rome that would allow her to connect with the early-morning flight to Strasbourg. The lamb smelt delicious. She rose and kissed George Vine on the cheek. 'Thank you for dinner,' she said. 'Do spend that AMB money wisely.'

STRASBOURG, FRANCE – 15 June

Joyce had been staring through the peephole for ninety-three minutes before anything moved in the corridor. His eyes, alternating against the fisheye lens, were dry and scratchy. His neck hurt. The knuckles he'd skinned on the doomed tree house were throbbing. The door felt greasy against his cheekbone. None of it mattered. In his right hand was the Sig Sauer, loaded and fitted with the suppressor, safety off. In his left was the door handle. He had only to throw open the door and fire the shot and he would go down in history as the man who eliminated Mossad's rogue assassin.

He would happily wait an eternity for that.

A door opened. He couldn't tell which one. Between the girl's apartment and the end of the corridor were just four more doors. If someone walked past on the way to the elevator, there was a one in four chance that –

The figure was unmistakably Yadin: fast-moving, erect, sepulchral; a dark figure in colour and manner. The shock of seeing him so close, so abruptly, momentarily confused Joyce. His mind flew inexplicably to the girl in the bathroom. Was she calm? Was she trying to escape? Could she identify Joyce to the police? Yadin was already past his field of view, footsteps nearly at the elevators, and still he couldn't move. It's too late, Joyce told himself, banishing the image of the bound girl. He's pressed the button. The elevator doors will open. Someone inside might witness the kill.

As he wavered, the elevator pinged and he knew Yadin was gone.

Raging at himself, Joyce moved to the windows and looked down on the small square in front of the apartment block. A scattering of couples sat sprawled on benches in the late-evening sunshine. Yadin emerged and walked quickly past them all. Joyce watched him disappear behind the neighbouring block, heading in the direction of the trams on Avenue du Général de Gaulle. Dejected, he went to check on the girl.

She was sitting, now, her arms twisted uncomfortably upwards. What was her name? It was too late to ask. 'Do you want some water?' When she shook her head, he said, 'I have to use the toilet. Sorry.'

He felt intensely unsettled in her presence, and he left the bathroom as quickly as he could. Returning to the window, he was stunned to see the unmistakable figure of Yadin walking back across the square. Had he forgotten something? No – a plastic carrier bag swung from his left hand. He'd been shopping, Christ! Popped out to the grocer's. Joyce started laughing. The man was human after all. He needed to eat. Needed to shit. And he could be killed just like anyone else.

The surge of adrenalin that overtook Joyce was exquisite. He'd never felt so alive, so powerful. A reliable weapon and the element of surprise: that was all you needed against a man carrying a plastic shopping bag. Walking out into the corridor, he felt invincible. Brazen. He didn't bother to hide the gun. There was no one around. Positioning himself directly in front of the elevators, he waited for the lights to reveal which one would give up his prey. As the digits over the left elevator climbed towards 6, he raised the Sig Sauer, eased down the safety and stared along the line of the suppressor at the steel door.

Yadin blinked at him, and Joyce's heart leapt to see the genuine surprise in that seasoned face.

'Step out. Hands clear of your body.'

Yadin walked forward, and Joyce moved with him, swivelling his firing stance like a god. The elevator doors closed.

'You are Gavriel Yadin?'

The man sighed. 'You don't want to do it here. Make a big mess in the hall.'

Joyce used his chin – not his weapon – to gesture down the corridor. The other man turned, arms well away from his sides. At the apartment door he said, 'I have to take out the key.'

'Left hand, very slowly,' commanded Joyce. He was ready for anything. The slightest misstep, a shudder of unsanctioned movement, and he would fire. He almost wanted it to happen, proof that he could triumph in the heat of the battle rather than cold blood.

But Yadin showed no sign of wanting to test his opponent's nerve. He unlocked the door – slowly, cautiously, compliant to a fault.

Joyce followed him inside.

She had been silent for nearly two hours. Simon Arkell could not think what had triggered the mood swing. In the European Quarter they had come close to an understanding. He had felt something in her, in himself, in the federal air. Then it was gone again, suppressed behind a north German mask. She had followed him back to the pension, lost in her own unknowable world, unresponsive to his offers of food or television. She had sat on the bed and stared out of the window, although there was nothing to see but the guttering and roof tiles of the neighbouring building.

He had left her to her thoughts and gone down to reception to check again for messages. Still nothing. What the hell was taking Madeleine's analyst so long? Without a weapon and Yadin's address he felt caged, useless. He'd called Danny then: five last-minute flight bookings from Cyprus on Friday, three of them single men; none of the names had shown up in Strasbourg. With no leads, Arkell had returned to the room and buried himself in a weighty history of Strasbourg's medieval period.

He had been lost in the past for some time when Klara finally spoke. 'It's true, isn't it?'

Looking up, he saw tears on her cheeks. How long had she been crying? He understood the question then. Quietly, he said, 'I'm sorry.'

She seemed to hover between two or three courses of action. 'I'm going out,' she decided. Climbing off the bed, she began rummaging through her bag.

'Shall we get some dinner?'

'I'm going to get drunk.' Out came a sequinned crimson T-shirt, a pair of white jeans.

He hesitated. 'What are you doing?'

'Having fun. Isn't that what single people do?' Irritably, she brushed away a fresh tear. 'My God, I've been sensible and faithful long enough.'

'Klara, this is not a good idea.'

'It wasn't a very fucking good idea to go out with him in the beginning, was it?' She unbuttoned her top, exposing a plain white bra. 'Don't come to me for good ideas.'

Arkell turned away as she unzipped her skirt. 'I can't let you go out on your own.'

'Do what you want. I'm going to find a bar with men who don't kill people for a living.'

If not this place, then some other. It could have been a Cypriot alleyway. It could have been a public toilet in Nizhny Novgorod. A student apartment in Strasbourg was as good a place as any. Gavriel Yadin was not a sentimental man. He had been raised by a woman who did not value sentiment, in a country that could not afford it. What did it matter where he was killed?

At least Death had found him planting his cabbages, as Montaigne would say. *Cum moriar, medium solvar et inter opus.*

In fact, Yadin was looking forward to death. He was not religious, had not glanced at the Tanakh since scripture class. He did not believe in an afterlife. Yet he felt there might be something, a serenity, a sense of release that the mind might slip into even as the body decayed and disintegrated. He wasn't confident that such a feeling might last longer than the time it took for the neural pathways to shut down, but he harboured a hopeful belief that a memory of that feeling might stretch somehow into eternity – that a faint essence of what had once been Gavriel Yadin might persist.

That the body left behind should fall in an Alsatian tower block and then lie in chilly limbo in a French morgue before ending up, an embarrassment, in some little-visited Tel Aviv cemetery was an outcome that did not trouble him at all. He was, more or less, ready.

Letting the shopping bag drop, he turned and faced the man who would kill him. 'All right,' he said quietly. It occurred to him, his only regret, that no one would now eat the fresh asparagus in the shopping bag. He raised his hands to the back of his head, squarely presenting his chest for a clean shot.

The British agent – perhaps that was another slight regret – eyed him suspiciously, and then with elation. It was not blatant, but with the door closed behind him the man was finally starting to relax into his victory. Yadin knew very well what a prize he represented. This man, this competent but characterless cog in a tired imperialist machine, would reap great reputation from killing the Mossad's rogue combatant. This one act would make his career. Yadin could picture him twenty years from now, the corner office and the double chin, a legend to the young intelligence officers whom he carelessly sent out into the field while he lunched with politicians and business leaders in search of underhand advantage.

Well, no matter. It made no difference whose finger pulled the trigger. The outcome would be the same.

But the man did not shoot.

He kept the Sig steady, aimed, left hand cupped under the right. He maintained his firing stance, right foot well back, the toe turned outwards. But he did not act.

Yadin felt the first splinters of doubt lodge in the tranquillity of his fatalism. He waited, watching a range of emotions play out on the other man's face – fascination, incredulity, exultation. He did not speak because there was nothing to say – should be nothing to say.

And yet, appallingly, the British agent started talking.

'So how were you going to do it?' he asked. 'Was it Mayhew or Andrade? They're both in Strasbourg. Which one was the target?'

To Yadin, the realization that this man was unworthy came in an instant. Such questioning was not useful interrogation; it was self-indulgent curiosity. He sighed inaudibly. It was impossible. He could not continue to pretend: it made every difference whose finger pulled the trigger. This manifest unprofessionalism was simply unacceptable.

'It was Andrade,' he said, to buy time while his mind switched from resignation to stratagem.

'When? At the plenary?'

Yadin shook his head. 'Impossible. The security around the Parliament will be impenetrable.' To the shaking of his head, he risked adding a rotating gesture with one arm – a representation of the police-ringed Chamber, perhaps: something to get his opponent used to a little movement.

'Then where? His hotel?'

This time he shook his head vigorously. 'It has to be public. That is the mission. Public destruction of the drug liberalizers. Restaurant Les Trois Rois.'

Surely now, thought Yadin, he has to ask the important questions. It was irrelevant how the assassin would have performed his task if the assassin was dead. The essential point was why, and on whose orders. Yet still the British agent failed to ask these things. It was as if he was star-struck, so blinded by the Kidon legend that all he could think of was method.

'How?' It would be laughable if the man wasn't holding a Sig. 'How were you going to do it?'

Yadin held his stare. He lowered his arms. 'The same way I have killed you,' he said softly.

A flicker of fear appeared momentarily, but the man summoned up a scornful smile. '*You* kill *me*?'

'Us both.' Yadin smiled back. He did not often smile, but it seemed tactically useful here. 'It is called cyclohexyl methylphosphonofluoridate. An organophosphate, a thousand times more toxic than cyanide. It is in the air we are breathing. Can you taste it? Like . . . sweet dew. You may know it as cyclosarin.'

'Bullshit,' said the man, but the smile was gone.

'I think you are aware of my visit to Cyprus? Kolatch is clever. Cyclosarin does not evaporate easily, but Kolatch built a pressurized capsule for this mission. It bursts on impact: a tiny aerosol explosion that spreads the toxin throughout a room. It is in our lungs. If you don't shoot me, we will suffer together vomiting and convulsions before full respiratory failure.' He shrugged. 'I hope you will shoot me.'

The terror that overcame the British agent was a source of simple professional satisfaction to Yadin. He did not often have to talk this much. He rarely needed to convince by power of speech. That he could do it well in English was pleasing.

'W-Where is it?'

That was the bait, swallowed whole. He only had to point. And as the Englishman glanced down at the floor, an instinctive and calamitous response, Yadin used the same arm to hammer a fist into the barrel of the Sig, knocking the gun sideways as his body pivoted and his foot crunched into his opponent's knee.

He followed the roundhouse kick with a total Krav Maga offensive. The English agent was younger, had been professionally trained, but it was already clear he was not proficient in field skills. Although he managed to throw a few punches while he groped for his weapon, this was not his true game.

It was over in less than a minute.

This time she walked well ahead of him, pointedly ignoring his attempts to soothe and settle her. At the bar in Rue des Tonneliers she drank steadily, accepting shots from strangers, buying drinks for dark-eyed students. Arkell nursed a single beer, watching her disintegration with feelings that he acknowledged went well beyond professional concern. When the music was ramped up and an impromptu dance floor established in a cramped corner of the bar, she turned to him with a brittle smile and said, 'So let's dance!' Her full lips were glistening; beneath those two confident front teeth her rounded chin trembled a little; one eye, heavy with shadow, was drawn a little wider, further accentuating the off-centre gaze.

He put down the beer. 'It's late. We should get back.'

'It's not even dark out there!'

She swivelled away and seized the wrist of one of the dark-eyed students, a boy in a paisley waistcoat and grubby houndstooth trousers. He followed her willingly. The music was trashy German pop, made worse by a substandard sound system. Klara's movements were a little ragged from the booze, but in tight white jeans, sequinned T-shirt and tilted fedora she made an undeniably appealing figure on the dance floor. She laid her forearms on the shoulders of her partner and teased his groin with occasional bumps from her own. Then, to the surprise of the student as much as those watching, she leaned in close and put her tongue in his mouth.

Arkell pulled her away.

'Jealous?' she laughed. She was still dancing, her arm rhythmically jerking in his grip.

'This is not going to help you get over Gavriel.'

'Stop treating me like a fucking invalid!' She wrenched free of him. 'If you want to play, let's play. Otherwise, go home!'

He looked around the ring of students that had formed – at the insolent grins of boys almost half his age. Philosophers, musicians, botanists with so much to learn. He saw her through their eyes: the hot older woman with lips tender red and eyes hungry as theirs.

'I'm staying.'

'OK, Englishman. Let's do it!'

She took his hands in hers and drew him close. The heat of her was engulfing. He'd forgotten what it could feel like. There had been little reason to dance in the last nine years. Little opportunity – at least, that he had chosen to take – to move in melding unison with a lithe and tempting body. She was beautiful. Her breath was a wild thing on his cheek. The urge to taste her was profoundly disturbing.

'We should go,' he muttered hoarsely, and this time she complied without a murmur, interweaving her fingers in his and slipping in his wake through the forgotten students.

Outside on the street, she tried to kiss him.

Awkwardly, he said, 'I'm not right for you.'

'God, I'm not asking you to marry me!' Her face darkened.

He didn't answer. Her fingers were still caught up in his, and he closed his hand around hers and dragged her away from the bar.

Klara cleaned her teeth, removed her make-up and undressed in furious silence. He stepped into the bathroom while she climbed naked into bed, and when he came out the light was off and the thin summer quilt was drawn tight around her. He collected the spare pillow and blanket and sat on the carpet, his back against the door. Sleep was only a distant possibility.

His mind had roamed to a dozen places and ages before she spoke. Her words, in the darkness, took on a disembodied character. 'I have to tell you why I can't help you any more.'

'You'll feel better tomorrow. This evening doesn't matter.'

'It's not about this evening.' After a long pause she said, 'If this story you told me is true then I can't any longer see Gavriel. Not as my lover.' Her voice was rigid. Void of warmth. 'But I understand now I have to choose my side. I'm not just some stupid girlfriend, you know. I have values. I have a sense of responsibility.'

'Klara, what's this about?' He considered turning on the light, but feared it might make her retreat into her shell once more.

'You tell me Gavriel is fighting against the people who want to legalize drugs, yes? And you are fighting for them.'

'I said he's trying to murder three politicians.'

She seemed to ignore that. 'My brother died with an overdose. Did you know that? When you came sniffing around my apartment dressed as a priest, had you already spied at my past and found that, yes, I in fact have lost someone I loved?'

He stared into the darkness. 'I had no idea.'

'He was a selfish bastard sometimes, but very talented. I loved him, like anyone is going to love an older brother who can do anything. He played the saxophone . . . *Ach*, it doesn't matter. He had a good job in a bank, buying and selling companies. Then someone at work got him into coke. He had difficulty to calm down after a big night in the clubs so he smoked spliffs. That didn't work so he tried stronger stuff. Skunk. I didn't see him for three months. He showed up at my university, a mess: he had quit his job, given up his apartment. He needed a place to stay, crashed with me, did a lot of coke. It made him frantic – he scared me. I caught him smoking crack. He was changed: no more lightness, no more generosity. Just suspicion and resentment. One time he passed out on my bed and shat himself. I can still smell it. He stole my money and denied it. When I accused him, he punished me by ripping up my study notes. He left without telling me.

'We searched for almost one year. The police found him dead in a . . . you say "squat house"? He was living with two Turkish street cleaners and two Russian "artists" who were cheating welfare. They hid his body in a cupboard, inside a plastic sack to stop the stench. One of the Russians was arrested for fraud and the house was searched. This is how they found him. My brother was so stupid, but I don't blame him. I don't blame the squatters. I don't blame his job or the people he worked with. I blame the drugs. End of story. I'm not going to continue a relationship with a man who kills people for his job. But Gavriel is trying to stop the arseholes who want to increase the use of drugs – and you are trying to help them. It's not difficult to choose between you.'

The realization that something had gone badly wrong in Europe struck Madeleine Wraye as she was approaching Beirut Rafic Hariri international airport in a battered taxi. She had been unable to reach Joyce on his mobile before or after the dinner with George Vine. She tried his home number, listening numbly as Sophie Joyce cheerfully announced, 'He's had to go abroad for work. I'm afraid I'm not allowed to say where.'

She called Arkell immediately. 'Hang on,' he answered. The sound of a door opening and closing. 'Klara's just gone to sleep. She's not in a great way. Don't want to wake her up.'

'Is everything all right?' she began, stalling her own bad news.

'We'll get there. What about your end? I haven't heard from

your analyst yet about Yadin's whereabouts. Time's running out.'

'I think he may be in Strasbourg.'

As she stepped into the cool of the terminal building, Wraye heard the silence from France as loud as colliding ships.

Eventually: 'This guy have a name?'

'Joyce. Edward Joyce.'

'He's got Yadin's location?'

'I believe so.'

'And he's bringing it to me?'

Wraye sighed. She was going to have to apologize for someone who worked for her, and she hated that. 'Probably not.'

Arkell was catching up fast, but he wanted it spelt out. 'He thinks he's going to do this himself?' The incredulity in his tone was, she had to admit, entirely justified.

'Look, Simon, I'm sorry. Joyce is a fuckwit. But he's my fuckwit. Whatever trouble he's got himself into—'

'Get me the address,' interrupted Arkell. 'I'll find another weapon.'

Edward Joyce came round to find blood in his left eye. He knew it was blood because his distorted vision was pale red. His forehead felt wet. The blood was trickling from somewhere near his hairline. Beyond that, he couldn't analyse any further. Both his hands were tied behind his back.

He tried shifting position. Nothing moved. Whatever he was tied to was unequivocally solid and stationary.

Yadin's face loomed red and unfocused before him. 'There are things you need to tell me,' he murmured. 'I'm sorry. There will be some pain now.'

There was already pain. A throbbing in Joyce's skull was complemented by aches in his stomach and face. But the agonizing assault that came out of nowhere at that moment obliterated those more familiar impressions. He had never felt anything like this. Despite all the training, the grim accounts from those few officers who'd seen real torture, he hadn't imagined anything close to this. He didn't even know what it was that Yadin had done to him. He didn't care. As he screamed, all that he could think was: *Stop!*

There was something in front of his face. Held between finger and thumb, what exactly it was Joyce couldn't tell. It was red, but then everything was red. Displayed for a second longer, it dropped out of sight. Joyce suspected the thing, the unidentified object, had once been a part of him, but he was too groggy and too swamped by the aftershocks of pain to work out which part.

'Are there more like you in the building or outside?'

Shaking his head sparked a debilitating nausea in Joyce. It was as if he'd tripped a switch, waking the entire length of his intestine, turning it into a writhing serpent of bile. Only when he tried opening his mouth to throw up did he realize it was already open and stuffed with wadded material. A momentary image of the girl in the nearby apartment came to him. Still bound, still gagged. She might be stuck there for days now.

It was his first acknowledgement that he was not going to leave the apartment alive.

Had he vomited? He was confused. It seemed he hadn't. From a distance, he heard Yadin say, 'We'll make sure of that', and thought he was talking about the same thing. Then the murderous pain struck again. More acute, more drawn out.

Where was it coming from? His whole body was rigid, charged. The scream that sounded so muffled to his ears echoed alarm-loud through his brain. He couldn't work out where the damage was, couldn't make himself care. *Stop. Just stop.*

His eyes were tightly closed. If there was another gory trophy Joyce did not want to see it. A vision of Sophie, smiling that concerned, loving smile she always wore when she knew something was wrong. 'Again,' she said. 'Is there anyone with you? In this building or outside?' Her fingers tugged the wad from his paralysed mouth. She seemed genuinely anxious to hear the answer.

'No,' he rasped. 'It's just me.'

It made her happy, that answer. He could see now that she was perched on the edge of the tree house. His tree house. Perfectly level, every baton screwed in place, the wood polished and shining in the sunlight. Maya was balanced on a window sill, laughing to herself. Jasmine was storming up the ladder and down the slide, up the ladder and down the slide, a perpetual cycle. *Look at me! Daddy, look at me!*

'You're not the one who followed me in Cyprus.' There was a frown in Sophie's voice, despite the lovely smile. 'Are you?'

'No,' he freely admitted.

Was he smiling? He felt like he was smiling. A quick double slap on his face made him open his eyes.

Yadin was gazing tiredly at him, a kitchen knife liberally bloodied in his right hand.

'I have a family,' said Joyce. The chill of awakening consciousness spread through his veins. It seemed to stop his heart. 'I have two beautiful daughters. Five and three.' There were tears running down his cheeks, he realized, and for once in his life he didn't feel ashamed. 'She's called . . . They're called . . . M – . . . Jasmine and Maya.'

'Good,' said Yadin. 'That's good.' He leaned forward and patted Joyce's wet cheek with the red blade of the knife. 'Let's talk about the man in Cyprus.'

At 1.25 a.m., Avenue du Général de Gaulle was empty, and the apartment blocks to the east of it mostly dark. Arkell knew better than to make assumptions about the sleeping patterns of residents near a university, but as he crossed the square in front of Yadin's tower block he seemed entirely alone in the city. The night was always a calming time for him, when the complexity of urban life fell away and he felt again the silent crunch of African sand beneath his boots.

Instead of a Legion rifle, he held a Colt Defender 9mm concealed inside a folded jacket. Carlo had not been able to source a weapon in Strasbourg, and Arkell had had to drive across the Rhine to meet a man from Stuttgart halfway. The Colt was all the guy had. If Arkell needed to use it, at this time of night, the noise would be heard across half the city.

So. A swift exit would be called for. He adjusted the hood of his sweatshirt against the CCTV cameras around the tower block entrance. The lock on the toughened glass door was electronically controlled and protected by a wide lip of steel. No subtle way in. He used the butt of the gun to crack the lower glass pane and his jacket-wrapped fist to punch out the fragments. No alarm, at least none audible. Nevertheless, the CCTV might be monitored. Mentally, he started a stopwatch.

Arkell took the fire stairs, preferring the solid certainty of six flights to an elevator that might be under remote security control. He took three deep breaths at the top to steady his right arm. The jacket he let fall in the stairwell, holding open the door. You never knew what might matter. An apartment door was slightly ajar. Dark inside. Not the right one. He took the torch from his pocket – cheap plastic, the best on offer at the petrol station near the border. Yadin's door was locked, a standard nightlatch which Arkell picked in an instant. Easing the door open, he padded silently inside.

He could smell blood straight away. An immediately familiar stench that he hadn't encountered in years. Closing the door behind him, nudging the latch with the slightest metallic whisper back into place, he switched on the torch.

The living room was empty, the kitchen area clean and apparently unused. One bathroom and two bedrooms made up the rest of the apartment. Arkell knew with certainty that the smell of blood came from the furthest bedroom. Nevertheless he checked the other rooms first, taking care to shine the torch beam into every corner and behind each door. Then he walked into the second bedroom and threw on the lights.

Nobody.

Arkell lowered the Colt, made the weapon safe and slipped it into his pocket. It was clear Yadin was no longer present. Nor was Joyce, in any meaningful sense. The evidence of his prolonged agony was laid out in a neat row on the nightstand, bloodied pink, oddly artificial-looking. Cause of death was equally unsubtle. His throat had been slit, ear to ear.

Always deliberate.

Arkell wondered if this was a message aimed at him personally. The nightstand made it plain that Yadin now knew everything Joyce had known about his mission. About him. What *had* Joyce known? Wraye would never have shared his real identity. But Joyce would have been able to describe Arkell's appearance, detail some of his attributes and methods. He would have revealed how much they knew and did not know about Yadin and the people who had commissioned him. And he would have told Yadin about Klara.

Only then did Arkell remember the one thing that should have occurred to him as soon as Wraye rang: Joyce knew his address in Strasbourg.

He called Klara's mobile. It was switched off. He tried the pension, but there was no answer. Stopping only to check Joyce's pockets, he rushed out of the apartment, wiping the door handle and lock clean as he went. In the corridor, he paused. That other apartment, door still slightly ajar in the middle of the night . . .

He went in fast, gun extended, a blitz search that brought him to the dark bathroom and the collapsed girl in under ten seconds. Untying her, he filled the mug with water and allowed her two sips before asking roughly in French, 'The man who did this . . . blond or dark?'

'Blond,' she rasped.

Arkell was out of the building and driving fast long before she was ready to call the police.

Gavriel Yadin stalked through the black Strasbourg night, his few items of clothing, his equipment, and the two packages from Kolatch in a backpack loosely slung over one shoulder. The

British agent's gun went in the canal. His passport, phone and wallet would be mailed in the morning to a domestic address in north London in case they were of interest to Kartouche.

When Yadin came to the cathedral, he paused a while and rested his forehead against the Vosges sandstone. He wished he could feel God's presence, that God might come briefly into existence to make sense of all this. Tonight he had welcomed Death. The subsequent killing had made far less impression on his soul than that sense of his own ending. He had killed many times, had feared death on occasion, but that was the first time he had looked into his own grave with something bordering on relief. And it had made him stronger.

Let's take the strangeness out of death. Let's get used to it. To practise death is to practise freedom.

Pressing his hand against the smooth stone, he pushed himself abruptly away from the Christian wall. The knuckles were bruised. He allowed himself two painful minutes to think about Klara Richter, then put her from his mind. Professional concerns first; he would deal with the private outrage later. Priorities. He needed sleep. To check into a Strasbourg hotel now would be to lay a blazing trail for the authorities. How hard would it be to run a search of single men who had taken a room without a reservation in the hours following a murder? In such cases, when there was a clear operational need, Yadin felt no compunction for the actions that must follow.

Selecting a modest apartment above a bakery in Rue des Juifs, he forced the lock on the street entrance, bolted the door behind him, went upstairs and shot the young couple as they slept. His suppressed HK made only four curt cracks in the silence of the bedroom. Yadin took the one pillow that was still white and went to sleep on the couch next door.

Simon Arkell bounded up the stairs of the pension with no thought for the sleeping guests. The door to the room was half open. He felt a sickening sense of reprise. Dark inside. He stopped on the threshold, convinced she was already dead, shocked at the paralysing effect of that thought.

He barely knew her. Basic compassion and professional concern aside, what the hell did it matter?

She was dead, and Yadin was poised to shoot him the moment he walked in.

He threw on the lights. Klara was alone, crumpled on the end of the bed in a long grey T-shirt, clutching a pillow to her chest. She dropped her face immediately. A sob, muffled. There was a livid red weal on her arm.

Arkell locked the door and checked the bathroom. He swept his gaze across the floor, the wardrobe, the light fitting, the TV. A Kidon combatant had been here. Anything was possible.

Finding nothing, he laid the Colt on the desk and sat beside her. 'What did he do?' he asked softly.

The top of the pillow was wet with her tears. 'He's right to be angry,' she whispered.

'What did he do, Klara?'

She raised her head to stare thunderously at him. 'He came here and found me sleeping in another man's bed.'

It was almost an accusation, but Arkell barely heard the tone. He was looking at her jaw, her cut lip, her swollen eye. 'Oh,

Christ,' he murmured. He raised a hand to the bruises but she jerked away from him. 'Klara, I'm so sorry.'

'Why? This has nothing to do with you.'

'It's my fault. I put you in danger. He could have killed you.'

She seemed uncertain. Without a hat, she looked naked, young, especially vulnerable. 'He would never hurt me.'

'Look what he just did to you!'

'It's nothing,' she said, getting up and walking to the bathroom.

Arkell followed her. She was washing her face. He passed her a towel and watched her wince as she touched it to her jaw. Her off-centre gaze, reflected back at her in the mirror, was lifeless.

'Klara, he could have blinded you, broken your jaw.'

She shook her head in dismissal. 'You've never been in love, have you? You make mystical connections with dancing women five hundred years ago, but you've never grown up enough to feel anything real.'

Arkell marched out of the bathroom. He began throwing clothes into her bag. 'Get dressed. We're leaving in five minutes.'

When Klara reappeared, she said, 'I'm going to bed.'

'He's coming back. If not for you then definitely for me. We have to find another hotel.'

'He's not coming back,' she sighed, climbing into bed. 'And he's not interested in you.'

'He knows I'm after him now.'

'He doesn't blame you. He doesn't . . . resent. He said something about a ditch in Cyprus. I didn't really understand. He said a wolf has to be a wolf.'

Still holding her bag, Simon Arkell gazed down at her sprawled body. The shape it formed of the thin summer quilt was dune-like, the hard edges of her hip and knees softened into flowing curves that might have been carved by the wind. Her arm was exposed, the red welt glowing against the white linen. 'Klara, get up.'

'You leave if you're afraid.'

'I'm not going to let him hurt you again. Get up.'

She didn't reply.

'Klara . . .'

'Turn out the light, will you?'

He hauled her to her feet. Her cry was more startled than angry.

'Get dressed.'

'Fuck you. Let go of me!' She struggled in his grip, then abruptly gave way. 'God, oh God, oh *God* . . .'

She was shaking violently, he realized. 'I'm sorry,' he began, releasing her, but now Klara's arms locked around his back.

'I'm frightened,' she whispered. 'I'm frightened for him. What you'll do to him.' She hesitated. 'I'm frightened *of* him.' Looking up, she added, 'I'm frightened of *you*.'

'You don't need to be frightened of me.'

'When you came crashing in here with a gun . . .'

'Klara, I'm not going to let anything happen to you.'

Her off-centre stare briefly straightened into a perfectly symmetrical flash of hope. A last shudder ran through her. He took hold of her arms to steady the nervous, trembling energy. This time, when she quaveringly went up on tiptoe, he kissed her.

She dropped down fast, as if shocked by the touch of his lips. He drew back, an uncertain retreat.

Both stood motionless.

She looked away. 'I'm sorry I said that thing about your wife.'

He felt the emptiness of his arms, the uselessness of his hands. He needed something to grip – a chair, a weapon, anything. 'I don't remember what you said.'

'I made an assumption . . . that she left you.'

'Oh.' He blinked. 'No, I don't think she would ever have left me.' The taste of her was still on his lips, but the meaning of that taste had evaporated.

'How did she die?'

'Car crash,' he said straight away, from habit, and then wished he'd paused long enough to consider telling her the truth. Most probably he wouldn't have done; but he'd have liked to imagine the possibility, if only for a second.

'Was she . . . ?'

Klara didn't seem to know how to finish the question, so he offered a kind of answer. 'She was grounded. Real. To be honest, I was a bit of a mess before I met her. She sorted me out. We used to go climbing together: she was scared at first, but she put her trust in me and that was the most incredible feeling . . .' He pictured Emily as he'd first seen her, in the Covent Garden piazza, alone among that winter crowd applauding the shivering violinist. Watching her, he'd been compelled to clap too, and she had caught his eye and smiled her gratitude. 'She was the best thing that ever happened to me.'

'She sounds . . . amazing.'

'She was. Yes.' His forehead was aching. 'It . . .' He paused. 'The terrible thing is, I think I was relieved when she died.'

Frowning, Klara said, 'You don't mean that.'

He wondered if he should just walk out the door and keep walking until he lost control of his limbs. It would be one way to deal with the chaos inside.

'I adored her, I did. But our life together . . . By then it had already become something else. Wedding planning. Drinks with the neighbours and Christmas with the in-laws. Kitchen extensions. I went abroad with work and I felt *free*. I was always looking forward to the next trip because it meant escaping the conversations about tile colours and what time of year, given the school calendar, would be best to conceive a child.

'When she died, a part of me died with her. I doubt now I'll ever be the person she made me want to be. But another, essential part of me that had been slowly suffocating was . . . resuscitated.' He met her off-centre gaze then. 'Independent. Alone. That's the part I've been surviving on for years now.'

She put her hand to his cheek. 'So you are vulnerable,' she whispered.

Her skin, wet against his. Too late he realized he was crying.

One finger worked its way over his lip. She drew him to her. 'That was all I needed to see.'

STRASBOURG, FRANCE – 16 June

Her first visit had been with Tony Watchman, back when they were still young enough to find even France exciting. The requirement was vague: with members directly elected at last, the European Parliament was starting to assert itself; it had claimed a greater control over the EEC budget and had recently drafted a 'Treaty establishing the European Union'; Thatcher's Cabinet wanted insight into the dominant power bloc, the Confederation of Socialist Parties.

A possible asset had emerged, a corruptible aide to a French Socialist Party MEP. He needed to be wined and dined and seduced into the arms of the Service. But the political risk was enormous. SIS could not be seen to have authorized an operation against the elected representative of a close ally. Watchman and Wraye were selected as expendable new recruits who could be disowned. To muddy the waters still further, a false-flag operation was devised. They were to play CIA officers passing themselves off as Canadian lovers on a wine tour of the Rhineland.

The truth was they worked together extremely well.

It was almost embarrassing, in retrospect, to think how naturally she had counterpointed Tony's wide-boy cockiness, how readily she had smoothed over his still-rough edges. Their legend – college sweethearts, trouble with her father, high hopes of a job for him in Silicon Valley – was a breeze. She got the Canadian vowels better, but when it came to meeting the asset Watchman produced a more authentic US accent – he had an old friend in South Carolina, he said, whom he used to imitate for laughs. They looked and sounded just the way competent American spies should look. And they made perfect lovers.

The truth was there was chemistry between them.

Chemistry, but no sex. She was too alive to the dangers of being seen, in that early age of female Intelligence Branch officers, as one of those women. Easy. Available. Yours for a promotion, a good posting, a commendation on the next staff appraisal form. But Tony had made it clear he wanted her. And for a brief while, in Strasbourg, with wine and adventure and the elation of a successful mission coursing through her veins, she had wanted him too.

Madeleine Wraye insisted on meeting at Illkirch Lixenbuhl, the final stop on tram line A. 'I'm known in this town,' she said. 'Too many MEPs with too much history. I'd just as soon they didn't link me with a gruesome murder.'

'Won't the French keep it quiet?'

'I doubt they can. It's too good a story. Especially with the girl next door tied up all the while. Hope to God Joyce's FCO cover holds.'

Arkell drained his coffee and ordered another. The café was dreary but the service was quick and silent. 'At least we know Yadin is here.'

'We knew that yesterday. I didn't need to lose an officer for that.' She gave an involuntary groan. 'The stupid little arse! He was actually doing quite a good job for me in England. Christ knows what I'm going to say to his poor wife.'

'You've told the Canadians?'

'And the Brazilians. Both security details are fully aware of the immediacy of the threat.'

'Yadin will expect that,' said Arkell. 'He'll still make the hit. Do you have the premiers' schedules yet?'

'Andrade flew in last night. He's holed up in an undisclosed hotel somewhere in the countryside. ABIN aren't sharing his location even with me. Very sensible of them. Mayhew arrives later this morning. He'll exit the plane via covered stairs directly to an armoured car in a convoy of four identical vehicles. Full police outrider escort for both parties to the Parliament. The whole building has been swept for explosives, and nobody other than MEPs and long-serving technical and translator staff will be allowed in all day. No cleaners, caterers, police, spin doctors, researchers or bag carriers. Short of a missile attack on the Parliament, they should be safe until after the address.'

'No missiles,' said Arkell. 'It's going to be chemical. Most likely at close quarters.'

'An aerosol, a scratch as someone brushes past—'

'An umbrella,' he smiled.

'At least there won't be any of those in this weather.'

'What about drinks or food?'

'Both premiers know not to touch anything. Their teams have brought everything their guys will consume with them. They won't even be drinking sealed EU mineral water.'

'OK, so we can assume Yadin won't strike while they're addressing Parliament. What's next on the schedule?'

Wraye grimaced. 'They split up. You can't watch both. Mayhew is hosting a private view of photography from the War on Drugs at the Halle des Fleurs. Showing us complacent Europeans in pitiless black and white what our narcotics policies mean for the good people of Latin America. Meanwhile Andrade is speaking at a reception for the pharmaceutical industry at the Centre de la Paix—'

'Opposite side of town.'

'That's right. The idea is to generate interest in the commercial possibilities of legalized narcotics. No one has better lobbying power than Big Pharma: if they can get the directors of GSK,

Pfizer, Merck and Roche on side, it'll do a lot for the Think Again cause.'

'And then? Where are Mayhew and Andrade staying?'

'They aren't. Now that we know Yadin is definitely here, both have agreed to fly out straight after the events.'

'That simplifies things.'

'Except for one problem.'

'Andrade or Mayhew,' he nodded. 'Which one is the target?'

'Have you asked the girlfriend?'

He looked at her in surprise.

'Miss Richter. You said he got to her last night.'

Arkell started laughing. 'There's no way he would have told—'

'Men do all kinds of stupid things.'

'Madeleine, she had no clue what he was until I broke it to her.'

'Don't be so sure.'

'I am sure. I looked into her eyes. She'd never dreamed he was anything more than a jetsetting businessman with a wife and kids back home. She was in pieces.'

Wraye said simply, 'Ask her.'

Arkell sat back, crossed his arms. 'Fine. I'll ask her. Can you get me into those events? Plus one?'

She frowned. 'You're not planning to take her?'

'It's an idea, but no. I'm going to take an associate. You've met her – she was your driver in Italy.'

'The pretty one.'

'It helps in these situations. Takes the attention off me.'

'Depends who's looking.'

'You'll need names for the guest list. Use Andrew and Susan

Meredith. We have passports and driving licences already. Well tested. No flags. I'll send you the photos.'

'What do you want to be?'

'Venture capitalist,' he answered. 'Forum Associates. I've used it before, know the language. And it works for both events – Forum has interests in Pharma.'

'If they check with Forum?'

'Andrew's on the website. He recently made partner. Not a great photo, but it's close enough. Anyone answering the phone will know him as the one who travels a lot but brings in investors and occasionally makes it to the Christmas party.'

'How the hell?'

'I helped the founding partner out of a nasty case of extortion.'

Wraye nodded appreciatively. 'You've really managed quite well without the Service, haven't you?'

'Speaking of which, where are we on ASH?'

'Down to three. Vine, Watchman and de Vries. All had the opportunity to edit your Porthos message. Two of them have a strong motive; Watchman, who doesn't, is circumstantially linked to Ellington's death. Vine has actually met Yadin, although he claims he didn't know who he was.'

'Which one do you think it is?'

'I'm not going to speculate. There are a couple more lines of investigation to pursue when I get back to London.'

'You realize Joyce will have told Yadin all about you? Which means ASH is probably already planning your disappearance.'

She stood up, leaving a twenty-euro note on the table. 'Go find out which guest list you need to be on.'

* * *

Gavriel Yadin was also seated in a Strasbourg café. Unlike Wraye and Arkell, he drank only mineral water. Before a hit, he preferred to keep his bloodstream free of any drug, even caffeine. He was watching the comings and goings at the rear of the venue. Already, a cordon of officers from the Police nationale had secured the entrances. Metal detectors were in position at each door. Plenty of metal was being carried into the venue, but all of it – cutlery, sound equipment, lights – was being laboriously checked by specialists from the Direction Centrale du Renseignement Intérieur.

A caterer's van drew up. Yadin noted the name and opened up the internet browser on his smartphone. The caterer's website was studded with praise from delighted customers, including most of the European institutions in Strasbourg. He went straight to the contact page to find the company's phone number.

'I'm sorry,' he said in French that was good enough for this purpose, 'I'm serving at a lunch today, some business thing, but I've lost the address.'

There was a pause before a curt voice asked, 'Is it BNP Paribas?'

'That's it.'

'Number twelve Rue de la Morne. Hurry. You'll be late.'

Arkell was relieved to find Klara still at the pension. She had been out: there was a copy of *Le Figaro* open on her knees, and a half-eaten pain au chocolat on the side table. Her bruises had been artfully veiled with foundation and concealer.

She met him with a shy smile and a kiss. He held up a white straw trilby; its narrow brim was curled at the back, and a cornflower-blue sash girded the crown. 'Just in case you feel like making a concession to the summer weather.'

Staring at the hat in silence, she seemed frozen with indecision. Then a broad smile broke out and she snatched it from his hands with girlish delight. 'It's beautiful,' she said, whipping off the black fedora and replacing it with the trilby. She looked up at him, face perfectly, powerfully symmetrical for once. 'Thank you.'

He allowed himself to enjoy the moment a heartbeat longer, then said, 'I have to ask you to do something. You know Gavriel is in Strasbourg. You know why he is in Strasbourg. The two men he has been ordered to kill are in town today, leaving tonight. He will have the opportunity to kill only one of them. I need to know which one.'

She blinked in amazement. 'You think he told me?'

He shook his head. 'I think he gave you a way to contact him.'

'And you want me to ring him and say, "Hey Gavriel, please excuse me but who are you thinking to kill tonight?"' She laughed tonelessly. 'Sure, I'd be happy to ask. We could all three of us video chat.'

Arkell accepted the sarcasm. 'It would be enough to know where he'll be.'

'So you can murder him!' she blazed.

'So I can stop him murdering.'

'And help a million more people get hooked on drugs.'

'Klara . . . you don't really want to be responsible for the death of an elected premier, do you? Whatever his politics?'

She stood up, wrapped her arms around her taut body. In a quieter voice, she said, 'Without a phone number . . .'

'All I'm asking you to do is say you'll meet him. Say that you're sorry, that you're confused by all the lies I've fed you. That you want to meet him tonight.'

She shrugged helplessly. 'How can I? You want me to climb on the roof and shout it?'

'Listen to me, Klara. He is very, very good at what he does. If I'm not there to stop him, he *will* kill one of these men. Andrade, Mayhew – they're both reasonable politicians with loving families, trying to do the right thing. If Gavriel kills either one, the damage to their country, their children, will be catastrophic.'

Klara sat back down. Without seeming to realize it, she picked up the newspaper and returned it to her knees, spreading it carefully with flattened palms. 'He didn't give me a phone number,' she whispered.

Arkell waited.

'He didn't.' She pressed her right hand to her forehead, began rubbing with slow, unthinking strokes. 'But there is an email address.'

The email that dropped into Yadin's phone mailbox had been re-routed through three different cyber-laundering services, nominally located in Austria, Jordan and Malaysia. Yadin ignored the slight vibration signalling the new message. He was busy shopping – or at least giving the appearance of shopping – in the mall across from the BNP Paribas offices. Another caterer's van – it wasn't the same one; he'd checked the plates – was parked outside. He'd watched two men and three women in matching uniforms ferry platters of salads and cold meats between van and bank. Neither of the men, regrettably, looked anything like Yadin. One, however, was approximately the right size.

The woman stepping at that same moment off a TGV from Paris was known to her parents and brothers as Julia Hanbury. There was also a Facebook account in that name, through which she kept in touch with Melbourne friends. No one in Europe called her that. Not any more. Not since a British guy whom she knew probably wasn't named Andrew Meredith had charmed her into sharing some confidential client numbers at the job she once had. Andrew – it was just easier to think of him as Andrew – had taught her the thrill of living with a range of names. She'd never used Beth before, and she doubted she would again. It didn't fit her. It was the British woman who'd inspired it, the one with the thighs: she looked like a Beth.

Occasionally Facebook's Julia Hanbury remembered to post details of the dull accountancy job that had taken her via Sydney and New York to Utrecht. She also posted about the lovely Dutch boy who kept her there. From time to time, one of the Melbourne gang would float the idea of a visit. She always found ways to put them off. Just too complicated to navigate around the no-longer-existent job and fictional boyfriend, not to mention the fact that she hadn't set foot in Holland in four years. Andrew had generously offered to pay for an apartment in Utrecht so she could maintain her 'story', as he called it. But it was just as easy to have her parents' letters and seasonal gifts forwarded from the Utrecht PO Box and have calls to her Dutch number redirected to whatever network she was currently using.

Andrew paid her way too much as it was.

That was why she didn't sleep with him. It would be weird when he was paying her so well for all the fun stuff she got to do. That, and also he'd never asked.

She'd reckoned he would when he kind of married her. That was fun, seeing his name in her new passport. But he was all business about it. And when they shared a hotel room as a honeymoon couple in Dubrovnik, he slept on the floor despite her not-so-subtle hints. She'd woken in the middle of the night and found him gone.

She felt oddly jealous that time. Like it really was their honeymoon and he was sneaking off to some local girl. She knew perfectly well he wasn't: he had been very explicit about the kind of work he did and the danger it might put her in. But still, it hadn't felt great.

She had married him a few more times since then. He liked going on honeymoon. She actually couldn't remember all the names she'd been given. She'd learned to get comfortable with her own company in fancy hotel suites. And she quite enjoyed messing up the sheets to keep the staff from wondering.

When they weren't on a job, he called her Siren. He'd asked her right at the beginning of it all, over those fateful cocktails in Utrecht, as the envelope of client numbers lay smouldering on the table between them, what name she wished she'd been given. 'Siren' just popped out of nowhere. A ridiculous name, but she loved hearing it on his lips. It made her feel capable of anything.

She walked out of the station into the Strasbourg sun and there he was, the same tentative smile he'd worn when he first approached her in that Utrecht street. Kissing her on one cheek, he took her bag and the zipped carrier containing three evening dresses of different cuts and lengths. He wouldn't know which one to choose, but he would tell her the kind of event and she would take it from there. They were well rehearsed at this – almost like a married couple.

She smiled, to herself as much as to him. 'Hello, Andrew.'

'Siren. Thank you for coming.'

'Did I have a choice? I think it's in my contract.'

'What are you missing? Any hot dates?'

'I'm in retreat, as you well know. The only men in the village are well over seventy, and they drink far too much cheap cognac to be any use to me.' Her Australian accent only really emerged these days when she was messing around. 'But there's at least one masterpiece I'll never finish now, that's for sure.'

'I promise it's worth the sacrifice.'

'So do I get to shoot anyone tonight? Seduce a sleazy Euro politician? Plant a bug in a defence minister's bathroom?'

'Just polite conversation and looking beautiful, I'm afraid. The guy I'm after will be watching the lone men more carefully than the couples.'

She sighed as she threw an arm around his back. 'One day, Mr Meredith, you will finally appreciate my talents. Come on, let's get a cab. You don't know it yet, but you've treated me to a seriously nice room at the Hyatt, and it looks like I've got time to make good use of their spa.'

'Sounds like a reasonable incidental expense. Especially as there's a risk you might spend tonight in a police cell.'

'Ah, sweetie, you always say that. One of these days it'd better happen.'

* * *

The bankers' lunch did not last long. Times had changed, it seemed, even in France. The catering staff loaded stacked platters and crates of dirty crockery into the van, and were then dismissed. Yadin tracked the two men to a tram station. Through the glass pane of the carriage behind theirs he watched the lanky guy get off at Homme de Fer. The two waiters did not shake hands or give any other sign of friendship as they parted. Not that it made any difference, but Yadin always noted such things. The other man stayed on the tram for five more stops, then walked four blocks to an apartment building. Yadin kept his distance, but the waiter never looked round. As they approached the building, he accelerated his pace, perfectly timing his arrival to catch the swinging door.

The waiter, standing at the elevators, glanced round but made no comment. Yadin gave him a silent nod. They stood unmoving, side by side, watching the glowing number above the steel door. His target began to look uneasy only when Yadin got out on the same floor and chose to walk in the same direction along the empty corridor. He stopped to let him go past, and Yadin stepped neatly alongside him and seized his windpipe between finger and thumb. The important thing was not to get blood on the clothes.

The waiter gasped hoarsely, rigid with fright. 'You can still breathe and you can still move,' Yadin assured him in whispered French. 'Is there anyone in your apartment? Answer quietly.'

'No,' he wheezed.

'Open the door. Nothing will happen to you if you cooperate.' It interested Yadin, who had long studied human psychology for its practical applications, that most people chose to believe such statements, even when they came from strangers who had just assaulted them.

With some difficulty, the waiter extracted a set of keys from his pocket and stumbled towards one of the doors. Yadin maintained his precise grip on the man's throat as he unlocked the door and edged inside. The tired flat was empty, but the mess in the kitchen suggested multiple dwellers.

Yadin closed the door with his heel, showed the man the automatic and then released his throat.

'Take off your clothes.'

'What?' The fear in the man's eyes intensified.

'I told you, nothing will happen to you. I want your clothes, not your body.'

Hurriedly, the waiter stripped. Yadin glanced into the three bedrooms. 'Which is yours?'

'On the left.' There was a growing tremor in his voice.

'Share it with anyone? Girlfriend? Boyfriend? Anyone going to go in there today?'

'No.'

He was fully undressed now. Even his socks and underpants lay in the pile beside him. A line of tattooed fish swam their way up his left leg. Love handles that had not been visible under his shirt spoilt the otherwise trim outline of a young body.

'Thank you,' said Yadin, gripping his thick chestnut hair and jerking his head back so that the neck snapped.

Yadin found the catering firm's identity card in the trousers. It would not be difficult to replace the photograph. He carried the body into the bedroom and shut it in the wardrobe. He decided against closing the bedroom door in case it was not the waiter's habit.

Such little things, he had been taught a long time ago, can make all the difference.

Klara Richter looked up from her crossword as Arkell opened the door. The black fedora was back, the straw trilby nowhere to be seen. She gave him a bright smile. Too bright. 'Hi,' she said.

'Hi.'

'So . . .' She went back to studying the paper. 'You have a girlfriend.'

Arkell swung round to face the mirror. Had Siren left a smudge of lipstick on his cheek? But there was nothing. 'Why do you say that?'

'At least one, I should say. One in France, perhaps. A few more in England. Any in Germany?'

'Klara, what are you talking about?'

She looked back up at him. Still that bright, over-cheerful smile. 'It's no big deal.'

'Good to know.'

'She's cute. Young for you, isn't she?'

He sat down on the bed, facing her. 'Did you follow me?'

'Isn't that what spies do? Seems like I'm not bad, yes? Maybe I should get a job with one of your fascist bureaux.' She filled in a clue. Arkell would have bet money it was not the right word. 'You should look round more. I think maybe Gavriel followed you too. Maybe he also followed you in that taxi. I didn't need to. I know that story.'

'Klara, what is this about?'

'Nothing. I'm happy for you.'

'She's not my girlfriend.'

'OK. Good.'

'We work together.'

'Sure. Fine.'

He shook his head in bewilderment. 'When you got bored of following me, did you check your email?'

'Yes, I did.'

'And?'

She shrugged. 'We're meeting.'

'Where?'

'He said 9 p.m.' She hesitated, and for a moment Arkell seemed to see straight into her tortured soul. 'Café des Grecques.'

Arkell grabbed a city map. 'Show me.'

She did her best to look uninterested, as if she could barely be bothered to cooperate. But her finger came down with precision on a street to the south-west of the old city.

Arkell stared at the bright new copper nail varnish on her neatly trimmed fingernail. 'Are you absolutely sure?'

Both events were due to start at 8 p.m. Standing alone at 7.35 on a street corner midway between the two venues, her face turned away from passing cars, Wraye felt more than a little tense. Watching Arkell approach in a dark suit with a sylph-like figure in grey silk on his arm did not help. This woman had seen her naked, remembered Wraye with irritation. Knowing that she would be writing the cheque for that expensive couture only heightened her annoyance.

'You still don't know?'

'I'm still not sure,' he corrected her. He did not try to introduce Siren.

'What did Richter say?'

'She said Yadin would meet her exactly one hour after the start of the events, one block from the Centre de la Paix.'

'So it's Andrade.'

'Maybe.'

'A block away!'

'Exactly. One block from a presidential murder scene? One block from the centre of police attention for the next month?'

'You think it's a misdirect?'

'Klara was . . . There was something wrong.'

'Could he have called her?'

Arkell shook his head. 'I've still got her mobile cloned.'

'You wrote the email for her, didn't you? Was there anything in it that might have tipped him off?'

'Nothing. But she may have sent a second email explaining what we want to know.'

'So he steers you to the wrong venue, leaving him free to take Mayhew.'

'Unless he's double-bluffing,' interjected Siren.

'Thank you,' said Wraye icily.

'It is a possibility,' acknowledged Arkell. 'The misdirect is a little obvious when you think about it.'

Wraye looked at her watch. 'You're on both guest lists,' she told Arkell, 'which I can assure you was no small feat.' She held up two pairs of tickets, one in stiff white card, the other in the style of a black-and-white news story. 'It's 19:42. Make the call.'

* * *

Yadin had been inside the building for close to three hours before he revealed himself. The venue was part of a larger property, incorporating offices, an EU member-state delegation and an independent art-house cinema that still received EU funding only because one of the commissioners had a weakness for meaningful movies shot on grainy celluloid. The cinema was closed for the day, but the business tenants had protested vigorously at the idea of an enforced holiday, and no one had dared suggest kicking the member-state delegation out.

Nevertheless, DCRI officers had swept the entire building the night before, and all day had been checking the identities of anyone entering.

Yadin had taken no satisfaction from the ease with which he'd passed through the security cordon. There were any number of ways he could have done it unaided, but Kartouche had offered a simple convenience and he had accepted it because to do otherwise would have been proud and unprofessional. Kartouche's organization possessed capabilities and contacts beyond even those of the Mossad. And although Yadin liked to work alone, to depend on his own judgement and competence, it was, he recognized, foolish to refuse genuinely useful assistance. It usually took the form of intelligence: security arrangements for the Tobago broadcast; the premiers' French schedules; the structural plans of this building; possible profiles of the man who was hunting him. But in this case, Kartouche had pulled a different kind of string, and at 17:09 the Police nationale officer guarding the entrance to those business offices had looked at his watch, looked again a minute later, and then had very deliberately walked around the corner of the building. He was back at his post twenty-five seconds later.

Yadin had accepted that convenience. For the rest – talking his way past the shared reception, breezing in smart grey suit through the offices of three different enterprises, disabling the alarm on the emergency exit into the stairwell that connected with the venue – these things he did for himself.

At 20:03, now dressed in the waiter's black trousers and white shirt, Yadin removed the cork from a wine bottle. The bottle was from the same vineyard and of the same vintage as the cases he had seen unloaded that morning. Strapping one further object carefully to his wrist, he checked its mechanism before buttoning his sleeve.

For some time he had been listening to the noises coming from the other side of the uppermost emergency exit door: shuffling, throat clearing, heel tapping, the occasional acknowledgement of a radio call. The top storey held the venue's administrative offices and storage rooms, and aside from the man guarding the emergency exit it seemed to be empty. Mentally sliding into the necessary language and accent, Yadin rapped on the door and uttered the lone sentinel's call sign: 'Sierra Four'.

The shuffling and heel tapping stopped. 'Who's that?'

'Tango Whisky. Open up, Sierra Four.'

A pause. It was possible the man would do what he ought to do – radio for instructions. But no one likes to look stupid. 'Tango Whisky? Which unit is—'

'Will you open the damn door? It's a furnace in here.'

Sierra Four hesitated just a few more seconds. At least he had his weapon out, reflected Yadin as he hurtled through the opening door and drove his rigid knuckles into the man's throat. Even if he hadn't flicked the safety lever.

Yadin pocketed the officer's radio and concealed the body in a cupboard full of flipchart easels. Retrieving the bottle of wine, he closed the emergency door and made his way to the elevators.

Now that he was inside, the danger lay not with the security team but with the staff of the catering firm. The workforce might be casual, made up of students and other passing bodies, but they would know who else was working the job. And there would be supervisors keeping a close eye on anyone in a logo-stamped white shirt. For an event like this, it would be a particularly close eye.

So Yadin did not hurry into the main reception space. Instead, he waited in a darkened adjoining room full of stacked chairs and folded conference tables. Twice the radio, set to a low volume, called for Sierra Four. Twice he mimicked the dead officer's intonation and accent to give the all-clear code. When the lights next door dimmed, and the premier began speaking, Yadin switched off the radio, picked up the bottle of wine and eased open the door.

'Ladies and Gentlemen, *muitos obrigados*, thank you for coming,' said Murilo Andrade, larger than life in a bulging dinner suit. 'I hope you will find this evening interesting, thought-provoking, even profitable.' He smiled at the polite laughter from the assembled pharmaceutical leaders. He knew their industry well, having helped set up a very successful Brazilian manufacturer of generic medicines – pharmacologically almost identical to the branded compounds that had made these global corporations rich, but on sale, once the relevant patents had expired, for a fraction of the cost. These people didn't like him very much back then. Perhaps they would warm to him tonight.

'Your business,' he began, 'is about making people better. But increasingly, in this age of statins and beta-blockers, it is also about preventing them getting ill. If you need justification – to your shareholders, your employees, your families, your god – for developing, manufacturing and selling safe, taxed narcotics, that is it. Your participation in, and your eventual control of, the recreational drugs business will stop people getting ill. More, it will stop them dying.

'There is no more regulated industry on earth than yours, and there is none that better understands the mechanisms of human biology and the tolerances of our bodies. With your expertise in pharmacodynamics, toxicology and neuropharmacology, you have the ability to create patentable formulations rich in neuroprotectors and stripped of the molecules that aggravate addiction. If anyone can make these substances safe for those many millions who insist on consuming them, it is you.'

Looking around the darkened room, Madeleine Wraye scanned every face near the president. Three or four might almost have been Yadin – with make-up, with a wig, with a false nose. She edged a little closer to one likely candidate.

'Your industry has been repeatedly, sometimes unfairly, vilified – for excessive profits, for unethical marketing practices, for compromised clinical tests. Through years of hard work, you have put most of that behind you. And now you are thinking: why in God's name would we expose ourselves to all that shit again? Marketing *heroin*? Selling crack to the daughters of congressmen and senators? Is he *louco*?!'

One of the Yadin lookalikes, a waiter, drifted discreetly amongst the laughing, charmed directors, topping up glasses of red wine. Wraye watched his progress until he disappeared from view.

President Andrade had moved on to talk about dosage and labelling.

She prayed Arkell had made the right choice.

'Ladies and Gentlemen, thank you for coming.' Terence Mayhew was a ghostly figure in the darkness, only the left side of his gaunt face illuminated by a spotlight. 'You are not going to enjoy this evening, I guarantee. The images you are going to see, the stories you are going to hear, are sickening. There's no other word. Sickening. And all the more so because they portray events that need never have happened. Would never have happened, if we as a society had not got ourselves into such a convoluted moral mess.

'There are stories we could tell from all over the world, but tonight we are going to concentrate on Latin America. Every nation in the Americas looks to Europe for its heritage. As mine looks to Britain and France, the southern nations look to Spain and Portugal. But there are other roots: Greeks, Germans, Italians, Poles, Welsh, Lithuanians . . . all made new lives in Latin America. Mexico . . . poor Mexico . . .' He gestured to a darkened shape in the centre of the exhibition space, shrouded in cloth. 'Mexico, colonized by Spain, occupied by France and ruled by an Austrian. You are our Past and you continue to shape our Present. Latin America desperately needs Europeans to understand the consequences for its people of this trade which they both prohibit and fuel. In the name of Anneke van der Velde, a truly great European, I beg you to open your eyes!'

A light came on at one end of the hall, and a solitary black-and-white image leapt out of the darkness. As every guest strained to interpret the confusion of limbs and twisted metal, no one noticed a door behind them silently open.

'Cali, Colombia. Her name was Adelita. The little boy was Rodrigo. The smallest body is a girl. La-la, she was known as. Her face was removed by a single explosive bullet *after* the car bomb had exploded. Miraculously, she had survived the blast, but it seems one of the *carteleros* objected to her crying.'

Another light. 'Tijuana, Mexico. Twenty minutes earlier, this was a wedding party. The bride's father was a senior police officer who made the mistake of being incorruptible. That's him hanging from the tree. The bride was raped by twelve men and left to bleed to death within sight of her still-breathing father.'

Gavriel Yadin moved unobtrusively through the crowd of eurocrats and fashionistas, of semi-famous French actresses, German Mittelstand business owners and Spanish labour leaders. The pictures and the stories made no impression on him, other than in their effect on the people around him. Few guests, even those with empty glasses, took any notice of him. He topped up the occasional drink, but otherwise concentrated on reaching a certain spot near the shrouded mass in the centre. He already knew what lay under it.

'Puerto Plata, Dominican Republic. The man on the ground is Juan Miguel Santos, a fisherman with a big family and a lot of bills to pay. He made a little on the side – we're talking perhaps sixty dollars per month to buy clothes for his kids – storing packages for a gang that smuggle cocaine to Europe in banana shipments. Another gang didn't like the first gang so much, and they took it out on Juan. The girl clinging to what's left of his chest is Esmeralda. She's twelve now, hasn't spoken in eighteen months. A sweet little kid, her life ruined because of economic incentives our laws have created. Are you hearing this, people? Is this an English-speaking audience?' He was shivering with rage now. 'Europe did this! *We* did this! Do you understand how fucking appalling this whole business is?'

Mayhew too was making his way slowly towards the shrouded centrepiece, as picture after picture was illuminated around him. Bolivia. Trinidad. Panama. Colombia again. Paraguay. Barely controlling his anger, he set out in bleak terms the human tragedies behind them all. And meanwhile Yadin worked his way imperceptibly towards the same spot, a macabre moth drawn to a roll call of violent death.

Then, a hand on his arm. A Danish accent. 'Pardon, may I have some of that?' Yadin paused, conscious of the tall blond man with the radiant wife, but more conscious of the empty bottle in his hand.

Reluctantly he muttered, 'One moment, please.'

The catering tables lay in the other direction. He had no choice but to turn round. Mayhew was, by his calculation, three pictures away from the final reveal. Each picture was taking about eighty seconds. There was time.

Still, he could not hurry. Could not give people a reason to notice him, or draw the attention of the other catering staff.

And the crowd seemed denser now, more reluctant to part for him. Less navigable.

'. . . five bullets to the chest. Already dead. But still they cut her head off and used it – folks, I'm really not kidding – as a football.'

Two pictures left. Running out of time. What did the thirsty Dane matter? He was already out of sight. Yadin turned back, chose a different route that would bring him to the same destination without passing the Dane.

'. . . which, as you know, is a popular tourist resort. Or was, until these guys started throwing body parts into the bars and cafés. Antonio was just one of many low-paid civil servants who ended up . . .'

One picture left. As Mayhew set out the story behind it, Yadin edged past three captains of German industry and positioned himself with a clear line of sight to the point he knew Mayhew must reach.

'These, ladies and gentlemen, are just a few of the many human consequences of Prohibition. Cigarettes kill people, it's true. Alcohol kills people. But these legal, regulated substances only kill the people who choose to consume them – and never like this.'

All around the hall, the spotlights were extinguished. The images were gone. The single remaining light on Terence Mayhew also caught the end of a white rope, lowered from the gantry above. As Mayhew walked the last few steps to it, the people around melted back, leaving nothing but air between assassin and prime minister.

Moving imperceptibly, Yadin drew back his sleeve.

'So now I leave you with one last exhibit.' A spotlight lit up the shroud. Mayhew took hold of the rope. 'Ciudad Juárez, Mexico. People were disappearing as competition to transport drugs into the US intensified. A lot of people, most of them innocent of any crime more serious than giving the wrong drug runner shelter or a meal.'

Yadin tilted his hand back, clear of the line of fire. He almost smiled to see Mayhew so caught up in his own words, every nerve tuned to his subject. There was a strong likelihood he wouldn't even notice the needle-thin dart pierce his flesh, such was his passion. And if he did, it wouldn't matter: by then everyone would be focused on something else.

'They were found, eventually, in a mass grave twenty kilometres from town. Hacked to pieces, decayed, desecrated. This, Europe, is the reality of Prohibition!'

As Mayhew tugged on the rope, hauling away the shroud, and as the spotlight that had faithfully followed him went cold, the only claim on anyone's attention was the hellish recreation before them all. So realistic were the dismembered corpses in amongst the piles of sandy Mexican earth that many of the onlookers imagined they could actually smell the fetid putrefaction rising off each unthinkable figure.

No one was focused on the prime minister. It was the perfect moment. Except that suddenly Yadin found himself thinking again of that blond guy with the Danish accent, of a face glimpsed in a Hamburg elevator, even of a silhouette amongst the shadows of a Cypriot alley. British, ex-military, according to that fool of a dead agent.

Known only as TALON.

He straightened his left forearm, gripped the bulb trigger between finger and thumb –

'Me again,' said a voice beside him, not at all Danish now, as a great weight crashed down on his arm and that single, lethal dart shot uselessly into the scuffed floor.

Yadin reacted physically long before he'd had time to acknowledge the disaster. The defence was the same he'd practised a thousand times with his instructor in Tel Aviv, and then later in London and Colombo and wherever else the chance to refresh his skills and sharpen his reflexes presented itself.

His whole body rolled with the momentum of his arm – *The assailant has knocked the weapon from your hand and broken your tibia: respond!* – and his shoulder came down and launched up again into his opponent's chest. It should have cracked his ribs, but the guy managed to swivel, absorb the blow. *Respond! Respond! Respond!* Follow up with elbow, fist, elbow. It was a fight he could have won, but there was no time. The commotion, only two seconds old, had already drawn the attention of Mayhew's protection detail. A lot of guns were about to point his way.

Yadin turned into the darkness and ran.

When the lights came on, Arkell saw Siren hurrying towards him, even as four heavy Canadians grabbed him and pinned him to the floor. *Go*, he was able to mouth, and she obeyed, as he had always insisted she must if this situation ever arose.

There was no sign of Yadin. 'Close the doors,' Arkell said urgently. 'That was Gavriel Yadin. Seal the building!' The men holding him were Royal Canadian Mounted Police officers, he guessed – members of the Protective Policing unit. They did not seem to recognize the name, nor care much what he had to say. They were focused on their prime minister, being rushed out of the hall. 'Listen to me. The man who's trying to kill Mayhew is in the building.'

There was no response from the grim-faced officers.

'Hurry! Alert your perimeter. Don't let anyone leave!'

The guests parted as four Police nationale officers approached. There was a whispered conference between the two law-enforcement groups. With the French guns on him, Arkell was released. One of the new arrivals stooped over him and said in English, 'Come with me please, sir.'

There was no point fighting any more. Too many seconds had elapsed. Yadin was gone. Lost in the crowd. Headed out of town. Off into the Alsatian sunset with Klara. After all, she was conclusively his. Tonight had proved that. She had chosen her side.

The Legion deserter looked up at the French officer and smiled stoically. 'Sure,' he said.

They did not take him to a police station, but instead held him in an office upstairs. He stripped off his tie and ripped jacket. The air on the third floor was humid and stale. The two police officers detailed to guard him looked on from the doorway, eyes expressionless and weapons pointed just a little away from him. He didn't try to talk to them.

Eventually two plain-clothes detectives arrived.

'*Votre nom, monsieur?*' There was a hint of brandy on the breath of that one.

'I'm sorry, I don't speak French.'

'Your name?'

'Andrew Meredith.' Another identity that would have to be shredded. A pity. Forum Associates had been particularly accommodating.

'Nationality?'

'British.'

Little notes were made in a little book. 'You were an official guest at the reception?'

'The invitation's in my pocket.' He gestured lazily to the jacket that lay strewn across some administrator's desk.

The silent partner checked the card, along with the passport he found in the same pocket. A grudging nod.

'Who were you fighting just now?'

'I didn't know him.'

'Why were you fighting?'

'The guy had wandering hands. Is it against the law to defend the honour of your wife in France?'

'Your wife is downstairs?'

'I imagine she's gone back to the hotel.'

'The prime minister's bodyguards said you spoke about "killing Mayhew".'

Great, thought Arkell. *Thanks, guys*. 'You've got that wrong.'

'How is it wrong?'

'When they jumped me, I tried to explain it was a little personal disagreement. Neither of us was trying to kill Mayhew. That's what I said.'

Both detectives nodded gravely. More notes were made.

'It seems one of the bodyguards is missing.' With a look that suggested he expected no good whatsoever to come of the question, the detective asked, 'Do you know anything about this?'

Arkell shook his head apologetically.

'Mr Meredith, what is your political ideology?'

'*Seriously?*'

'Do you have an opinion of Prime Minister Mayhew's politics?'

He realized then that they were simply going through the motions. There had been a violent incident in front of a distinguished premier on French soil. Questions had to be asked, if only for form's sake. Wearily, he resigned himself to manufacturing some suitable answers.

'What is your business interest in narcotics, Mr Meredith?'

'Have you ever been convicted of a criminal offence?'

'Have you been to Canada?'

Over the course of an hour, they asked nothing beyond what was necessary for the purposes of diplomacy, and Arkell told them nothing they did not expect to hear from an inconvenienced British financier. As they were drawing to a close, however, a flushed, squat man in a dishevelled linen jacket was shown in. He conferred hurriedly with the lead detective, who shrugged and turned to Arkell.

'This is Mr Bleeck from Dutch police. He would like to talk to you informally. Do you have any objection?'

'Do I have a choice?'

'For the moment, yes.' The detective's manner became confiding. 'Perhaps he will request a detention through official channels if you say no. It will be easier to talk to him now, I think.'

Mr Bleeck looked on, nodding vigorously. 'It would be a great help to me, Mr Meredith.'

'Fine.' The identity would have to be shredded, but for now he was still living the Forum cover and venture capitalists generally cooperate with the authorities.

'Thank you,' murmured Bleeck. He glanced at the detectives. '*En privé, s'il vous plaît.*'

The French officers shared a look. They rose and beckoned to the uniformed guards. 'Thank you, Mr Meredith. Please, no more fighting in France.'

The Dutch policeman was shabby and tired, a little overweight. 'My name is Chief Inspector Mikael Bleeck,' he began. 'I am the senior coordinating officer for the investigation into the death of Prime Minister Anneke van der Velde. I have two hundred and seventy-three officers working all hours; I have an unlimited budget and extraordinary powers to detain and question anyone in the Netherlands. I have the absolute cooperation of all units of the Dutch military and intelligence services, and I am receiving unprecedented support from Interpol and most Western police forces. The resources at my disposal are immeasurable. Despite all of this, the only real lead I have to find the killer is you.'

He sat down, apparently exhausted by this opening salvo.

'Wasn't it a heart attack?' said Arkell.

Bleeck ignored the question. 'Tonight, a guest in the same room as Prime Minister Terence Mayhew, Anneke van der Velde's partner in the Think Again initiative, declared, "That was Gavriel Yadin."'

Arkell looked blank.

'Is that what you said, Mr Meredith?'

'What was the name again?'

Bleeck frowned as he repeated himself.

Arkell made up his mind. 'Never heard of him.'

'Two members of Mr Mayhew's protection detail – men highly trained and very perceptive – heard you say the name. It's in the police report. An Interpol alert was triggered,' he added, as if this detail might make it true.

'Sorry. Maybe it was someone else?'

'Mr Meredith,' he said sternly. 'Our prime minister was murdered in front of the world. I think you understand this. Our government is in chaos. Our stock market has crashed. The Dutch people expect me to find answers. If you know anything about Gavriel Yadin, if he was here tonight, you have to tell me.'

Arkell calculated what a curious venture capitalist would say. 'So this . . . *Yadin* is an assassin?'

'Last night, there were three murders in Strasbourg: a newly wed couple shot in bed, and a British diplomat brutally tortured in the university quarter. Gavriel Yadin's DNA was found at both crime scenes. That is why I am here. Please. You know this man. I have four teams researching him, but you *know* him. What can you tell me? Anything at all could be valuable. We have to find him.'

'I'm sorry,' Arkell said with finality. 'I've never heard the name.'

Bleeck stared at him, his face a picture of crushed hope. Arkell felt genuinely sorry for the guy. But there was no point – Yadin was gone.

The door opened and another man strode in. Arkell

recognized him from the cluster of Canadian officers that had rushed Terence Mayhew out of the exhibition hall. His face was an unhealthy white. Without introduction, he declared, 'I need to talk to this gentleman alone.'

'I haven't finished questioning—' began Bleeck.

'Yes, sir, I believe you have.'

Bleeck stared at the rigid-jawed Canadian and the door he held open. He looked back across the desk, a last plea in his eyes.

'Sorry,' smiled Arkell. 'Wish I could help.'

Bleeck laid a business card on the desk. 'In case you remember anything.'

The Canadian shut the door too quickly behind him. He did not sit. Flattening two large, heavily veined hands on the desktop, he said, 'One of my men is lying dead in the next office. His neck is broken and his trachea has been crushed. Would you know anything about that?'

Arkell considered him. 'Before I answer,' he said quietly, 'please identify yourself.'

'I'm asking the questions.'

'And I'll answer them when you give me a name and RCMP rank.'

A moment's hostile hesitation, then: 'Shel Margrave. And it's not RCMP. I'm with the Canadian Security Intelligence Service.'

'Shel Margrave is CSIS Deputy Director, Operations.'

'That's right,' he said, newly suspicious.

'Now on close protection duty?'

'In this instance, my presence was necessary.'

'So you know about Yadin.'

'Yes, I do.'

'Shame the RCMP officers didn't,' muttered Arkell.

The CSIS director's face tightened. 'The protection detail had the briefing they needed – physical description, photograph, skills profile. They know the threat as TARQUIN. There are sensitivities about the name.'

'You don't want to piss off Mossad.'

'I'd like to hear how you know so much, sir.'

Arkell ignored that. He felt suddenly angry. Yadin was gone, and there were no more leads. For the time being, he chose to blame this man. 'It's a pity you didn't brief them fully. If the officers who detained me had recognized the name they might have prevented his escape.'

Mirroring his rising temper, Margrave snapped, 'Just who the hell are you, anyway? And don't give me that venture capitalist crap. You spend way too much time in the gym for that.'

'I believe I currently work for you,' said Arkell bitterly. 'Indirectly.'

Margrave stopped still. He sat down, wonderingly. 'Madeleine Wraye's guy?'

'Not great communication between CSIS and RCMP, is there? She put me on your guest list. I'm surprised you haven't managed to establish that in the three hours I've been stuck here.'

Margrave murmured, 'I'll accept that criticism.'

'Yadin was in the room. You showed the PMPD officers a photograph? He was right in front of them. He took a shot at their principal, for Christ's sake! Don't believe me? Some kind of dart. The weapon was attached to his arm. Go search the floor around where I was held. Do it carefully. Full hazmat protection.'

Eyes never leaving Arkell, the Canadian spoke a few terse words into his radio. 'And you engaged him?'

'Until I was prevented from doing so,' said Arkell.

'You should have declared yourself beforehand.'

'That's what you're paying for? A polite, official chap who goes around introducing himself?'

Nodding ruefully, Margrave said, 'A Kidon marksman missed his target at close quarters?'

'Maybe he was having an off day.'

'Right. Well, I guess we owe you.' Margrave stood up. 'Seeing as you're working for me, this would be a good opportunity for a progress update. Without wishing to tread on Madeleine's toes, I'd like to hear anything you've got on Yadin, any contact you may have had with him or his associates, and particularly where we go from here. But I'm already late. Would you object to driving and talking?'

'Driving and talking?'

'There's a man I'd like you to meet.'

Shel Margrave's ID gained them immediate access to the airside of Strasbourg airport. He drove the black SUV right up to a Learjet parked some way from the terminal building. One of the waiting Police nationale officers took charge of the vehicle as they stepped out. 'Come on,' he called back to Arkell, starting up the steps.

The freelance spy, who for nine years had survived on his wits, stayed on the tarmac. 'I don't get into strange men's aeroplanes.'

Margrave looked round. 'What are you afraid of? We're Canadian: we don't do rendition, for God's sake.'

'This may sound paranoid, but members of more than one intelligence service have tried to kill me.'

'Join the club. Look, you're more useful to me in Europe than Canada, which is where this plane is headed in about twelve minutes. I'll kick you off in time, I promise.'

With that he continued up the steps and disappeared from view.

The SUV had driven off. Arkell gazed along the taciturn line of French police officers guarding the Canadian plane. He felt just a little foolish standing there on his own.

He took the steps at a run.

'This is him?' said a voice.

Arkell blinked quickly in the bright cabin lights. There were too many people; they blurred together. But he recognized the voice. He'd heard it at length that evening.

Margrave was the closest. 'Yes, sir.'

'Different than I expected.'

The speaker stepped forward. Arkell allowed himself a quick inventory of the others present – PMPD, CSIS, chief of staff, press secretary, various harmless aides – before focusing his attention on the prime minister.

'What do I call you?'

'Might as well stick with Andrew Meredith for now.'

Mayhew glanced over his shoulder. 'Where is that thing? Bring it here.'

A PMPD officer pushed through the aides, gingerly holding a clear plastic bag by one corner. Inside was a fine steel dart, bent out of shape.

'Give it to me,' said Mayhew impatiently. 'I'm not going to

prick my damn finger.' He took the bag and held it up to Arkell. 'Our people will analyse the contents back in Ottawa. Any idea what they'll find?'

'Something unusual,' said Arkell. 'Ya—' He stopped himself, with a glance to Margrave. 'TARQUIN went to a specialist for it. That's a tiny dose. There aren't many poisons that will kill you with a few drops.'

'We might as well get it over with,' said Mayhew gruffly. He extended a hand. 'Thank you for saving my life.'

'Thank me when I've eliminated the threat.'

The prime minister let his arm drop. 'I'll do that. What are your chances?'

'Honestly? I've missed the best opportunities. Here, Cyprus . . .'

'TARQUIN was in Cyprus?' Mayhew turned to Margrave. 'Did the Service know that?'

'No, sir.'

'The Dutch?'

'If they did, they didn't share it with us.'

'You seem to be a step ahead of us, at least. Who's behind it?'

Abruptly an image came to Arkell of three men in a police line-up: George Vine flanked by Tony Watchman and Martin de Vries, all dressed in prison fatigues. 'I'm afraid we—' He was interrupted by a ringing phone. 'I'm sorry, do you mind?' he said, reaching into his pocket. 'It's after midnight. No one calls this late unless it's important.'

The prime minister shared a look with Margrave.

Arkell glanced at the screen. It was Danny. 'What is it?' he muttered, turning away from the others.

'Hello to you too,' came Danny's excited voice.

'Little busy, Danny, I'll—'

'No, no, don't hang up! I found your guy.'

'*What?*'

'See, I was surfing a few travel systems, trying some back-door tricks, double-checking those names. I mean Strasbourg is boring *as shit* at night. So, anyways, one of them came up. José Cumes. He's back in the air again.'

'Where's he going?' breathed Arkell.

'Wait a secondo, hombre. This one isn't a scheduled flight. He booked a last-minute private charter out of Strasbourg. Cessna Citation. You want to know how much this baby set him back?'

'Where, Danny? Where's he gone?'

'OK, hold on . . . Here you go. It's still France.' He sounded disappointed. 'Tarbes. Landed midnight-oh-five.'

Arkell lowered the phone. Tarbes? Where was Tarbes? It rang a bell, but why? He looked back at Mayhew. 'You're not planning any other events in Europe, are you?'

'We leave for Canada soon as you and I are done.'

'And President Andrade?'

'Back to Brazil tonight. Why, what's up?'

'Nothing, I . . .' *Why Tarbes?*

One of the aides leaned forward timidly. 'Actually, sir? I think Mr Andrade is making an extra stop before he heads home.'

'He didn't mention anything to me.'

'Sir, I could be wrong, but I was sharing ideas for the next Think Again conference with one of his speech-writers and he happened to mention that one of the things the president has always wanted to—'

‘Christ, where’s he going?’ demanded Arkell.

‘L-Lourdes,’ said the aide. ‘He wants to celebrate Mass in Lourdes.’

Right after wheels-up, Mayhew went to bed in the private cabin at the back of the jet, but Simon Arkell remained locked in discussion with the RCMP and CSIS officers. It had taken a matter of seconds to confirm on his smartphone map what he already knew: Lourdes, one of the pre-eminent pilgrimage sites in the Roman Catholic galaxy, lies just a few miles south of the provincial town of Tarbes, in the foothills of the Pyrenees. The other end of France.

It had taken even less time for the prime minister to agree to a small detour.

‘This was not planned – we agree about that?’ Nathaniel Henderson was the Assistant Commissioner in charge of Protective Policing for the RCMP. ‘This is a last-minute move. Go after Andrade to make good his failure tonight?’

‘Doesn’t mean he’ll be any less effective,’ Arkell assured him.

‘What do Andrade’s people say?’ asked Margrave of the young woman beside him. It had been Sergeant Sarah Winter’s job, as inter-services liaison officer, to make the call to her opposite number in the Brazilian camp. ‘Not a lot yet. Roberto was asleep already. Pretty unhappy to be woken. They thank us for the information.’

Arkell leaned forward. ‘Andrade’s schedule in Lourdes?’

‘He has to check with his boss, who’s also asleep, whether he can share that data. Definitely Mass in the morning. Definitely departing for Brasilia before midday. The rest is currently need-to-know. They're already settled in a hotel round the corner from the Sanctuary, with full security in place. Andrade will have a Gendarmerie escort from the moment they leave the hotel to the steps of their plane. Roberto is confident there are no vulnerabilities.'

'Does anyone here know Lourdes?' asked Arkell.

'I do,' said one of the CSIS officers. 'I volunteered there before college. Spent a summer as *hospitalier*, welcoming pilgrims, wheeling the sick to services, stuff like that.'

'Describe it.'

'I have to say, it's kind of ideal assassin territory. Big open square Andrade's bound to walk across, forested hills all around with commanding views over the basilicas and grotto. A sniper could hide anywhere in those hills and fire as many rounds as he wanted. No danger he'd be caught.'

'There's a grotto?' sighed Henderson.

'It won't happen like that,' said Arkell. 'TARQUIN's weapon is chemical. A poison. He'll want to get close. The question is how he'll deliver it.'

'That's a no-brainer,' said the CSIS officer straight away. 'Andrade's going to Mass, right?'

'Right.'

'Then it's the Eucharist.'

'The *what*?' demanded Henderson.

'Of course,' said Arkell. 'The body and the blood.' When Henderson still looked blank, he added, 'Communion bread and wine.'

'Jesus Christ,' swore Henderson.

'Well, yes, exactly. At least to Catholics.'

The Assistant Commissioner missed Margrave's smile. 'It won't just be Andrade taking communion.'

'No,' agreed Arkell, 'and TARQUIN won't want collateral deaths. At least not in public. He'll look for a way of spiking only the wine or the wafer that Andrade takes.'

'An accomplice in the clergy?'

'An altar boy?'

'A single doctored wafer, kept aside for the president?'

'Something on the rim of the cup, one side only? The priest turns the cup for Andrade?'

The ideas and theories kept coming until Sarah Winter, scrolling through a document on her satellite-linked tablet, interrupted. 'Um, excuse me? It might not be the Eucharist. I mean, there are other possibilities. I have the president's schedule.'

'Go on,' muttered Henderson.

'The Mass will be held in the Rosary Basilica at 9 a.m. But before that, Andrade visits the Grotto of the Virgin, and before that . . .' Winter looked up almost apologetically. 'He's taking a bath.'

FOLKESTONE, ENGLAND – 17 June

Madeleine Wraye could see that the three men standing in the lay-by beside the Eurotunnel exit road were armed. It was 3 a.m., still dark, and they were deliberately positioned behind a parked Austrian camper van, out of view of the CCTV camera. Few people would have noticed, but Wraye knew what to look for and with the passing headlights the slight bulges formed by their handguns were just visible.

Stepping out of her rental car, Wraye felt suddenly drained. Five hours' hard driving from Strasbourg to Calais, with the added strain of wondering how soon ASH would come for her. Because Arkell was right: ASH must know by now. Joyce had had plenty of information to give up under Yadin's blade: her name, her CSIS contract, a dangerous interest in GRIEVANCE and Ellington's death, a shortlist of suspects. What Vine, de Vries or Watchman might have guessed from her questions, ASH now had confirmed courtesy of an idiot analyst who thought he could play with the big boys.

It had become a straightforward race: unmask ASH before he eliminated her.

As the three men in suits and shoulder holsters approached, she straightened, determined not to show her exhaustion. The last stragglers from the shuttle were driving past. In a moment it would be dark again, save for the nearby glow of a hundred Terminal lamps. No witnesses, other than a couple of sleeping Austrians in a camper van.

Which would be worse? Murdered on the orders of the father figure who had recruited her, the partner who'd taken his first SIS steps alongside her, or the unloved exile whose career she'd fought so hard to defend. Vine, Watchman, de Vries. Which would hurt more?

'This car needs to be returned to France,' she said. She wasn't sure why she had begun that way. Perhaps it was the lack of sleep: she hadn't seen a bed for three nights. Perhaps it was fear. 'Can one of you take care of it?'

Were they in fact Austrian tourists in that camper? It had a large aerial, mirrored windows – a perfect surveillance vehicle. She pushed the thought aside. The three men were glancing from one to another. A decision was reached and the tallest stepped forward.

'There'll be an Avis office in Calais by the ferry terminal. You have your passport?'

'Yes, ma'am.'

'My case is in the boot. Would you mind?' She turned her attention to the two cars parked at the end of the lay-by. Both were sleek black Vauxhall saloons. 'Which am I taking?'

One of the other men held out a key. 'The forward vehicle, ma'am.'

She nodded. 'Stay with me as far as Guildford. If you spot a tail or any kind of threat other than uniformed police, take it out. On no account use your weapons unless you're fired upon – just crash the fuckers into a ditch, understood?'

Now that she had protection she drove at a more leisurely pace, conscious that she was tired enough to be a danger to herself even on the largely empty M20. Traffic was heavier on the M25, where she kept to the inside lane and concentrated on working out what to say. She watched the sun rise on the A3; minutes later the other Vauxhall flashed its lights twice and exited via a slip road. By the time she reached the silent village just outside Godalming, a beautiful summer morning had developed.

Pulling into the driveway of the stone cottage, Wraye parked beside a bright green Mini and turned off her engine. There was a good-sized lawn with a scattering of fruit trees, a paddling pool and a crooked wooden platform on which stood a half-built Wendy house. Pink crayon faces decorated the stilts and sides of the platform. She closed her eyes and allowed herself precisely one minute to damn Edward Joyce for his unutterably imbecilic and moronic stupidity. Then she removed her jewellery, cleaned off her Strasbourg make-up, and filled her mind with all the good and clever and admirable things he had done, the competent work, the brightness and hopefulness and loyalty of the man.

Madeleine Wraye pulled her stiff body out of the car and went to wake up his widow.

LOURDES, FRANCE – 17 June

It was many years since Murilo Hernandez Andrade had felt this good. Good in the moral sense. In the pure sense. He was not, he had long accepted, a good man. He knew he was going to hell. That did not mean he could not do good things. With Think Again he was trying, really trying, to do a good thing. But he could not stand before St Peter and say, 'I have not stolen, I have not coveted, I have not committed adultery. I have not killed.'

No, with certainty, he could not say that.

He had lived well. Recently, very well. He had taken commercial and social advantage of his position at various levels of government. He had drunk some of the best whisky in the world, in quantities and mixes that made a mockery of the meticulous efforts of its distillers. He had snorted cocaine off the buttocks of Brazil's finest prostitutes. It had made him feel super-good.

But he had not felt *good* until today.

Standing alone in the modest grotto of Massabielle, hand pressed to the hallowed rock, Murilo Andrade looked up at the statue of the Virgin and marvelled at the wonder of St Bernadette's visions. How he envied her. (Envy! Even here, he was sinning.) At fourteen, Bernadette Soubirous had witnessed divinity and brought the good news to millions. At fourteen, Murilo Andrade had started down a path that would condemn his soul to everlasting damnation.

It had begun as a thing of beauty. Tall and unusually developed for his age, the boy who would one day rule a BRIC powerhouse did that simple and wonderful thing: he made love. It was not his first time; his father, as was common practice in the north-east of Brazil, had taken him to a whorehouse a few months earlier to initiate him. What more natural thing could there be than to share what he had been taught with his consenting girlfriend?

If fathers in Pernambuco are overly permissive with respect to their sons' sexual adventures, the very opposite is true for their daughters. It is quite simply not acceptable, amongst a certain class of north-eastern family, for a daughter to be anything other than a virgin on her wedding day. They must flirt, of course, wear provocative clothes and dance like Venus crossed with Catwoman. But they must not go to bed with a man. So seriously is the matter taken that boyfriends are not infrequently shot dead by vengeful fathers.

In some ways, Murilo Andrade was lucky to be alive.

When he found out, Livia's industrialist father chose a different form of punishment. With the regretful acquiescence of Andrade's parents, who were appalled at the prospect of this rich and powerful man pursuing a vendetta against them, he beat the young Romeo with a cane until his bare flesh had split open in a hundred places.

The scars had been a concern this morning. At the baths, after an extraordinary delay caused by his protection team insisting on a last-second switch of bath in case the water was poisoned (the sacred, healing water of Lourdes, my *God*!), he had been introduced to the two Hospitalité volunteers who would bathe him.

'You will see things,' he told them in bad French, 'that I do not wish to be known.'

They responded with compassionate but dismissive nods that assured him nothing observed in the baths was ever discussed. And so, once the curtain was drawn on his bodyguards and a wet towel had been wrapped around his waist, he allowed them to lower his great disfigured body into the icy water that had welled from Bernadette's spring. It touched him, that water, as nothing in his life. The cool, clean essence of the Virgin soaked through his skin and into his bones, his brain, his burdened heart. It was the beginning of letting go.

He would not have done it for the caning alone. At fourteen, in that culture, he believed he deserved it. But that was just the start of his punishment. Senhor Pereira insisted that the boy who had defiled his daughter must now marry her. They were minors; with both sets of parents in a kind of collusion, the young couple had no choice. Murilo was taken out of school and sent to work in the Pereira shoe factory, two hundred kilometres away, cutting leather in a fusty workshop. He was forbidden physical access to Livia until his sixteenth birthday, when he met her again on the steps of an altar. Denied his education, bound for life before God to a woman he no longer knew, Murilo Andrade was allowed one night to make love to his distraught wife before being sent back to the factory.

Something in the young Andrade just snapped. And one scalding day, during a visit to the shoe factory, something in the neck of Senhor Pereira also snapped. There were no witnesses. In the end the police called it an accidental death.

No witnesses but God. Yes, Andrade knew he was going to hell.

Thanks to his wife's considerable inherited wealth, Andrade had been able to begin afresh. He went back to school, then college, then law school. And with Livia's share of the Pereira fortune he funded his political campaigns, first at the municipal level while he pursued a career as a patent lawyer, and then at state and federal level when his charisma, intelligence and determination began to draw a following.

There had been corruption, yes, of course, and debauchery and excess. But really, why not? He was condemned anyway. And yet he did feel good now, washed almost clean of his sins in the chill waters of Lourdes. Almost pure enough to stand here, in this revered spot, and share a little of the sanctity of Bernadette.

For the first time since he'd broken Pereira's neck, he felt righteous.

* * *

From his position behind the Sanctuary of the Rosary Basilica, Simon Arkell – who had broken three necks in his life without the slightest concern about eternal damnation – watched as the Brazilian close protection officers oversaw the preparation of the Eucharist. They were taking no chances. The chalice and paten had been carefully cleaned and then cleaned again under their supervision. New wafers, wine and water had been hurriedly procured from one of the smaller chapels by the river. Only the chaplain, a man who had lived and worked in Lourdes for twenty-eight years, was permitted to handle them, and then only under the strictest observation.

On the recommendation of Assistant Commissioner Henderson, the Brazilian team had given Arkell an earpiece radio and authorization to move freely around the great Byzantine rotunda and the other holy sites: he had mingled with the crowd of pilgrims singing 'Ave Maria' at the baths; he'd walked ahead of Andrade down the hellish line of *brulières*, scanning the faces of the *feutiers* who perfunctorily scraped fat candle stubs off the fiery grids; at the grotto, he had stood a little to the side, maintaining a clear view of the meadow and buildings across the Gave de Pau. The Brazilians had not given him a weapon. That had come from Margrave as he stepped off the plane.

'Lose it permanently when you're done,' the CSIS director had said, keeping the Glock, shoulder holster and spare clip out of sight of the airside staff at Tarbes-Lourdes-Pyrénées. 'If the French find it on you, you did *not* get it from a Canadian.'

Arkell was confident that Yadin was not inside the windowless building; every possible hiding place had been searched, and he had personally checked the face of every person entering the church. But there could be an accomplice. Stalking around the perimeter of the nave, past the fifteen side chapels with their mosaic depictions of the mysteries of the rosary, he kept a close watch on the expressions and gestures of the worshippers near the president. The Basilica's domed construction, with no pillars blocking sightlines, made surveillance easier. His eyes followed Andrade up to the Sanctuary, and he tensed as the host and the wine were swallowed. Nothing. The president rose, crossed himself, and returned to his pew.

The gentle whisper of professional Brazilian voices in his ear faded beneath the much louder ensemble of a thousand joyous Catholic singers. It didn't matter. He didn't understand much of the Portuguese anyway. If something was important they'd tell him in English. Andrade was getting carried away, tears in his eyes as he sang. Arkell envied the strength of the congregation's faith – if not their actual beliefs, built on the claims of a nineteenth-century teenager. He forced himself to focus. Where was he, right now, that resourceful Israeli? And what was he planning?

A withered sacristan approached the president with a glass vial. This part of the ceremony was most definitely not on the official schedule. Pressing the transmit button on his radio he said urgently, 'I don't care how therapeutic that water is, do not let Andrade drink it, touch it or even so much as inhale it.'

Standing on the threshold of the Rosary Basilica, Murilo Andrade paused a moment to enjoy the brilliant sunshine and the magnificence of his surroundings. To either side, sweeping stone ramps led up to the neo-Gothic Upper Basilica on the great Massabielle rock behind him. Ahead lay the broad expanse of Rosary Square, with the Esplanade des Processions beyond. Halfway down the esplanade, a long line of blue bath chairs pulled by youthful volunteers, sweltering in matching yellow tabards, transported the sick to a service of thanksgiving in the monumental underground Basilica of Pius X. In the distance, the ancient château fort loomed high over the town.

A few moments from now he would be locked in a car, and then a plane for maybe twelve hours. Despite his bodyguards' pleas to keep moving, he allowed himself this short moment of luxury.

A crowd had gathered in Rosary Square, held back by two lines of municipal police manning hurriedly assembled steel barriers. Word of the Brazilian president's unannounced visit had got around, and even in a town famous for more spiritual concerns there was no shortage of curious onlookers. Scouts in neckerchiefs and shorts jostled with tourists and sunburnt *stagiaires* for a view of the controversial premier. Andrade smiled to himself at the unease this holy mob would be causing his detail. He felt unsympathetic after the business with the water. Did they not understand that the Immaculata herself had instructed pilgrims to 'drink at the spring and wash in it'? Well, he had washed; now it was time to drink. But the officers were resolute, and Andrade had given way rather than cause a scene in church.

The cars, with their motorcycle police escort, were waiting in front of the statue of the Crowned Virgin. He wished they had not driven right into the centre of the Domain. Earlier, they had parked discreetly just inside St Joseph's Gate, and he had happily walked the short distance to the baths. Now, it seemed, security concerns had trumped religious decorum. His protection detail hovered either side of him as they started down the narrow corridor between the steel barriers, using their bodies to spoil the aim of any gunman lurking in the crowd. The officers were all tall: if not quite as wide around the chest as Andrade, they certainly matched him for height. He felt, as often on these occasions, like he was walking inside a moving cage.

A flash of yellow and green caught his eye. Someone unfurling a Brazilian flag over the barrier to his left. A charming gesture! It was a young woman, a nurse in white uniform with a long black cape and two red ribbons crossing her chest. Her white headscarf, in the style of a nun's veil, struggled to contain a curly abundance of flaming copper hair. Was she a compatriot, come all this way like him to honour Nossa Senhora? Or a friendly local, showing support for the visiting leader?

'*Licença . . .*' he murmured to the officer next to him, edging diagonally towards the flag.

The man tried to dissuade him. But Andrade did not feel like being caged any more. It was this very officer who had snatched away the vial of sacred water, embarrassing both the old sacristan and himself. Petulantly, Andrade brushed him aside.

Along with her Brazilian flag, the nurse was holding a red rose. She really was very pretty, in a sweet, devotional kind of way. Andrade offered his most winning smile. '*Bom dia, senhora. Como se chama?*'

She hesitated charmingly. He had always had a weakness for red hair. '*Adriana, Senhor Presidente. Adriana Lecouvreur.*'

He was delighted. He'd named his own daughter Adriana! '*Nome bonito*,' he declared happily as he took the proffered flower.

She made a little suggestive motion, bringing her hand towards her nose, inviting him to do likewise.

Really – how charming!

The president of Brazil raised the blood-red rose until its thick, velvety petals were brushing his upper lip – and inhaled.

In mid-sentence, urging the Brazilian officers to remove the flower at once from their principal's hand, Arkell saw the woman in the nurse's outfit turn and look towards a figure at the edge of the square, by the foot of the northern ramp. He was dressed differently from the night before, and was wearing a pale straw hat, but there was no mistaking the posture or the profile.

Arkell had left the Basilica ahead of the president, had taken up position among the *Malades* benches on the north side of the square to watch for Yadin. Now that he saw him he knew it was already too late.

He did not wait for Kolatch's poison to take effect, but sprinted towards Yadin, who saw him immediately and started running. Dangerous to pull a gun here, with twitchy French cops all around. Instead he yelled into the Brazilian radio: 'North side of square! I need back-up! And grab the nurse!' But he knew that the moment their principal fell the close protection officers would think only of CPR and ambulances. He was on his own.

Yadin ran straight at a pair of motorcycle gendarmes, the

rearguard of the president's motorcade, parked in the shade of a large linden tree near the Reconciliation Chapel. They saw him coming and half-rose out of their seats. One put his hand on his holstered pistol.

Yadin shot them both while running. The four gunshots echoed across the square, but at that same moment a collective gasp arose from the crowd lining the barriers, swiftly followed by shouts and one unearthly scream. It seemed to many that the shots and the collapse of the president were connected. Only a few people near the Reconciliation Chapel noticed the small, violent sideshow at the edge of the square.

The bullets lifted one gendarme right off his motorcycle. His partner teetered in his seat, somehow balancing the bike as his heart stopped beating. Yadin hauled him backwards, deftly slipping into his place before the motorcycle could fall. Firing twice at Arkell, he roared off down the tree-lined walkway.

Arkell had expected the shots, had dropped to the ground at the right moment, and now launched himself towards the remaining motorcycle. The engine was still running. Heaving the machine upright, Arkell climbed on and shifted into gear. Yadin had reached the end of the walkway and cut up to the esplanade, heading for the cluster of pilgrimage crosses and St Michael's Gate beyond. By now, other gendarmes on the ramp and in the square had noticed the fate of their colleagues. Those last two shots had cut through the commotion around the president.

As Arkell sped away in pursuit, half a dozen different police and Gendarmerie officers got a good clear look at his face.

WIMBLEDON, ENGLAND – 17 June

He had been untraceable in the preceding days. A retired civil servant who eschewed email and mobile phones, Sir Matthew Milford had chosen to spend three blissful weeks touring the mausoleums, mosques and madrasas of Samarkand and Tashkent. The pilgrimage had put him in a generous, benevolent frame of mind, and consequently he was more than usually inclined to be helpful to his unexpected visitor.

He remembered her, of course; serving on the FCO Management Board at the time of her dismissal, the rumours of a stitch-up by colleagues jockeying for the Chief's job had reached his ears. She was officially still an outcast, and on a different day he might have taken a dogmatically official line. But the mosaics of Uzbekistan had inspired in him a new hope for humanity, and this was after all a woman who, by common Whitehall consent, had served her country with distinction.

'Rupert Ellington? Yes, certainly I remember him. What a sad time that was.'

'You knew him well?'

'Does one ever know your sort well?' he smiled. 'I liked him. We played tennis together, and he was generous with his time when my children wanted to try his guitar. I would say we worked well together.'

Madeleine Wraye, while perhaps a little frayed around the edges, looked as resolute as always. Whatever she was doing with herself these days clearly agreed with her. She was taking only tiny sips, he noticed, of the cardamom coffee his wife had prepared for them. But she had complimented the cups he'd bought in Tashkent. Sir Matthew had been unable to resist the mesmerizing blue Ishkor glaze of the Rishtan ceramics, though God knew he had enough coffee sets to entertain a sheikh's entourage.

'More sugar?' he offered.

Declining politely, she said, 'I'm sorry to bring it up, but do you remember what was going on the day he died?'

Frowning, Sir Matthew began to sense an object behind this unlikely social call. 'I do, I suppose, yes.'

'It's a long time ago. Why has it stuck in your memory – apart from Rupert, of course?'

'There was a bit of a panic on that day. I rather wondered, the next morning when I heard the news, if it hadn't brought on the aneurysm.'

'What kind of panic?'

Sir Matthew hesitated. 'Is this something you're looking into for someone? Should I be checking with King Charles Street before talking about it?'

'I'm afraid they'll tell you to show me the door. Call it unfinished business, Sir Matthew. Something rotten in the system that I owe it to the Service to sort out. I'm not asking you to tell me anything you consider more than nominally secret.'

He contemplated that. It really was a very long time ago. Madeleine Wraye was essentially on the same team, notwithstanding the quibble over data security or whatever it was. And Deborah seemed to like her, which long experience had suggested was a pretty good indicator.

'It was a panic without foundation, as it turned out. Brought on by one of your lot. Anthony Watchman rang me with an urgent terror alert. They'd picked up chatter about an imminent attack on a British compound near Old Diriyah. A bit frightening, if I'm honest, after the Khobar Towers bombing. Anthony painted a most alarming picture of jihadis overrunning the place on explosive-rigged motorbikes. So we were rather busy that day, liaising with the Saudi security forces, installing extra barriers and so on.'

'Tony called you personally?'

'I thought it a bit strange myself. Poor Rupert, I'm afraid it put his nose out of joint rather. I suppose Anthony felt that with such a serious and imminent threat he had to get the Ambassador's attention PDQ, although of course if Rupert had come to me with the same information I would have dropped everything.'

'This may seem an odd question, but did Rupert have anything else going on that day?'

'No time for anything else,' he laughed. 'Can I offer you a fresh coffee? The bloom's gone off that one, I'd say.'

'Thank you, no. I don't need to take up much more of your morning, Sir Matthew. Just one other question. Did Anthony Watchman send you something by courier that day?'

'Goodness, how would I recall a thing like that?'

'Perhaps related to the terror alert?'

He paused. 'How odd! Yes, that's right. I'd completely forgotten. The geranium man.'

'*Geranium* man?'

'Sorry, I should explain.' He laughed at the memory, dormant for a decade. 'Deborah planted splendid great urns of geraniums outside the gates of the Residence. Actually quite tricky to grow in Riyadh, for some reason, but she pulled it off. When Anthony's man turned up with the file on the supposed motorcycle terrorists – who never materialized, by the way – the night watchman said the first thing he did, before even ringing the bell, was take a close look at the geraniums. In the pitch dark too. Deborah was rather chuffed by that. Most visitors barely noticed them.'

She was a funny sort, reflected Sir Matthew after his uninvited guest had left. Professional and quick-witted – bit of a loss to British Intelligence, actually. Yet he couldn't be quite certain he trusted her. At least she hadn't asked about anything confidential. He wasn't entirely sure, on reflection, exactly what she had asked.

Driving out of Wimbledon, Madeleine Wraye was so distracted that she almost didn't notice the restaurant. Only the vivid safari colours of Potjiekos drew her mind back to the present and made her pull abruptly onto the pavement.

On impulse, she walked in. Two waiters dressed in springbok-adorned polo shirts were laying tables for lunch. A woman, the manager perhaps, was at the bar, poring over a ledger.

'I'm looking for one of your waitresses. I don't know her name but she works Sunday evenings.'

The woman glanced up, jaundiced and distracted. 'We're closed Sundays.'

Wraye stood motionless. 'Every Sunday?'

'Yup.'

'Is there another branch that—?'

'Nope.'

She looked at the modest scattering of tables. In her mind's eye, she very clearly saw de Vries and van Rensburg in the corner, lamenting the state of British foreign policy over boerewors and bobotie, even though she now knew it couldn't have happened.

Oh, Edward. What were you thinking?

HAUTES-PYRÉNÉES, FRANCE – 17 June

Somewhere far behind, half the gendarmerie were following. Slower to navigate the crowded, narrow streets of Lourdes, their cars had lost a lot of ground by the time they reached the dual carriageway south. Their sirens were fading, and at the pace Yadin had set they were never going to catch up. Arkell wondered whether the motorcycles had GPS trackers: the gendarmes might, if they were exceptionally well organized and had units in the right mountain villages, be able to establish a roadblock between Yadin and the Spanish frontier. But he wasn't going to count on it.

Yadin knew how to use a bike. Christ, he was nimble. The Legion hadn't taught two-wheel skills, but Arkell had amused himself experimenting during a week of downtime in Pakistan. He wondered if motorcycles featured in the Mossad's training programme and decided they almost certainly did. The Kidon manual probably set out a bunch of useful instructions: how to come alongside a moving vehicle and attach a shaped charge; how to remove oneself fast from the scene of a murder; how to fire a handgun while doing 160kph on winding roads.

Arkell had no intention of trying that.

Gavriel Yadin cut across an alluvial plain, then followed the winding course of a river as the mountains rose around them. They roared through a gorge where twelve cars crawled behind a flock of cyclists in brightly coloured spandex. Yadin accelerated past them all in the face of oncoming vehicles, forcing Arkell to follow him through terrifyingly narrow gaps. The roadway was especially constricted in the gorge, squeezed between sheer rock and a tumbling river. Broad nets strung overhead to catch falling debris only added to the sense of claustrophobic enclosure.

When the gorge opened up, Yadin took a side road that climbed out of the valley. Maybe he wasn't making for Spain after all. Maybe he too was considering the possibility of roadblocks. Isolated gîtes and farmhouses flew past. Spray from a waterfall dampened Arkell's face and gave the tarmac a treacherous lustre. Startled drivers swerved out of their way. Ten minutes out of Lourdes, Arkell became aware of the changing temperature, the cooler breezes and occasional cloud overhead.

They cut through a dark birch forest and then, as the road levelled out, bounced over a cattle grid and raced on across open pasture. In the distance, the rumble of a helicopter, layered over their engines. Cows with heavy bells, an Alpine scene, grazed placidly around them. An estate car was parked on the grass beside a picnicking family. Beyond them, three cyclists had abandoned their bikes to rehydrate and take photographs.

Something was bothering Arkell. The woman with the poisoned flower – Yadin's accomplice – she had seemed . . . not familiar, exactly, but reminiscent of some earlier memory. Arkell had not got a clear view of her face; he had seen a glimpse of reddish hair, and that flash of puppyish pride in the set of her chin when she gazed towards Yadin. But by then, he was already turning to see what she saw . . .

The helicopter came into view: blue and white, the colours of the gendarmerie, but it was too far to the west. So much for GPS trackers. A quick glance at the dash, and a low-fuel warning light caught his attention. Yadin's odds were improving fast. Arkell considered trying a shot, but the range was impossible. He needed an opportunity fast.

It came just a few minutes later, approaching the snowy granite peaks that marked the Spanish border. Their route had carried them over a high ridge, where gusts of wind tested the balance of both riders, and Yadin was now accelerating down a zigzagging road into the valley beyond. Red-topped snow poles marked out eight hairpin bends. An opportunity – but a risky one.

The grassy hillside was liberally scattered with boulders and scree. Not a healthy environment even for an off-road motorcycle equipped with suitable tyres, forks and suspension. But what the hell: he was out of fuel anyway. As Arkell dipped low around one bend and saw Yadin racing towards the next, he went for it. Coming upright he leaned immediately to the other side, describing an elegant S-track that launched him off the road and landed him with a jarring thud on the rock-strewn slope.

Navigating a tortuous course between boulders and fissures, Arkell reached for the Glock. The muscles of his left forearm bunched and trembled with the effort of keeping the bike steady. He was less than halfway to the next stretch of the zigzag before he was spotted. Yadin accelerated and pulled out his own weapon.

The navigable stretch of hillside was coming to an end. The way down was blocked by a mass of granite boulders. Arkell had hoped a route would open up between them, but as he bounced and skidded and slalomed towards it, the array of boulders remained solidly unbroken.

Tightening his grip, readying himself for the impact, Arkell drove straight at a slanting outcrop of rock, using it as a ramp to lift him into the air so that his spinning tyres bounced once on the flattest of the boulders and he was propelled blind onto the tarmac below.

As he dropped onto the road, right in front of Yadin, both men fired. Then Arkell was crashing down the next stretch of hillside, and immediately he was in trouble.

This slope was steeper, densely scattered with boulders and pitted with fissures and crevices. His brakes seemed to have barely any effect. By some miracle he escaped the worst of the fissures, and he took the rest at an angle that kept the wheels from catching. Steering between the boulders, slowing, just about making it . . .

Until a loose stone bumped his rear wheel onto a patch of scree which sent the bike sliding sideways and round and down until he went over.

He landed hard, just managing to pull his legs clear as the machine crashed down and hurtled on into a boulder. The crunch and howl of twisting metal was terminal.

Arkell allowed himself a few seconds to deal with the pain in his head, his hip, his right knee. As he lay there, more points of injury became apparent. Lacerated forearm, knuckle abrasion, shoulder contusion. The growing list was not helpful. He lifted his head to look for Yadin, but lowered it immediately as a wave of nausea struck him. A little bump to the skull. He'd had those before. It would pass.

Reloading, he gazed back up the hill.

No sign of Yadin.

Nothing was broken. He could move both legs, with some complaint from the right knee. He could flex all his fingers and toes. Gingerly rolling sideways, he confirmed that his spine was undamaged. Vision fine. The rest was unimportant. No bullet holes in him, although when he crawled over to the misshapen bike and turned off the engine he found one in the seat.

A new quiet. With the motorcycle silent at last, he could finally hear the Pyrenees – the punchy winds, the rustle of grass, the intermittent whistling call of red kites overhead. And in the distance, muted sirens and the low rumble of the Gendarmerie helicopter.

No sound from the other bike.

Crouched beside a boulder, he raised the Glock. Which way to point it? Yadin could be lying injured on the road above, or he could have continued on to approach from below. One way or the other, he was close by. Had he ridden away, unscathed and uninterested, the sound of his engine would have been audible for miles.

Above or below?

Arkell laid his left hand flat against the ground, picturing the Gascon smugglers and Basque separatists and subsistence herdsmen and Vichy militia and horseback lovers who had passed over this spot. That brief connection settled him, dulling the pain.

A sound. A small rock, perhaps only a pebble, skittering across the percussive hillside. Still a little disoriented, he was fairly sure the noise came from above.

On principle, Simon Arkell hated staying still when the enemy knew his location. Better just to go have it out. He tested his muscles, readied himself, checked the Glock. Then he started running.

Sprinting between the boulders, randomly altering his course up the hillside to make it as hard as possible for Yadin to target him, Arkell powered his way back up the hill. The sprint drew a fresh wave of nausea and redoubled the pain in his skull and knee. But he had lost interest in his physical state. He wanted to know. He really, urgently wanted to know.

Had he got him?

Something made him shift his gaze, and he saw to his astonishment the figure of a man cresting the ridge far up beyond the switchback road. Moving with speed and purpose; no limp, no obvious injury. Sprinting up to the road, Arkell saw the other bike lying crumpled about two hundred metres from the intersection point. Things were looking up. Arkell knew mountains. He had spent *long* months marching through mountains. Whatever endurance tests the Mossad put their Kidon recruits through, it was highly unlikely they featured quite so much mountain time as the Legion's programme.

Smiling broadly to himself, despite the lingering nausea and aches, Simon Arkell set off at a steady jog up the hillside.

LONDON, ENGLAND – 17 June

Three left. Vine, de Vries, Watchman.

Linus Marshall used to say there was no such thing as truth in Counter-Intelligence: everything rested on the interpretation of tiny, ambiguous fragments of evidence; the art lay in assembling the most plausible story to fit those fragments. The trouble was, decided Madeleine Wraye, there were three equally plausible stories on the table.

Martin de Vries, driven by a hatred of narcotics and the urge to avenge his dead sister, with unrivalled technical access to the machinery of SIS, caught in a lie about his knowledge of Arkell's return from Yemen. The fact that Joyce had fabricated evidence against him did not make him innocent.

Tony Watchman, whose career owed much to attacks like GRIEVANCE, linked to Yadin – in this latter-day wilderness of mirrors – by Rodrigo Salis's murder. He'd dispatched a last-minute courier to Riyadh on the day of Ellington's death – with a vial of poison to be cached for Yadin in the ambassador's geraniums?

George Vine, the only director known to have met Yadin, with a proven financial tie to one of GRIEVANCE's major beneficiaries . . .

She paused on Vine. Where was the link to Think Again? If AMB was Vine's sponsor, and Vine commissioned Yadin's assassinations . . . what might AMB have against drug reform?

An idea . . . A possible motive. AMB was one of the USA's primary contractors in Afghanistan and the Middle East, trusted by the Department of Defense to deliver a private-sector solution to a tough government problem. Might not the DoD's buddies at the Department for Homeland Security also draw on their services?

The facts weren't hidden, as her search engine swiftly revealed. They just weren't that widely known. It had never been a big news story. The replacement of US Coast Guard and Customs and Border Protection staff and equipment by AMB assets had been so gradual as to seem largely uncontroversial. First, as in war, AMB had supplied logistical support and facilities management. Its security teams had taken on some of the administrative burden of processing captured smugglers and drugs. Then the company had begun to operate a few of the USCG's cutters on a sale-and-leaseback basis, still with uniformed Coast Guard personnel on board but with AMB hands on the engines and tiller. A new division had been set up to pilot non-weaponized drones along the US–Mexican border fence; its monitoring staff had successfully directed Border Protection officers towards smugglers building ramps or firing contraband over the fence from catapults and pneumatic cannons. Another division was tasked with detecting tunnels, using a range of ground-based and satellite technologies.

Finally, in an era of government cutbacks, and with a compellingly priced offering, AMB had been contracted to take over many of the routine counter-narcotics patrols both at sea and on land. Just another case of creeping privatization in the ongoing process of downsizing the federal government. At a time when the space programme was being outsourced, and even air traffic control and the postal service were being sized up for sale, it was not surprising that routine supervision of the War on Drugs had been entrusted to the private sector.

In the contested streets of Iraq, AMB had built their reputation for efficient and orderly fulfilment of contractual obligations; along the extensive southern border of the US, they were collecting on that reputation, quietly channelling a sizeable proportion of the Homeland Security counter-narcotics budget into their own coffers. And what would happen to that multibillion-dollar revenue stream if Think Again's reformatory agenda reached Washington? Yes, AMB had every reason to wish Anneke van der Velde, Murilo Andrade and Terence Mayhew silenced.

Wraye's phone rang: it was one of the two international news-scanning organizations she paid to alert her to events of relevance to her work. She listened to what the researcher had to say and brought up the BBC News homepage. The shaky smartphone footage from Lourdes showed only the president staggering and collapsing, although a couple of gunshots could be heard in the background. He was holding a rose, she noticed; he didn't let go of it, even as he fell. It was almost beautiful.

HAUTES-PYRÉNÉES, FRANCE – 17 June

The cirque was majestic, a great natural amphitheatre at the head of the valley, a geological bowl adorned with packed snow and waterfalls. Swathes of pine forest reached partway up the gentler slopes, but the rest was sheer granite, stepped cliffs with only the occasional small plateau to interrupt the vertical rock. Beyond rose the highest peaks in this region of the Pyrenees – the Spanish frontier – a forbidding wall of near-vertical rock.

No villages, no roads, nothing but raw, unforgiving splendour.

They had been running towards the cirque for over an hour. The Gendarmerie helicopter had come into view occasionally, but never close enough to spot them. Arkell had matched the other man's formidable pace, always keeping the distant figure in sight but resisting the temptation to try to close the gap. They had settled into a kind of unspoken agreement: there would be no desperate racing; the outcome would be a question of stamina alone.

Looking up at the great Palaeozoic crest of rock that lay ahead, Arkell couldn't believe Yadin meant to go over it. Spain might be slightly safer, the police a little less determined to catch a French cop killer, but the risk of tackling that rock face without any gear . . . Surely it was easier for a man of Yadin's talents simply to disappear in France.

Unless his objective was not to escape. Could it be that this contest with a well-matched opponent had become more important to the Israeli?

For the first time, Arkell considered seriously the possibility of going up that rock face dressed in clothes intended only for a formal evening event in Strasbourg.

Yadin's path led through a meadow of purple and yellow wild flowers, and then across a pebble-strewn river. They were getting close now; the sound of tumbling water was growing loud. A small pine wood obscured the lower reach of the main waterfall, but the upper section sparkled in the early-afternoon sun. A cloud of fine spray caught by the wind dispersed into nothing. The river was a relief after six hot kilometres. Arkell allowed himself a few seconds' pause to gulp the deliciously cold water.

Clearing the treeline, he blinked rapidly against the light. The waterfall was two hundred metres away, a thundering rush of ice-cold snowmelt. And there at its base was Yadin, half lost in the spray, staring directly at him.

The man waited a moment longer, then turned and vanished behind the cascade. Arkell slowed down. Whatever else, there was surely no need to run any more. Yadin wasn't going anywhere but up. At last Arkell understood: the waterfall would obscure Yadin's progress up the rock face, protect him from a ground shot. It also made the physical challenge of the ascent that much greater, and Arkell had by now acknowledged the importance of that factor to his opponent.

He was starting almost to like the guy.

Grinning, he ambled across the banks of gravel and fluvial debris and the grimy packed snow that covered the ground. The spray, this close, was blinding. There had been little undercutting, even over millennia, of the hard granite face. Only a slight gap separated water and rock – enough to provide air to breathe and a semi-dry surface to climb.

Edging forward, Glock in hand, Arkell peered upwards. Little light penetrated the curtain. No movement, other than the constant rush of foaming water. Just a bare, bleak wall disappearing into near darkness overhead.

A scrape in the moss, three metres off the ground. Arkell climbed onto a boulder to get a closer look. The mark was fresh, the rock dry and clean where the moss had been stripped away. By Yadin's boot? There was the first handhold, there the jutting pimple he'd used to step up. Arkell examined it closely. A trace of mud marked the edge.

Tucking the weapon into his waistband, he set his own foot on the same fragment of rock and started climbing.

The ascent at first was not difficult. The granite was sheer, but there were plenty of fissures to grip or to wedge a fist inside, and a few protrusions here and there for a foothold. He kept scanning the rock face above, searching for movement in the gloom.

No Yadin.

The waterfall closed in around him as he approached the overhang. Water flooded the rock face on both sides. Yadin must have forced his way through the water to one side or the other. But which way?

In the darkness beneath the overhang, it was hard to make out the bumps and holes on which his life depended. Glancing down, he saw the shallow plunge pool and the boulder debris of the talus far below. It would be an instantly fatal fall. He imagined Yadin, up here in the darkness, gazing down at him while clinging for his life to these few meagre holds.

Which way? Running his fingers over the rock face, Arkell could find nothing at all to grasp on the left side. To the right, an inadequate crimp. He formed a rigid claw over it and felt around with his foot for some kind of toehold. Nothing within reach except a narrow fissure. He couldn't fit any part of his shoe into it, but maybe . . .

Retreating to his earlier holds, he took off his shoes and secured them under his belt. With some difficulty, he managed to jam his smaller toes into the fissure. He leaned close into the wall, let go of his last secure hold, and trusted his weight to his toes. Switching hands on the crimp, he swiftly spread his right fingers to search the rock beyond. A long stretch, almost to the watery curtain, found a robust chickenhead.

Easing his toes out of the fissure, he let himself swing one-handed from the new hold.

A soft spatter of droplets cut through the fine mist, dampening his face. His bare feet found a narrow ledge that seemed to extend into the waterfall. Switching hands, he reached sideways with his right arm to assess the force of the flow. Not good.

He found a sharp-edged fissure for his right fingers, and eased his way along the ledge. The barrage of ice-cold water on his shoulder, then on his head, unbalanced him, and he lay flat against the rock for a few seconds to get used to the rushing, disorientating flow. He could see nothing at all now. The cold was paralysing. He had endured colder conditions, but not when his life depended on the precise functioning of his fingers and toes.

Sliding his right foot sideways, he measured another half metre of support before the ledge came to an end. Beyond that, the slick wet rock face was bare.

Cursing, he balanced on his left toes, left fingers crimping that sharp-edged fissure, while his right hand and foot searched the rock face beyond for some kind of hold. It was completely smooth: no way to climb any further. Already the icy torrent battering his skull was bringing on a headache. Go back? Try the left route? He wasn't at all sure that retreat past the chickenhead would even be possible.

Arkell opened his eyes beneath a visored hand and let them adjust to the glow of light coming through the waterfall. It was perhaps another two metres to the edge of the water. He could see just the faintest outline of the dry rock face beyond.

Crouched down, left foot poised on the end of the ledge, he let go of the fissure above and focused all his energy into his left leg. The icy water was already causing him to shiver violently. It was time to move.

Thrusting hard, he propelled his body upwards and sideways. With eyes creased almost closed, he could just make out the rock face rushing past. Then he was out of the waterfall, in bright, clear sunshine, and starting to fall. As the curve of his trajectory steepened and his vertical speed accelerated, he glimpsed a rough and fracturing ledge. His right fingers, drawn into a claw, lunged at it, grasping and scratching for a hold. A piece of granite came away, and with it his fingers, but his left hand was ready to take their place, forming a tenuous clamp on what was left of the ledge.

It held.

He hung, motionless, and gazed around. Three metres to the right, a buttress he could reach via an indent and a jug. Eighty metres below, the scree-covered ground. And just thirty metres above, hauling himself onto a granite outcrop: Yadin.

Still hanging from one arm, Arkell whipped out the Glock and fired three rapid shots. His aim, squinting against the sun, was slightly off. Fragments of granite burst from the mountainside. He corrected for the error and fired again. But Yadin had rolled forward onto the outcrop and disappeared. Stuffing the Glock back in his belt, Arkell twisted sideways, stamped on the indent to get a hold on the jug and swung himself onto the buttress.

God, it was good to be able to see again.

Beyond the buttress, the rock face curved inward, and Arkell eased his way round to a gully out of Yadin's line of fire. The gully led more or less straight upwards for fifty metres, with big dry rocks jutting out on either side. In comparison with the rock face he'd just left, it was the equivalent of an express elevator. A child could have scrambled up it.

It was a chance to close the gap.

Simon Arkell hauled himself from rock to rock, kicking off one boulder to pounce onto another. The cold of the waterfall was wearing off. New energy coursed through him. If he could just get higher than Yadin . . .

He emerged from the top of the gully onto a scrap of rough, sloping ground that still bore a few traces of dirty snow. The grass that clung to it was thinly spread and coarse. With the Glock in his right hand, Arkell crawled to the edge and gazed across to the outcrop.

No one there.

His feet were throbbing from a dozen sharp edges, and he paused to put on his shoes. Then he continued upwards.

By two o'clock, Simon Arkell was starting to worry. He had kept the entire local area of the cirque under constant observation, yet had seen no sign of his quarry. Each time he crested another rise or peered over a new ledge, he expected to spot the Israeli scaling the next stretch of rock. But there was never anything but patches of old snow and the occasional eagle using the mountain updraughts to rise lazily into the sky.

He began to wonder if the other man had outsmarted him, had found a way down, was already ambling towards the nearest village. Arkell was thirsty. The sun was brighter at this altitude, unrelenting. His clothes had long since dried out in the gusting winds: there was no moisture to be sucked from a shirtsleeve. He considered the residues of snow, streaked with black, and decided he was not yet that thirsty.

He had traversed slowly across the cirque to intersect what he believed to be Yadin's route, but could find no sign the other man had ever been here. At this altitude there was little noise from the waterfall, and Arkell spent long minutes trying to detect the scrape of scree on rock, or the tumble of a dislodged pebble. But if Yadin was moving anywhere nearby, he was doing it without making a sound.

Arkell kept climbing.

There was something about the little meadow that made him pause. A welcome plateau between two challenging bluffs, it was green and lush compared to the sparse patches of grass scattered elsewhere on the cirque slopes. It would have been a beautiful place to come with a packed Gascon lunch and a case of cold beers, if it wasn't so hard to reach.

No movement. No sign of the man. Arkell lowered his weapon.

It seemed, then, to fly from his hand. His right arm was flung outwards as an intense pain tore through it. The sound of the gunshot he registered almost as an afterthought. The Glock had landed several metres away. He needed to leap towards it, drop to the ground, work out Yadin's position – three tasks already in his mind, not quite carried out when the second round struck his left leg and he collapsed.

Simon Arkell did not have time to crawl towards his weapon. Closing his mind to the searing pain, he saw a man already standing in the place it had landed. The man's own gun rested neatly against his thigh, the trigger finger of the right hand flush against its barrel.

That finger tapped twice on the metal, a contemplative action. Arkell raised his eyes to gaze into Gavriel Yadin's bleak face. The assassin looked tired. Capable, but tired.

He picked up the Glock and hurled it far out over the valley.

'Shouldn't have done that,' managed Arkell through the pain. 'Some kid will blow his toes off.'

Yadin made a brief phone call. His words were inaudible to Arkell. Then he walked the eight paces that separated them and gazed down at the crumpled figure. 'What's your name?'

'I can't remember.'

Yadin drew back his foot, and kicked him very precisely on the entry wound on his thigh.

It took Arkell a moment to get his breath back, but when he did he managed a convincing laugh.

Yadin watched him expressionlessly. 'Your friend in Strasbourg gave a good description of you. He knew your approximate age. He believed that you once worked for SIS, but he did not know your name and could not find your file.'

Poor Joyce, thought Arkell. He must have suffered a lot worse than this.

When Yadin kicked his leg a second time, he just grinned.

The Israeli sighed. 'In fact, this question of one name or another name is not interesting to me. Others find it interesting but now, after this long climb you and I have made, I do not care. I have a different question. It was you in Cyprus?'

Arkell nodded, clamping his jaw against the waves of pain coming from his thigh.

'My question is only personal: I . . . sensed someone in the restaurant in Limassol. Was it you? Did you come in?'

'Yes.'

'But you didn't act.' He glanced sideways at the sound of an engine. 'Why?'

'Guess I'm not cut out to be an assassin. Maybe you could give me some pointers.'

Yadin was quiet for a while. Somewhere overhead, the noise of the engine grew, accompanied by the thud of rotating blades.

'You let me finish my dinner,' said Yadin. He holstered the Sig Sauer. 'I will let you finish your . . .' He gestured around the cirque, the towering rock walls, the precipitous plunge to the valley floor. '. . . excursion.'

A black and yellow civilian helicopter came into Arkell's field of view, dropping neatly onto the meadow behind Yadin. Spanish registration. An efficient exfiltration; no doubt the original rendezvous had been at a somewhat lower altitude.

'You're good,' said Yadin, with a last look at the route they'd both climbed. He hesitated before turning to the aircraft, gazed once more at Arkell. A trace of something like regret in his eyes. 'Unfortunately, not good enough.'

Simon Arkell lay on his back, bleeding into the Pyrenean soil, and watched the man he was supposed to have killed fly the short distance out of French territory. As the helicopter disappeared behind the great snow-capped crest, and the silence settled once more over the cirque, he started to wonder just how much it was going to hurt to get off that mountain.

* * *

The answer, he discovered, was a great deal. Hobbling across the meadow, testing that wrecked leg, was murderous. Controlling his breathing made the pain a fraction more bearable. He paused to bind both wounds with pieces of his shirt, buying himself a little respite before trying again. The second round had pierced one of the flexor muscles in his thigh but he could still extend his knee. He could walk, after a fashion.

His arm was less functional. Yadin's first round had passed straight through his forearm; he couldn't tell if it had clipped a bone on the way. He could move his fingers a little, but when he tried to take hold of a rock to ease himself into a gully, his grip gave way. Something fairly important was clearly compromised.

So . . . one arm and one and a half legs for the descent. At least he didn't have to shoot anybody. And he didn't have to go through the waterfall this time.

From the edge of the meadow, Arkell had been able to plot an alternative route that would lead him via a stream where he could drink, and then well away from anything else aquatic. With a maximum of three points of contact, one of them very weak, above all he needed dry surfaces.

For the most part, his route turned out to be sound. He teetered alarmingly on some of the narrower ledges, and half-expected his left leg to give way completely on a critical hold. The muscles in his left arm were worn out with the strain of taking all his weight, and his left fingers struggled to straighten after some of the crimps. Yet he was descending – slowly and painfully, but with measurable progress.

Only twice did he wonder if he would make it. The first doubts came when a punishing wall descent led him to a ledge from which there was no onward route. It was past 5 p.m., he was shattered, he'd lost blood, and he felt like sitting down on that ledge and staying down. It took him several minutes to summon the strength to get back on the wall and retrace his holds until he found a navigable line.

The second crisis of faith came when he looked down and saw the rows of gendarmes massing at the base of the cirque. Had they responded to reports of gunshots? Or had Yadin summoned more than a helicopter with that satellite phone? Either way, Simon Arkell found it very hard to call up the will to complete his treacherous descent. Because now he was picturing the crashed motorcycles just a few kilometres from here, and the officers who had witnessed him ride off on one of those motorcycles, fleeing the scene of a triple murder. And he knew that whatever story he came up with as he fought his way down those last two hundred metres – even if it was the absolute truth – there was no way he would be spending tonight anywhere other than a particularly secure French jail.

TOULOUSE, FRANCE – 17 June

Forget the quality of the food and the level of decorum in political debating chambers, Arkell decided, the measure of a civilized country was the way it dealt with presumed cop killers. If it treated their wounds *before* allowing enraged officers to beat them up, then it was truly civilized. Simon Arkell still had a lingering love of France. It was hard to shake off entirely the gruff loyalty to the tricolour instilled by the codes and songs of the Legion. So he was glad that the behaviour of the authorities in this case lived up to the faithful view of *La Patrie* that he and his comrades had once held.

The doctors did not speak to him at all, did not offer the slightest word of reassurance as to the long-term prospects for his damaged arm and leg. Yet he could see that they were taking care to do the job right – putting him on an antibiotic drip, debriding and cleaning the wounds meticulously, adding relaxing incisions to counter muscle swelling, sewing with small close stitches that would leave only a minimal linear scar – whatever they believed him to be.

He thanked them courteously in English. At no point did he utter a word of French to anyone.

There was little point at this stage making protestations of his innocence. As soon as he was seized at the base of the cirque, two officers of the Police nationale were called forward to examine him. He recognized them both from Rosary Square, and it was obvious they recognized him too. Both gave an unambiguous nod to the arresting gendarmes.

It was possible Margrave – even Mayhew – might be willing to vouch for him, but they were en route to Canada when the shooting occurred and could not have testified that he *hadn't* murdered someone. The Brazilian team were probably already on their way home, and with their president dead they would have little time or inclination to help a foreign spy. They might even wonder if he was implicated, this unknown figure thrust upon them just before Andrade was assassinated.

Only one person could sort out this mess. As the gendarmes escorted him from the Toulouse University Hospital to the

Gendarmerie Commissariat; as they placed him in a cell and removed his shoes and personal effects; as they beat him about the face and stomach with their fists; as they summoned colleagues to pummel him until he was on the floor; as they did all of this, he said only one word, over and over: 'Telephone.'

Eventually, when parts of his body had started to jerk spasmodically, and he was clinging to consciousness only out of a bloody-minded determination not to let them see him faint, they gave it to him.

'It's me. I'm not in Strasbourg any more.'

He did not use her name or his own. It was the middle of the night and she had been asleep, but she immediately grasped the need for obscurity. 'So I gathered from our Canadian friend. Are you still where he left you?'

'Unfortunately the gendarmes have me. They think I killed two of their number.'

She paused. 'That *is* unfortunate. Particularly for you.'

'Quite.'

'So you didn't get him, then?'

'No.'

'Two down, one left.'

'I'm sorry. I realize you must have lost confidence in me.'

'I wouldn't say that. You're playing tough odds against a thorough opponent. Turns out he'd poisoned the holy water in church, and the original bath. The flower was a lucky final shot on goal after you'd thwarted his first two attempts.'

Arkell glanced at the blood seeping through the bandage on his forearm. No doubt, the thigh wound had been similarly reopened by the gendarmes' boots. 'I know him now. I've spoken to him. Believe me, I *am* going to get him.'

'I'm counting on it.'

'Are you able to straighten this out with the French?'

'Actually, it occurs to me that it might be quite useful to leave you in their custody.'

He tensed. 'Meaning?'

'You're in the system now. First time in nine years. It's an opportunity.'

'Hard to see from where I'm standing.'

She ignored the tone. 'I haven't managed to identify ASH. I have an idea who he is, but I've got no proof. Three contenders, all with possible motives and opportunities, and no other line of inquiry to pursue. We need to make ASH show his hand.'

'I don't see how I can help from a Gendarmerie cell.'

'It's simple.' He could hear the smile in her voice. 'Tell them who you are.'

'*What?*'

'If ASH ordered your death, don't you think he'd be intrigued, to say the least, to hear of your resurrection?'

Arkell's fingers gripped the receiver. 'Don't *you* think,' he said, managing to keep his voice even, 'that's a dangerous play? The first thing ASH will do is demand my extradition. He's bound to have a million strings he can pull with Paris. I'll be handed over in chains. How long do you think I'll last then?'

'Extradition takes time. He'll be impatient to see you.'

'That doesn't help me when eventually I end up in that windowless vehicle headed for some remote corner of Yorkshire.'

'It won't come to that,' she told him confidently.

'What makes you so sure?'

'Because as soon as you have ASH's identity, you're going to tell the gendarmes who you *really* are.'

Silence between them. The two corporals watching him saw a great smile break out on his face.

'It's your Get Out of Jail Free card. Gendarme jail, anyway. The rest is up to you.'

'All right,' he said. 'One last thing. The woman in Strasbourg. *His* woman. Is she still there?'

'As far as I know.'

'Can you check?'

'Of course. What's up?'

'Just make sure she's OK.'

TOULOUSE, FRANCE – 18 June

The interrogators were in full uniform. Their epaulettes identified them as a major and a captain. They sat in frosty silence before a steel table, and made no gesture when Arkell was brought in. He was placed opposite them and his manacled hands were secured to a ring on the table.

The captain spoke first, eyeing his bruises and cuts and the dried blood on his forehead. 'You have not been ill-treated.' It was not a question.

Arkell admired his effrontery. 'No.'

The major produced a passport. 'You are Andrew Meredith?'

'No.'

Taken aback, he opened the passport and examined the photograph. 'This is you, yes?'

'It's a false passport.'

The two interrogators exchanged a look.

'You are travelling illegally in France for what purpose?'

'I'd rather not go into that.'

A thin, unfriendly smile. 'Would you prefer to explain why you killed two gendarmes?'

'Wasn't me.'

'And President Andrade of Brazil?'

'Again, not me.'

'We have plenty of witnesses who saw you, Mr Mered—' He stopped. 'What is your real name?'

The suspect smiled. 'My name is Simon Arkell. I am an officer of the British Secret Intelligence Service. I am sorry, but I cannot answer any more questions until you have notified my superiors of this arrest.' The smile broadened. 'Would you like the telephone number?'

Madeleine Wraye made a single call that morning, to Linus Marshall.

'There's going to be some news for the Service today from France. Rather surprising news, concerning a deceased officer of ours. It might come via the DGSE or DCRI, or it might come directly from the Gendarmerie. Do me a favour, Linus, make sure three of your colleagues get to hear the news immediately. Call them up, sound shocked, amazed, whatever comes naturally – just make sure they get the message. Ready with a pencil? George Vine, Tony Watchman . . . and Martin de Vries.'

* * *

Alone in his cell – he was left unmolested now – Arkell wondered if ASH would simply pull one of those many strings and have him killed right away. It seemed unlikely the gendarmes would do anything that couldn't be covered up. Shooting and stabbing were out. But poison was a distinct possibility. He had drunk plenty of water before the interrogation, having determined to consume nothing at all once he'd given up his identity. Then there was always the trip on the stairs and the broken neck. He flexed his one good arm. Let them try.

Food was brought on a tray, and removed untouched an hour later. Otherwise, there was no contact with anyone. Those gendarmes he did glimpse looked distinctly uneasy. No one spoke to him.

In the end, Arkell was surprised how quickly ASH came. He must have used the Hercules, or requisitioned one of the government's few private jets. When he was led back into the interrogation room and once again manacled to the steel table, Arkell looked into the familiar eyes of the SIS director and found himself wondering what story the man had devised to explain this unscheduled trip.

Perhaps he no longer needed to explain himself.

'So you really are alive,' marvelled the man from the Secret Intelligence Service, when the gendarmes had left.

'I'm sorry to disappoint you.'

'On the contrary, you've impressed me.' Tony Watchman leaned back in the stiff institutional chair, eyes generous with admiration. 'I haven't heard a whisper all this time. Talk about deep cover. You should give a lecture at the Fort one of these days. I know I'd learn something.'

'I may not be available.' He raised his manacled hands.

'Don't worry about that,' Watchman said, folding his arms, the picture of relaxed satisfaction. 'We'll sort out the French. They're being very helpful. Falling over themselves to apologize for beating you up. We'll get you back to London in no time.'

'And then?'

'Then? Sorry, mate, your employment was terminated. These things happen when you're dead. But if you want back in, I'm sure it won't be a problem.'

'Are you serious?'

'Simon. *Simon.* You were always a good officer. This makes you a star. It would be an honour to welcome you back into the fold.'

'And Ellington? My wife? Saeed Bin—'

Watchman had swiftly raised his hand, and Arkell found himself obeying its authority. The Director of Counter-Terrorism gazed around the drab room. 'Where would you place your microphones?' he mused. In a whisper so low Arkell barely caught it, he added, 'I regret your wife's death. Sincerely. I liked her.' After a pause that might have been intended to feel commemorative, he resumed with his normal cocksure voice: 'You and I have a lot to discuss. Let's not share it with our French friends. When last I heard, you were in possession of some interesting intelligence from Saudi. Given that you have not, in fact, been dead all this time, I ask myself why that intelligence has never come out. I conclude it is because you understand the considerable sensitivity of that intelligence, and are too responsible and mindful of your duties to the Service to discuss it. That makes me think you and I can work together. That makes me think you have a bright future in the Service, in my section. Or, if you prefer the freelance lifestyle, there are lucrative options. I employ capable men to do difficult things.' He glanced pointedly at Arkell's bandaged forearm. 'I believe you met one of them in the mountains yesterday. You may feel you have other loyalties, but whatever your history with the lady, the brutal truth is she's a spent force. Out in the cold. The really interesting work – the really interesting rewards – only I can offer.'

Arkell let him finish. He had once respected Tony Watchman for his blunt efficiency and straight talking. But had it actually ever been straight talking? Was it all just artfully presented bullshit, as hollow and self-serving as this transparently bogus proposition?

'Here's an idea,' said Arkell, leaning forward and lowering his voice to a whisper. 'The French are looking for the killer of a visiting head of state. You're sitting here, right under their noses. Suppose I was to point them towards a possible connection . . .'

Watchman stood up, a tight smile giving him the look of an animal baring its teeth. 'Simon. It's not going to happen. You're not going to tell them anything.' He walked to the door and rapped it sharply. 'We're finished, thank you.' He glanced back at Arkell, straightening the line of his suit. 'I'll see you in London.'

Simon Arkell had assumed those words – *You're not going to tell them anything* – were intended as an order. Now, he realized they were a statement of fact. Apart from the non-commissioned gendarmes who escorted him back to his cell, no one came near him. He had planned to speak to the next officer who looked in, but none did. His cell lay at the end of a long corridor, and no one came within speaking distance.

So much for Wraye's clever plan.

He tried reaching them. Through the bars, he called to anyone who ventured into the corridor. He spoke in French – there was no need to hide it now. He even yelled the essence of his confession. But it seemed the gendarmes had been told not to hear anything. His food was brought by a North African woman in cleaning overalls who spoke no French at all. He tried what was left of his Arabic on her, but she scurried away without meeting his eye.

It was beginning to dawn on Arkell that he might actually be handed over to Watchman without any further contact with the gendarmes: without once getting the chance to use that Get Out of Jail Free card.

So he started singing.

Au Tonkin, la Légion immortelle
A Tuyen Quang illustra notre drapeau,
Héros de Camerone et frères modèles
Dormez en paix dans vos tombeaux.
Au cours de nos campagnes lointaines,
Affrontant la fièvre et le feu,
Oublions avec nos peines,
La mort qui nous oublie si peu.
Nous, la Légion

The French Foreign Legion has many cherished songs, but 'Le Boudin' is its official march. And any legionnaire not engaged in marching – at eighty-eight steps per minute – always stands to attention on hearing it.

Arkell stood thus now. He remembered every word. More than that he remembered, in a flood of nostalgia, the intense pride those lyrics engendered in every man who sang them. He repeated it over and over again, watching the faces of those gendarmes who passed through the corridor. He watched them pause, and then hurry on. Until one man – a desk sergeant, perhaps fifty years old – entered the corridor and stopped still.

It wasn't quite standing to attention, but Arkell knew he'd found his man. He put all he had into the second verse, the spirit of Indochina, the triumph of defeat in Mexico, everything the Legion stood for. It was true: he had been commended for his singing by the NCOs. Such things are taken very seriously in the Legion.

The desk sergeant was mouthing the words. His back had straightened. His legs had edged together. As Arkell drew the song to a heartfelt close, the man's voice joined his for the last bars.

Silence in the corridor.

The man was struggling with himself. Trying to decide what to do. He started forward two paces, stopped still. Then, perhaps remembering his former courage, his younger self's bravado in the field, he cleared his throat and said, 'We are forbidden to talk to you. But I will do what I can for you, my friend.'

He turned to go.

'Wait!' shouted Arkell, in French. 'My Legion name is Jonathan Reeves. I served only three years.' He paused while the other man frowned, then spelt it out: 'I am a *deserter*.'

* * *

They came for him three hours later. Arkell was impressed: he had expected a great deal of official wrangling to be necessary, and then a five-hour drive from Aubagne. He vaguely remembered there was a recruiting centre in Toulouse; perhaps these legionnaires were stationed there.

A gendarme unlocked his cell. He stood back respectfully as the four legionnaires seized Arkell and led him out. They wore green berets and standard duty fatigues – no white kepis or green and red epaulettes for the deserter. A sous-lieutenant, by his looks the only Frenchman among them, watched disdainfully from the corridor.

A scattering of Gendarmerie officers and deputies turned out to watch the procession. It is not every day that the Foreign Legion comes calling. The gendarmes must have been persuaded he was no cop killer, Arkell realized, to be letting him go. Perhaps new evidence had come to light. Perhaps Watchman had fabricated some alibi, some story as to his role and activities in Rosary Square.

But the Gendarmerie is a branch of the French armed forces, just like the Legion. They knew where their loyalties lay. Called upon to choose between the arrogant demands of British spies or the strict honour code of French brothers-in-arms, the gendarmes had no difficulty deciding to whom they should release their prisoner.

Outside, it was dark. Arkell had only a rough idea of the time. As the legionnaires led him to an army truck, he held up his manacled wrists and asked, 'Are these still necessary?'

The sous-lieutenant nodded to a gendarme, who summoned

the key. Arkell thanked the man who removed the handcuffs. He was shoved into the rear of the truck and his four escorts climbed in after him. The sous-lieutenant barked quick, superfluous orders – *Le regarde! Silence!* – before stepping into the cab.

It is a long way from Toulouse to the Legion's headquarters in Aubagne, near Marseille. The route passes the medieval town of Carcassonne and the Roman town of Nîmes. It passes Arles, where van Gogh painted, and the Rhône delta, and the Camargue wetlands. Arkell saw none of it. What he did see, by the feeble light of a single bulb on the roof of the truck, were the faces of the men guarding him.

They were bored. Moreover, they were very young, two of them perhaps just eighteen. The age he had been when he joined. They held their weapons with the attention he would expect – and they would be ready to use them if necessary. They were well spaced around him, with enough distance to ensure he couldn't try anything underhand. But the boredom was getting the better of them. And he noticed something else: they were all surprisingly interested in him, more so than he would expect for a deserter. The sergeant was hiding it well, but the two youngest privates were openly staring at him whenever they believed him to be looking elsewhere.

Arkell had become very good at sensing when he was being watched.

Had the gendarmes recounted his exploits in the Pyrenees? Had they suggested that he might be implicated in the death of President Andrade? That he was a British secret agent? It didn't matter; their unguarded curiosity was an opportunity.

Around three hours out of Toulouse, he leaned forward and spoke to the youngest. 'Why am I so interesting to you?'

The boy flushed, and looked to the sergeant for guidance. The older legionnaire shrugged, a permissive gesture. Gazing wonderingly at Arkell, the private asked, 'Is it true, after you deserted, you walked through a camp of two hundred men to return your clarion?'

Arkell smiled. The opportunity had just broadened considerably. These men were green – the private still needed to work on his French, and even the sergeant looked more practised in parade drill than live-fire situations. Arkell had a pretty good idea what might distract them.

'Oh, I didn't *walk*.'

'How? How did you do it?' The admiration was laid bare now. He might be a deserter, but he was also a legend.

'You know,' sighed Arkell, with his best Legion gruffness, 'I can't even remember. I couldn't do it now. Too old, weak. And with these bullet wounds . . .' He gestured vaguely at his thigh and right arm.

There was a pause. They looked from one to another. It was the second youngest private who took the bait.

'*Bullet wounds?*'

This time, Arkell's smile was on the inside. For the watching legionnaires, he adopted an air of desolate gloom as he rolled up the sleeve of his stained shirt. 'They didn't tell you? I was shot here . . . and here . . . just yesterday. I can hardly walk. This arm, the doctors say I will never use it again.' By now he was unrolling the stiff, blood-caked bandage around his forearm. For effect, he tore the last section away, ignoring the twang of pain as a scab was ripped off and fresh blood started to flow.

Mournfully, he dabbed the blood away with the handful of bandages.

It didn't take long. These were professional fighting men who had yet to see for themselves what a bullet could do to human flesh. For any young soldier, there is a gruesome fascination in studying that first battle injury. Arkell remembered his own induction into the realities of weaponized ballistics. The victim, a Croatian recruit, took a stray round in the gut during a training exercise. Arkell, still a boy really, had been close enough to feel very, very lucky.

The youngest private moved first. He edged a little closer to stare with naked fascination at the bleeding hole in the prisoner's arm. Two of the stitches still held; the others had ripped free. Arkell, apparently lost in thought, looked up as if surprised by their interest. 'Oh!' he muttered. 'It's not much to see. A little blood. The hole in my leg is bigger . . .'

That was all they needed. The four men gathered around, three of them standing, clutching the side of the truck for support, peering in the dim light at the hole left by Yadin's first round.

And that was all Arkell needed. He hit the sergeant first, a massive punch from his left fist that sent the man sprawling back across the truck. In the same moment he kicked the legs of the corporal from under him, then seized his rifle and used it to club first one private in the face and then the other in the side of the head. Standing swiftly, he stomped on the corporal's chest, winding him, and swung the butt of the rifle against the rising sergeant's head. The brutality, in the context of the Legion, did not seem unreasonable. There might be a broken jaw or cracked rib among them, but nothing that they would not risk in the normal course of training. It would be good experience for them.

Smiling almost fondly, Arkell stepped over the groaning soldiers and gazed out at the dark autoroute. Thankfully there were few other vehicles around. Still, this was going to hurt. Grabbing a flask of water, Arkell balanced on the tailgate and leapt into the night.

The impact was severe. The forward momentum got the better of his parachute roll, and he struck his injured arm, and then his head, on the ground. Lying dazed in the slow lane of the autoroute, he knew he had to move. Headlights were approaching. Any second now, one of the legionnaires would raise the alarm and the truck would double back.

In fresh agony, disoriented, elated, he grabbed the water flask and stumbled off the carriageway into dark wasteland.

LONDON, ENGLAND – 19 June

The call came as Madeleine Wraye was just waking up, refreshed and well rested at last.

'Hello London.'

She sat up straight, instantly alert.

'It's Watchman,' said Arkell. 'ASH is Watchman.'

She breathed out long and hard. 'Where are you?'

'Not in France.'

'Well done. I knew you'd make it. Do you need anything?'

'About two weeks to recuperate, then another crack at Yadin.'

'You've got ten days. Recuperate fast.'

'What's happened?' He sounded tired, but newly excited.

'I know where Yadin is going to target Mayhew.'

'A public event?'

'Andrade's funeral in Brasilia. Mayhew is giving the eulogy. Outdoors.'

There was silence on the line. Then he surprised her by asking, 'Where's Klara?'

'We don't know. She was still in Strasbourg yesterday. My people observed her eating a lonely dinner in the restaurant next door to your pension. She looked "troubled", they said. By this morning she was gone. I have someone watching her apartment in Hamburg in case she turns up there. Simon, she's not becoming a distraction, is she?'

'I'll see you in Brazil.'

Madeleine Wraye repacked her suitcase and filled her handbag with sealed envelopes of US dollars. She added four passports in different names. She checked the locks on the filing cabinets and activated the detonators concealed within each one. It was time to abandon Markham Square, at least until Tony Watchman was behind bars or in his grave. Once word reached him of Arkell's escape, not even the discreet pair of ex-soldiers downstairs would be enough to protect her.

Wraye did not intend to wait around for a visit from either SO15 or Gavriel Yadin.

PART III:

THE KILL

ENGLISHMAN'S BAY, TOBAGO – 27 June

It made no sense at all to stop off in Tobago on the way to Brasilia. From Milan, Arkell had to fly to New York, and then on to Trinidad for a local connection to the smaller island; for the second leg of the journey, he would need to return to the US, transiting Miami before heading south again. The total journey time was close to sixty hours and the six flights would together cost over three times the price of a direct route. Uncomfortable at the best of times, it would be particularly unpleasant with two very recent gunshot wounds. But Arkell was a romantic when it came to geography, just as much as history, and in geographic terms Tobago was only a little bit out of the way.

He did not expect to discover anything that Chief Inspector Bleeck and the many other law-enforcement and security-service officers investigating Anneke van der Velde's death had not already unearthed. He was not, anyway, much interested in the DNA traces and partial fingerprints that might still linger at Belvedere House. He didn't need forensic proof to confirm the facts they already knew. He wanted only to experience the place where Yadin had started it all.

Perhaps, too, he was drawn to see where Klara had lived for a week with the man he was on his way to kill.

To that end, he checked into Emerald Sea Resort. It was the kind of sprawling complex he would usually have avoided, but it offered all the amenities he needed to begin to rebuild his damaged body. The sea was warm, the grilled fish were plentiful and delicious, and the fitness centre had all the kit necessary to isolate each damaged muscle. A teenage guest watched, entertained, as Arkell lifted a full six kilos with his right arm. After two days, he was up to eight kilos. By the end of his short stay, he could manage ten.

Running was still a challenge. The beach at Emerald Sea was a kilometre-long stretch of firm sand – ideal for exercise. Any other time he would have pounded up and down it with boyish exhilaration; now it was a trial to make it from one end to the other, at a slow jog, leaning heavily to spare his left leg. Most of his exercise he took in the sea. For once he paid attention to local warnings about Atlantic currents and undertow, and did not venture out of his depth.

In the downtime, he made good use of the resort's hammocks to rest his aching arm and leg, though his abstemious orders of fresh lime juice, coconut water or raw egg were a disappointment to the terrace barman, and his solitary habits a regret to one or two female guests. He held occasional conversations, but only with the staff and only on one topic.

None of them minded talking about the guest who had later drawn such interest from the foreigners in suits. Yes, they remembered the girlfriend. No, she hadn't said much. Neither was a big talker. At dinner, they sat opposite each other – some couples preferred to be side-by-side. No one remembered them holding hands. Did she seem to love him?

Well . . .

Some said yes; some said no. She was loyal, they could agree on that. She obeyed him without question. And when he looked at her with that hungry stare, she looked back the same way. But sometimes, when he wasn't looking . . . It was as if she didn't even want to know him.

Every morning, Arkell phoned Carlo and Danny. Both were searching, in their different ways, for Klara. Carlo's expertise lay in the informal contact, the casual acquaintance encouraged with a dose of Arkell's money to pass on police reports, interrogate municipal databases, reveal information, share gossip. Beyond the immediate circle of her Hamburg colleagues and friends, however, he had uncovered no trace of Klara Richter. And Danny, with his cyber fingers in a million online pies, was faring no better. She had not booked an airline ticket, or crossed a controlled border, or used a credit card – at least not in her own name. There had been no further calls on her monitored mobile since Strasbourg. And if a fugitive had travelled from, say, Spain, for a rendezvous with Klara in, say, western Germany, Simon Arkell simply had no way of knowing.

On his penultimate day in Tobago, Arkell rented a car and visited Belvedere House. He made no appointment. Technically, the site was still a crime scene, but the two Trinidadian cops on duty were so bored that they welcomed his authoritative manner, flashed Interpol ID and polite questioning. He had bought bananas at a roadside stall in Les Coteaux and he shared them with the policemen while complimenting them on the shine of their boots. After that, they were ready to show him everything.

The house itself was locked up. The policemen led him through the gardens to an outhouse, where they described in animated detail the suitcase of hiking clothes that had been discovered beneath a pile of roof tiles.

'Mind if I have a look around?' said Arkell in his most assured commanding-officer voice. 'No need to accompany me. I know you have to guard the house.'

The men seemed disappointed, but they nodded their assent and watched him limp into the forest.

For Arkell, the policemen were already forgotten. He was thinking only of Yadin. The Israeli had trod this ground, passed these trees, his mind set on one of the most audacious political assassinations ever devised. Was there a trace of that strangely detached, almost regretful man still lingering in the air?

He walked a zigzag path, not bothering to search for spoor that the almost daily rains would have obliterated. His concentration was fierce, so much so that he did not notice his limp had disappeared. What ache was left in his thigh made no impression on his consciousness. The half-light penetrating the canopy seemed luminous to him. Yet there was no Yadin. No scent, no sensation of the man he had faced on a high Pyrenean meadow.

Birds unknown to him flashed through the upper foliage. Towering bamboo dripped memories of that morning's rain down his neck. The terrain was awkward, with exposed roots and thick red mud that required careful navigation to protect his healing limbs from a fall. By the time he reached the great tree with the branch overhanging the fence, the back of his shirt was damp with sweat. A couple of heavy lianas would have provided an easy way up that trunk. A cluster of rotting bromeliads on the ground might have been dislodged from the branch. Arkell stood a short distance back, imagining the assassin balanced up there. Sitting? Lying. A good vantage point to remain for a while, hidden among the parasitic greenery, listening for possible threats.

Arkell studied the ground beneath the branch. A few broken twigs and seed pods were pressed into the damp earth. A parachute roll would do that. And there, two slight indentations, edges softened by many rains, barely still visible. Heel marks? It could be fantasy; those blurred holes might be nothing more than the remnants of some small animal's excavations. An agouti hunting for roots. Nevertheless, Arkell crouched and pressed the fingertips of both hands into those two dents in the forest floor, and he closed his eyes and felt Yadin.

A man like the grave. Eaten away by his own remarkable ability. A dark void at the heart of his being. Intense weariness. Was that what a lifetime of killing did to a human being?

Arkell remained like that, unmoving, long enough to bring one of the policemen looking for him. At the man's uncertain cough, he opened his eyes and rose. They walked back to the driveway without exchanging more than a dozen words.

Afterwards the cop wondered aloud to his colleague whether the man from Interpol had smoked something in the rainforest.

He was different. He was . . . bigger somehow.

A little frightening.

MONPAZIER, FRANCE – 27 June

The Dordogne village in which Siren had set up temporary home was all right as far as it went. It was picturesque, obviously. That was the point. She was there to make pictures of picturesque stuff, the way you were supposed to in France. Monet had his garden and haystacks in Giverny, van Gogh his sunflowers and irises in Arles; she had her Gothic arches in Monpazier. So far she had painted the arches from fourteen different angles, sometimes in bold, pitiless outline, sometimes with an obliging fruit vendor in the foreground to soften and add colour to her subject. Fourteen competent canvases. Perhaps a few that might be considered good. Perhaps.

It was, in a way, her dream come true. Her grandmother had instilled in her a passion for the art of a continent thousands of miles from Melbourne, and during her time in Utrecht many weekends were spent visiting the Rijksmuseum, the van Gogh museum and the Mauritshuis, with occasional longer journeys to Paris, London and Berlin to feast on their great collections. Often, hunched over an annual report or sunk in the gridded hell of some unfathomable spreadsheet, she had wished herself five hundred miles south, in a straw hat and smock, paint-smattered and liberated, creating instead of analysing. Now she had her wish, she was living the dream, and it was . . . well, not all there.

To be brutally honest, she found it quite boring.

Maybe if she were a better painter, if she'd liked her work more, it might have been different. But the dream of so many years was turning out to be somewhat underwhelming. For a start, it was uncomfortable. She hadn't expected that. With no breeze or shade, it was too hot; she found herself sweating most of the time. And the little canvas stool that had looked so cute in the art shop was turning out to be an instrument of slow torture. For another thing, she felt self-conscious, sat in front of an easel that she now saw was too elaborate, with her half-cocked work on display for all to judge. And it was not as if the village had embraced her to its cultural breast. The only Monpaziérois who bothered to talk to her were trying to sell her something. They saw her as a tourist, she realized. And weren't they right?

A practical person, Siren was quick to think through the problem and look for a solution. She needed to relocate to a different village, with a more artistic community, and refreshing winds, and subjects that better suited her talents. She needed to go back to the art shop and buy a cheaper easel and a more expensive stool. She needed to remember that art was not supposed to be fun – it was a torturous endeavour that led to marriage breakdowns, penury, harsh criticism, even madness, ear loss and the asylum. If she wished to create great art, she needed a different mindset.

But she had a growing suspicion that the location, the tools, the talent and the mindset weren't the problem. She suspected the problem was really one of timing. She was living a dream that she had outgrown. Five years ago, this life would have been perfect. But it was no longer what she wanted.

So when a short, fat British man with owlish glasses approached her as she was swabbing the sweat from her neck and wondering how to rescue this car crash of a canvas, she seized on his proposal in an instant. Yes, indeed, she was free.

No, it wouldn't be too much trouble to fly to Brazil. The man handed her an envelope of spending money, an air ticket in the name of Susan Meredith, a Rio hotel reservation – 'Andrew's on assignment, so call him when you arrive but not before' – and wished her bon voyage.

LONDON, ENGLAND – 28 June

'I have something for you. Something that can put you straight back into Counter-Intelligence, maybe higher if you want it.'

She had appeared unannounced beside him on the Victoria line, taking his arm and forcibly piloting him out of the carriage at Pimlico. 'Tony Watchman. I'm going to hand him to you on a plate. Apple in his mouth and parsley behind his ears, but first I need something from you.'

'Madeleine, I will not be party to wild accusations against senior members of the Service by discredited ex-employees.'

'Have I made an accusation? Last time you hinted at certain corporations getting into bed with Service directors. I've identified the director; I need you to tell me what companies are linked to him.'

'I'm just Audit now—'

'Bullshit, Linus! You're a spycatcher to your bones. What do you have on Tony?'

The former Director of Counter-Intelligence and Security hesitated. Two officers of the British Transport Police had appeared on the platform. A gust of air signalled the approach of the next train. If they didn't get on it, the officers' attention would be drawn. One thing Linus Marshall instinctively avoided, both as a spy and as the son of Jamaican immigrants, was drawing the attention of the police.

'Christ, it's just a name. What harm can that do?'

He said it in a rush: 'AMB.'

The train rolled into the station but she ignored it. 'You're thinking of George Vine.'

'I am not! George has a local arrangement with their Dubai office, but that's chickenfeed. Early warning stuff we'd probably give them anyway through CIA. They toss him a bit of cash, that's all. It's Tony who gets the red carpet treatment in Louisville.'

The train doors opened. Marshall started towards them.

'Wait, Linus, I don't get it. What's the connection?'

'David Atticus.' The doors were beeping. 'I've told you more than enough. Go look at Tony's regimental records for the rest.'

MIAMI, USA – 28 June

By chance, Arkell picked up Siren's message between planes at Miami International airport.

'Hi there! I know you said not to call early, but just wanted to let you know I've arrived in Rio and it's super-gorgeous here, so thank you ahead of whatever horrible hardship you have lined up for me. Speak soon, darling husband.'

His fingers, on the screen of his smartphone, felt icy numb. The call went straight to voicemail. 'Siren, wherever you are, get out of there. I did not send you to Rio. You're in danger. Get out now, go to a police station or an embassy, then call me.

Do not trust anyone who approaches you. I'm coming to get you.'

There was a Rio flight leaving in two hours that still had availability. Arkell bought a ticket and rang Danny.

'There's a woman I need to find urgently in Rio de Janeiro,' he began.

'Sounds wrong but fun.'

'This is serious.' He was thinking fast. How had they found her? Strasbourg: Yadin had seen them together. A glance at the guest list for her cover name, which would lead to the Hyatt. Then a tail to wherever she was living. 'She's called Susan Meredith. If you can locate her mobile phone—'

'Whoa, hold it! In *Brazil*? I'm not a magician.'

'Then find me a hotel reservation.'

Next he rang Carlo. 'Siren's been taken,' he said. 'I need a weapon – in Rio. Do you know any—?'

'Leave it with me,' said Carlo. 'Text me your flight details and someone will meet you.'

He tried Siren again. Voicemail. He rang again and again for the next two hours, until he had boarded the plane and been warned twice by the stewardesses to switch off his phone. A night flight, but Arkell was unable to sleep. He drank his first alcohol in a week, a straight brandy that he couldn't taste and which did nothing to dull his fear. In fact he felt sick. For eight hours, over the Caribbean, the Amazon basin and the Brazilian plateau, he played out scenario after scenario, trying to second-guess what a professional killer might do with a sweet young woman from Melbourne.

RIO DE JANEIRO, BRAZIL – 29 June

Three things happened in quick succession when Simon Arkell arrived in Rio. First, a text message from Danny: *Leblon Internacional.* In the arrivals hall hung with black crêpe, Arkell spotted a man with a placard displaying one of his older aliases. A car was waiting, in it a locally made Taurus OSS with two magazines. While they drove to Leblon, Arkell familiarized himself with the Brazilian gun's elaborate safety system and the unusual single-action/double-action trigger. Then the third thing happened: his phone rang.

'Mr Arkell.'

It was strange hearing that name again. Even Madeleine Wraye hadn't used it. In nine years, no one had spoken it aloud in his presence. Now, the rogue Kidon combatant had his identity, and that made him feel vulnerable.

Arkell had long used a grey hat service to reroute all his mobile calls through a variety of scrambling systems that effectively prevented tracking by GPS interrogation or triangulation. A generic ringtone overrode any local variant that might give away his location. Arkell had turned up the air conditioning to full power before answering, blocking out ambient noise from the city. He told himself it was late afternoon and he was somewhere in Italy.

'Yes.'

'This is Gavriel Yadin.'

'I'm impressed you found this number.'

'In fact, a friend of yours gave it to me.'

Here it comes, thought Arkell. You don't know. You don't

know he has her. You have no idea. 'Friend?' he said blankly.

'Let me save you some time. I have listened to her voicemail. I know you are coming here. Perhaps you are already in Rio. Perhaps you have the address. We are at the Leblon Internacional, room 4008. Come soon. And please – don't bother the police: Mr Watchman has many good friends in this city.'

'Can I speak to her?'

'No.' The line went dead.

He stared out at the billboards in sombre black and white, paid for by respectful international corporations, at the highway filled with cars fluttering black pennants from their aerials, at the people milling on the pavements, sombre and bereft of the usual Carioca spirit.

'I'm sorry, I don't know your name,' he said to the man Carlo had sent.

'Felipe.'

'And you speak fluent English?'

'Yes, it's quite good now.'

Arkell held up the Taurus. 'You know how to use this?'

'Sure.'

Hoping that the man didn't have a wife and children, he said, 'Tell me what else you can do.'

Simon Arkell limped through the gilded foyer of the Leblon Internacional without a glance to the doormen or receptionists. He paid no attention to the elaborate flower arrangements, or the monstrous and shapeless scrap-metal sculpture that dominated the space. He noted, but did not linger on, the faces of the guests and travel reps seated on the crisp white couches and gathered around the elevators. None appeared to be a threat. But Tony Watchman's people never did. Grey, forgettable figures, the freelancers employed by the Counter-Terrorism section were adept at loitering unchallenged in the hairiest parts of the world.

He stepped into an empty elevator. No one tried to join him.

He stood outside room 4008 for some time, thinking about the man who had lain on that rainforest branch. He closed his eyes and brought to mind the passing glimpse into the man's character he had drawn from the damp earth of Tobago. He thought about the kills that had defined Yadin's career, the sense of weariness, the deadened soul. Then he adjusted the sling on his right arm and used his crutch to rap on the door.

It was not Yadin who answered, but Klara.

He hid his surprise, his shock. She looked pained rather than apologetic, although her first words were, 'I'm sorry, Simon.' She was wearing his white straw trilby.

'At least now you know my name.'

He followed her into the room, and there was Siren, hands bound behind her back, a noose around her neck anchoring her to the fitted wardrobe. Dressed but shoeless, she was able to sit on the carpet, just, with the rope not quite taut. Yadin stood beside her, a handgun dangling casually by her cheek. Her eyes were red and puffy, and her whole face was an unhealthy greyish hue. The chafing on her neck suggested she had been in that position for some time.

Yadin looked at the crutch. 'Is that necessary? You made it off the mountain without it.'

'Doctor's orders.'

'Take off the sling, please.'

'You shouldn't have come!' cried the woman on the floor.

'It's OK, Siren.' With clumsy movements, he eased his right arm out of the sling and let it hang by his side.

'Siren?' said Yadin. 'That's your name? Well, you've lured your sailor, very good. No more singing now.'

'You can let her go. I'm not armed.'

'The crutch.'

Arkell let it fall, along with the sling.

'Klara.'

She picked up a pair of speedcuffs. At her approach, Arkell said, 'Go easy on my right arm. Your boyfriend wrecked it.'

His words made her fumble the cuffs. Her movements were nervous and awkward. 'Put your hands behind your back,' she said, her voice subdued and a little scared. 'Palms outwards.'

'That's really going to be a problem for my tendons.'

Unsure, she looked to Yadin. He only stared back, unrelenting.

'Palms outwards,' she insisted.

Sighing, he complied. But as she reached for his right wrist, he snatched the cuffs from her, seized her by the hair and thrust the point of one cuff's rotating arm against her throat. 'I can rupture her carotid just like that. You know I can.'

Yadin had not moved. 'Yes.'

'Let Siren go.'

But Yadin was looking at Klara. 'You said he started to like you?'

She was trembling against Arkell's body. Her nodded reply was frantic.

'Then why is he threatening to kill you?'

'Untie Siren,' demanded Arkell. 'You've got me here. Let her go.'

'What kind of man is he?' Yadin showed no sign of alarm, only curiosity. 'You spent time with him. Do you think he is bluffing?'

'Please, Gavriel . . .' She was close to tears.

Yadin glanced up at Arkell. 'Your arm has recovered fast.' He came close to smiling, then rubbed his eyes as if suddenly tired. 'Just kill her. Then we can continue.'

'Oh, Jesus,' whispered Klara.

'This is surprising, *Schlampe*? Did you think I would want you back?'

'Gavriel, I didn't—'

You believe I don't know what happened in Strasbourg? That I couldn't discover the truth in thirty seconds from the maid?'

'Please . . .'

'You won't kill her?' he demanded of Arkell, pressing his gun against her forehead. 'I remember now: you aren't "cut out" to be an assassin. All right. Move. I'll do it for you.'

'Simon!' Arkell couldn't be sure whether the scream came from Siren or Klara. He stared transfixed at the weapon. It was a Heckler and Koch USP. The hammer was back, the safety was off; he didn't dare lunge for it.

'No? You don't want me to kill her?' Yadin seemed to consider the idea, then glanced round at Siren. 'Shall I kill that one instead?'

Steadying his voice as best he could, Arkell said, 'You don't have a suppressor. A gunshot will bring half the hotel up here.'

'This is Rio,' said Yadin nonchalantly. 'Make a choice. Which one do you care less about?' He flicked the HK barrel between the two women in playful inquiry.

Arkell did not look at Siren – did not want to see her face. 'You're a professional. You don't need to do this.'

'You're not going to save your loyal assistant? Does this bitch mean so much to you?'

Arkell lowered the steel cuff from her throat. He let go of her and stepped away. Klara stayed rooted to the spot. Snapping the speedcuffs first on one wrist then the other, he turned to display his hands locked behind his back.

'On the ground,' said Yadin. 'Face down.'

He knelt, favouring his bad leg, then rolled sideways into a prostrate position that allowed him sight of the others. Siren was in tears, silent but broken. Klara still stood motionless, as if transfixed.

Yadin slapped her hard. 'Wake up,' he said in German. 'Take this.'

Arkell stopped breathing. Having insulted, accused and hit Klara, Yadin had just handed her the gun. He seemed unassailably confident of her loyalty. But surely . . . ? Klara held the cocked and unlocked weapon as if it were some alien thing whose function she barely understood. Arkell stared up at her, willing her to make the brave choice –

'*Bist du verrückt?* Point it at him.'

She responded to the order with a frightened jerk, supporting the gun with both hands and aiming it waveringly in the area of Arkell's torso. He hoped she realized how little pressure that single-action trigger would need to fire the chambered round.

'It's all right,' he said softly. 'I'm not going to move.' He wasn't convinced she heard it.

Yadin collected a white hand towel. To Siren he said, 'Open your mouth.'

She looked for guidance to Arkell, who nodded. Yadin stuffed the towel into her mouth and clamped his left hand over her jaw. Simultaneously, his right hand took hold of the rope around her neck. With his knee against her back, he pulled the noose tight.

She exploded into movement, her legs flailing and her body jerking to get free of him. But his grip on her was unbreakable. Her muffled screams were hardly louder than the thrashing of her bare feet against the soft pile carpet. Arkell was much louder. He yelled one word urgently and repeatedly: 'Stop! Stop! Stop!' When that had no effect, he tried threatening, reasoning – pleading.

'You made your choice,' said Yadin. 'But you can cry about it if you want. The rooms around us have been emptied today.'

'You need her alive to make me cooperate!'

'I don't think so.'

'Stop it, Gavriel, please, stop,' cried Klara. 'Don't do this.'

An inhuman sound came from deep within Siren. The HK in Klara's hand was hanging slack. Arkell leapt upwards, onto his knees, onto his feet.

'Klara!' roared Yadin.

She brought the weapon swiftly back to Arkell. 'Get down!'

He met her desperate stare, tried to understand it, tried to draw out the compassion in her.

'I will fucking shoot you!'

'Please, Klara . . . She's done nothing.'

'Down! Right now!' The USP was pointed at his left eye.

He got down on the floor as the life was steadily choked out of a woman called Julia with whom he had once flirted over a set of accounts in Utrecht.

Yadin seemed uninterested in the stand-off. His focus was back on his victim. Her face had turned a purplish red and her eyes were darting crazily about. Tiny blood vessels had burst in the delicate skin of her eyelids and in the whites of her eyes. Her long ash-blonde hair looked eccentrically neat above her thrashing body, Yadin's iron grip on her jaw preventing her head moving at all. Her skirt had split, and her shirt was wet with sweat. The relentless, useless thumping of her feet against the carpet was both proof of life and herald of death. Watching it all, mouth slightly open and eyes fixed, Yadin breathed a little faster.

When Klara spoke, she was barely two paces from him, and he seemed genuinely surprised to find her there. 'Stop it, Gavriel.'

He looked at the weapon in her hands, its barrel defining a line to his hip. 'You want to shoot me?'

Without speaking, she laid the gun on the carpet. 'Stop it,' she repeated. 'This does nothing for you.'

'Get away from me,' he growled, turning back to Siren, whose legs were beating the ground with less strength now.

'She's just a child.' Her voice cracked. 'There's no satisfaction killing a child.' She knelt beside Siren, facing him. Unbuttoning her shirt, she pulled the collar back, exposing her long, taut neck. 'I'm here now,' she whispered. 'You don't need her.'

Suddenly furious, Gavriel Yadin uttered an animalistic groan and seized her throat with both hands. He swore at her in a tumultuous conflux of Hebrew, German and English as, beneath him, Siren found a last ounce of strength to spit the towel from her mouth. While Klara folded under Yadin's exasperated assault, Siren shook and stretched her neck until the rope loosened a fraction and she could breathe again.

Yadin tossed Klara to the ground. From his pocket, he drew a clasp knife. Siren saw the blade and screamed. He cut the rope, picked up the semi-automatic, and dragged her into the bathroom. With Klara wheezing on the floor just a couple of metres from him, Arkell watched the bathroom door in despair, waiting for the shot that would end Siren's life.

It never came. When Yadin walked out of the bathroom, he was carrying a hotel phone, ripped from the wall. He slammed the door behind him and snarled at Klara, 'She's alive, OK? Are you satisfied? Does that meet with your approval? Now get the fuck out of the way while I talk to this guy.'

Talking, at least in the beginning, involved no speech as such. Instead, Yadin began by pinning Arkell's feet under a heavy couch. He ordered Klara to sit on it, and with his prisoner thus anchored he searched him thoroughly. He checked his pockets, his ankles, the backs of his knees, his groin and the small of his back. He was careful always to keep his hands out of reach of Arkell's teeth and fingers, even as he checked his sleeves, collar, armpits and hair. The sling and crutch were briefly examined, found to be authentic, and tossed aside. When he was satisfied that Arkell had brought nothing of any consequence into the room – no weapon or radio or device of any kind – he moved to the drinks cabinet.

It was well stocked; the Leblon Internacional was proud of its five stars, and determined to hold on to them. But Yadin was less interested in the bottles than in the equipment provided to dispense and adorn their contents. With the air of a connoisseur he selected a few items and gathered them into the empty ice bucket. Sitting beside Arkell, he laid out his haul: a Hawthorne strainer; a wooden muddler for crushing limes; a stainless-steel bar spoon with a small garnish fork on the end; five plain wooden cocktail sticks; a pair of ice tongs; a corkscrew and a small serrated knife.

'I'm going to make you a bet,' said Yadin. 'We won't need the knife.'

He was calm again, that air of weariness returned, all suggestion of uncontrolled, perhaps carnal, violence banished. Arkell did not look at the items arrayed on the carpet. He was determined to maintain eye contact with the man who was about to torture him.

'You're an interesting guy,' said Yadin. 'Did you know our lives have crossed before? Of course you did – that's why you took this job. Mr Watchman sent me your file the first time he asked me to kill you.'

'The time you *failed* to kill me.'

Yadin's gloomy expression intensified. After a pause, he said, 'A Legion *deserter*.' When Arkell betrayed no reaction, he said, 'But you lasted three years. This should be an interesting challenge.'

'Are you going to ask me any questions? You never know, I might answer them. Then you can mix us both a drink instead of misusing hotel property.'

'A former intelligence officer? How can I believe anything you tell me voluntarily?'

'They always say torture doesn't work.' Arkell almost managed a smile.

Yadin contemplated him. 'You like to read history, I think. Did you know that Montaigne wrote about torture in the sixteenth century? He understood the problem: why should we think pain will make someone tell the truth rather than force him to lie? He saw it as a test of endurance rather than truth.'

'Wise man. You should take note.'

'In case it helps, I'm sorry your wife died. Unfortunately now I have to hurt you again. Mr Watchman is concerned about information you may have, and which you may have passed to others. You know what information I am talking about?'

Arkell nodded.

Picking up the cocktail strainer, Yadin detached the metal spring from the rim and began to uncoil it. 'This is going to be the subject of our discussion. Mr Watchman would like to know who you have given this information to, and whether you have written anything or made any kind of audio or video testimony concerning it. In particular, he would like to know how much you have shared with Madeleine Wraye.'

'It's all documented, in the safe keeping of a law firm. Updated last week to include Watchman's role. In the event of my death it goes straight to the BBC and the *Guardian*.'

'But you're already dead.' Was there a ghost of a smile there? 'How would they know?'

'I check in weekly. Every Tuesday morning. If I don't call two weeks running, they push the button.'

The spring was now fully uncoiled. Yadin had wound the steel wire neatly around his left hand. 'Every week you must make a call? For nine years? I don't believe your spirit is so easily tied down.'

'Sure you want to take the risk?'

'For the moment, it would waste our time to talk more. You know how this works: it is necessary that you come to the point where you want nothing more than to tell me everything Mr Watchman needs to know. For that you must hurt. You must feel your body is splitting apart. It's the only way. Are you ready?'

Arkell had wanted to waste time. As much time as possible. He had tried summoning help once and it had not come. The cavalry had not been ready. He needed to delay proceedings as long as possible before trying again. But Yadin was in no mood to prevaricate.

'It's possible you will pass out, like your friend in Strasbourg. To stop you choking on your tongue, we must take precautions.' Picking up the ice tongs and the strainer, stripped of its spring, he rose and stepped out of Arkell's sight. 'How should we do that?'

'I've never passed out in my—'

Before he could finish the sentence, something hard and cold was thrust into his mouth. He bit down, too late. Against the roof of his mouth, against his tongue, he felt the sharp, round edges of the cocktail strainer rim. He couldn't close his mouth without cutting into his palate.

Yadin advised, 'Don't fight it. This is for your own good.' He picked up the clawed tongs. Arkell felt his tongue seized and pulled forward, scraping against the strainer rim. When it was protruding from his mouth, Yadin unwound a length of the steel wire around his hand. 'Don't move now.'

The grip on his tongue was too strong even to whisper the signal. When the steel wire punctured the side of his tongue, he pushed his mind to Chad, to Pakistan, to Cyprus. He recalled the Legion beatings in Corsica and Djibouti, the gunshot wounds in the Pyrenees, and he told himself that this was not as bad. While Yadin forced the wire deeper into his tongue, penetrating right through from one side to the other, he made himself relax every muscle in his body, absorbing the shocking pain and neutralizing it. It was just one more injury.

The wire kept threading through the meat of his tongue until even lengths hung on either side. Yadin twisted the ends together to form a loop, then removed the strainer and experimented pulling on his prisoner's tongue. The sensation was monstrous: Arkell felt as if his flesh would rip open. If he could only withdraw his tongue back inside his mouth, he could close his teeth on that wire, gain some measure of control. But there was no let-up.

'What?' Yadin, irritated, was looking over his head. Klara. 'Close your eyes if you have a problem with it.'

He couldn't speak like this – couldn't make more than rudimentary coughs and grunts. Did Yadin really mean to torture him without letting him speak? Had he left it too late to call for help? The Heckler and Koch was nowhere to be seen – lodged in a pocket, out of reach on a side table; it was the perfect moment for an intervention, and he could do nothing to make it happen.

'What shall we start with? Corkscrew? Spoon? Baton?'

With a deft motion, Yadin twisted the loop of wire beneath Arkell's chin, pinning his extended tongue against his lower teeth. He picked up the long spoon and ran his fingertip over the garnish fork on the end of the handle.

'Where do you fear injury most? The eye? The ear canal? Under the fingernails?' He let the question hang in the air. 'We have time to experiment.' With one knee planted on Arkell's upper back, he ran the miniature tines of the fork over his cervical vertebrae. Pressing the fork lightly between two vertebrae, he mused, 'Would this paralyse you, do you think?'

The fork continued up his neck to the hairline, where it veered to the underside of his ear. Those sharp little prongs lingered there, probed a little as if curious, then dropped an inch down his jawline. They hovered a moment against the bone, and then –

The first penetration was not as bad as Arkell had feared. It hurt, but no more than any other flesh wound. The overwhelming sensation was one of intrusion – having a foreign object burrow into the critical junction of jaw and neck was more disturbing than painful. Until Yadin found his target.

Simon Arkell had no idea what nerve had been hit in that hideous surgery. He could only shut down his mind and steel himself against the spasms that threatened to rip his tongue from its wire skewer and which, he felt sure, would have broken his back if Yadin had not been there to hold him down.

A few seconds to recover. Then Yadin jabbed the nerve again.

It felt like he was inserting that toy fork deep into the jawbone – into the brain cavity, even. Arkell realized his mouth was full of towel. What sounds he must have been making. The shockwave of pain returned, and his entire frame shook. Raw, unsurpassable agony liquefied the bones and sinews that held him together.

He did not pass out, but neither was he completely there. The distortion in his perception of time became apparent when he realized that Klara had been whispering urgently in German for some while. He could see nothing but the carpet, out of focus, stretching into the far distance. If he rolled his eyes to the left, he could make out the serrated knife and the corkscrew, unsullied, awaiting their turn. The drip of blood from his neck was the only physical sensation. Where was Yadin? There was no pressure on his back, no voice responding to Klara's words, which he half-understood to be pleas on his behalf.

Something like an aftershock passed through him, sending his muscles rigid, sparking new protests from his damaged arm and leg. As he settled back against the floor, he became aware that the carpet beneath his face was damp with sweat. The ache from his abused jaw grew steadily, ripped flesh and bruised bone claiming attention now that the sound and fury of the traumatized nerve were fading.

Yadin was crouched in front of him. 'Klara believes I should allow you a chance to speak. She thinks – I am not confident she is right – that you are ready to tell me what I need to know.'

He considered Arkell's strained, sweating face a while before leaning forward to pull the towel from his mouth. He unwound the wire clamped around Arkell's lower jaw. Where was the semi-automatic? Not in his hand, anyway, not immediately ready to fire, and that was all that mattered right now.

'So. Speak.'

Thank you, Klara, were the first words that passed through his mind. There was only one word he planned to say aloud, but he took his time readying himself for it. His throat was congested; he cleared it with a short coughing fit. He tried moving his injured tongue, practised shaping the word. He filled his lungs, steadied his shaking jaw, imagined the sound of it –

'*STOP!*'

The room had been so silent in the seconds beforehand that the word – the signal – seemed even louder than it was. A heroic roar, the stage cry of a pantomime giant, it echoed – at least in his unsteady mind – around the hotel. It sounded ridiculous, an overblown non-sequitur, a nursery objection to the most adult of ill-treatment. But it served its purpose.

Yadin knew immediately what the word meant, what it was intended to summon from beyond the confines of his improvised torture chamber. He leapt sideways, out of Arkell's sight, lunging for the weapon he had felt confident enough to lay down. Before he could reach it, the door was kicked open, and Arkell shut his eyes.

He could do nothing, with his hands still cuffed together, to save his ears.

The M84 stun grenade detonated two metres from him, deafening him completely. All sense of balance gone, he opened his eyes and watched with elation as Yadin soundlessly crashed into a table. It had been too much to hope for: the Israeli had not closed his eyes. Blinded, his weapon lost, Yadin was doing the only thing he could – blundering across the room in search of his escape exit, a connecting door to the next room.

'Shoot him!' Arkell yelled, unable to hear his own words, unable to see the man they were directed at.

Yadin was almost at the connecting door. Would Felipe have

the guts to do it? It was one thing to toss a flashbang, another to shoot an unarmed man on the urging of a near stranger.

Yadin looked back, blinking hard. In a movement almost too fast to see, he'd crouched and pulled a thin knife from a sheath on his ankle.

'Shoot him now!' The words felt mangled by the wire hanging from his tongue.

Yadin threw the knife. For Arkell, it was all happening in a surreal vacuum of silence. Had a gun fired? Had the knife found its target? He'd remained flat on the ground, not wanting to add to the confusion, but now, fearing for Felipe, he kicked upwards and felt the couch shift easily – Klara was no longer on it. Leaping to his feet, he saw her stumbling after Yadin. By the door Felipe and another man, both in black body armour and riot helmets, were aiming handguns at the fleeing assassin. Yadin's knife was buried in Felipe's thigh.

Neither man was willing to fire, and when Arkell looked back he saw why: Klara was in the way. Flailing around, half-blinded, trying to reach Yadin. He was at the connecting door, fumbling for the handle. Arkell ran forward, with the Brazilians, all of them converging on Yadin as he got the door open and turned to grab Klara. Lifting her up, as if she were nothing more to him than a piece of furniture, he threw her with full force at his pursuers.

Hands still cuffed behind his back, Arkell could do nothing to protect her – or himself – from the impact. Her body smacked into his chest and, as the connecting door slammed shut, he collapsed beneath her.

'Corridor!' he gasped, breath knocked out of him. Had the

Brazilians heard? They were struggling with the door, locked from the other side. Felipe's partner tried to kick it down.

'Go to the corridor!'

Now they heard him. They ran out of the room, footsteps still silent to Arkell. He looked to Klara, who was clutching her neck.

'Are you all right?' The words felt clumsy, slurred by the wire skewering his tongue. Klara didn't hear them any better than he did. He pulled himself up and made eye contact with her. 'OK?' he mouthed, the wire rendering even that simple gesture grotesque.

She nodded. 'Siren!' he called. 'Come out.'

Lying on his side and arching his back, he forced his cuffed hands under his buttocks and brought one foot and then the other over the speedcuffs. He stood and looked around for the Heckler and Koch. It was lying on a side table. Siren appeared from the bathroom, pale and still in shock. The noose around her neck hung loosely below the burn marks it had left.

'I can't hear anything for now,' he said. 'Can you hear me?'

She was staring in horror at the wire hanging from his mouth, at the grisly hole in his neck. Pulling herself together, she nodded.

'Get Klara to untie you. She can't hear either. Then find the key for these cuffs. She probably knows where it is. Don't let her leave.'

He stepped through the open door, gun raised in his cuffed right hand. No one in the corridor. The fire stairs. A few drops of blood on the carpet. He pulled open the door and looked down. Impossible to hear anything more than a dull hum.

He started down the first two flights of stairs, but stopped when he caught a flash of movement. Never before had he been deaf in a combat situation. It was unnerving. Leaning cautiously over the rail, his balance still unsteady, he looked down and saw two black figures walking despondently up.

He made the weapon safe and headed back to the room.

'You're not about to trust her?'

Siren was outraged. The full force of her anger was lost on Arkell's debilitated hearing, but the expression on her face left no room for doubt. Klara stood up and walked to the windows.

A mirror above the bar reflected back the grisly state of his mouth as Arkell worked the steel wire slowly through his tongue. Blood flowed from each side, and he had to pause regularly to spit into a highball glass. 'She wants to help.'

'She pointed a gun at you while her boyfriend strangled me!' Siren's words sounded a long way off, tinny and muffled.

'She saved your life.'

'More than you were ready to do when that monster gave you the choice.' Angry at herself now, Siren drew closer. 'Will you let me do that?'

'It's done,' said Arkell, tossing the wire on the bar.

'Then can we please go find a doctor?'

He looked round, concerned. 'Is your throat—?'

'Not *me* – you!'

'I'm fine.'

'There's a bloody great hole in your neck. You are *not* fine.'

Rinsing his mouth with vodka, Arkell spat in the glass and turned to the Brazilians. 'Felipe, Marcos, you've risked your lives. You deserve to walk away now, but I'm going to ask you to come with us. You've seen his face. You too, Siren. We'll need all the eyes we can get in Brasilia. Will you help us find him?'

The two Brazilians nodded without hesitation. Siren said, 'Of course I'm coming, you stupid bastard, but that woman—'

'Thank you,' said Arkell, cutting her off. From his wallet he took a clutch of $100 bills and handed them to Felipe. 'I'm going to talk to Klara now. Go to hospital and get that leg sewn up. And take Siren with you – have a specialist look at her throat. Then find us a plane to Brasilia. Private jet if necessary. I'm not in the mood to fly economy.'

Siren was staring at him furiously. She didn't speak as she found her shoes and tidied her hair in the bar mirror. When Klara offered her a scarf, she took it without so much as a glance at the other woman, wrapping it around her bruised neck. 'You're making a mistake,' she told Arkell as she left. 'Don't turn your back on her for a second.'

More blood had collected in Arkell's mouth, and he sat down with a bottle of mineral water and the ice bucket. He spat into the bucket, gargled water, spat again. Klara sat opposite him, back uncomfortably straight and legs pressed together. She watched him as a child might watch a large and drunken stranger – with rapt attention and a hint of fear.

'How's your neck?'

She flexed it unconsciously. 'OK.'

'Can you hear me all right? We can shout if necessary.'

'I can hear you.'

He offered her the water. When she declined, he drank half the bottle.

'My colleagues will tell me the same thing Siren just did. We should lock you up.'

'You should.'

'But you're prepared to help me find and kill Gavriel Yadin.'

She looked down. 'I can't say I want you to kill him.'

Arkell set the ice bucket on the floor as a spittoon between his feet. 'Klara, why are you here?'

'He contacted me. He said he needed me.'

'So you flew straight back into his arms?'

'Yes.'

'That night in Strasbourg, what we did together . . . That was all fake?'

Swallowing, she said, 'I understand why you think that.'

'If you still love him—'

'I don't still love him.'

'So sure?'

There was no reply. Arkell stood up and moved to the closet. He began rifling through Yadin's clothes, searching the pockets, checking the lining of the jackets.

'Look, Klara, I'm not going to lock you up. But Siren's right: it would be crazy to involve you tomorrow if I can't trust you.' Two empty cases were stacked beside the closet; swiftly he unbuckled each one, running his hands into every crevice and corner. There was nothing inside. On the desk was a sheaf of maps: Brasilia and Rio. The open safe held a set of keys, seven thousand dollars in cash, a passport in the name of René Salvin and a plane ticket to Brasilia. No weapons, no poisons, no dossiers incriminating Tony Watchman. A thorough search of the bed, light fittings, furniture and bathroom yielded nothing.

When she spoke, it was so quiet he had to ask her to repeat herself. The ringing in his ears seemed to be getting worse. 'I said, I never wanted you to be hurt,' she said stiffly.

'You had nothing to do with it. I came for Siren.'

Klara shrank back into her chair and stared at the floor.

'When I first met you,' he said, sitting down again, 'you gave me the impression you knew nothing about Yadin's job.'

'You gave me the impression you were a priest.'

'*Did* you know? Or have you just come to accept the idea?'

She muttered something inaudible. Impatiently, he told her to repeat it.

'I didn't know.'

'So you discover you've been sleeping with a hired killer and within a week you're back in his arms?'

'I slept with you too.'

He sat back, repulsed. 'You see no difference?'

'Weren't you hired to kill?'

Unable to answer, he spat blood into the bucket. Was there no difference? Was he in danger of turning into Yadin? He had been so young when he killed for the Legion, for Wraye. Too young to know better, perhaps. Until Emily died. There had been no formal renunciation, no symbolic laying down of arms. He had simply stopped killing. For nine years. Would Yadin's funereal existence be his own fate if, wiser now and more mindful of the value of life, he started again?

Klara stretched her neck painfully and said, 'Haven't you ever . . . ?' She stopped. 'I – I know there's a difference.' Raising her eyes at last, she said, 'Haven't you ever felt close to someone you shouldn't?'

Meeting her gaze, he hesitated.

'You know you should leave, shut them out, but you stay. You let them get close to you. You let them take hold of a piece of your heart.'

'Klara . . .'

'So imagine, please, Simon, how much harder it is when you only now find out who they are and what they have done. Especially when you can see they still love you very—' She stopped herself. 'When you *think* they still love you.'

'You can't believe . . . Klara, he just abandoned you.'

'I know.'

'He could have broken your neck.'

'You think I want to care for him?' She was suddenly indignant. 'A *murderer*? You think I want to feel anything for either of you?'

Arkell sat rigidly upright. He would not go down that road. He would not become Yadin. More blood was pooling in his mouth, but he chose to swallow it rather than reach for the ice bucket. 'I'm not asking you to promise me anything,' he said softly. 'I just need to know how you'll react if you see Gavriel again.'

'It's going to take time,' she said. 'I don't want him in my head, OK? Not after this. But he's been there so long, he's part of me. Do you understand? I have to exorcize him, cut him out like cancer. I'm trying to be honest with you.'

'"Like cancer" is good enough for me.'

They sat a long time in silence. Arkell could not say exactly when their gaze ceased to be antagonistic and instead relaxed into something like shared understanding. He became aware that a warmth had permeated his tired, damaged body, and with it a sense of unfathomable optimism that he hadn't felt in many years. His fingers moved unconsciously to his injured jaw: the pain had been growing steadily as the tension drained from his limbs.

Klara said, 'Let me look at that,' and before he could object she was next to him on the couch, easing away his hand and using mineral water and a cocktail napkin to clean the caked blood from the wound.

He could not turn his head to look at her as he wanted to. Feeling her fingers on his skin, he tensed again, unsure now what to do with his hands, his elbows, his feet.

'It's bad,' she said, and kissed his jaw.

He looked at her then. Her disquieting lips, wet with mineral water and a scrap of his blood, shivered slightly, a whisper from his.

'You have to see a doctor.' When he didn't react, didn't move, she said, as if by way of negotiation, 'I'll come.'

And suddenly, with holes in his neck and tongue, bullet wounds in his arm and leg, and nine long years lost to anonymity, he felt ready to break down.

BRASILIA, BRAZIL – 29 June

Through the night they poured into the capital. To a city laid out in the image of an aeroplane, the people of Brazil came in cars and buses, on motorcycles and the roofs of garbage lorries and cement trucks. Makeshift camps of mourners mushroomed along the 200-metre-wide central reservation of the Monumental Axis, the immense ministry-lined avenue that formed the fuselage of the aircraft city. From Mato Grosso and Amazonas, from São Paulo and Rio Grande do Sul, from Ceará, Alagoas and Pernambuco, they had travelled days and nights to a capital most had never seen before to pay their last respects.

In a guest bungalow behind the Canadian embassy, Simon Arkell read the AMB file late into the night. Klara was asleep in the room next door, but Madeleine Wraye stayed up until he had finished. In silence, they walked outside to a darkened tennis court, away from the possibility of Canadian bugs.

'David Atticus served in the US Marine Corps at the same time Tony was in the Royal Marines,' she explained. 'They met through a Pentagon exchange programme, hit it off immediately, shared adventurous expeditions up mountains and over polar ice caps, debated politics in the mess. Best buddies, inseparable even by an ocean. So it's odd that the friendship seemed to come to an abrupt end soon after Tony joined the Service. No more family visits, no friendly calls.

'Atticus stayed on as a Marine, rose to the rank of major, then was recruited by AMB to revamp their security division. He performed extremely well, in part because he seems to have had inexplicably good information about threats and opportunities in some tricky parts of the world. From there it's all speculation, except that Tony has been known to slip off to Louisville from time to time when visiting Langley. And he has twice been observed meeting with Atticus in DC. Strange, given that there has been no overt interaction between the two of them for decades. We can only presume that Tony has been feeding

Atticus and AMB critical SIS CX for over twenty years . . . and for at least half that time has been commissioning some very black work on their behalf.'

'What's in it for Watchman?'

'There's no obvious money trail – Tony hasn't been buying mansions – but AMB will have made it worth his while. Escrow accounts and stock portfolios Tony will collect on when he leaves the Service, same way we compensated Soviet defectors who stayed in post. I wouldn't be surprised if Tony owns a fair chunk of AMB by now. He certainly deserves it, given the military contracts they won as a direct consequence of GRIEVANCE.'

'And now Think Again is a threat to their counter-narcotics business?'

'Revenues from domestic border patrol operations have overtaken the combined Middle East and Afghanistan contribution. The Homeland Security work is too important to allow people like Mayhew to turn the heads of congressmen with talk of legalization. It also explains a riddle. Just before he showed up in Strasbourg, Yadin executed a drug baron by the name of Rodrigo Salis who had been eluding AMB's Gulf operations by shipping cocaine into the US via West Africa. AMB's credibility now depends on their success in curbing cocaine flows, and Salis was not helpful in that regard. Tony Watchman paid him a visit, I would guess to encourage him back into the more traditional smuggling routes that fall within AMB's purview. It didn't work, so Tony had him killed.' She smiled sourly. 'I fear for the safety of all drug barons who dare to channel their product around the AMB net.'

'How much evidence do you have for all this?'

'Very little. So if you find Yadin tomorrow, do try to extract what you can while he's still breathing.'

'I'm not sure he knows much.' He paused. 'I guess he could testify to the executions Watchman ordered.'

Wraye looked round sharply. 'This isn't going to trial. You know that.'

'Bad choice of words. If I catch him alive, Yadin can share what he knows with our interrogators.'

'If you catch him alive in Brazil, it won't be our interrogators that go to work on him.'

'All right, but –'

'Simon, you understand we cannot discuss Anthony Watchman with CSIS or ABIN – or anyone else, for that matter. He's a British problem, a *Service* problem, that you and I are going to resolve. However interested the Canadians and Brazilians might be in the identity of Yadin's master, you do see why we can't air this particular dirty laundry?'

'Of course.'

'So then you understand why Yadin cannot be captured alive on Brazilian soil. Why it is your duty – as well as your *right* – to kill him.'

He looked away. 'Of course,' he said again.

BRASILIA, BRAZIL – 30 June

'What we have to accept is that the threat to our prime minister's life is not the topmost security concern in the minds of our Brazilian friends.' Nathaniel Henderson gazed around the alert faces of the Prime Minister Protection Detail and Margrave's CSIS team. 'Enemy action has taken down their president. The vice president has assumed the office. He and the other three individuals able to fulfil the role of acting president will be present in the Praça today. A single attack could eliminate all four of them, plunging Brazil into a constitutional crisis. We will have the full cooperation of the federal police, ABIN and the military police – we just shouldn't expect to have much of their attention.'

'So we're looking for this guy in a crowd of thousands,' said one of his officers, 'in a city we don't know, with law enforcement who don't speak our language or share our priorities.' Like his colleagues, he was grim-faced and wan. Daybreak was still a few minutes away. All of them had been awake since 4 a.m.

'Might not even be him we have to worry about,' said another. 'He used an accomplice in Lourdes.'

'The Praça is so exposed,' said a third. 'Couldn't we move this thing indoors?'

'The only buildings around the square are government facilities,' said Henderson. 'Their windows and rooftops will be fully controlled by the Feds.'

'And if TARQUIN impersonates a Brazilian officer? In a police uniform, he could get himself a sweet sniper's position on the roof of the Supreme Court.'

'Or he impersonates a presidential guardsman. Or a congressional aide. Or a grieving relative. Shit, apart from a few seconds of side-profile video, we don't even know what he looks like!'

Henderson held up a hand to halt the growing discontent. 'We're going to have some help with that. Some of you have met this gentleman before.' He turned to Arkell. 'You want to bring in your friends?'

Simon Arkell opened the door. Felipe, Marcos, Siren and Klara walked in. Both women looked tense; he wondered what had passed between them.

'These folks have all seen TARQUIN close up,' said Henderson. 'They have kindly volunteered to accompany us today.'

'No disrespect,' interrupted one of the RCMP officers, 'but who are these guys? How exactly do they know TARQUIN?'

'Fair question,' said Arkell. 'Siren is my assistant. Yesterday we had an unpleasant encounter with . . . TARQUIN. Felipe and Marcos, both former members of the Rio state military police, came to our rescue. They had no knowledge of TARQUIN until yesterday.' He hesitated. 'And this is Klara, who . . .' He caught Siren's damning stare, and was aghast to find himself blushing. 'Who . . .'

'The man you're looking for was my lover.'

Astonishment marked every face in the room. Siren's glare turned triumphant. A CSIS officer hurriedly swept up and concealed a set of papers laid out on one of the tables. 'Who the fuck let her on site?' muttered someone.

'You had a physical relationship with TARQUIN?' demanded Henderson.

Nervously, she tugged at her charcoal beret. 'For four years.'

Turning on Arkell, the PMPD chief said, 'Clearly this individual must be excluded immediately and detained for her own protection until the threat is past.'

But as two RCMP officers started forward Shel Margrave, who had been silent thus far, said, 'If you don't mind, I'd like to hear from the lady.'

Henderson looked thunderous. 'We're on a tight schedule. We don't have time to—'

'It seems to me,' observed Margrave, 'that we have almost no usable intel on the man we're trying to find. Ms . . .'

'Richter.'

'Ms Richter knows him a thousand times better than anyone else in this room. If she is willing to help us identify him, perhaps she might also share with us some insight into the man's character. That would seem to me as good a use of the next ten minutes as a weather briefing or whatever else it is we have scheduled before we head on out there.'

Henderson shook his head in silent protest. Of Arkell he demanded, 'Do you vouch for her?'

Madeleine Wraye stepped forward. 'I vouch for her.'

'All right, then,' said Margrave. 'Ms Richter, please, tell us what you can.'

Under the hostile gaze of more than twenty intelligence and police personnel, the apprentice physiotherapist from Hamburg seemed momentarily dumbstruck. Glancing helplessly at Arkell, she stammered, 'I – I don't know what I can tell you. I'm only now finding out the truth for myself.'

Gently, Arkell suggested, 'You could describe how you met.'

She shook her head. 'That's too sad.'

'OK, enough,' interrupted Henderson. 'If we have to wait for Ms Richter to get over her feelings for this murderer—'

'I *am* over him!'

The outburst drew a fascinated silence from the room.

'Don't you people understand it's not easy? Finding out the worst possible truth about someone you love . . . knowing you have to stop loving them . . . but you can't just switch it off in one day. I don't think any of you understand this. I *loved* him! He was intense, angry, withdrawn. But he was . . . he is human. And he can be kind, generous. There is so much intelligence in his eyes and depth in his soul. More than I see in any of you. I know you have to kill him today. Perhaps that's right. Perhaps it's what he wants. There is something in him that is new. Like he's empty. How do you say . . . a *death wish*? No, that's not what it is. But maybe now he looks forward to death. I don't know if he was ever afraid before. I know he will not be afraid of anything again.'

'What makes you say that?' asked Margrave. 'Has he talked about fear?'

'It's the way he moves, the way he breathes. Sometimes in Rio I thought he had stopped breathing completely.'

'I'm getting a picture of an increasingly unstable individual,' murmured one CSIS officer.

'He's not unstable,' said Klara simply. 'But I think he has been depressed for a long time. Before, I believed it was a midlife crisis, but now . . . knowing what he is . . .'

'Do you have any idea what's he planning today?'

'No.'

'See any equipment while you were with him? Long cases, perhaps? Syringes? Bottles? Strange devices?'

'Nothing.'

'Did he meet with anyone?'

'In Rio there was a man. He approached us in a café on Avenida Atlântica. They knew each other. The man was called . . . Olavo. Gavriel told him we were busy and he should come to the hotel the next day.'

'And did he?'

'I don't know. I wasn't there most of the time.'

'Why not?'

'Gavriel sent me out every day: "go shopping", "go to the beach", "take a tour to Pão de Açúcar". He didn't want me around. Maybe he was sick of me. I don't know.'

'When you returned to the hotel from these excursions, was anything different? New luggage? Had the toiletries in the bathroom been moved?'

'No.'

'Signs of cleaning? Grease or oil marks?'

'Nothing like that. Only . . . once there was an odour.'

'An odour?'

'Like . . . in science class.'

'Some kind of chemical? Chlorine? Ammonia?'

'No, not chemistry. I remember the smell from the physics classroom. More like a . . . burning smell.'

The Canadians stared at each other in bemusement. 'What physicists burn stuff?' remarked one.

An RCMP officer at the back of the room cut through the speculation: 'She's talking about solder. That burning smell you get from a soldering iron.' He paused. 'TARQUIN is doing electronics.'

'Jesus,' growled Henderson. He turned to Arkell. 'Was there anything electronic in the room when you searched it? Transistors, switches, any little components at all?'

'No.'

'Has he built himself a vest? He's depressed, she says. Looks forward to death. Are we dealing with a suicide bomber?'

'It's a possibility,' mused Margrave. 'In his past life he encountered a few.'

'Can we find out who this Olavo guy is? If he came to the hotel, maybe there's CCTV.'

'ABIN are all over TARQUIN's hotel room,' said Sarah Winter, the officer responsible for liaison with the Brazilian intelligence service. 'They're checking the faces of everyone entering the hotel during his stay. A big job – thousands of people coming and going.'

Margrave nodded. 'Have them prioritize anyone arriving and leaving within two hours, carrying a bag or a case, on . . . what day would this have been?'

'Wednesday,' answered Klara.

'Wednesday. And check their files for any local hoods with access to explosives by the name of Olavo.'

Henderson turned to his own team: 'This doesn't mean we stop looking for the guy with the dart gun or syringe. But Ms Richter has given us a valuable steer: we also need to keep our eyes open for bags and bulky jackets. We all know how to do that.' He looked at his watch. 'Time to move.'

It was agreed that Arkell would search alone. Siren and Klara were paired with CSIS officers, Felipe and Marcos with members of the RCMP, but Simon Arkell was given a tacit carte blanche to operate autonomously. He was also given a radio, a car and, unofficially, another Taurus.

He parked on a grass verge near the magnificent Praça dos Três Poderes – the Square of Three Powers. Much of it had been cordoned off for the ceremony, and a solid line of Federal District military police held back the mass of grieving citizens already thronging this nexus of Brazilian government. On one side of the square stood the Supremo Tribunal Federal, which housed the Judiciary, a glass-fronted building with an overhanging flat white roof supported on curved flying buttresses. Opposite it, a broad ramp led up to a wider building of similar design, the Palácio do Planalto, office of the president. And set back from the square, keeping its distance from the other two powers, was the iconic Congresso Nacional: twin skyscrapers poised between two flawless white hemispheres – the bowl-like Chamber of Deputies and the domed Senate.

Beyond the Praça, on a patch of congressional lawn through which the red Cerrado soil was clearly visible, Arkell knelt and pressed his fingers to the dirt. For a moment he tuned out the chatter and the police megaphones and the media helicopters, and settled his mind on the man who was somewhere in this city, readying himself to murder a prime minister. His tongue still throbbed, his jaw ached. And as he recalled Gavriel Yadin's hands on Klara's neck, he told himself that Wraye was right – the killer had to be killed.

It did not occur to him to think of Siren's neck, although she was standing not far from him, beside the only entrance to the Praça's restricted zone. She had not slept for the pain in her throat.

'So what's the deal with TARQUIN's woman?' asked the CSIS officer accompanying her. 'Is she gonna face charges?'

Not looking away for a second from the line of faces queuing for admission, Siren replied, 'I really have no idea.'

'Couldn't help noticing you're both wearing scarves, even though it's baking here.'

In answer, Siren pulled up the edge of hers. The officer whistled softly. 'He's not a nice man,' she said, readjusting the scarf. 'So when I spot the bastard, don't feel bad if you need to shoot him.'

A short distance away, Marcos was walking with an RCMP officer and a federal police officer between two lines of soldiers from the Presidential Guard Battalion. They marked the route that the coffin – and Prime Minister Mayhew – would take from the Palácio do Planalto to the centre of the Praça. In their crisp white trousers, blue tunics and red-plumed, gilded shakos the soldiers looked like something out of the Napoleonic Wars. But Marcos was only interested in their faces.

Stiff-legged, leaning on a stick, Felipe was performing the same task within the restricted zone, searching among the mourners around the perimeter, the policemen lining the cordon and the international camera crews for the man who had left a knife in his thigh.

Klara Richter, in an embassy car three blocks away, felt nauseous with fear. The CSIS officer assigned to babysit her, a genial sandy-haired Vancouver man named Douglas Malloy, noticed her shaking hands and offered to pull over.

'Some air?' he suggested. 'Would a walk help?'

'I'm fine,' she murmured.

'This is a brutal gig for you, eh?' Margrave had chosen him for this role on the strength of something he hadn't done: there had been no judgement in his eyes when Klara's history had emerged. He was known for – and, in CSIS, not universally trusted because of – his generous spirit.

'You can say that.'

Malloy drove at a stately pace along Via Sul Dois, behind the southern row of ministries, then crossed the Monumental Axis by the sunken cathedral. On both sides of the great central avenue, mourners flowed in their thousands towards the Praça. Some had dressed entirely in black. Others wore black armbands. Many carried placards bearing Andrade's portrait. Klara and her CSIS minder scanned every face in sight.

On Via Norte Dois, they ground to a halt behind a blockade of taxis and minibuses carrying mourners to the Praça. Malloy eyed the generous verge. 'With diplomatic plates we could get away with a little cross-country, but it's not very respectful.'

Klara slumped in her seat. 'Whatever you want to do.'

'I guess we're unlikely to achieve much. Might as well watch the show from here.'

They gazed out at the crowded pavements. Brasilia was not normally a city of walkers; designed for cars, its affluent population and generously spaced layout made pedestrians a minority. For once, however, those on foot had the advantage. Klara smiled, briefly forgetting her fear, at the sight of two little boys using their Andrade placards as swords.

Then, all of a sudden, she sat bolt upright.

'You OK?' began Malloy.

'That was him!'

She was out of the car and pushing through the crowd in the same instant. Malloy shouted after her but she was already lost in the mourners. Hurriedly, he navigated the car onto the kerb and leapt out after her.

The press of people all around him was disorienting. A placard caught him in the eye. Two sullen men knocked him back when he tried to push through. Brandishing his Canadian diplomatic credentials achieved nothing. Starting to panic at the thought of losing Richter, telling himself that the proximity of TARQUIN was sufficient grounds for extreme measures, Malloy whipped out his semi-automatic. He held it alongside his Foreign Affairs and International Trade ID, pointed skywards, as he bellowed at the mourners. The weapon had the desired effect, although Malloy felt sick to his stomach drawing it in the midst of all these people.

Dashing through the crowd, he finally caught sight of Klara.

She was halfway across a parking lot jammed with tour buses from distant cities. Cards revealing their origins – Fortaleza, Curitiba, Campo Grande, Porto Seguro – shared dashboards with black ribbons and framed portraits of the dead president. The coaches blocked Malloy's view: he couldn't see anyone resembling TARQUIN. Klara looked back and urgently beckoned him on.

Malloy hit the transmit button on his throat microphone. 'Possible TARQUIN sighting north of Via Norte Dois. Pursuing on foot with Richter.' He was extremely fit: talking while running was not a problem. Rushing after an unseen assassin through ranks of obscuring buses, on the other hand, was a very big problem. His training called for him to wait for back-up. But he couldn't lose the German woman.

She was standing on a patch of waste ground just beyond the last tour bus. He came alongside her, breathing hard. 'Where?'

She pointed to a large construction site of red earth, stacked girders and scattered PVC piping, on which an eight-storey building rose in unadorned concrete. Malloy saw him straight away. The man was crossing the deserted site at a relaxed jog, a small black case in his hand. When he reached the steel fence surrounding the skeletal building, he paused at a gate and hunched over the lock. A moment later the gate was open and the man was inside the building.

'TARQUIN sighting confirmed,' said Malloy. 'Construction site two blocks north of Palace of Justice.' He looked round to the twin towers of the Congress, rising over the anonymous ministry annex buildings, and a hint of alarm crept into his voice. 'Be advised there is a probable line of sight from the top of the construction to the Praça.'

At the edge of the Praça dos Três Poderes, Simon Arkell turned and looked to the north-west. In the middle distance, he made out the top two floors of a dull grey building. No glint of glass in its windows and no aerials, aircon units or water tanks on its flat roof. A nearby crane confirmed the impression of a building under construction.

He turned up the volume on the CSIS radio and started running.

In the Palácio do Planalto, Shel Margrave was conferring with his ABIN opposite number, while keeping one eye on Terence Mayhew. The Canadian prime minister was at the other end of the reception suite, sharing a few words with the new president. A muted television showed the arrival of the military transport plane bearing the coffin and the Andrade family.

He excused himself at Malloy's first report. When the second came, he asked tersely, 'Did you see his face?'

'Negative,' responded Malloy.

Margrave made a swift assessment of Malloy's account: it might be accurate, it might not. The prime minister was still indoors – they had time. 'Soames, get over there. Malloy, I'm going to need facial confirmation before I divert any more officers away from the Praça.'

Gerard Soames was a capable officer and a good man to back up Malloy in a dangerous situation. But he was an unfortunate choice in one respect. At that moment, he was on the south side of the Praça, attempting to clear a piece of grit from his eye. It was too trivial an issue to mention, and he acknowledged and accepted the assignment without hesitation. But the grit was a problem, and he needed to deal with it before he could go into a hostile situation. It took him less than two minutes to remove his contact lens, sluice his eyeball with the solution he always carried, and replace the lens. And it was barely another three minutes before he'd worked his way through the crowd to the north side of the Praça. But those five minutes were critical. Because in that time, the few designated pedestrian routes across the cleared Via Norte Um had been sealed by grim-faced police officers ahead of the funeral cortège. These were Federal District military police, and they did not react constructively to Canadian diplomatic credentials. Where Arkell had been able to run straight across the great avenue, Soames was curtly told he would need to make his way at least half a kilometre to the east, through dense crowds, before he would have a hope of crossing to the north side.

* * *

They reached the steel fence and Malloy said, 'Wait here. There'll be more officers along shortly to take good care of you.' With his weapon cradled in both hands, he nudged open the gate.

Klara caught his arm. 'Don't you want him alive?'

'If possible, ma'am.'

'Then I have to come with you. He'll listen to me.'

'I can't risk you in there.'

'Why not?' she said fiercely. 'I was only important to identify Gavriel. I've done that.'

'You're a civilian. I can't involve you in a firefight.'

'There won't be one if I'm there!'

Malloy hesitated. He was not the kind of officer who actively sought the chance to put his weapons training to the test. The idea of confronting a Mossad assassin was not something he relished. The possibility of a negotiated surrender was appealing.

'All right,' he said. 'But stay behind me at all times.'

Inside the steel fence, tools and materials lay where the construction workers had left them the previous evening. Two forklift trucks stood abandoned beside a concrete-lined pit. Malloy picked his way through the debris and entered the skeletal building via a makeshift bridge of rough planks over the drainage ditch that ran around the foundations. He heard the woman follow, her clumsy footsteps too loud on the planks. Ahead, a rough concrete doorway opened onto a dark passage littered with lengths of timber and reinforced steel. Removing his sunglasses, Malloy edged forward, advancing with careful steps through the construction wreckage.

Klara whispered, 'Can I call to him?'

He looked back. 'We need to establish whether—' He broke off. She was staring past him, open-mouthed.

Swivelling round, he had time only to see a dark figure at the end of the passage, legs apart, hands clasped together at eye level. 'Oh,' he said reflexively, as two bullets tore into his throat.

He died on his back, vaguely aware of the Richter woman crouched over him, wishing he'd found time that morning to call home.

Simon Arkell heard the gunshots, despite the roar of helicopters overhead and the distant rumble of a million voices. He leapt a ditch and sprinted to the perimeter of the building site, scrambling over the steel fence rather than wasting seconds searching for a gate. Through a congregation of inert diggers and trucks, he spotted the plank bridge leading into the building. Fresh clods of dirt clung to the dusty wood. He slowed only to steady his breathing and adjust his eyes to the gloom inside, then launched himself into the dank passageway.

Klara was huddled on the ground next to Malloy's body. His radio was in pieces, his weapon nowhere to be seen. Arkell crouched beside her.

'Dead,' she sobbed.

'Are you hurt?'

She looked at him as if he was insane. 'That man is *dead*! Gavriel *murdered* him!'

He took her hand, felt it trembling. 'I know,' he said softly.

'He shot him right in front of me. His . . .' She couldn't finish the sentence. 'Simon, he was right in front of me.'

'It's OK. We'll get you out of here. Come on . . .' He helped her up. 'What did Gavriel say to you?'

She staggered slightly. 'He said . . .' Her brow creased. 'He said . . .'

Arkell helped her across the plank bridge. 'Did he go upstairs?'

Flinching at the bright sunlight, she looked at him in alarm. 'You're not going up there?'

'Sit here,' he said, guiding her towards a broad girder. 'More officers are on their way.'

'So wait for them,' she said, newly frantic. All of a sudden her arms were around him and her shivering body was pressed against him. 'Simon, for God's sake, what is *wrong* with you people!'

It almost would be possible, he felt, to do nothing more – to settle into this moment and forget the rest. Forget Yadin and Wraye and Tony Watchman, and the bombing of Dault Street that killed Emily. This was enough. *She* was enough. He lowered his mouth to hers and kissed her. 'I'll see you very soon,' he promised.

At the edge of the flat concrete slab that, for the time being, formed the top of the building, Gavriel Yadin set up his tripod. Made of carbon fibre, it rose just sixty centimetres high and weighed less than half a kilogram. The kit it supported did not weigh much more, although it had cost several thousand dollars. Kneeling behind it, Yadin closed his right eye and put his left to the rubber eyepiece extender. The image through the powerful lens was sharp and vivid. Nudging it across the Brasilia skyline, Yadin found the Congress and, beyond it, the Praça dos Três Poderes.

It fascinated him to see the sheer number of people who had gathered to observe a wooden box and listen to a speech in a language most of them would not understand. The power of death.

So frequent and so ordinary.

We travel through life never thinking about death, and then it happens – someone important dies, and we are outraged, horrified, paralysed with shock! But an emperor died of a scratch from his own comb and a young man in Dordogne was killed by a tennis ball.

It does no good to go on living. It will do nothing to shorten the time you are dead.

He turned his attention to the device beside the tripod. Already powered up and ready to operate. He need only connect it.

Then, a voice somewhere behind him: 'You know, I really hoped I might find you here.'

Terence Mayhew's eyes were glazing over. He could not concentrate on the pages before him. It didn't matter – he knew the speech by heart. This last review was really just to reassure his aides, and to escape further idle chatter with his Brazilian hosts about their pensions predicament.

He was not distracted by the prospect of assassination out there in the Praça dos Três Poderes. He had long reconciled himself to that possibility. In fact he was not thinking about Yadin, or the Andrade family, or his security team, or anything to do with this whole damn tragic business. His mind was instead wrestling with the dilemma presented by his youngest cousin.

Mikey.

He had never liked Mikey.

He pulled out his phone and looked again at the text. Simple blackmail, that's what it was. The timing could not be coincidental. He wanted $20,000. The demand was couched in sugary family language of course. *Got no one else to turn to. If you can't help me, I just don't know what I'll do . . .* Except that Mayhew feared his sly little cousin knew exactly what he'd do, exactly where he could obtain a comparable sum of money if only he were prepared to tell his story. What a headline:

> DRUG-PUSHING PM PILFERS POLICE STASH FOR JUNKIE CUZ

A victimless crime, but he had been the ranking police officer in the station, trusted by his superiors and his community to uphold the law. He would never have considered it if his mother and aunt hadn't come to him together, two tearful matrons, begging for his help. Mikey's ripping the house apart, they said. He's going to set fire to something. He's going to hurt himself, they said.

He needs his fix.

It was so easy, that was the problem. Grass, pills, powder, junk – they had it all in the station. And if a little went missing, it was easy enough to make up the recorded quantities at the next crack house raid.

Hard to refuse the second time. *But Terry, if it was OK last week . . .* And the third, and the fourth, until Mayhew had found the balls to do what he should have done in the first place. Mikey had been 'discovered' by some brother officers in possession of crystal meth, and had been forced into a treatment programme. Mayhew made sure the charges ultimately went away.

Unfortunately, Mikey's problem did not go away. He was clean for just over a year, employed in a hardware store for very nearly four months. Then he fell apart.

Mayhew had moved on to a new policy role in Edmonton, and was able to say with clear conscience that he no longer had access to drugs. Never again did he pass illegal substances to his deteriorating cousin. Instead he propped him up with money. Minimal sums. Cash that was, all agreed, only to be spent on food and rent. When he stood for parliament, and Mikey happened to show up in his riding, the remittances increased slightly. When he rose to ministerial rank and started appearing regularly on television, there was another bout of inflation. But the financial burden was manageable, and Mayhew was able to tell himself that it was nothing more than a bit of charity, a tithe to support a less fortunate member of his family.

Not now. Not twenty thousand. This was naked extortion. And if he paid, there would be more demands, greater still. Mikey might be living in the gutter, irretrievably hooked on a multiplicity of substances, but his brain still functioned lucidly enough to keep the texts coming. What would happen when Mayhew could no longer afford to pay? He was not a rich man, and there is a limit to the credit a bank will extend even to a prime minister. When the money ran out, would Mikey graciously accept the fact and go quietly in search of other funding sources? If he did not – and Mayhew was certain he would not – then everything was in jeopardy. Not just his career but the government, Think Again and the entire legalization movement. *Drug-pushing PM pilfers police stash . . .*

For the first time in his life, Terence Mayhew asked himself whether it might not be better for everyone if Mikey was dead.

Three years in office had changed the policeman from Alberta. He had been required to make decisions, and as a result of those decisions men had been killed – for the greater good. He was, he felt now, capable of making an equivalent decision about Mikey, if he could persuade himself that his analysis of the threat was robust and his motives were pure. A junkie's wretched life balanced against vitally important social reform. Or was he just trying to save his own political skin? Keep himself out of jail? Such was the issue: he had to be absolutely sure why he was doing this.

Well, he *was* sure. That was the phenomenal truth of the matter. It seemed to Mayhew in a moment of revelation that he was able to think more clearly, even dispassionately, about the question of his cousin's fate – now that he himself was faced with the imminent possibility of assassination.

Gavriel Yadin did not react immediately. Across a rooftop littered with metal reinforcing rods – rebars – and pieces of timber, Arkell wondered if Yadin had even heard him over the noise of the TV helicopters. Was he so engrossed in his work, in the murder of a prime minister, that he had become oblivious to everything else?

From this height, it was possible to get a sense of the remarkable shape of Brasilia: the Monumental Axis as the fuselage, with the two wings of residential neighbourhoods sweeping out to either side. And at the nose of the aircraft, the Praça dos Três Poderes, with beyond it the great artificial Paranoá Lake, created to bring humidity to the parched highland city. Simon Arkell ignored it all to focus his aim on Yadin's back. The distance between them was perhaps thirty metres: not a straightforward shot with a handgun, but he could do it.

He should do it. Wraye had been unequivocal.

But a bullet in the back? The easy death the assassin seemed to seek – was that the justice Emily deserved?

'Put your hands on your head!' Wraye was going to slaughter him for this.

There was no reaction. Still that inexpressive back. With the Taurus rock steady in a two-handed grip, Arkell started across the roof. If Yadin showed the slightest sign of –

His desert boot clipped a rebar. It didn't trip him, but the impact on his foot and the noise of steel scraping over concrete caused him to glance down for a fraction of a second. When he looked up again, Yadin was on one knee and pointing a gun at him.

'Put it down,' said Arkell, furious at his own clumsiness.

'Or you put yours down,' suggested Yadin benignly.

'The Canadian security team is on its way here. You just killed one of their people. If you're holding a weapon when they get here, they won't stop to chat like me.'

'Then they are more intelligent than you.'

Arkell smiled grimly. 'Are you any smarter? You've had two opportunities to kill me.'

'And now you've given me a third.'

Minutely raising the elbow of his right arm so that his trigger finger felt perfectly balanced, Arkell said, 'You understand this is over? Mayhew won't be stepping outside until you're killed or contained. Whatever happens between us, you're not getting that shot.'

'We'll see.'

'Klara is downstairs. She doesn't want you dead. For her sake, Gavriel, put your weapon down.'

'A personal appeal. Nice. Would she want *you* dead?' He gave the slightest hint of a laugh. 'Maybe we should put our weapons down together.' The dark humour turned into a mocking grimace. 'For Klara's sake.'

'All right.'

Still keeping the Taurus locked on Yadin, Arkell crouched down. Very slowly, he began to lower the gun. The Israeli mirrored his movements exactly, separating his hands at the same moment, bringing the gun to rest on the concrete in perfect synchrony.

Their hands drew clear of the firearms and they stood up and walked towards each other.

'How is your neck?'

'On the mend.'

'Leg? Arm?'

'Better than I implied.'

'Good. Then this will be fair.'

Arkell thought again of Wraye's explicit order. 'I'm giving you the chance to surrender.'

'So I can rot in a Brazilian cell?'

'It might be a Dutch cell.'

Yadin glanced at the rebars scattered about the rooftop. 'Your file detailed some skill in bōjutsu.'

Arkell smiled. 'I thought you wanted this to be fair.'

Perplexed, the other man said, 'Have you learned nothing about me?'

His foot lashed out. There had been no warning, no shift in stance. The high kick caught Arkell in the chest, cracking two ribs and tumbling him backwards. He looked up to see Yadin seize a two-metre rebar. Another lay close by, and he grabbed it and leapt to his feet as Yadin lunged at him with the steel rod.

It was simplest just to dodge that one.

Yadin spun around, bringing the rebar whipping towards his head. He ducked, and as the metal rod skimmed his hair, he rolled his own rebar around and delivered a glancing blow to Yadin's hip.

The other man staggered. Retreating three paces, he turned and assumed a fighting stance, the rebar gripped diagonally across his body. Arkell swung his rebar one-handed up and back to rest on his right shoulder. He needed to make better allowance for its weight. That strike should have landed better. He had misjudged the force required to reverse the momentum of the steel.

Yadin let his rebar slide through his hands and then flipped it round to point the other end at his opponent. A standard kata move, all the warning Arkell needed that Gavriel Yadin had picked up a little bōjutsu training himself.

In response, Arkell turned side-on to the Israeli. Pivoting the rebar back across his shoulder blades in an easy, almost lethargic motion, he waited for the other man to move. When Yadin lunged, he rolled the rebar off his shoulders and round, seizing it with left hand close to right, and deflecting the lunge without difficulty. But Yadin was already twisting back for a new attack, and this time he had to block the rebar directly. As the two lengths of tempered steel clashed, he locked his wrists against the punishing vibration.

Yadin rocked back and struck again, then reversed the rebar to attack from above. Each blow Arkell parried, shifting faster and faster as Yadin built up momentum. Arkell could see the other man refreshing and improving his technique by the second. The next swing was a feint, and Yadin went for a direct jab to the throat. Arkell batted the rebar aside, but the thought of that steel pole skewering his neck made him angry. Rocking backwards, he spun the rebar, rolling it from one hand to the other, before lashing out and catching Yadin on the left shoulder.

The impact of hard steel on bone drew a roar of pain from Yadin, and Arkell knew the shoulder was broken. The Kidon combatant threw a look towards his automatic, but Arkell had anticipated him and moved quickly to block his path to the weapon.

'Stop,' he said, no longer thinking of Wraye's order. 'You need a hospital.'

One-handed, Yadin whirled the heavy rod in a vertical and then a lateral plane, flicking it with superhuman agility towards Arkell's face. The other jerked back, and was then shocked to see the rebar turn and accelerate downwards towards his knee. Off-balance, he couldn't pull his leg clear in time; to save his knee, he rocked forward and took the blow on his injured thigh. The crushing pain made his leg collapse and he dropped to the ground. Above him, Yadin raised the rebar spear-like and drove it hard at his face.

Arkell rolled sideways to escape the steel, sacrificing his grip on his own rebar. He grabbed a timber baton and used it to smack away Yadin's second thrust. As the rebar struck the concrete beside his shoulder, he seized it and wrenched downwards. Yadin kept hold, but he'd allowed himself to be pulled dangerously low and Arkell reached up and smashed the baton against the side of his head.

The timber broke in two and Arkell rolled clear. Another rebar lay close by. It felt thicker and heavier. While Yadin steadied himself, shaking his bleeding head, Arkell spun it in his left hand to accustom himself to the new weight.

The Kidon combatant's hair was matted with blood. His left arm hung useless by his side. The rebar lay at his feet but he did not attempt to pick it up. Instead, he straightened, his body stiffening. Arkell could sense the energy coiling inside him. Yadin had lost interest in bōjutsu. Badly injured, perhaps a little concussed, he was falling back on his most fundamental hand-to-hand combat skills, preparing himself for a last-ditch assault.

Simon Arkell gripped the cumbersome rebar diagonally across his body. It was heavy, too heavy to be truly effective. For a moment he considered running for the automatic. But his left leg could no longer be relied upon. If he stumbled, Yadin would finish him in seconds.

He breathed out, breathed in, and imagined he was fighting his way through mud. Imagined the effort it would take to move his arms. That was the force he would need to handle this overweight bō.

Yadin attacked.

It was a spinning hook kick, a tae kwon do move that took less than a second to execute. As Yadin twisted his whole body clockwise and his right foot started to lift, Arkell's subconscious anticipated the impact of heel against head. The rebar was on the wrong diagonal to block it – no accident – and so, even before his conscious mind had time to think it through, his hands were working with all the force in his arms to reverse the heavy steel bō and set it with milliseconds to spare in the path of Yadin's lower leg.

The choreography of a spinning hook kick dictated that it was the back of Yadin's right calf that hit the rigid bar rather than his shin. Otherwise he would undoubtedly have smashed his tibia. As it was, the rigid barrier destroyed his balance and ripped his calf muscle. Arkell spun the rebar once more and brought the heavy steel down on the nearest part of Yadin's falling body. It happened to be his right arm, and the sound of his humerus cracking was sickeningly clear over the noise of the media helicopters.

This time, the Kidon combatant made no further move. He lay on the concrete, breathing shallowly, his broken arm splayed wide.

Arkell picked up both guns. 'Stay down. We'll bring the medics to you.' Tapping the transmit button on his CSIS radio, he said, 'Arkell. TARQUIN incapacitated. Safe to proceed with ceremony.'

'Arkell, this is Margrave. Confirm TARQUIN no longer a threat,' came the instant, urgent response.

'Affirmative. TARQUIN is down.'

But even as he spoke the words, Yadin was lifting himself,

standing, facing Arkell with all the certainty and determination of before.

'It's over. You're finished. Stay down.'

Yadin barely seemed to hear the words. He stepped forward, his right leg shuddering as the torn calf muscle took his weight.

'I said *stay down*!' yelled Arkell, raising the Taurus.

As Yadin took one last step towards him, the noise of the shots seemed impossibly loud in that wide open place. He fell backwards, and instinctively Arkell went to him. One soldier to another. Soames, he thought angrily: reckoned I couldn't handle a man with two useless arms. He crouched beside the dying assassin, and something made him lay his hand on the man's wrecked shoulder.

Gavriel Yadin, killer of kings, looked up at him and smiled. There were small pink bubbles around his lips. His chest was a butchered mess. 'I'm happy it was you,' he said.

Arkell nodded. There seemed nothing useful to add.

'So frequent. So ordinary.' He was choking now. 'You've failed, but . . . you were better than we knew.' His eyes flickered. 'Found me planting cabbages.'

Arkell leaned forward. 'I've *failed*?'

But Yadin had no more breath to speak.

The muted scrape of rubber soles on dusty concrete sounded beside him as he closed Yadin's eyelids.

'That was unnecessary,' Arkell muttered. 'And stupid. We could have learned a lot from him.'

Then he noticed that the feet beside him were shod not in Canadian black brogues but rugged brown boots. Jerking round, Taurus raised, he saw there were three of them, all carrying automatic rifles. The leader gestured efficiently and unambiguously at the Taurus. Arkell laid it down.

He recognized all three – a passenger on the Dortmund train; the solitary businessman in the Strasbourg winstub; one of the tourists in the foyer of the Leblon Internacional – yet still he had no idea what to expect. No possible explanation for these new players arriving so late to a game he thought was over. But one confusion connected with another and he said, 'You were in Cyprus. You killed Kolatch.'

The leader nodded. 'It was necessary.'

'And Dejan?' The man had sandy hair and blue eyes. He looked nothing like Yadin. Still, Arkell guessed the truth. 'You're Mossad. Kidon. Cleaning up rogue agents and assets that have become an embarrassment to Israel. Boim put you on to me and I led you right to them.'

At the leader's signal, the other two men picked up Yadin's body.

'You're *taking* him? Why?'

'For burial in Jerusalem.'

Arkell did not try to hide his surprise. 'You just executed him! Now you honour him?'

'This man was a hero. He served his country.'

'So he ends up on the Mount of Olives despite murdering two national leaders and attempting to kill a third?'

'Is that what happened?' The leader waved his men on, and they carried the body down the steps. 'Van der Velde, perhaps, but Andrade was poisoned by a woman. And Mayhew . . .' The Kidon combatant gestured towards Yadin's kit, still arrayed at the edge of the slab. 'Do you see a weapon?'

An uneasy chill forming in his stomach, Arkell limped across to the tripod. It held a sleek black video camera with a long lens. Next to it stood a mobile satellite uplink, small enough to fit – with the camera – inside the ordinary suitcase that lay open beyond.

There was nothing else. No sniper's rifle, no rocket-propelled grenade. Just a simple means of recording and broadcasting an event that was already being recorded and broadcast by a dozen TV crews in the Praça. It made no sense.

'Then what—?' He turned to find the roof empty. When he hurried to the steps there was no sign of the Mossad team.

He picked up the CSIS radio and touched the transmit button. 'Arkell. Yadin's dead. But we might still have a problem . . .'

At the foot of the building, Klara never saw the Kidon team. Maybe they entered a different way. Maybe she was too distracted to notice them slip past. Gavriel Yadin was going to die: she had accepted the fact, but still it put her in a state of turmoil to imagine the killing. And that was not the heaviest burden pressing on her mind.

She stood abruptly and hurried across the construction site. She had to get to Margrave. Yadin's last words to her, when Malloy's blood was still wet on her fingers, came back to her. She raised a thumb to the passing vehicles. No one stopped for her. She started running south. Then a car swerved in front of her and Gerard Soames stepped out.

'Ms Richter?' He squinted as he drew closer. 'Is that blood?'

'Simon went after him,' she said in a rush. 'He went up after Gavriel . . .'

'I know. I heard on the radio.'

'What?' Klara staggered a little. 'What did you hear?'

Soames had the grace to hesitate. 'Arkell got him. I'm on my way to help clean up.'

'No . . .' She caught his arm. 'No, we have to go to Mr Margrave. Right now. There's something else.'

'What are you talking about? It's over.'

'It's not over! Listen to me. I saw him. I saw Gavriel. He told me to stay away from the square. You understand? He told me I had to be at least three blocks away. Why would he say that?'

Soames was not the sympathetic type. He did not like dealing with hysterical witnesses or members of the public. But he recognized a threat to his principal's life as well as any security professional. He glanced up at the unfinished building, and then back at the Congress towers beyond which lay the Praça dos Três Poderes. Even for a skilled sniper it really would have been a very long shot.

'Get in the car,' he said.

Margrave had called Wraye into a huddle with the Director General of ABIN. 'Your guy says it's safe. My officer is still a while away from the scene, and the cortège is nearly here. What's your assessment?'

'If Simon Arkell says Yadin is down, you can be sure he's not getting up again.'

'So we can proceed with the ceremony?'

'Shel, I'm not responsible for the prime minister's security. I can't comment on other possible threats. But you don't have to worry about Yadin any more.'

'All right, then.' Margrave took the news to Henderson, who relayed it to Mayhew at the other end of the reception suite. The mood of frustration that had been growing amongst the prime minister's aides quickly lifted.

As Margrave watched the prime minister pull on his jacket and pick up his speech, he heard a voice in his radio earpiece: 'Soames. Malloy is dead. I have Klara Richter with me. She has important information on a possible new threat. I'm at the rear vehicle entrance of the Palácio. Urgently request permission to enter.'

Another officer approached. 'Sir, I have something back from Rio. They've identified an Olavo on the Leblon Internacional CCTV.'

'Stand by, Soames.'

'Olavo Pires Filho. He visited on Wednesday. He entered the hotel empty-handed at 15:38 and left at 16:12 carrying a case.'

'Wait . . . He didn't bring TARQUIN anything?'

'Nothing that couldn't fit in a pocket. He was there to collect.'

'So who is he? Do they have a profile? Criminal record? Gang connections?'

'Nothing like that, sir. He's an undertaker.' The officer paused, bracing himself. 'He works for the firm that just put the president in his coffin.'

A crackle preceded Arkell's transmission: 'Yadin's dead. But we might still have a problem. All he had up here was a video camera and broadcast equipment. There's something else planned.'

Margrave looked round to see Prime Minister Mayhew and his wife joining the new president and the other state dignitaries at the entrance of the reception suite.

'Soames, I'm sending an escort to you. Get Richter up here right now.'

Madeleine Wraye had not wasted the opportunity for a private chat with the ABIN Director General when Margrave stepped away. A recent political appointment, she had not known him during her SIS days. Now, as head of the most important intelligence agency in South America, he was not only a valuable source of information; he was a potential client. Wraye didn't quite present her card, but in a few carefully judged remarks she made sure he was aware of her privileged place within the extended intelligence constellation.

At the same time, she was listening with growing apprehension to the CSIS radio traffic through an earpiece she kept discreetly turned away from the DG. 'Did you ever find anything on that woman in Lourdes?' she asked. 'The nurse with the rose?'

The DG looked grave and pleased at the same time. 'A new lead came in a short while ago.' His English was excellent, if strongly North American in accent. 'A photograph. We've been searching the social networks and blogs for pictures taken on the day. This one we didn't spot at first – the tags are in Polish, and the president's name was spelt wrong – but I am told it shows the woman clearly. We will circulate it later today. Perhaps you can help us with your contacts?'

'I'd be delighted to. May I see the picture?'

'After the ceremony.'

'Of course.' She paused, thinking of that video camera set up on a roof overlooking the Praça. 'Unless there's any possibility of getting a copy now?'

He looked at her curiously, then made a call. 'Two minutes and we will have it.'

'Thank you.' She excused herself and grabbed one of the CSIS officers. 'Who's with Arkell's assistant, Siren?' she asked.

'That would be Michael Raynes.'

'They're in the square?'

'Yes, ma'am.'

'Tell Raynes not to let her out of his sight.'

Photographs were being taken. The VIP party had swollen to more than thirty people. All of them needed to be placed in precisely the right order behind the president and the prime minister. A television showed the cortège approaching at walking pace down Via Norte Um. The crowds lining the avenue were silent and very still.

Margrave tore his gaze away from the solemn figure of Mayhew and demanded of his team, 'Is there any doubt about this? I mean, I'm not crazy . . . the smell of solder, the undertaker, the video camera, the warning to stay three blocks away: this means what I think it means?'

Soames saw his opportunity to be bold, to be helpful, above all to stand out: 'Sir, you're not crazy. There is an explosive device in that coffin powerful enough to take out not only Mayhew but all the camera crews in the square. Which means thousands of spectators as well, along with the entire Brazilian executive. Yadin intended to film and broadcast it all.'

'And detonate it?'

'My bet is there's an associate in the crowd. Like Lourdes.'

'They'd be killed by the blast.'

'Maybe they don't realize how big the device is,' suggested another officer.

'We're sure about this undertaker? Do we have a picture?'

One of his officers produced a tablet and summoned up an employee ID. Impatiently, Margrave pointed to Klara. 'Not me. Show it to her.'

Klara nodded at the photo. 'That's the man who spoke to us in Rio.'

Margrave stood quite still, eyes raised above them all, trying to make the impossible call. 'If I go to Mayhew now, what evidence do I have? A camera on a roof. An undertaker who happened to visit a popular Rio hotel. In the twenty seconds he's going to give me before he starts down that ramp to address the world, what else can I tell him?'

Soames, on a roll now, looked to Klara. 'The electronics, the undertaker meeting, the three-block warning . . . She's your evidence.'

Margrave nodded. He made his decision. 'Ms Richter, please come with me. I need you to be eloquent, concise and extremely convincing.'

The ABIN Director General touched Wraye's arm. 'It's arrived,' he murmured, handing her his smartphone. She looked once at the photograph on the screen.

'Thank you,' she said, handing it back. Her voice was entirely steady. 'I'm going to need to borrow something from one of your officers. Rather urgently, I'm afraid.'

* * *

Alone at the top of a half-finished building, Simon Arkell had already dismantled the camera and satellite uplink, confirming what he already knew. There was no weapon here. At a complete loss, he pulled out his phone. He'd felt it vibrate silently in his pocket while he was stalking Yadin. A missed call from Danny Levin.

He called him back. 'Do you have anything?'

Danny sounded ridiculously cheerful. 'Didn't you listen to my voicemail?'

His leg was hurting too much to endure Danny's high spirits. 'Give me the headline. Have you found anything on Watchman?'

'I've got a stack on Watchman. Jeez, what'd you think, I've been asleep?'

'Anything relating to Brazil or Yadin?'

'Nope, but there is one bizarro thing. I was looking through his connections, people he's hung out with, served on a committee with, shared a golf round with, whatever . . . Anything cached on accessible databases.'

'I haven't got time for this.'

'OK, OK, look . . . Cancer Research. Six years ago. He gave like some shitty amount, ten pounds is all, via a donations website to sponsor a runner called Clare Hopeflower.'

A beep signalled a new message. 'Danny, I'm in South America dealing with an assassination attempt. What the hell has a charity run got to do with anything?'

'See, the weird thing is, Clare Hopeflower has plenty of background datapoints: Bristol birth certificate, private school in Berkshire, driver's licence, German exchange programme, German Literature at Oxford University, couple of translator jobs in Brussels and a bunch of council tax and TV licence payments when she comes back to England. But everything stops four years ago. Like she died or something.'

'I'm hanging up, Danny.'

'Take a look at the picture I just sent you,' he said, a note of triumph flooding his voice.

Switching to speaker, Arkell opened the message and stared at the passport photograph in utter disbelief.

'So tell me that's not your favourite German chick.'

'Walk with me,' murmured Wraye to the ABIN DG. The VIP party were all assembled now, correctly ordered for precedence, at the top of the long white ramp that led from the Palácio do Planalto down to the Praça dos Três Poderes. The cortège had arrived at the foot of the ramp, and an honour guard of Independence Dragoons in white uniforms with red-plumed bronze helmets was preparing to escort the coffin to the centre of the square.

Her phone rang, and she took the call as they crossed the central hall.

'It's Klara!' Arkell's voice was forceful, clear, urgent. 'She's English, she's called Clare Hopeflower, and she knows Watchman. Don't let her near Mayhew!'

'Thank you, Simon,' she said calmly, hanging up and continuing on towards the front of the VIP column, where Mayhew and his wife stood together with the new Brazilian president. They were erect and solemn, aware that the media cameras below were already on them. Close-up images were showing on silent television screens just to their left.

CSIS Director of Operations Shel Margrave seemed to hesitate on seeing those news pictures, but only for a moment. With the woman he knew as Klara Richter at his side he walked quickly into frame as Mayhew started down the great ramp. 'Sir, a moment please!'

Brazilian aides and security personnel stepped forward as Madeleine Wraye, an unknown figure to them, carrying something metallic in her right hand, doubled her pace towards their president. But at a signal from the ABIN chief they let her pass. None of them noticed that the other woman was also holding something – a much smaller object, slim and cylindrical.

Wraye had seen it, however. As Clare Hopeflower raised her arm towards Prime Minister Mayhew, she whipped the borrowed Taser up to shoulder-height and fired.

The instant the two barbed electrodes hooked into the English assassin's flesh, Wraye dropped the weapon and held her hands up for the benefit of the close protection officers rushing towards her. Incapacitating pulses of high voltage electricity continued to rip through her target until the dart gun fell from her fingers and she collapsed. Reacting from instinct, long before he had fully understood the situation, Margrave caught her and pulled her clear of the VIP party.

All the world saw the brief interruption and the fainting woman. The tight framing of the TV images excluded the cause of it. Madeleine Wraye was careful to ensure she remained, as always, in the shadows.

On this day we celebrate the life and work of a great leader, a brave pioneer, and a dear friend.

Simon Arkell watched the initial interrogation in something of a trance. Three ABIN officers with faultless English but little insight into this unfathomable enemy got nowhere.

'Do you admit to murdering President Andrade by presenting him with a flower you knew to be poisoned?'

'Do you admit to conspiring to murder Anneke van der Velde, Murilo Andrade and Terence Mayhew?'

'What was your relationship with Gavriel Yadin?'

'Who are you working for?'

'How did you obtain the dart gun and poison?'

Clare Hopeflower did not answer their questions, and in the presence of Canadian and British observers they did not attempt to force answers from her. This was all for show, Arkell realized: the interrogators did not expect results from their restrained questioning. They would get them later, behind closed doors. His troubled, bewildering Klara sat silent on a bench in the corner of the windowless basement room, bare-headed, cuffed hands lifeless in her lap. The blood-spotted place on her shirt where the electrodes had pierced her side was just visible beneath her elbow. What hell was she about to go through?

Taking the ABIN Director General aside, Wraye murmured, 'You probably don't need us any longer, and there's a flight to Lisbon I'd like to be on this evening. Simon and I have some rather urgent business in London. But before we leave, would it be possible to have a quick word with Miss Hopeflower alone?'

Murilo Andrade believed above all else in furthering the best interests of the people – not only of Brazil but of all the world. So when he chose to make his number one priority the legalization of drugs, he did so in the interests of the people of the world, knowing that it would probably cost him his job. Now, it has cost him his life.

Under the suspicious gaze of the ABIN officers, Madeleine Wraye led the prisoner, escorted by Simon Arkell, into the nearest toilets, a capacious room with eight cubicles and a dozen urinals. 'It's unlikely to be bugged,' she said as she checked the cubicles, 'but we might as well take precautions.'

Arkell set all the taps running. 'Stand here,' he said. 'And speak softly.'

'We haven't told the Brazilians or the Canadians about Tony,' explained Wraye, in a voice that was easily muffled by the gushing water. 'I'm going to break it to the powers that be in London tomorrow. It would be helpful – though I assure you not essential – to have your testimony.'

Wraye took a paper towel from the dispenser and wiped the edge of the washstand. Leaning against it, she said, 'You walked into this situation with your eyes open, knowing you would be arrested and imprisoned. I presume, therefore, that you are expecting Tony to intervene somehow on your behalf. Perhaps he can compromise the evidence against you. Perhaps there is a deal to be done. More likely he has persuaded you to believe these things, even though he knows them to be impossible. I wouldn't be surprised if the Brazilians bring back the death penalty for the murderer of their president.

'Regardless of what you think is ultimately going to happen, in the short term things are going to get very nasty for you. Intelligence services in these parts have long histories – black histories. There are plenty of mothballed facilities and officers with the old skills. So I'm going to give you a choice. We can allow you to disappear into the Brazilian security system for the next few days, during which time you may lose your teeth, your fertility, your eyesight, even your memories. Or I can promise personally to stay with you, ensuring that your human rights are scrupulously observed, and call for all possible British diplomatic cover until such time as your long-term fate is decided. I will do this for you in return for ten minutes of straight talking. Otherwise, Clare, I believe I'm going to throw you to the dogs.'

The thing about drugs is that they will always exist and we will always want them. That is our nature. Murilo Andrade was a great leader, a brave pioneer and a good friend, but above all else he was a realist. Today, in his name, I am asking you to be realistic. End this decades-long futility of denial. We like drugs and we always will. For Murilo, let's come together to make them reliable, regulated and safe.

'So why don't we start at the beginning,' suggested Wraye. 'When and how did you meet Tony? What did he first ask you to do? And why did you take on a German identity?'

The gushing of water from twelve stainless-steel taps was strikingly loud in the pause that followed. Arkell watched them both as if through a distorting lens: the two women seemed impossibly far away. When the younger spoke, her voice took him by surprise. It shouldn't have done – it was to be expected. The neutral BBC accent was nevertheless shocking to him.

'I'm very sorry,' said Clare Hopeflower. 'I appreciate what you're offering to do for me, but I really can't discuss any of this.'

'Shall we try Gavriel Yadin? You can't be concerned about self-incrimination, surely, when you've already declared yourself to have been his lover.'

Hopeflower just shrugged apologetically.

'Presumably Tony asked you to become intimate with him?'

This time there was no reply at all. As the water thundered from the taps, Wraye changed tack.

'Let me try out a hypothesis on you, Clare. Something to prime the pump. It's a hypothesis with quite a few variables, the first of which is how Tony first encountered you. You applied to join SIS, he was a friend of the family, there was a road accident, you met in a bar – it doesn't really matter, and I'm sure we can find the answer with a couple of hours' digging. What matters is how he recruited you. Let's say this is approximately five years ago, and you're around twenty-three years old. By now, Gavriel Yadin has been working for Tony for almost a decade. He's pulled off some important executions, but his mood is changing, darkening. The satisfaction of the job well done is losing its appeal, and he's starting down the road to the angst and alienation that you, I believe truthfully, described for us this morning. Tony's a great reader of people; he would have seen the change in Yadin, and it would have worried him. What can he do to preserve his marvellous secret weapon? He needs someone who can simultaneously distract Yadin from his gloomy introspection and keep a close eye on him. A lover, in fact.

'There you are, young and impressionable. Tony sets out to dazzle you with his job title, his secrets, his awesome responsibility for national security, his access to Number 10, his undeniable charm. Above all, he stresses, this is essential public service. Someone very gifted is needed to live a double life. Do it for five years and the world will be your oyster. Tony will lay the keys of the kingdom at your feet. A fast-track career in SIS or the Civil Service? A top job in the City? A seat in Parliament, even? Tony can make it all happen.

'Of course, it was important you didn't fall for Yadin. Tony would have given you long lectures about that, impressed upon you the dangers of getting too close, brainwashed you to a certain extent so that I really don't think you ever did love your Kidon lover, did you? The poor dead chump. He's been manipulated and played for years. The question is, Clare – and this is where I want you to pay attention – have *you*?'

Arkell tensed as he watched his one-time teacher shift gear.

'Somehow in the last year – and this is another of those uncertain variables – Tony has managed to turn you from agent handler into full-blown assassin. My guess is the junkie brother who died of an overdose was real, that you have a major personal issue with the legalization agenda, and that Tony has exploited it to persuade you that killing presidents and prime ministers really is for the greater good. However he did it, the outcome isn't in doubt: you've become a remarkably effective killer.

'But this time the variable matters – how Tony persuaded you to kill is acutely important. Again, let me hypothesize: you see yourself as basically a good person, fighting a just war through dirty means. But for that to hold you would have to believe that the man directing you, inspiring you, acculturating you, was also basically a good person. You would have to believe he was working on behalf of the British people rather than, say, a foreign corporation with immense commercial interests in the illegal drug trade. You would have to believe the individuals he sent Yadin to kill were evil-doers rather than, say, loyal

British intelligence officers. And above all you would have to believe that, as head of Counter-Terrorism for SIS, his efforts were directed at combating terrorism rather than – let's be conservative in our allegations – facilitating it.

'Clare, when you were a teenager Tony Watchman helped bring about the deaths of hundreds of innocent civilians in Chicago. I'm a very good judge of character and I don't believe you knew this about him. If I'm wrong, you deserve everything the Brazilians are going to do to you. But if I'm right, Clare, if you've been manipulated and used and duped by a man whose real motives were hidden from you, then for the sake of your future, your children, your grandchildren, you have *got* to start talking to me.'

Arkell realized he was holding his breath. The hand Wraye had chosen to play had served SIS officers well over the decades: numerous high-placed assets had been recruited when forced to confront a moral failing in their previous allegiance. But it was a high-risk tactic. It depended entirely on the moral compass of the subject, and on their willingness to accept a total realignment of their world view.

In the case of Clare Hopeflower, alias Klara Richter, it didn't work. 'I'm sorry,' was her only answer.

'You'd take a lifetime in prison for that man?'

'I doubt it will be that long,' she said mildly.

'You naïve little fool!' shouted Wraye.

Arkell stepped forward then. 'Can I have a go?'

He sat on the floor below the gushing taps and after a moment's consideration she joined him. Taking her charcoal beret from his pocket, he handed it to her. She nodded silently, gratefully perhaps, and pulled it on. They leaned back against the washstand and stared at the cubicles. With Wraye's departure there was a tangible lightening of the atmosphere in the room, but still it was a while before either of them found the will to speak.

'Did you kill him?' she asked.

'No.'

'But he is dead?'

'So you do care.'

'What I said in Rio was true. I did love him. In a way. Not at first, but it's hard to play the role for so long without it becoming a little bit real.'

'Then if you and I had spent more time together,' he said with bitterness, 'maybe that love would have become real too.'

She bit her lip. 'Which of us are you talking about?' When he didn't answer, she added, 'We were both trying to deceive each other.'

'My job didn't require me to fall in love with you,' he said stiffly.

She looked down. 'Neither did mine.'

He stared in confusion at the cubicle opposite, projecting onto the door her smile as it had been in Strasbourg, trying to understand, to assess, to make sense.

'In Lourdes – I saw you. Not your face, but I saw you do it. You knew what was on that flower. You chose to murder him.'

'Do you use that word for the people you've killed?'

'Andrade was different.' But as he said it he remembered the face of the family man he'd shot in Kyrgyzstan, the farmer caught up in a rebellion in Chad, the teenage boy with the grenade in Somalia.

'Not to me.'

He stretched out his bad leg, trying to relieve the throbbing pain in his thigh. 'You're talking about your brother.'

'It's all true. Look him up. Andrew Hopeflower, 74 Medley Street, Chiswick. The whole sordid story is in the police file.'

'So drug legalization . . . ?'

'Stupidest fucking idea in history.'

The welling emotion in her voice, he realized with a shock, almost had him slipping an arm around her shoulders. What was it like to see a brother die so pointlessly? Simon Arkell had a sister, much younger; they had never been close, even before he chose to disappear. He couldn't begin to understand this still-bereaved woman. Or perhaps he could, he thought, remembering Tom Parke's white body, streaked with mud, bloodless flesh torn where the groundsman's rake had hooked him, laid out on the gravel beside the storm drain.

'There's nothing I can do for you,' he said.

'I know.'

'They're going to throw away the key.'

She stayed silent. He sensed a shiver run through her.

'Clare, how could you do it? How could you play the adoring girlfriend to an assassin for four years on the orders of a man like Tony Watchman?'

'We all have our different talents,' she said wearily.

'That's what you wanted? That's really the life you dreamed of when you were at Oxford – when any future was open to you?'

She shook her head. 'I didn't know what I wanted. After Andy died, things got confused. At least it was something I could do.'

'There's so much you could do!'

She smiled ruefully, and he wondered if he should correct himself: *so much you could have done.*

'Simon . . .'

'It's a miserable bloody waste!' he raged.

'It is,' she whispered, just audible over the gushing taps. 'But I didn't know you then.'

Something small and very delicate seemed to break inside him. To save himself, he said the one true thing that could reliably bring down the shutters between them. 'I still don't know you at all.'

LONDON, ENGLAND – 1 July

None of them spoke in the ABIN car on the way to Brasilia International, nor in the departure lounge, nor on the plane. They checked in separately, using clean identities unknown to SIS or Tony Watchman, and sat on opposite sides of the Business Class cabin.

At Lisbon Portela, Siren took the thick envelope with evident discomfort and headed for Arrivals. Arkell had persuaded her to try a few weeks' painting in Belém's mosaic and cobblestone streets – to give her dream one more chance – while recuperating at one of the city's finer spa hotels. In return, she had accepted his apology.

Wraye and Arkell had two hours to kill before their connecting flight. They found a loud video arcade at one end of the terminal where they could talk safely.

Wraye handed him a folded sheet of paper. 'Watchman's

London address. His wife and children are at the Buckinghamshire house for the whole summer. There's a girlfriend who may be around: Gemma, thirty-two, primary-school teacher. Tell her you're a private investigator hired by Mrs Watchman – that should scare her away. Tomorrow midday, I'll go to the Cabinet Secretary. It would be helpful if his body hasn't been found before then.'

'This is really what you want? Sure you wouldn't rather see him stand trial?'

'I might. But it would be impossible for the Service and catastrophic for the country. The JIC won't regret his passing when they hear what I have to say. Do it cleanly and quietly, and I'm confident there won't be much of a police investigation.'

'What about AMB?'

She smiled then. 'You didn't imagine we'd ever be able to touch *them*, did you?'

'Tell me you're not serious.'

'The darlings of the Pentagon and DHS? One of the great American commercial success stories of the last decade? Simon, do you have any idea how much AMB donated to Super PACs on both sides of the last election?'

'Are you forgetting GRIEVANCE?' he said coldly.

She matched his tone, yielding nothing. 'GRIEVANCE happened. It's part of our history. None of those people can be brought back to life by exposing AMB's role, of which, by the way, we have no proof. Full revelation would only terrify the West and confirm every prejudice and conspiracy theory in the Middle East. The best we can do is deny AMB further access to the Service's resources. Meanwhile, we quietly take down the man who made their crimes possible.'

He was staring at her as if he no longer recognized her. 'When did you become so timid?'

'We have to pick our battles, Simon.'

Shrieks of laughter came from three kids huddled around one of the arcade games. 'If there was more evidence,' Arkell said forcefully. 'The only reason I . . .' He stopped. There was no point.

Some things, he had learned over the course of nine years, were best done alone.

Before boarding the BA flight to London, they each bought a sun hat from a souvenir shop. All SIM cards went in a bin. At Heathrow they both disappeared into toilets for exactly fourteen minutes, re-emerging into a pack of passengers disembarking a flight from Dubai. They joined separate Immigration queues, using the rims of their hats to hide their faces from the CCTV cameras. Neither false passport raised any flags, but they had to remove the hats at the desks, and after that they moved very swiftly through the baggage hall and Customs.

In the arrivals hall, Arkell spotted a familiar face. Incredulous, he gave a quick warning shake of his head, and turned to Madeleine Wraye.

'There'll be more work,' she said.

'You know how to reach me.'

'Perhaps even a way back into the Service.'

He shook his head. 'I like it on the outside.'

'I thought you'd say that.'

'Madeleine . . .' His mind returned to that dimly lit room in a Strasbourg pension. To a kind of truth laid bare in the dead of night. 'How do *you* think he got Clare to do what she did?'

She eyed him darkly. 'I think he was pushing at an open door.'

She kissed him on the cheek and walked quickly away. Danny Levin, approaching, said, 'Who's she? No, wait, don't tell me. It'll be fun working it out.'

'Danny, how the hell?'

He grinned. 'So there's this thing you can do with incoming flights, where you—'

'Actually, there's no time. We've got to get out of here.' Arkell started towards the taxi rank.

'Awesome! Are we being hunted? In *England*?'

'It's a definite possibility.'

There was a queue, but Arkell pushed Danny to the front, saying, 'I'm sorry, he had a dangerous episode on the plane. I have to get him straight back to the clinic.' No one objected.

In the cab, Danny said, 'So, the Fräulein who wasn't a Fräulein: was that useful?'

'It was,' murmured Arkell distractedly. He was looking back at the terminal he'd never seen before, at the new roundabout and the perimeter road, at the car parks and hotels, at the number plates and speed cameras, at the road markings, the dusty trees, the white vans, the satellite dishes, the garden sheds built for cash in hand, the cranes and Velux windows and wind turbines, the imposing buildings in which music and pharmaceutical executives battled to cling on to their markets, the fast-food van in the lay-by, the glass tower of gleaming show cars, the crumbling churches and advertising billboards and tower blocks and muted skies. England.

He was home.

* * *

Simon Arkell entered the Shepherd's Bush house of the SIS Director of Counter-Terrorism at 16:38. It was empty, no sign of the teacher girlfriend. The alarm was sophisticated but manageable. The locks were straightforward. With the kit he had purchased from a small workshop in Mile End, they were open in under thirty seconds.

He had devoted several hours to dry cleaning in the tube stations, department stores and alleyways of the capital. Tony Watchman could call, for another few hours at least, on the extensive resources of SO15 and the Security Service to capture and contain the two people in Britain who knew his terrible secret. He could access the entire city's CCTV network, and make good use of the latest facial recognition software to locate and tail them both. Nevertheless, by the time Arkell reached Wraye's unofficial armourer in Willesden, he was confident no one was following him. By 16:30, dressed quite differently, with a hoodie to foil the cameras, he was sure of it.

He sat at Watchman's desk, Glock 17 and suppressor resting on the blotter in front of him, looking at the family photographs in silver frames. A grinning girl, perhaps twelve years old, on a horse. Another, younger but acting older, beside a pool. A small boy sitting on his mother's lap on a rattan garden chair. There were documents to photograph, locked drawers to pick, a computer hard drive to clone. He might have an hour before Watchman returned home, he might have five. It didn't matter. He could continue searching, collecting data afterwards. He could afford a few minutes to consider the wife and children of the man he was about to kill.

Had Watchman been sitting at this desk when he ordered Gavriel Yadin to murder a young couple in Dault Street? Had he been looking at photographs of his wife and baby daughter when he signed Emily's death warrant? Arkell shrugged off the questions. They made no difference. The handsome family made no difference. There was Saeed and Ellington, Emily and van der Velde and Andrade, and all the many, many victims of GRIEVANCE. And then there was a young English woman who might have been something extraordinary, drawn into murder and a lifetime in prison. The balance of justice was indisputable. The only question lay in himself as executioner.

Was he ready to kill for the first time in nine years?

He had learned something from Yadin, the assassin who sought a greater familiarity with death. He couldn't have put it into words. He wasn't certain the insight had anything to do with killing. Rather, the extreme manifestations of humanity. Of soul. Did that help? Was he ready? So much doubt. The blade poised behind the Kidon neck, the paralysis that had cost a president's life. Standing over Yadin's body, killed by another – was the feeling he experienced then relief or impotence? Perhaps they were the same thing. Was he ready? Relief was not what he sought. Had never sought. Revenge . . . restitution . . . or just a symbolic act to alleviate the pain of so much old and new sorrow. Klara-Clare, damned before she'd started living. Simon Arkell did not flinch from the photographs, from the daughters and the son and the trusting wife, as footsteps sounded on the gravel path outside, as a key turned in the lock, as his forefinger settled on the Glock trigger, and his answer, in that time-telescoping moment, was, categorically – yes.

ACKNOWLEDGEMENTS

I have never been a spy. To those individuals who know much more about the intelligence services than I do and have helped me get most of the details right, I am immensely grateful. No names.

Thank you to my early readers for their wise feedback and many good ideas: Richard Marriott, Andrew Wilson, Matt Nelson, Imogen Cleaver, Paul Cleaver, Felicity Bertram, Rosemary Macdonald and Eva Schaller. Jon Elek took on a challenging edit and made *Rogue Elements* a stronger book. My father, Alasdair Macdonald, who loved spy novels and lived just long enough to see his son write one, spent many happy hours arguing over the plot and checking my facts.

This book was a publishing experiment: Advance Editions contributors offered some great suggestions and corrected a few embarrassing errors. My thanks to Dave Halpin, Jim Ratzer, David Nordell, Bruno Shovelton, VX, Roo Cove, Katy Beale, Jessel, Richard Marsh, Liz Chapman, Al Jack, HarryW, Simonetta Wenkert, JP, Wellington, Jon Martin, Terry, Laura Watkins, Heidi Kingstone, Katja Buerkle, Chris Baker, Peter Glassman and Vince Houghton.